Chapter 1

Simply Impossible

AN UNOFFICIAL GRAPHIC NOVEL FOR MINECRAFTERS

THE CLUCKSHROOM CHRONICLES, BOOK 1

THE MINESHAFT MENACE

MEGAN MILLER

SKY PONY PRESS
New York

Sky Pony Press books may be purchased in bulk at special discounts for sales promotion, corporate gifts, fund-raising, or educational purposes. Special editions can also be created to specifications. For details, contact the Special Sales Department, Sky Pony Press, 307 West 36th Street, 11th Floor, New York, NY 10018 or info@skyhorsepublishing.com.

Sky Pony® is a registered trademark of Skyhorse Publishing, Inc.®, a Delaware corporation.

Minecraft® is a registered trademark of Notch Development AB.

The Minecraft game is copyright © Mojang AB.

Visit our website at www.skyponypress.com.

10 9 8 7 6 5 4 3 2 1

Library of Congress Cataloging-in-Publication Data is available on file.

Cover design by Brian Peterson
Iinterior art by Megan Miller

Print ISBN: 978-1-5107-6301-2
Ebook ISBN: 978-1-5107-6807-9

Printed in China

Dear Reader:

I know you are not going to believe this, because it is impossible. You will probably call me a liar and more people will believe you than believe me. But all of these events did happen, and I will tell you what, when, and how. I just don't know why.

Yesterday was a pretty normal day. After school, Oscar and Malik met up with me to play a couple of Minecraft Earth adventures in the park near the library.

As usual, Oscar and Malik were arguing. This time, Oscar was saying that ancient humans battled dinosaurs, and Malik was telling him there was no proof.

But I got them into the game finally, and we were doing pretty well. What happened next defies all logic. This story is pieced together from recovered Minecraft Earth files and recordings. I'm sharing this with you in confidence. I hope you can keep a secret.

-Kiri

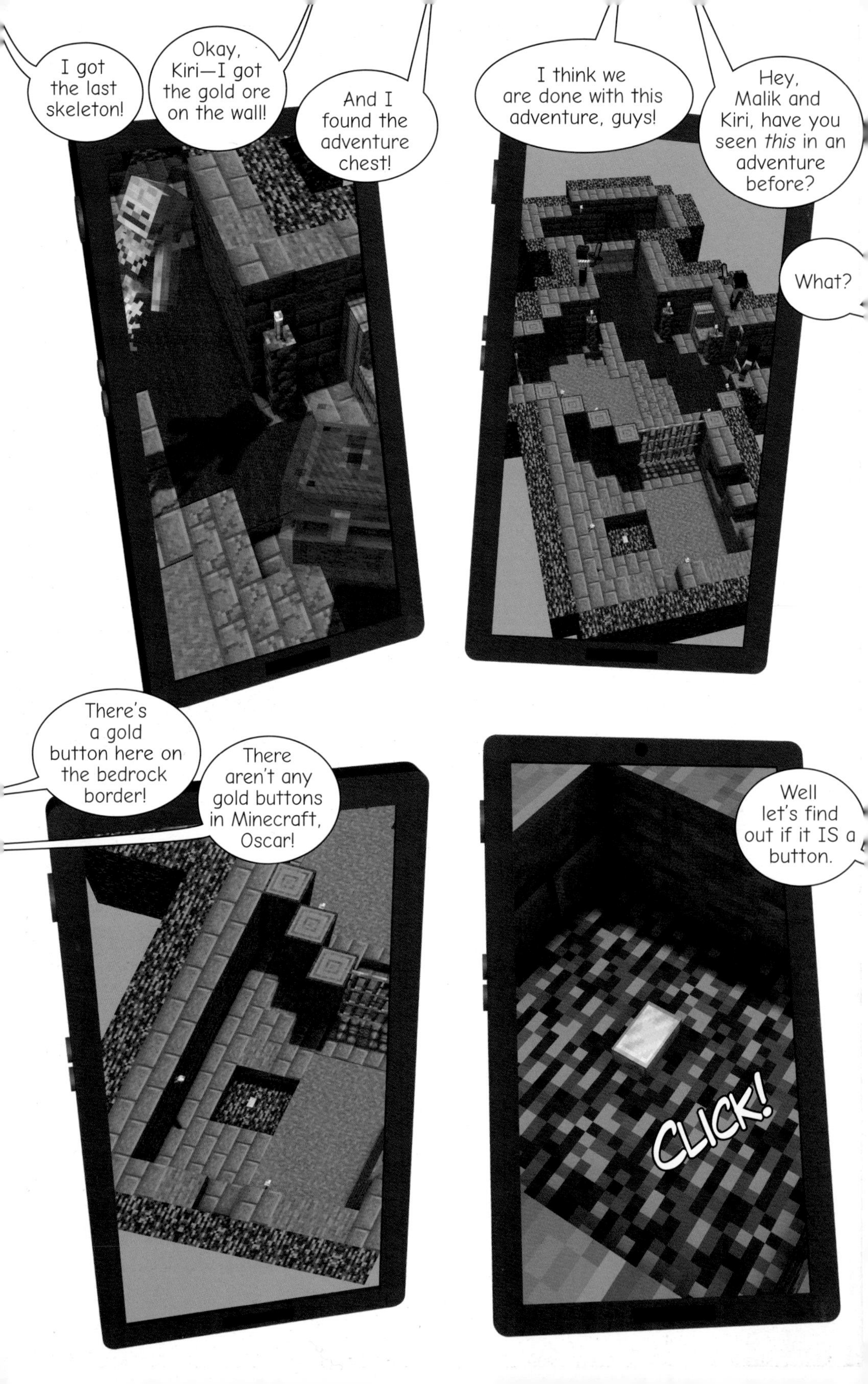

I got the last skeleton!
Okay, Kiri—I got the gold ore on the wall!
And I found the adventure chest!
I think we are done with this adventure, guys!
Hey, Malik and Kiri, have you seen *this* in an adventure before?
What?
There's a gold button here on the bedrock border!
There aren't any gold buttons in Minecraft, Oscar!
Well let's find out if it IS a button.
CLICK!

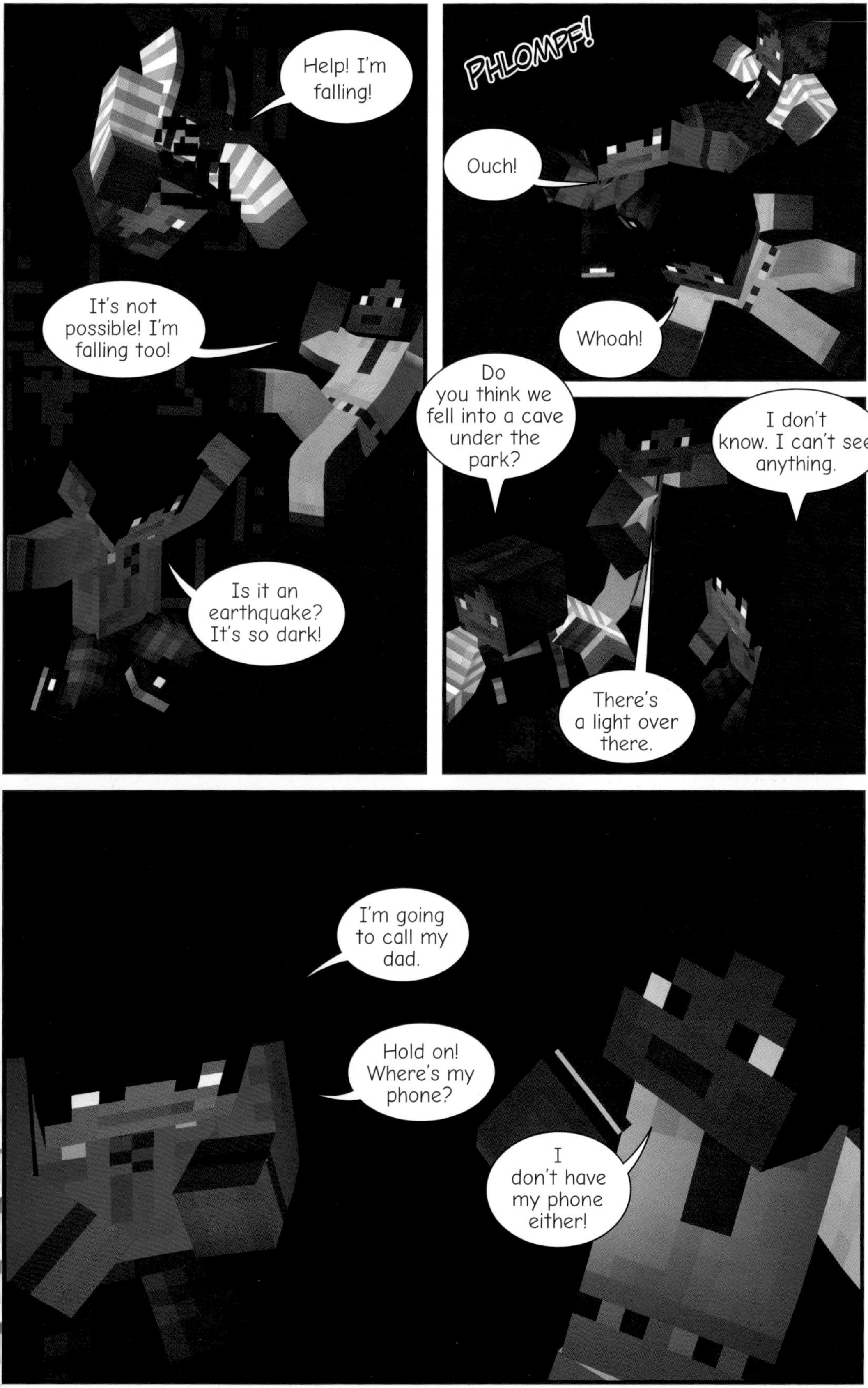
Help! I'm falling!
It's not possible! I'm falling too!
Is it an earthquake? It's so dark!
PHLOMPF!
Ouch!
Whoah!
Do you think we fell into a cave under the park?
I don't know. I can't see anything.
There's a light over there.
I'm going to call my dad.
Hold on! Where's my phone?
I don't have my phone either!

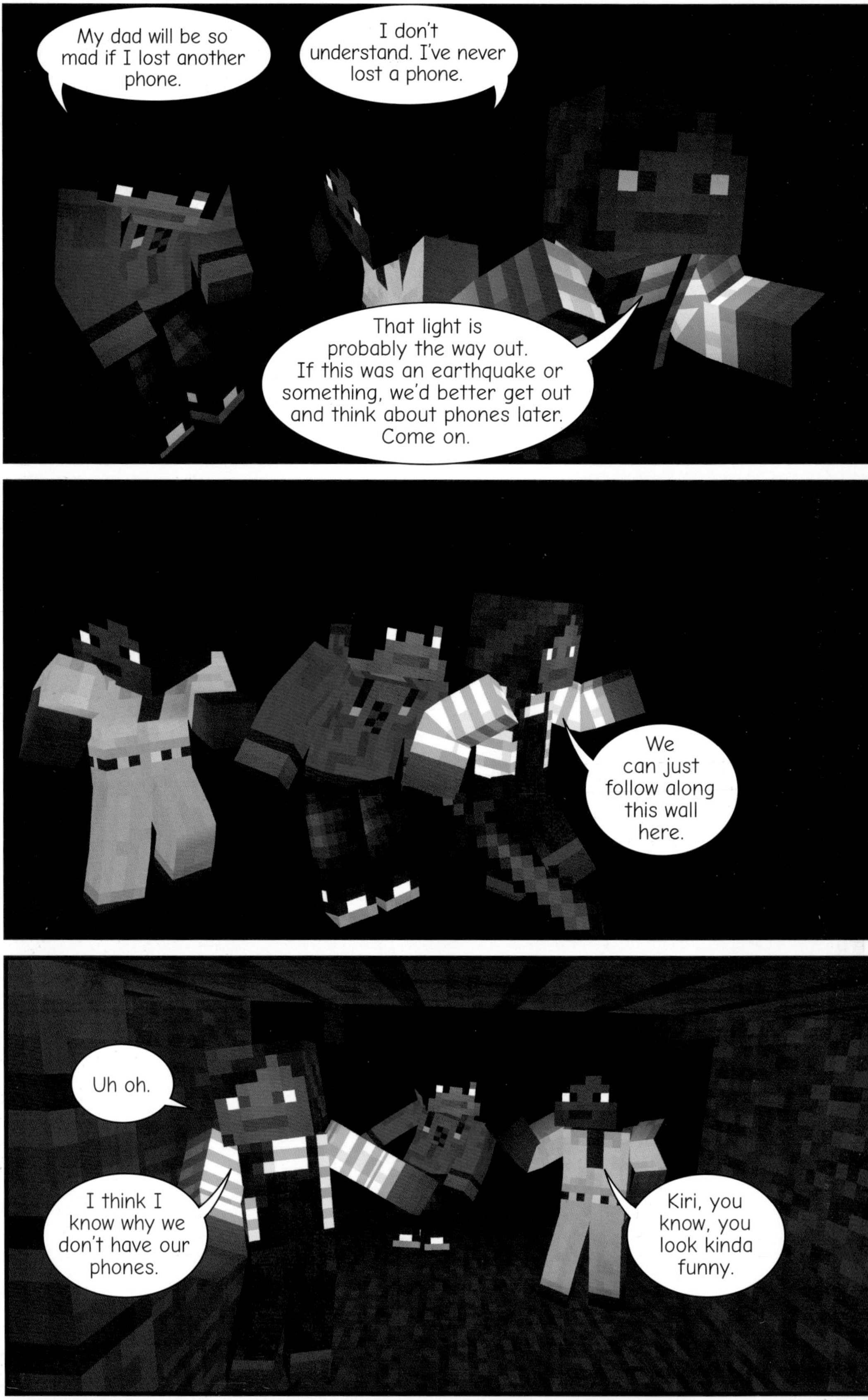
My dad will be so mad if I lost another phone.
I don't understand. I've never lost a phone.
That light is probably the way out. If this was an earthquake or something, we'd better get out and think about phones later. Come on.
We can just follow along this wall here.
Uh oh.
I think I know why we don't have our phones.
Kiri, you know, you look kinda funny.

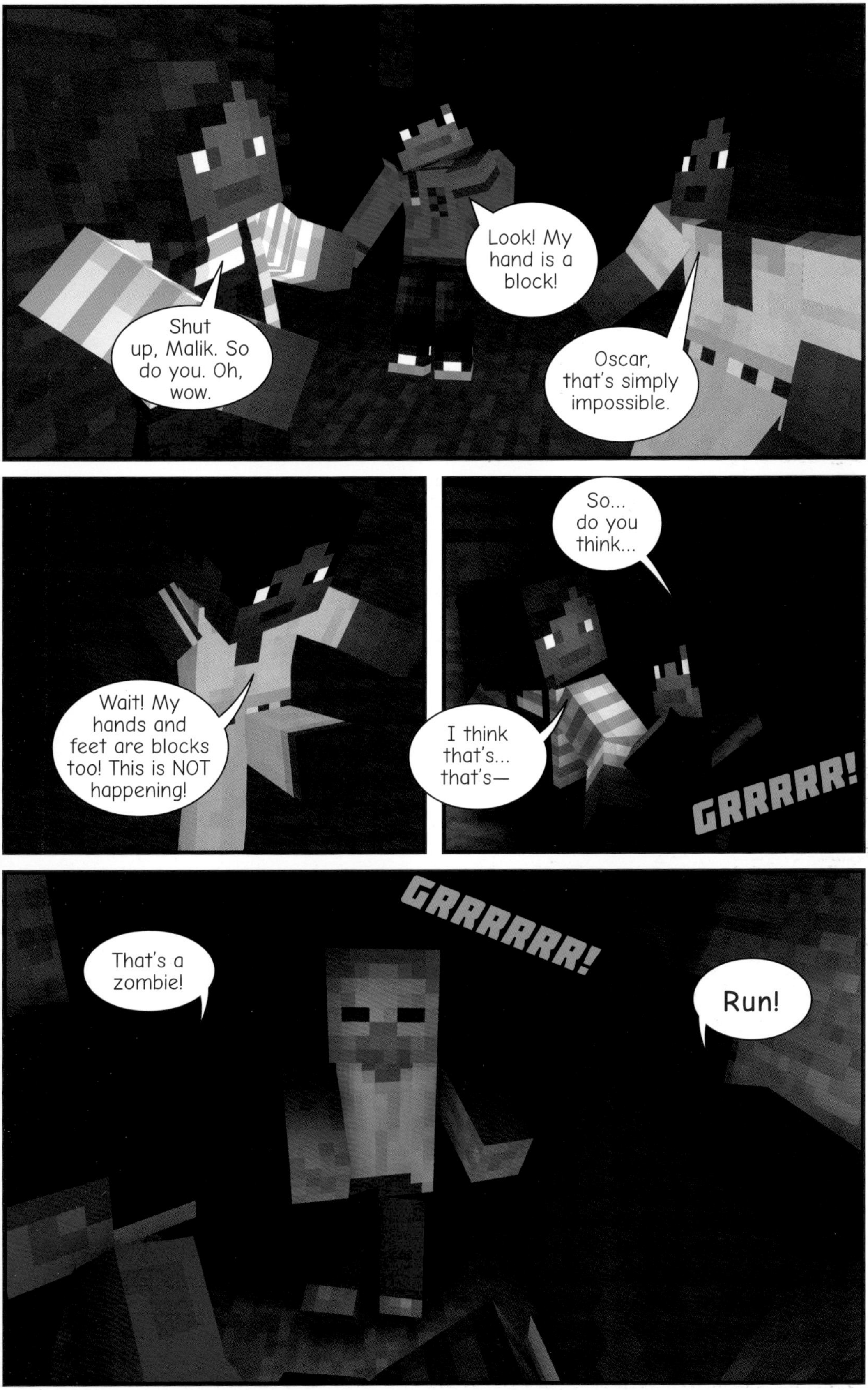
Look! My hand is a block!
Shut up, Malik. So do you. Oh, wow.
Oscar, that's simply impossible.
Wait! My hands and feet are blocks too! This is NOT happening!
So... do you think...
I think that's... that's—
GRRRRR!
GRRRRRRR!
That's a zombie!
Run!

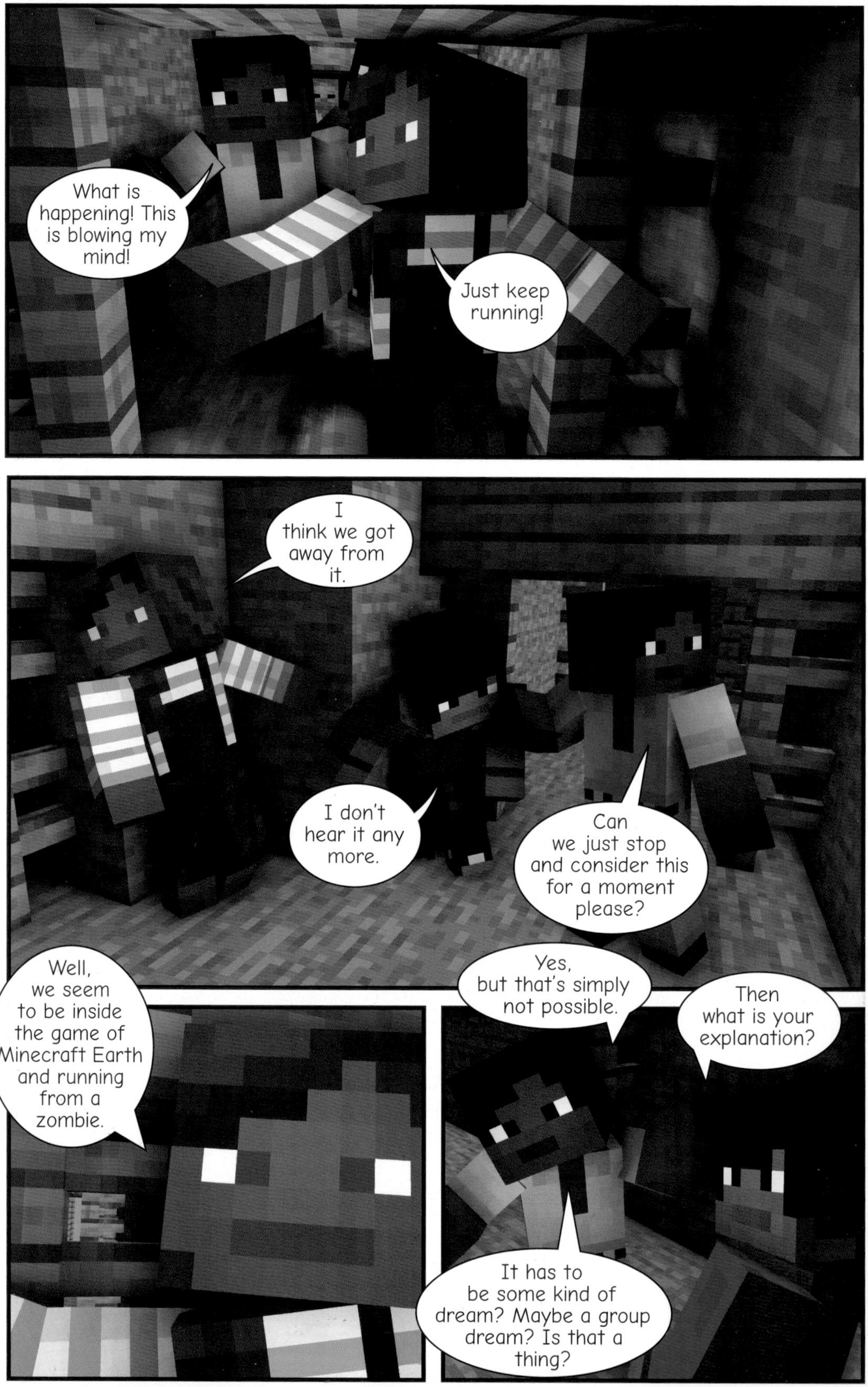
What is happening! This is blowing my mind!
Just keep running!
I think we got away from it.
I don't hear it any more.
Can we just stop and consider this for a moment please?
Well, we seem to be inside the game of Minecraft Earth and running from a zombie.
Yes, but that's simply not possible.
Then what is your explanation?
It has to be some kind of dream? Maybe a group dream? Is that a thing?

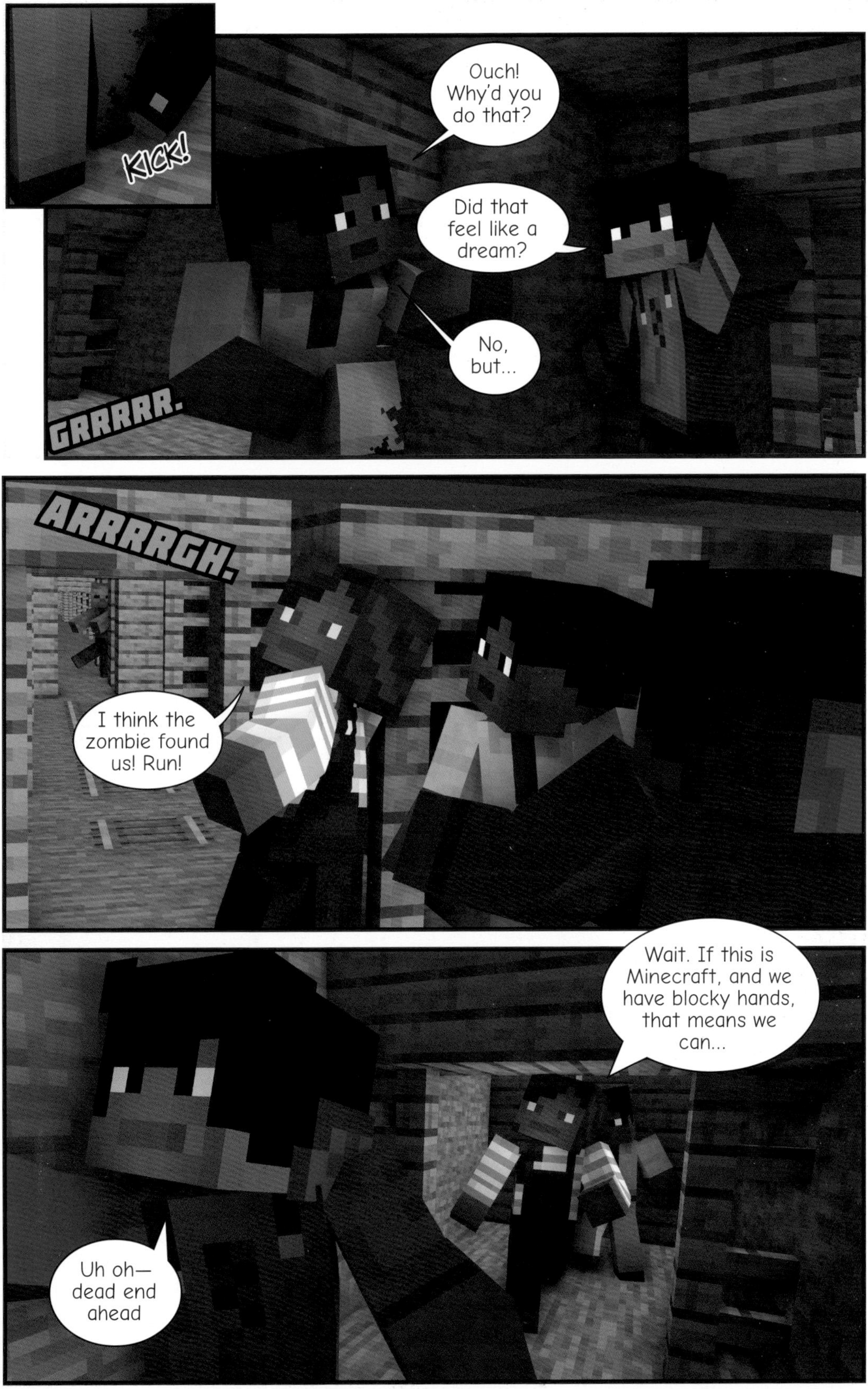
KICK!
Ouch! Why'd you do that?
Did that feel like a dream?
No, but...
GRRRRR.
ARRRRGH.
I think the zombie found us! Run!
Wait. If this is Minecraft, and we have blocky hands, that means we can...
Uh oh—dead end ahead

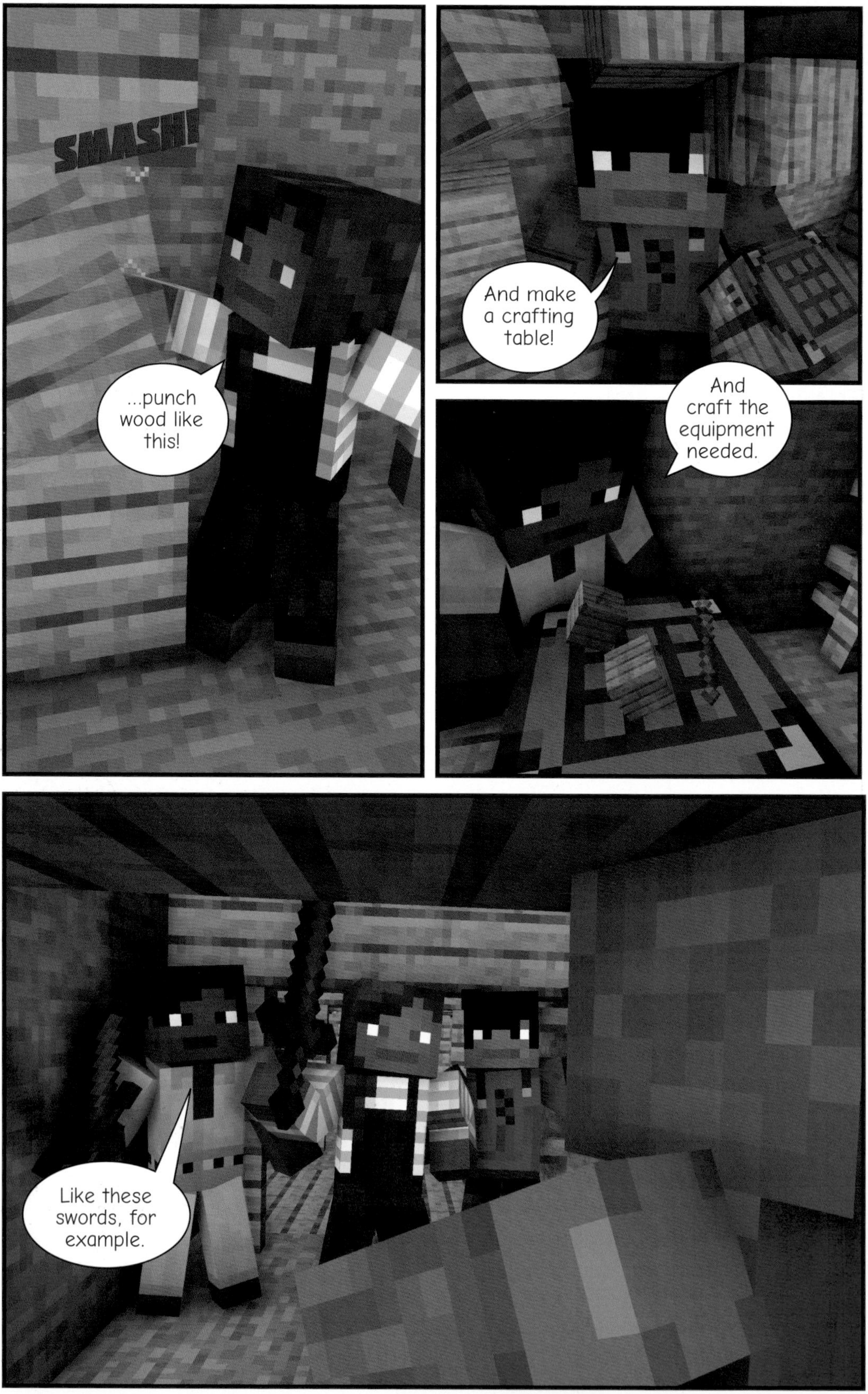
SMASH!
...punch wood like this!
And make a crafting table!
And craft the equipment needed.
Like these swords, for example.

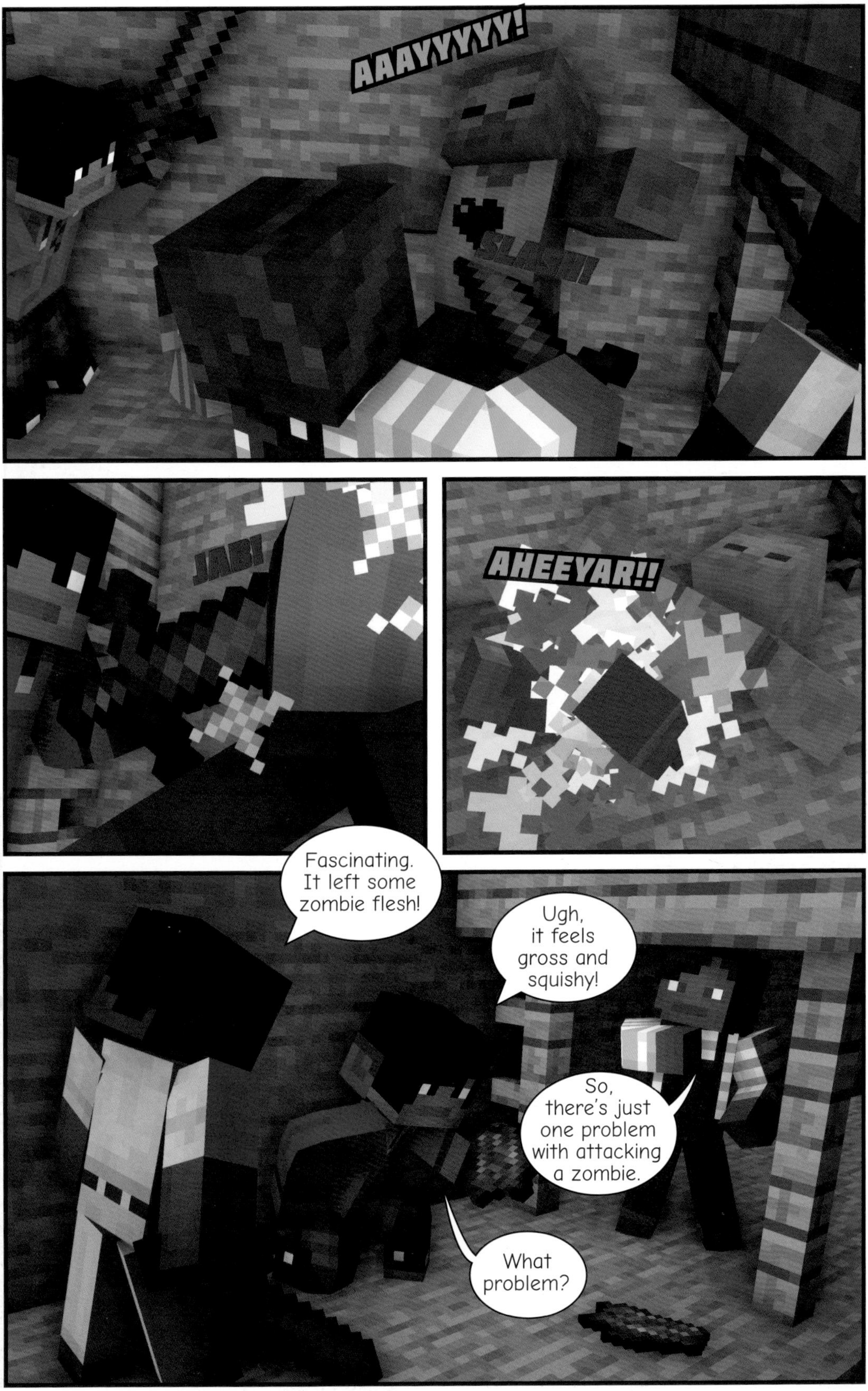
AAAYYYYY!
SLASH!!
JAB!
AHEEYAR!!
Fascinating. It left some zombie flesh!
Ugh, it feels gross and squishy!
So, there's just one problem with attacking a zombie.
What problem?

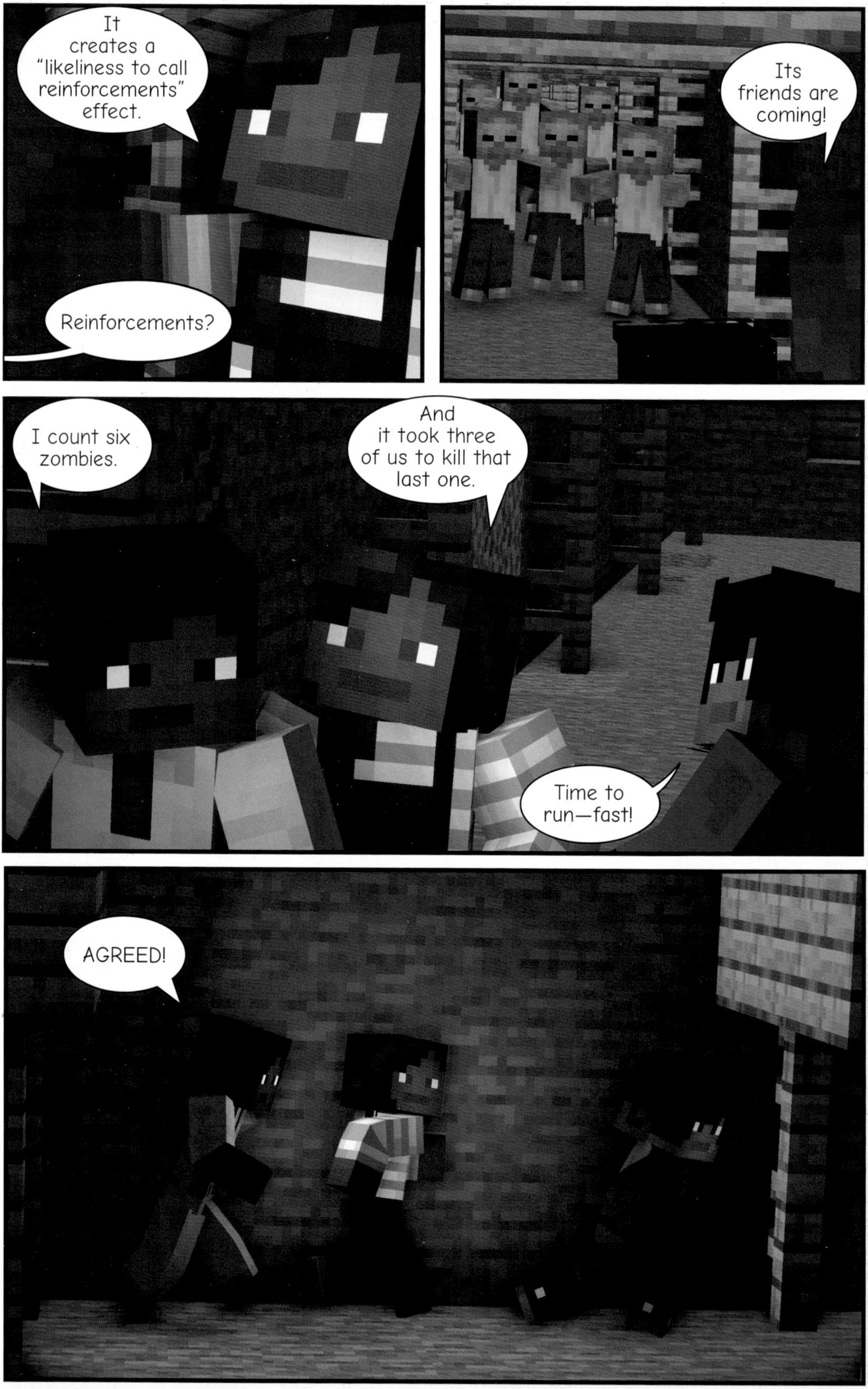
It creates a "likeliness to call reinforcements" effect.
Reinforcements?
Its friends are coming!
I count six zombies.
And it took three of us to kill that last one.
Time to run—fast!
AGREED!

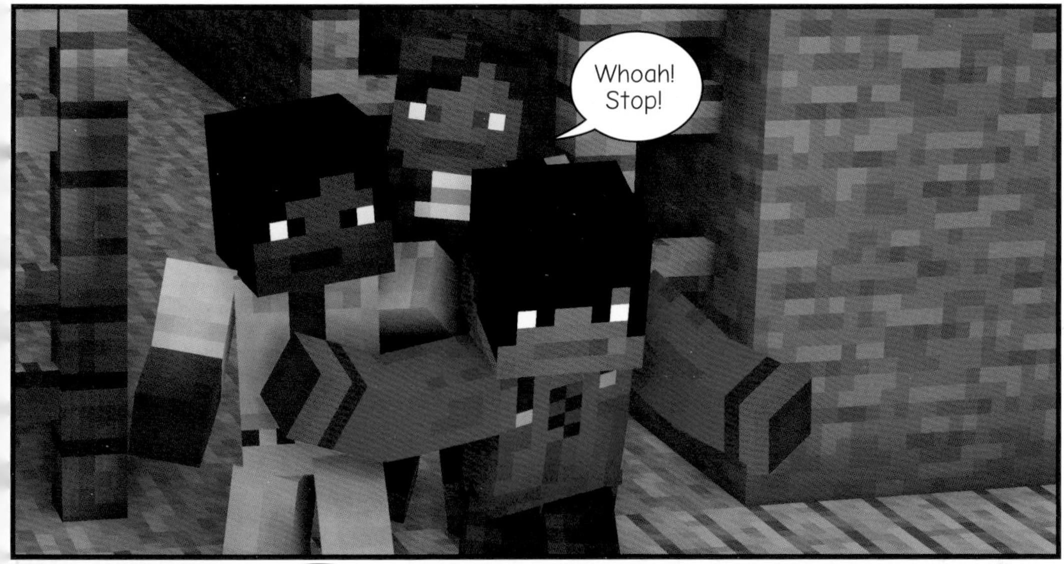
Whoah! Stop!

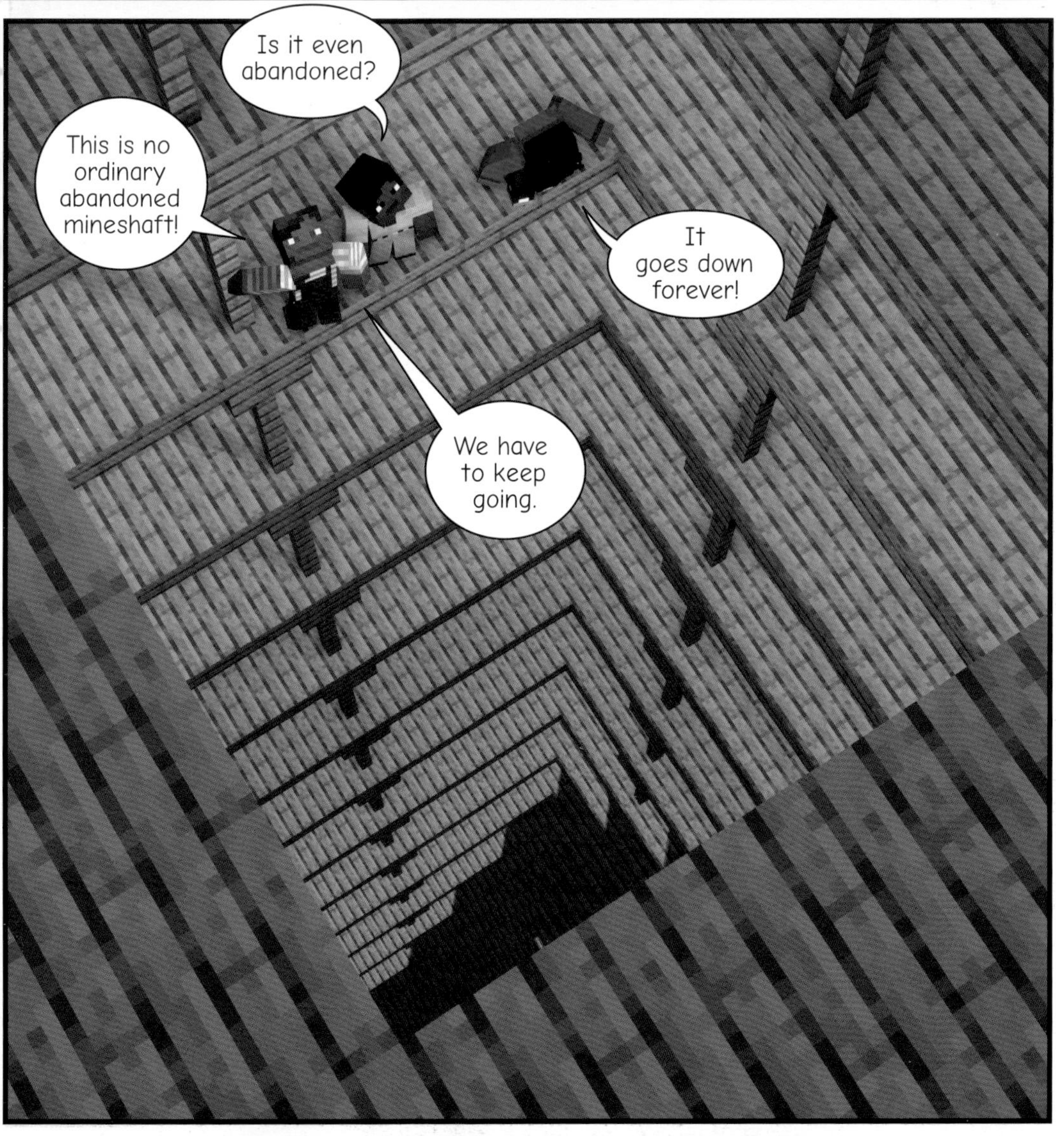
Is it even abandoned?
This is no ordinary abandoned mineshaft!
It goes down forever!
We have to keep going.

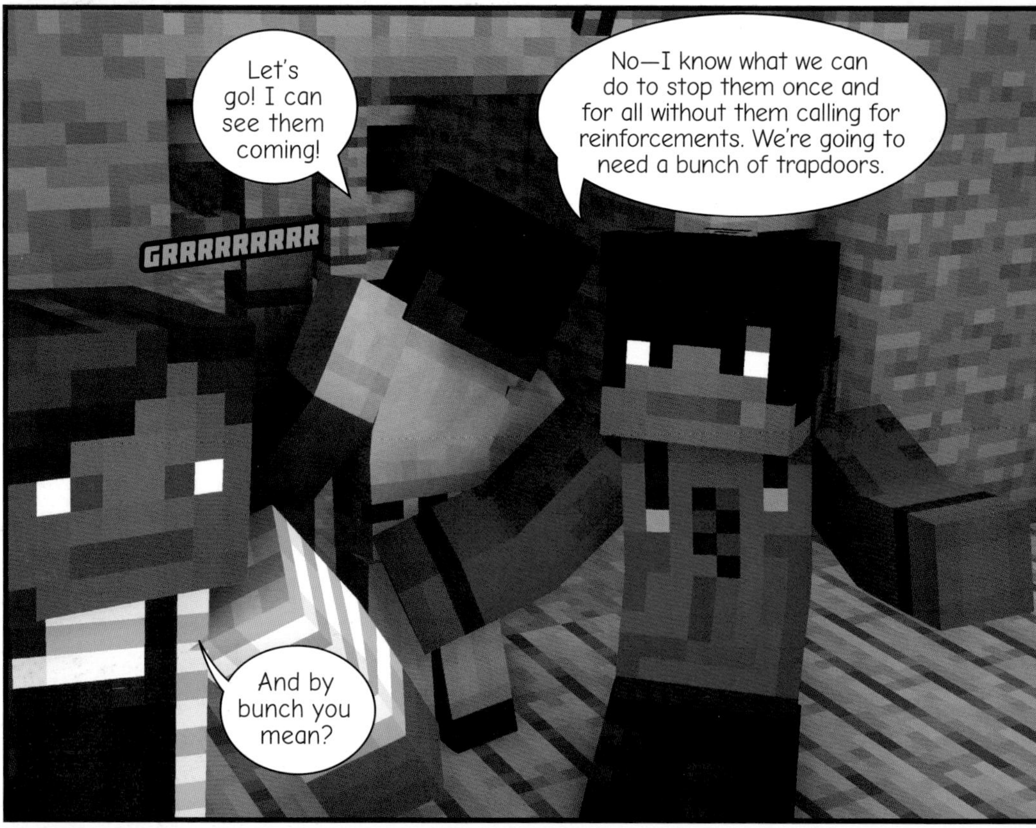
Let's go! I can see them coming!
GRRRRRRRRR
No—I know what we can do to stop them once and for all without them calling for reinforcements. We're going to need a bunch of trapdoors.
And by bunch you mean?
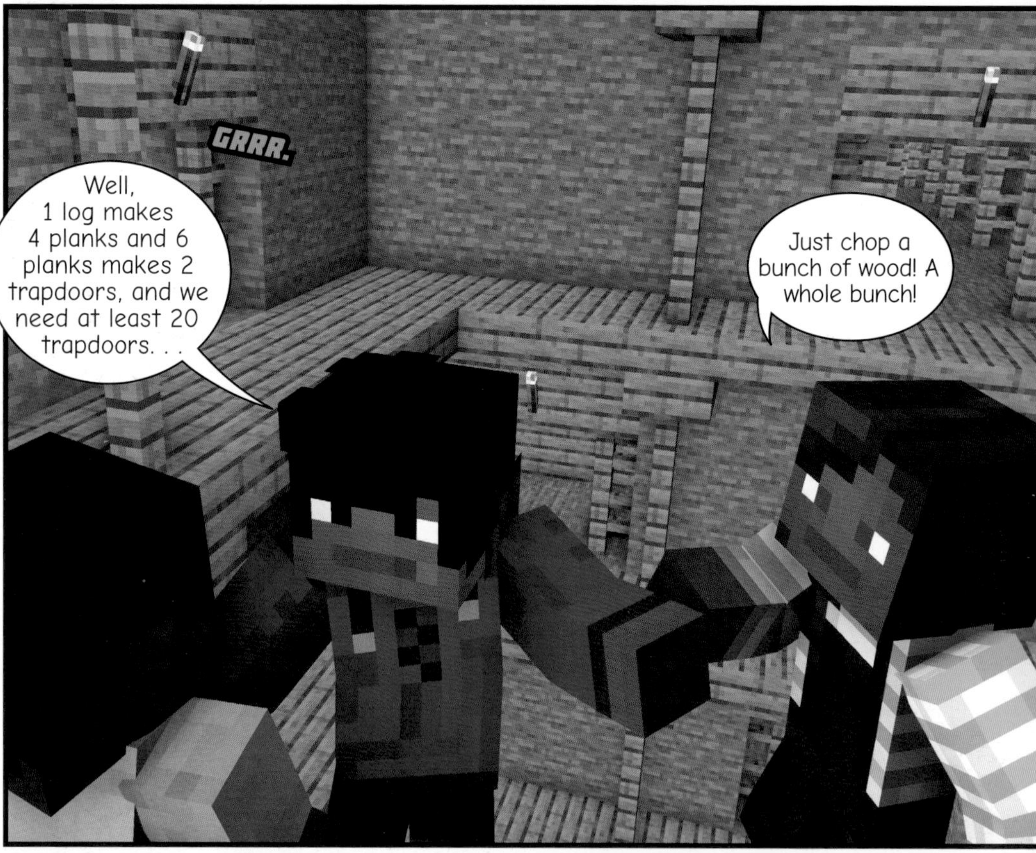
GRRR.
Well, 1 log makes 4 planks and 6 planks makes 2 trapdoors, and we need at least 20 trapdoors. . .
Just chop a bunch of wood! A whole bunch!

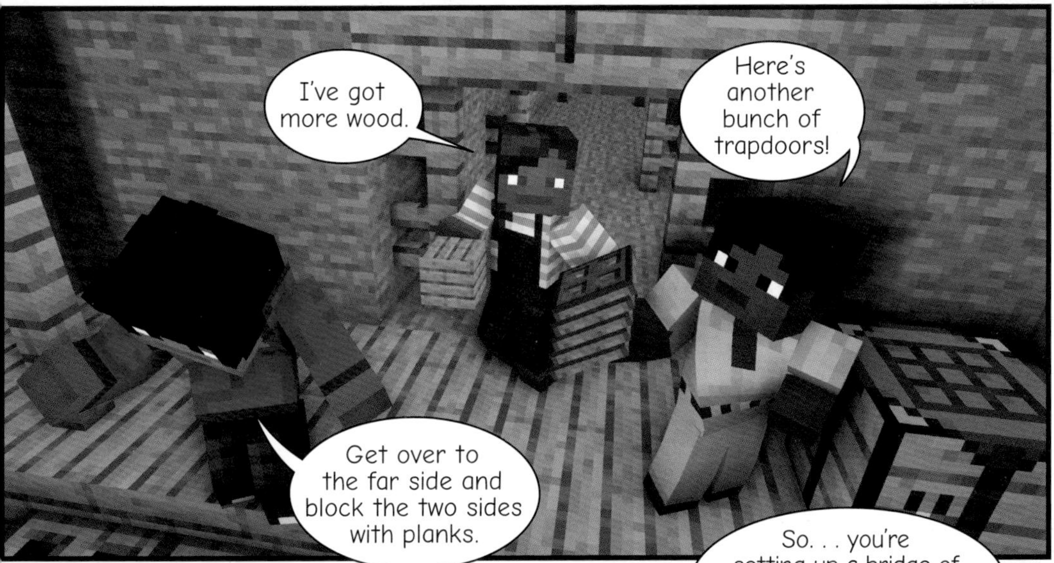
I've got more wood.
Here's another bunch of trapdoors!
Get over to the far side and block the two sides with planks.

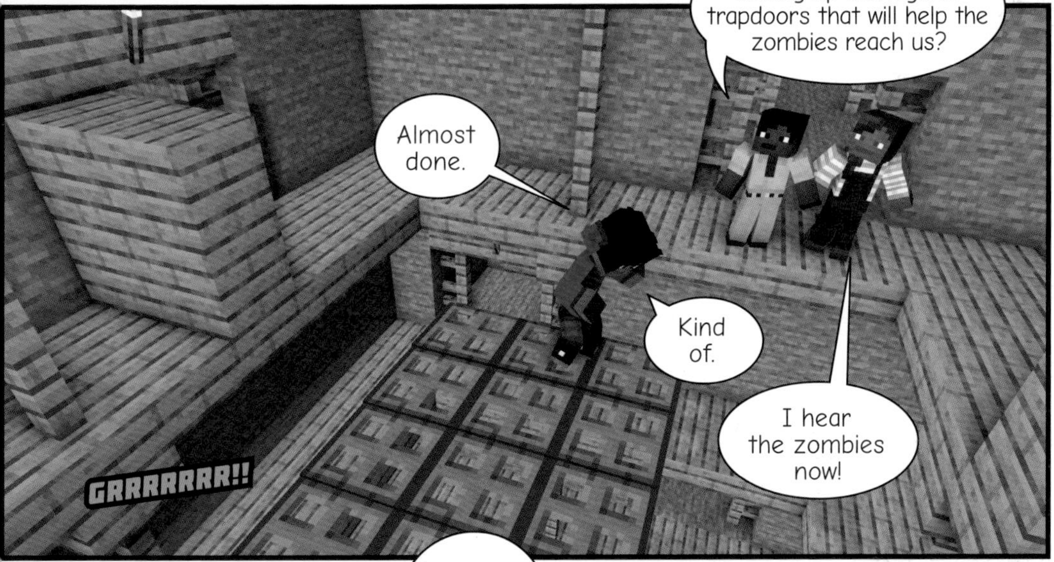
So. . . you're setting up a bridge of trapdoors that will help the zombies reach us?
Almost done.
Kind of.
I hear the zombies now!
GRRRRRRR!!

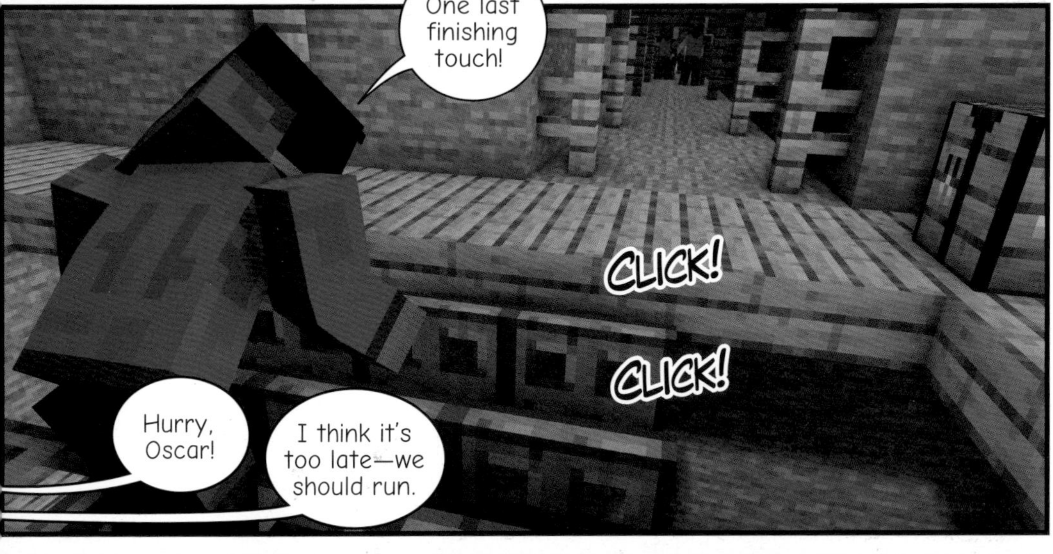
One last finishing touch!
CLICK!
CLICK!
Hurry, Oscar!
I think it's too late—we should run.

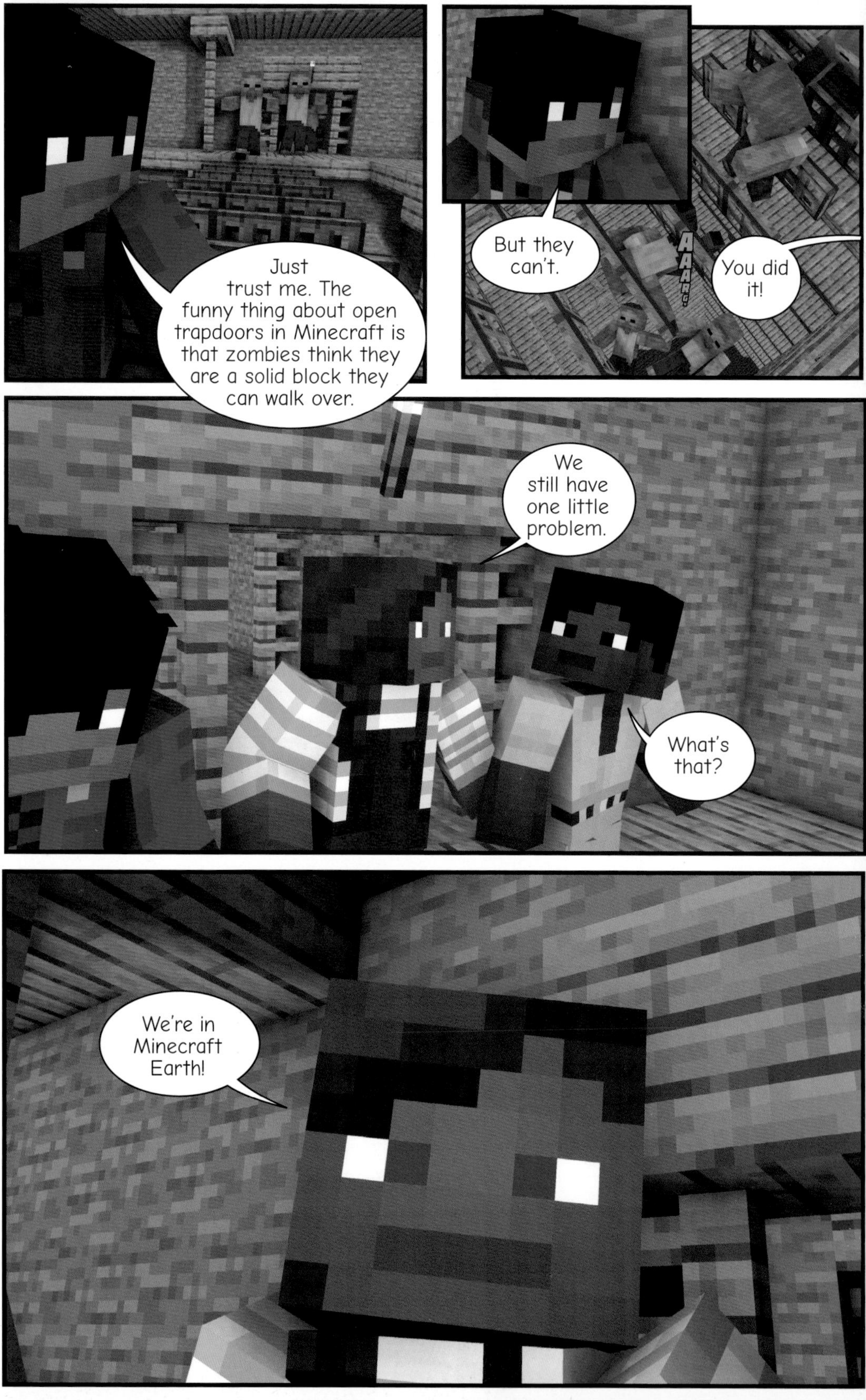
Just trust me. The funny thing about open trapdoors in Minecraft is that zombies think they are a solid block they can walk over.
But they can't.
AAARG!!
You did it!
We still have one little problem.
What's that?
We're in Minecraft Earth!

Chapter 2

Escape by Minecart

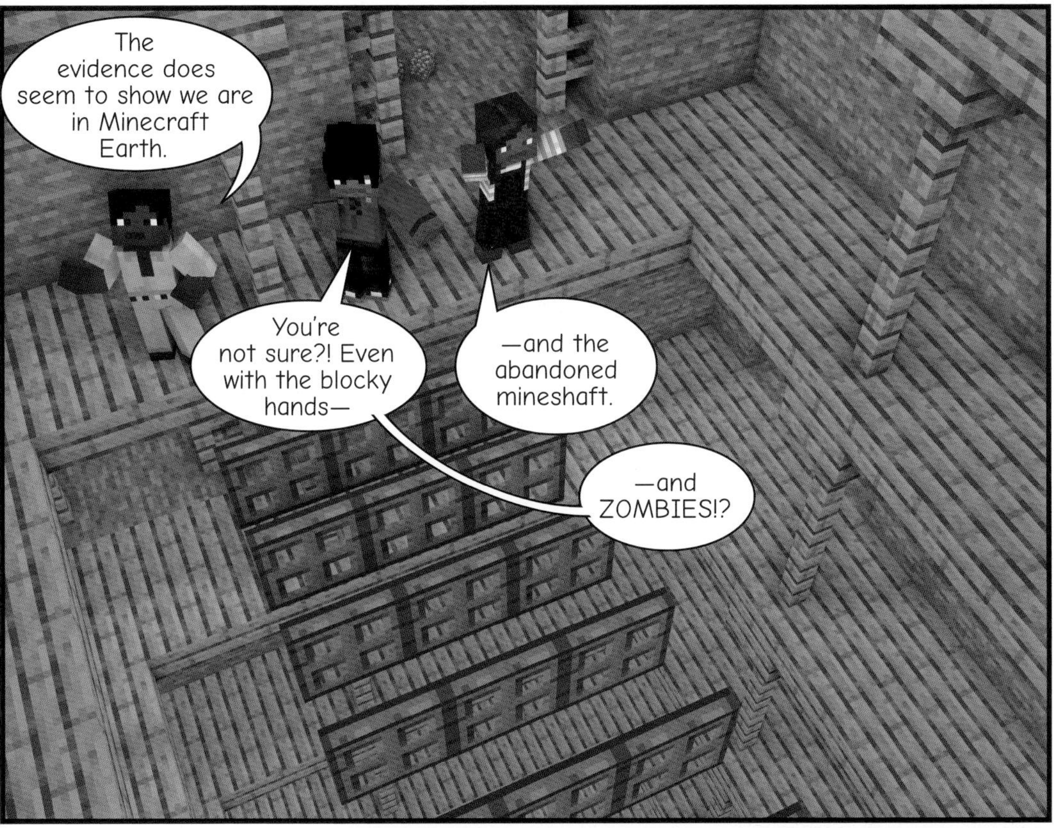
The evidence does seem to show we are in Minecraft Earth.
You're not sure?! Even with the blocky hands—
—and the abandoned mineshaft.
—and ZOMBIES!?

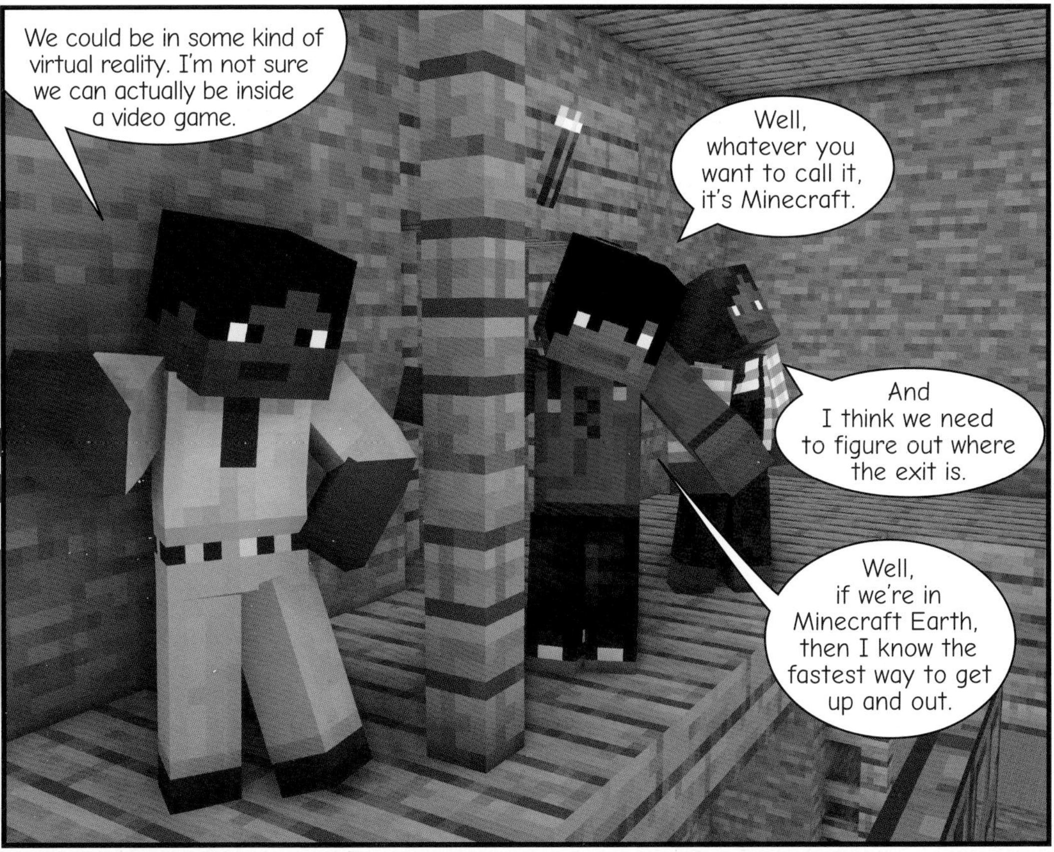
We could be in some kind of virtual reality. I'm not sure we can actually be inside a video game.
Well, whatever you want to call it, it's Minecraft.
And I think we need to figure out where the exit is.
Well, if we're in Minecraft Earth, then I know the fastest way to get up and out.

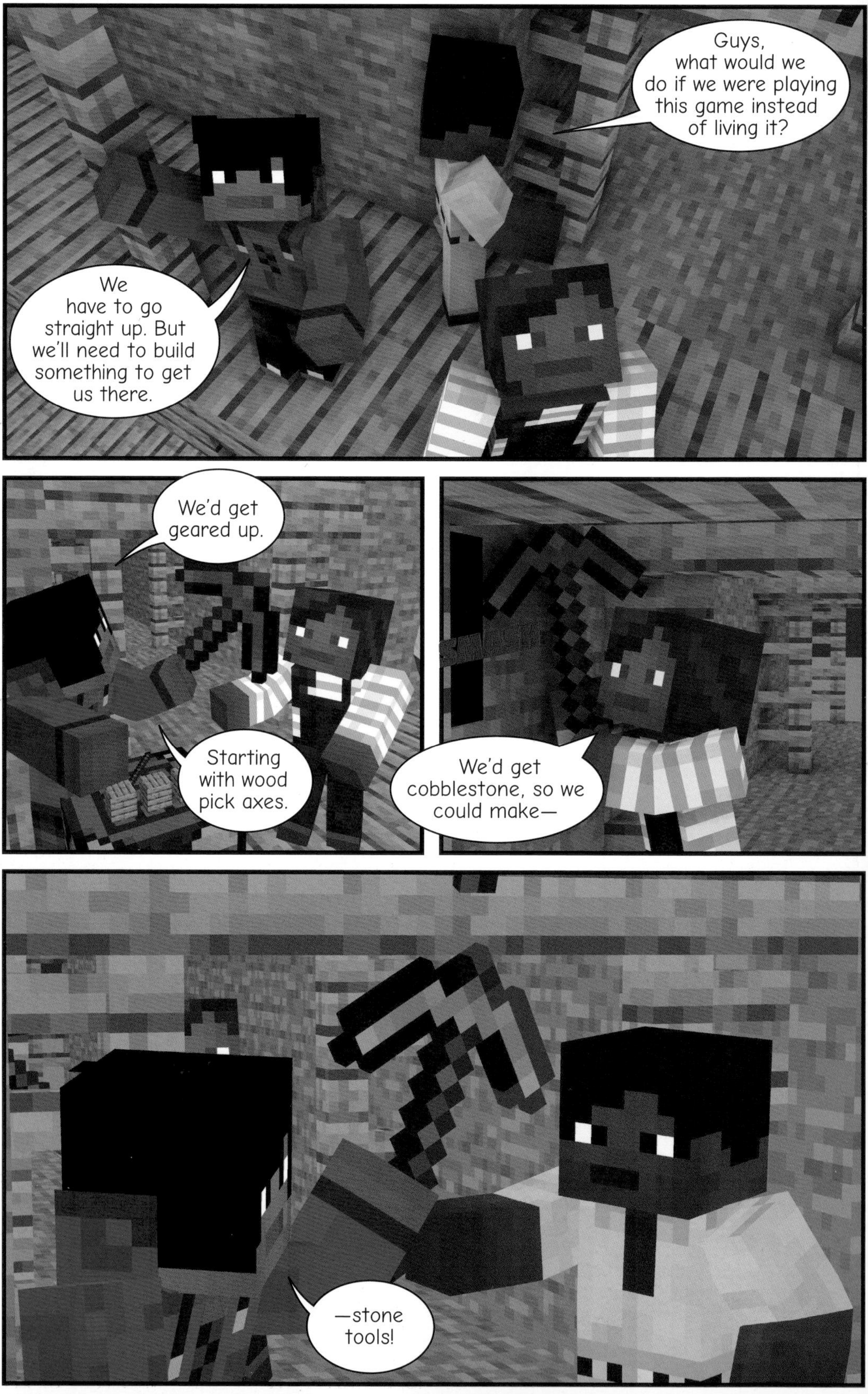
Guys, what would we do if we were playing this game instead of living it?
We have to go straight up. But we'll need to build something to get us there.
We'd get geared up.
Starting with wood pick axes.
We'd get cobblestone, so we could make—
—stone tools!

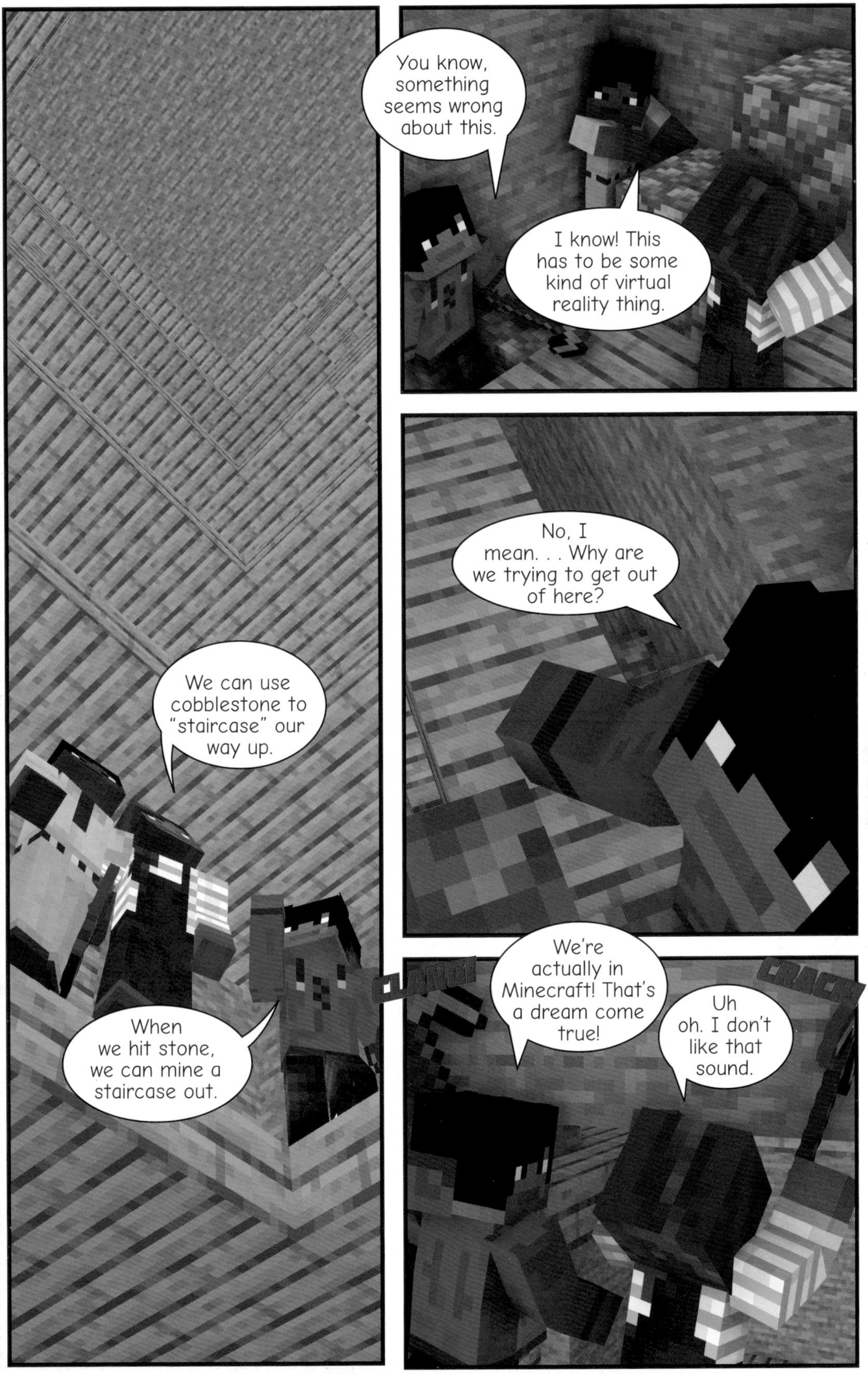
We can use cobblestone to "staircase" our way up.
When we hit stone, we can mine a staircase out.
You know, something seems wrong about this.
I know! This has to be some kind of virtual reality thing.
No, I mean. . . Why are we trying to get out of here?
We're actually in Minecraft! That's a dream come true!
Uh oh. I don't like that sound.

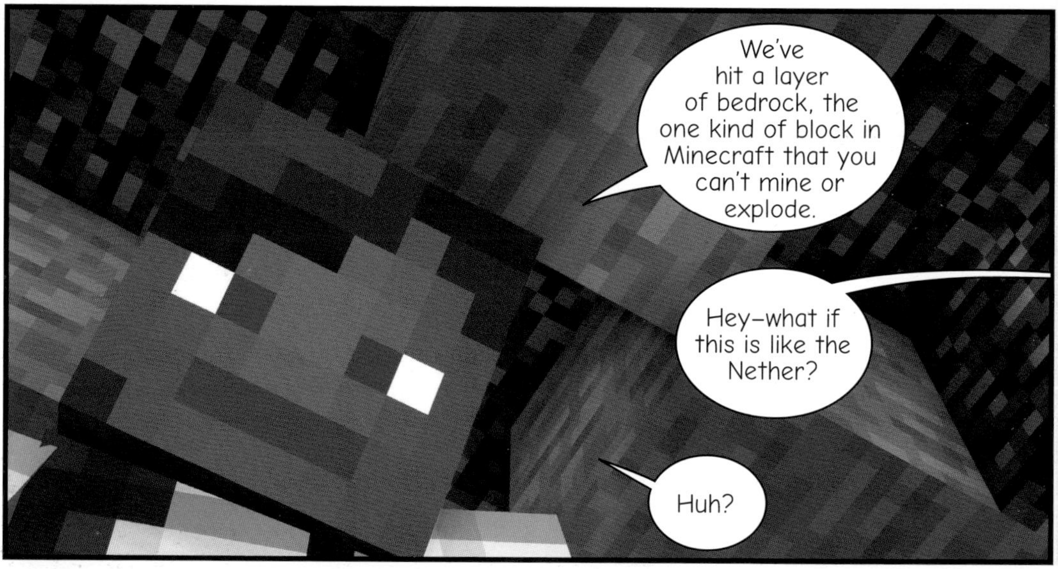
We've hit a layer of bedrock, the one kind of block in Minecraft that you can't mine or explode.
Hey–what if this is like the Nether?
Huh?

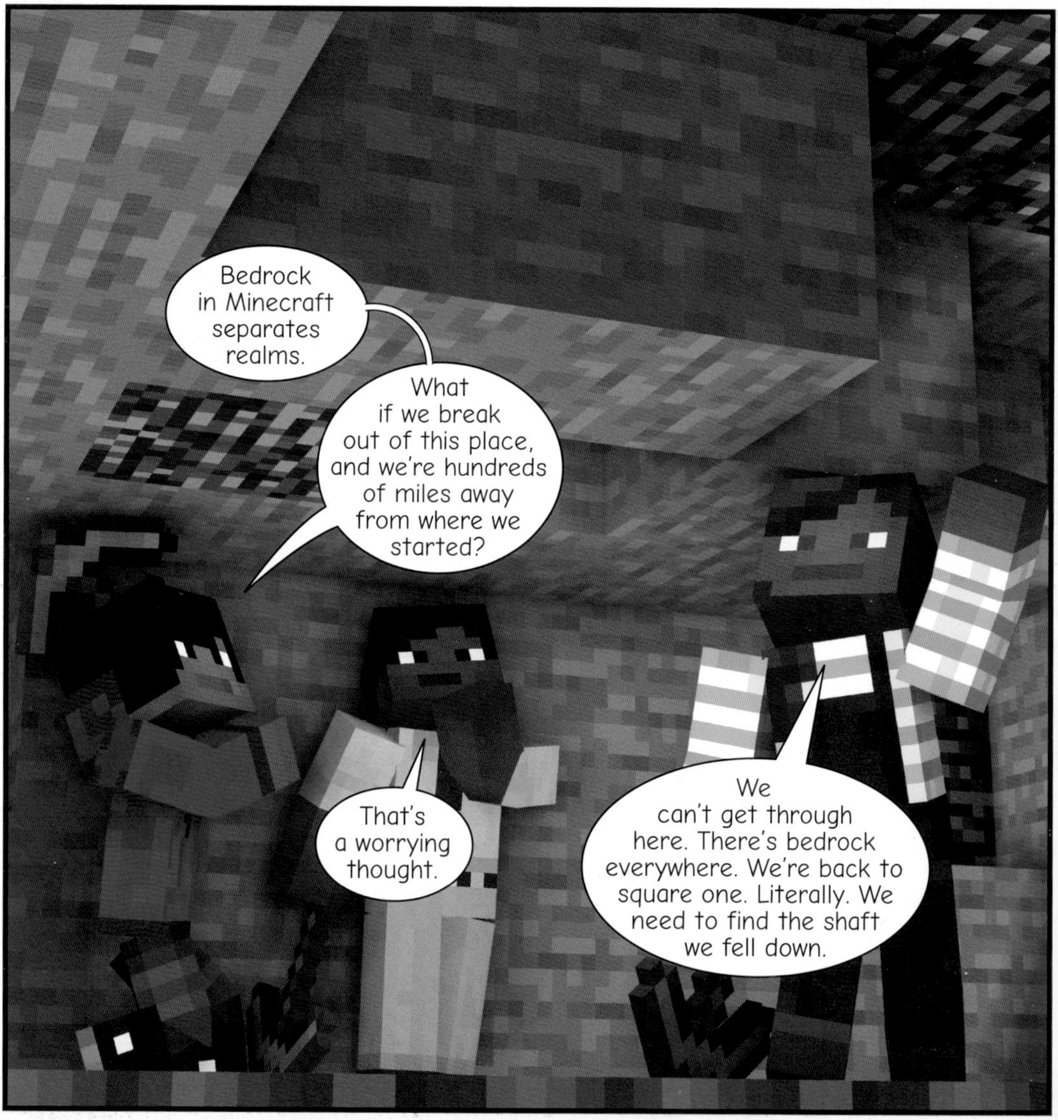
Bedrock in Minecraft separates realms.
What if we break out of this place, and we're hundreds of miles away from where we started?
That's a worrying thought.
We can't get through here. There's bedrock everywhere. We're back to square one. Literally. We need to find the shaft we fell down.

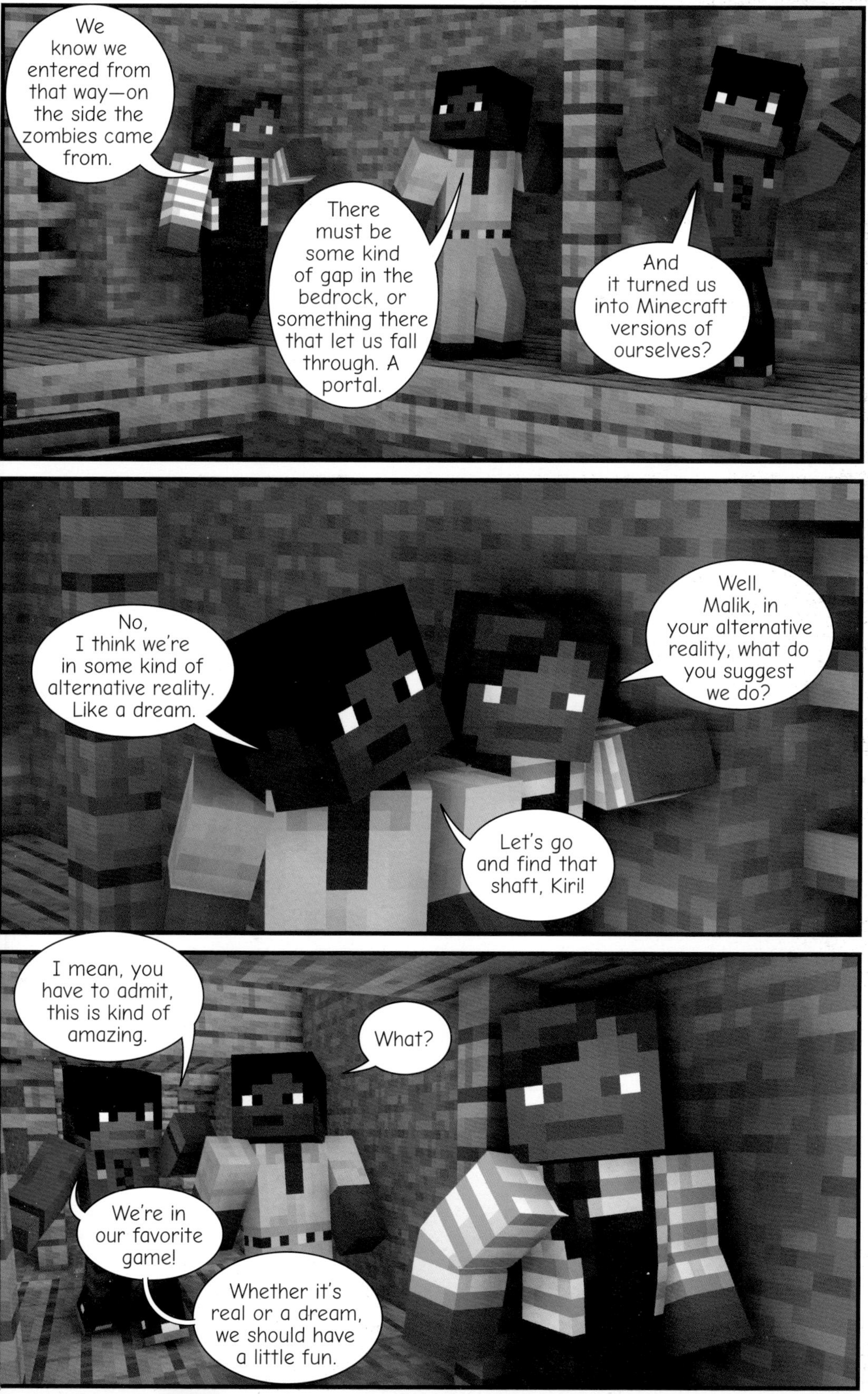
We know we entered from that way—on the side the zombies came from.
There must be some kind of gap in the bedrock, or something there that let us fall through. A portal.
And it turned us into Minecraft versions of ourselves?
No, I think we're in some kind of alternative reality. Like a dream.
Well, Malik, in your alternative reality, what do you suggest we do?
Let's go and find that shaft, Kiri!
I mean, you have to admit, this is kind of amazing.
What?
We're in our favorite game!
Whether it's real or a dream, we should have a little fun.

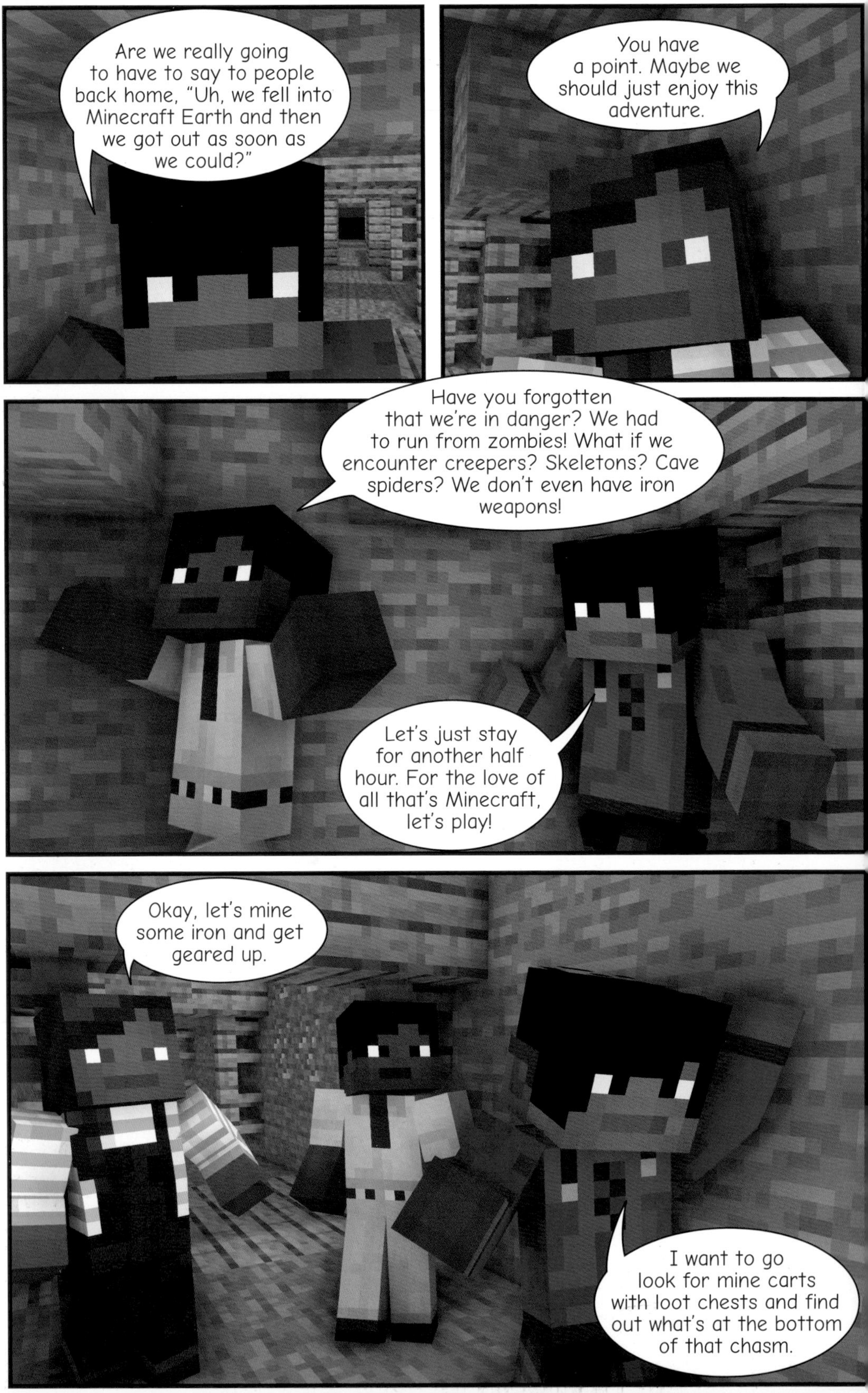
Are we really going to have to say to people back home, "Uh, we fell into Minecraft Earth and then we got out as soon as we could?"
You have a point. Maybe we should just enjoy this adventure.
Have you forgotten that we're in danger? We had to run from zombies! What if we encounter creepers? Skeletons? Cave spiders? We don't even have iron weapons!
Let's just stay for another half hour. For the love of all that's Minecraft, let's play!
Okay, let's mine some iron and get geared up.
I want to go look for mine carts with loot chests and find out what's at the bottom of that chasm.

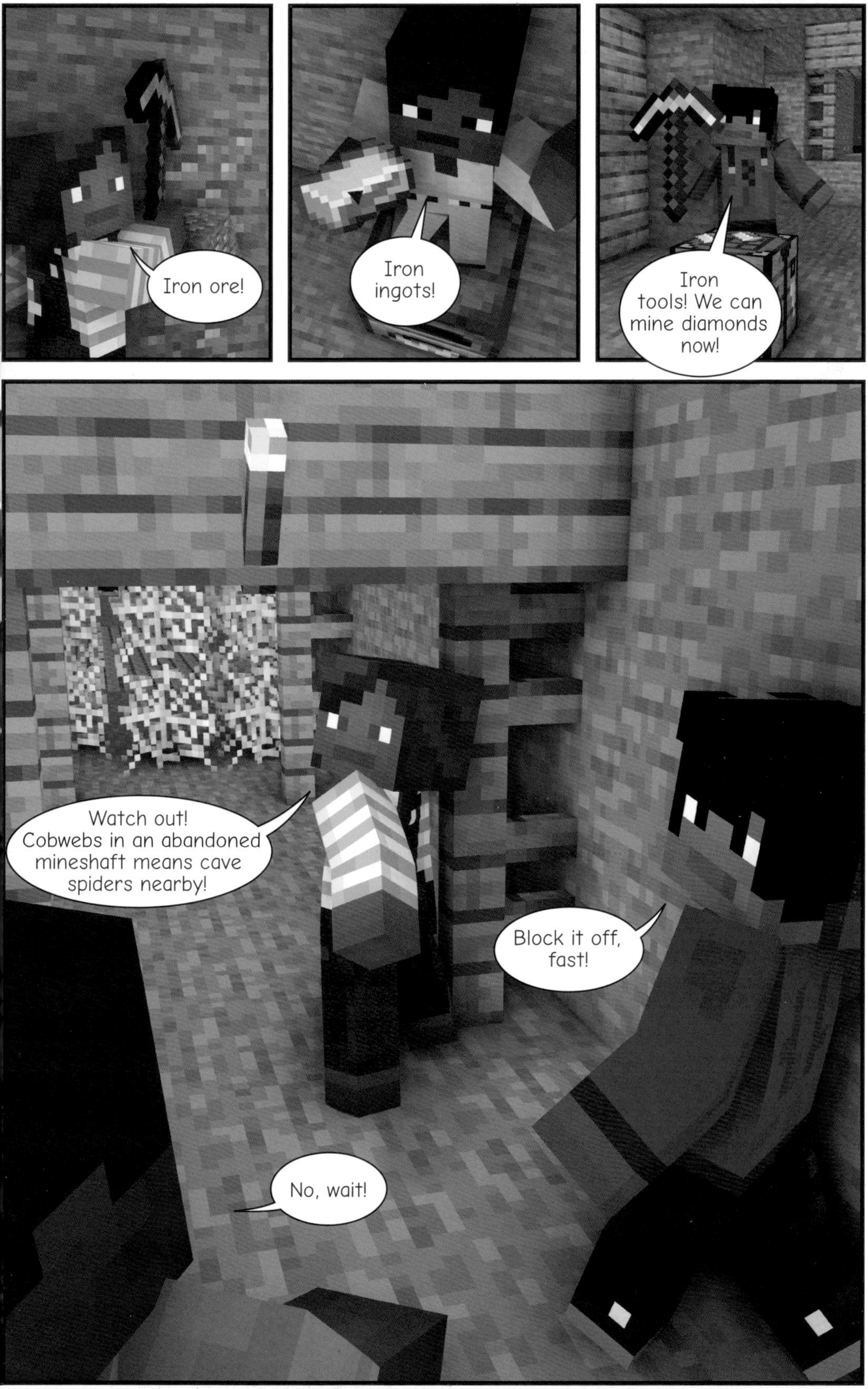
Iron ore!
Iron ingots!
Iron tools! We can mine diamonds now!
Watch out! Cobwebs in an abandoned mineshaft means cave spiders nearby!
Block it off, fast!
No, wait!

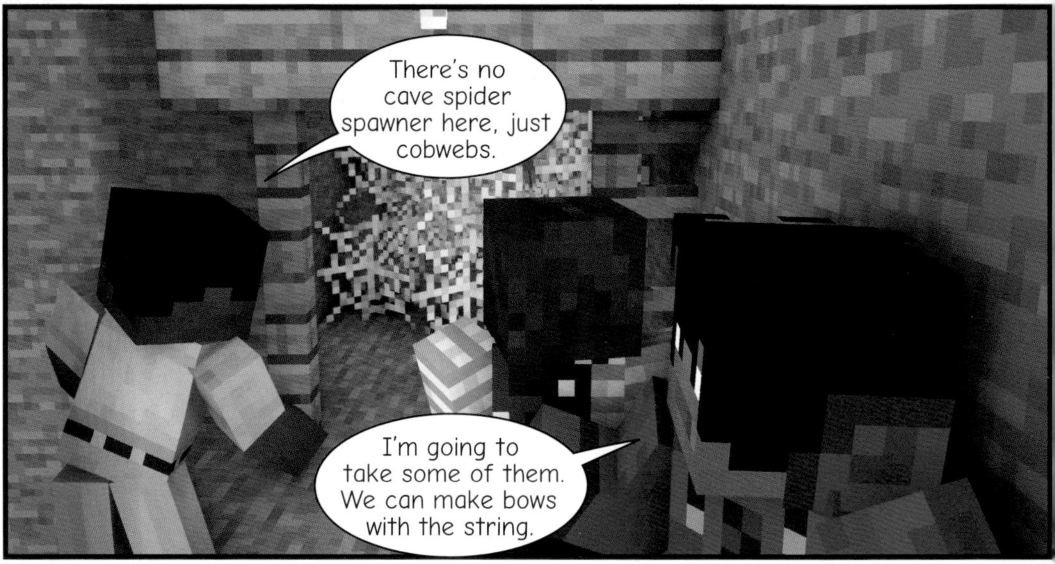
There's no cave spider spawner here, just cobwebs.
I'm going to take some of them. We can make bows with the string.

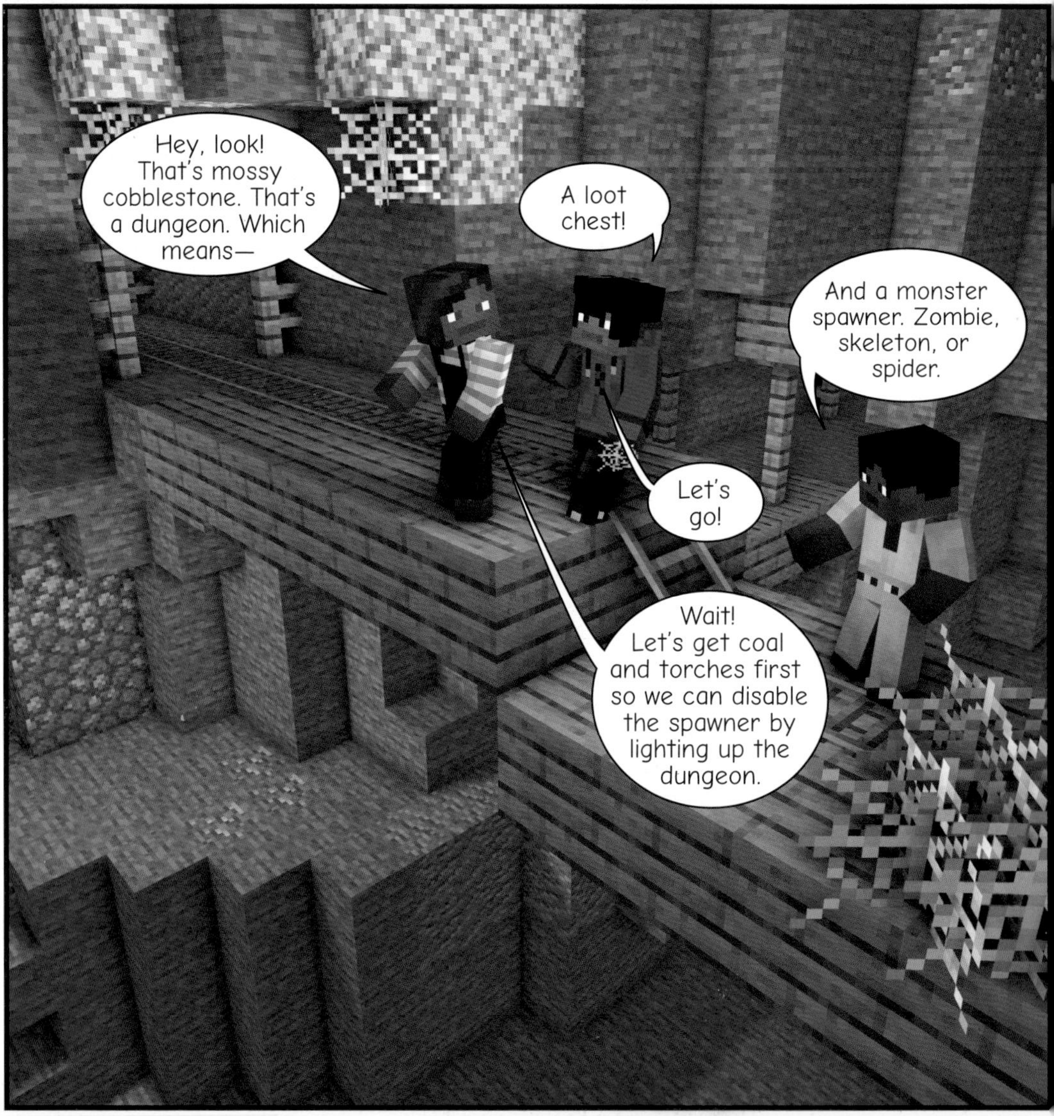
Hey, look! That's mossy cobblestone. That's a dungeon. Which means—
A loot chest!
And a monster spawner. Zombie, skeleton, or spider.
Let's go!
Wait! Let's get coal and torches first so we can disable the spawner by lighting up the dungeon.

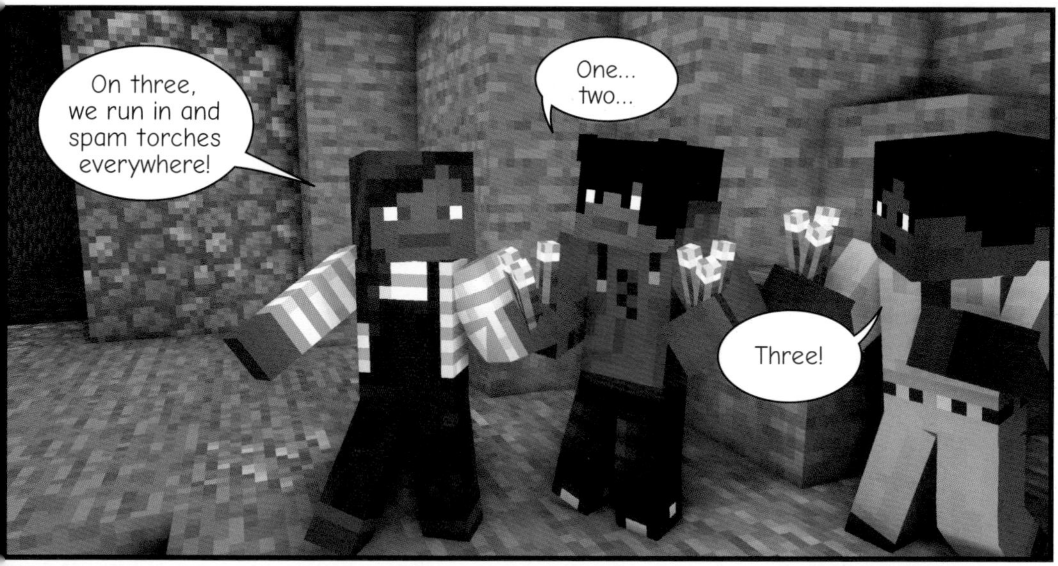
On three, we run in and spam torches everywhere!
One... two...
Three!

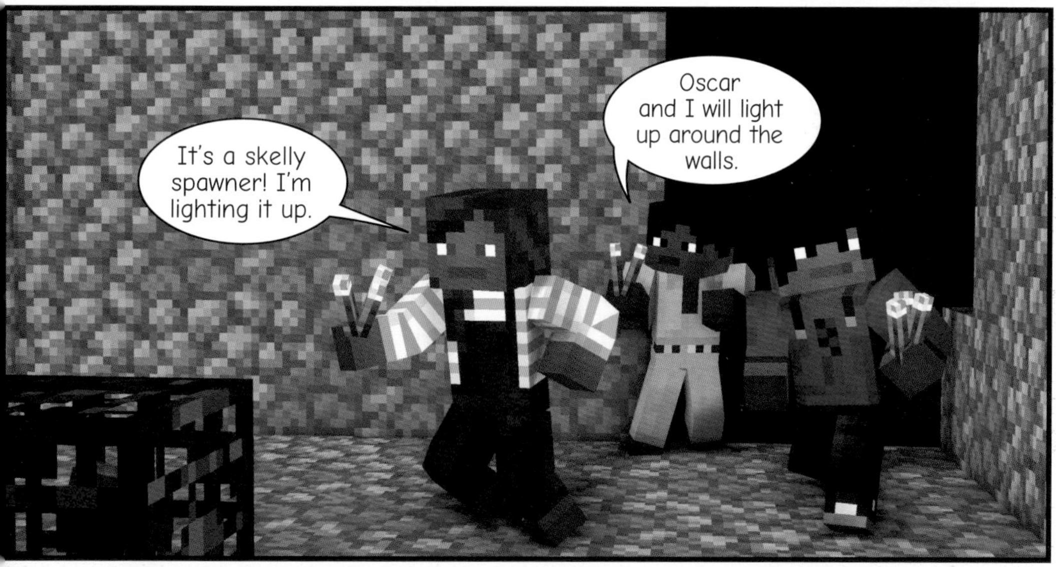
It's a skelly spawner! I'm lighting it up.
Oscar and I will light up around the walls.

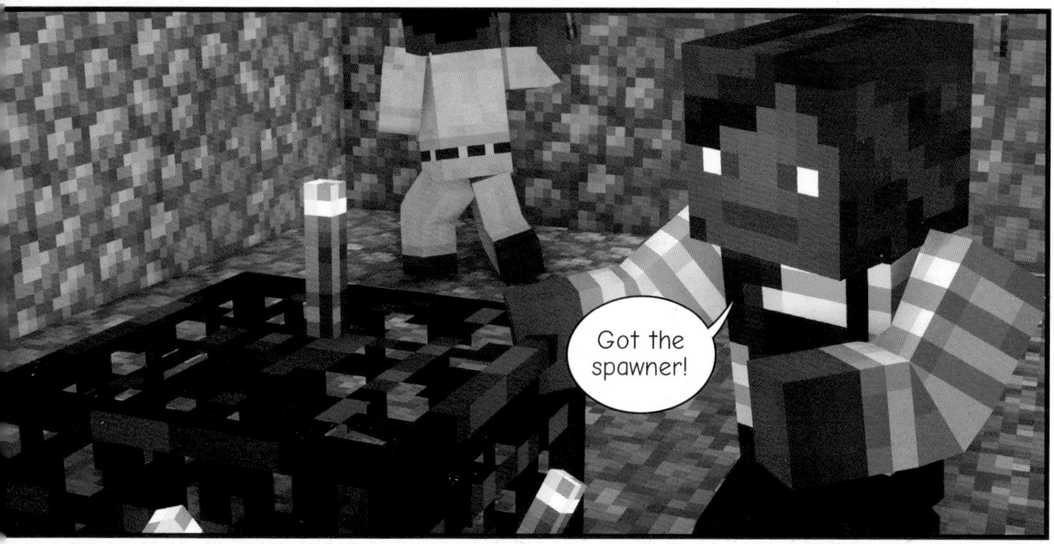
Got the spawner!

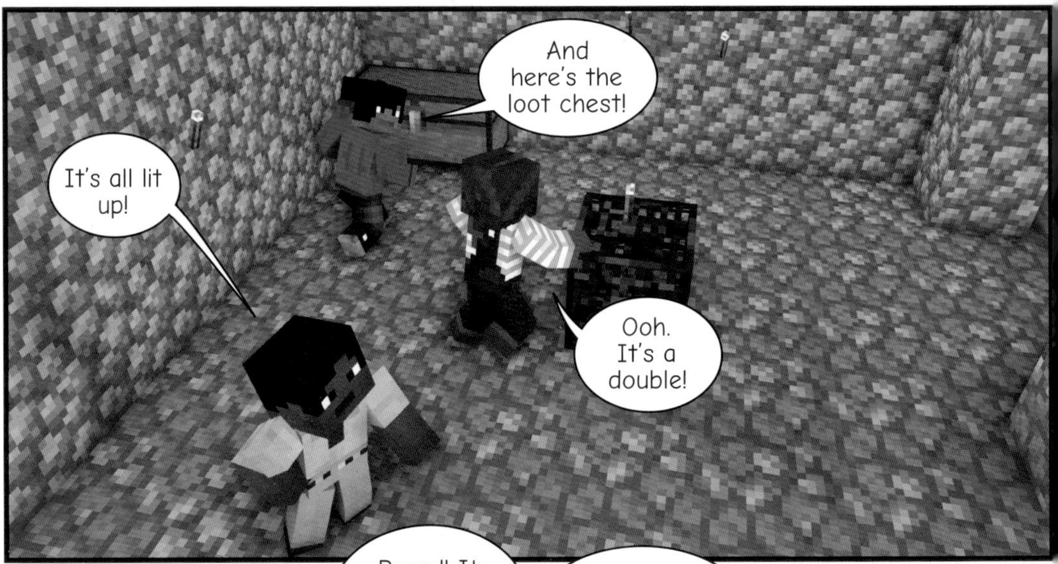
And here's the loot chest!
It's all lit up!
Ooh. It's a double!

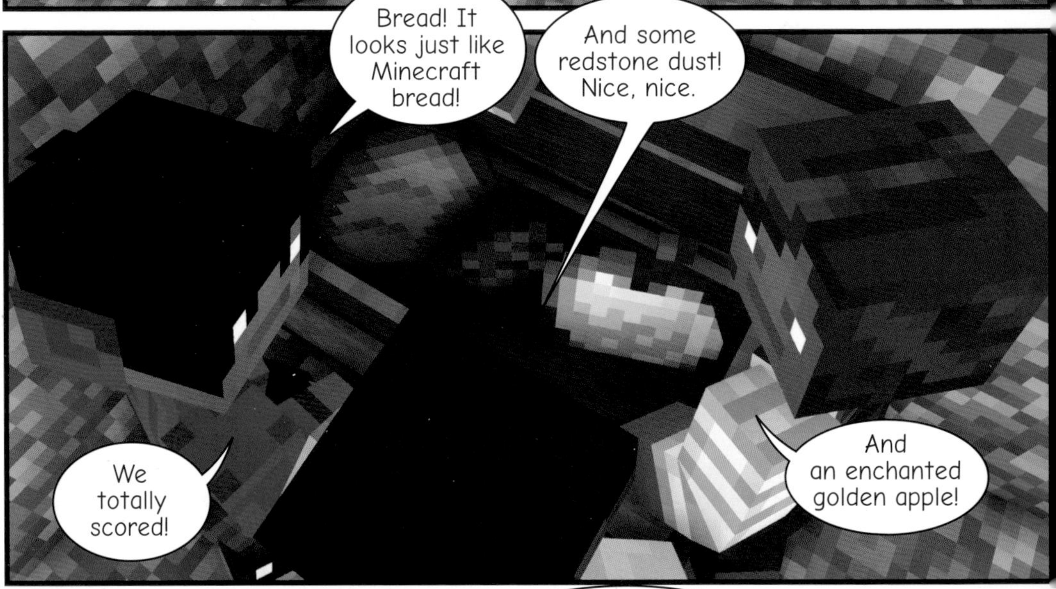
Bread! It looks just like Minecraft bread!
And some redstone dust! Nice, nice.
We totally scored!
And an enchanted golden apple!

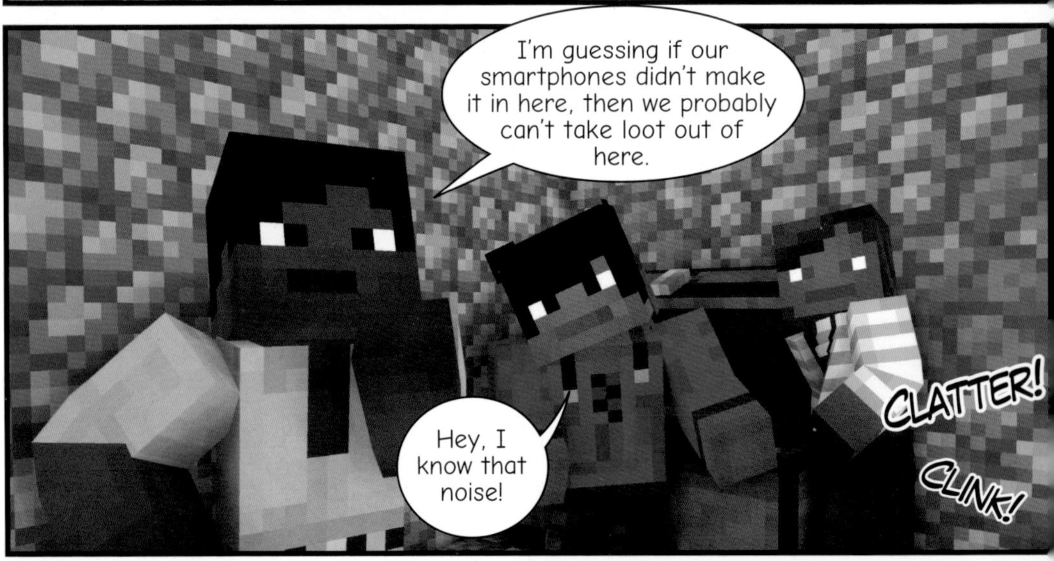
I'm guessing if our smartphones didn't make it in here, then we probably can't take loot out of here.
Hey, I know that noise!
CLATTER!
CLINK!

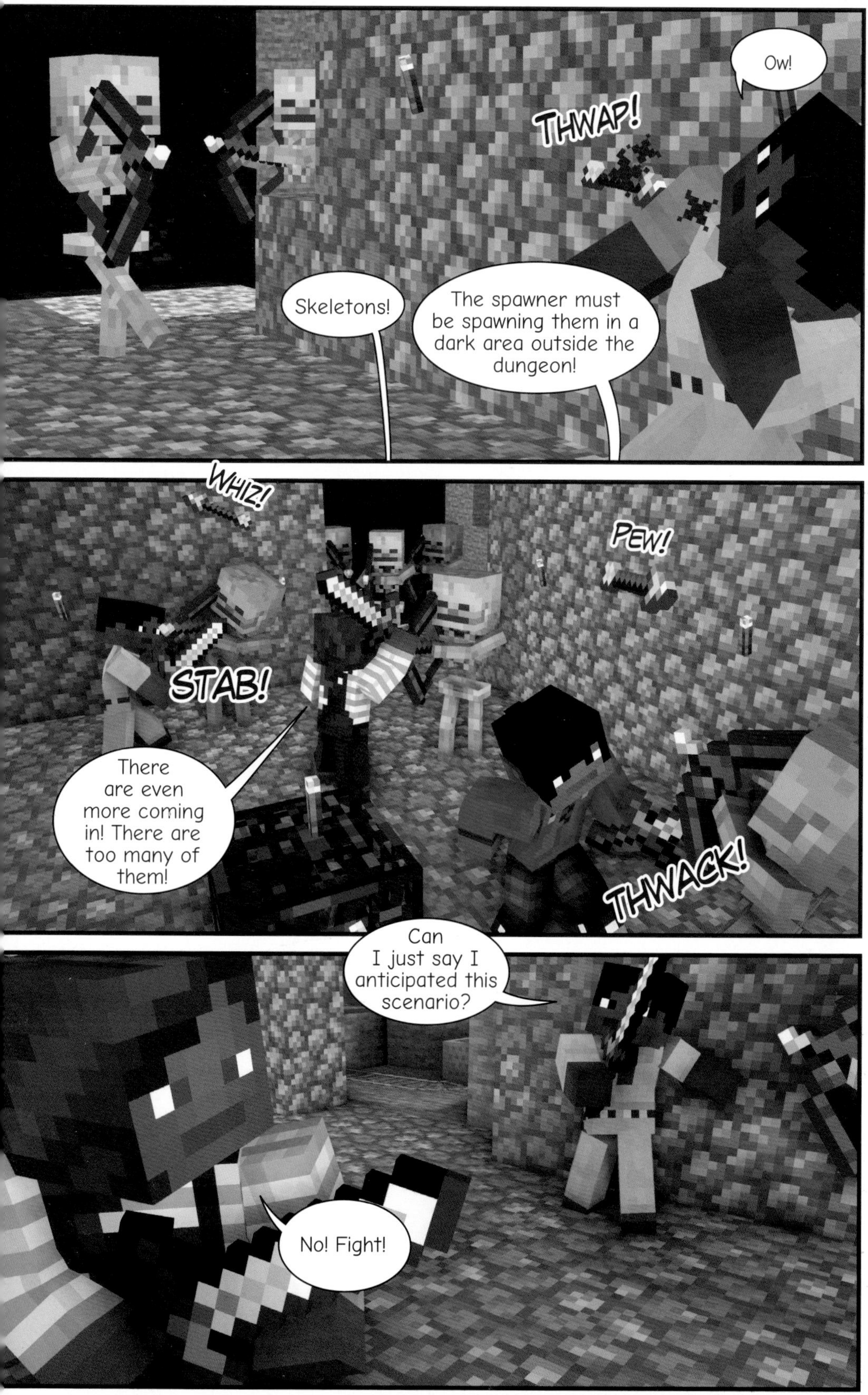
Ow!
THWAP!
Skeletons!
The spawner must be spawning them in a dark area outside the dungeon!
WHIZ!
PEW!
STAB!
There are even more coming in! There are too many of them!
THWACK!
Can I just say I anticipated this scenario?
No! Fight!

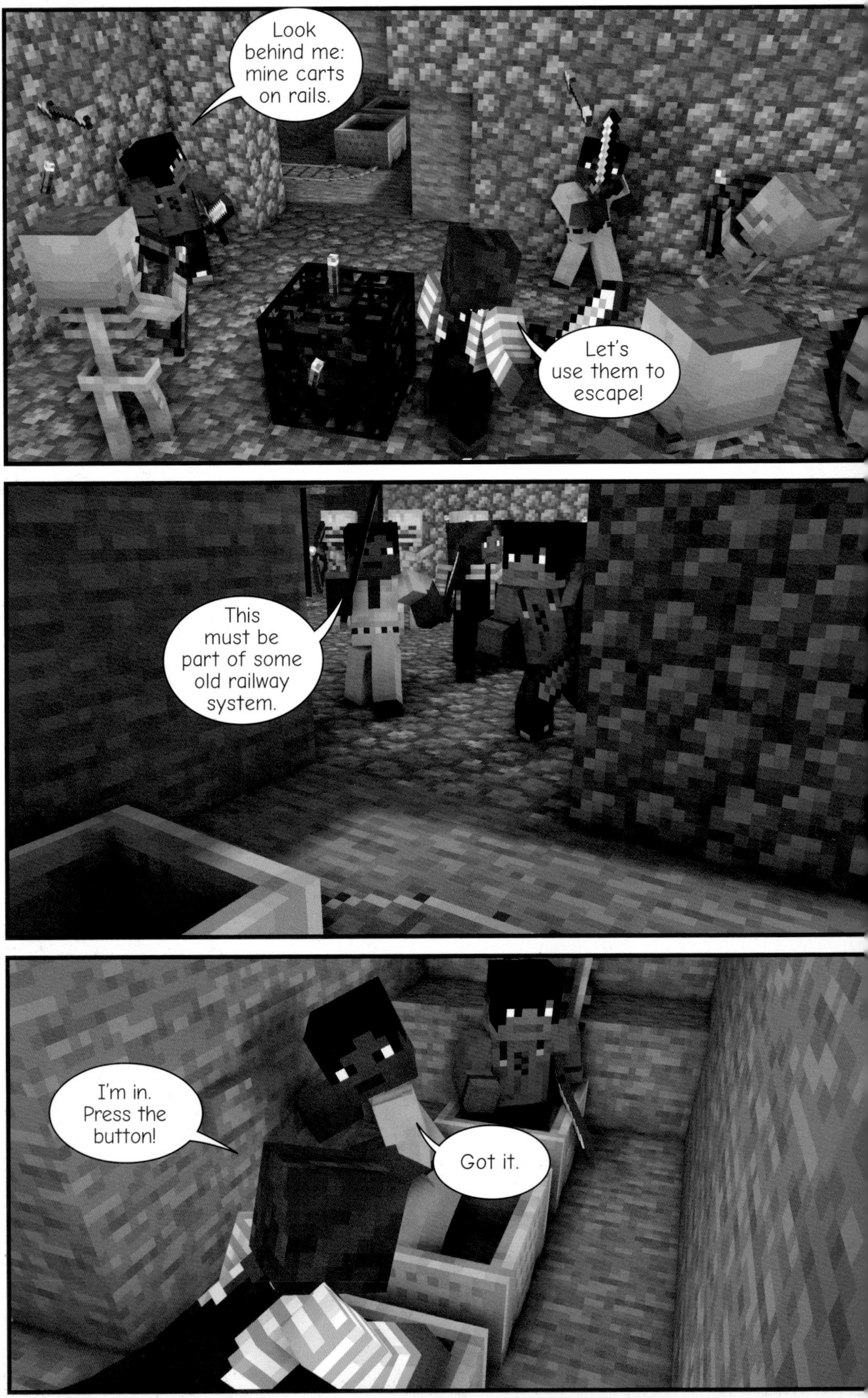
Look behind me: mine carts on rails.
Let's use them to escape!
This must be part of some old railway system.
I'm in. Press the button!
Got it.

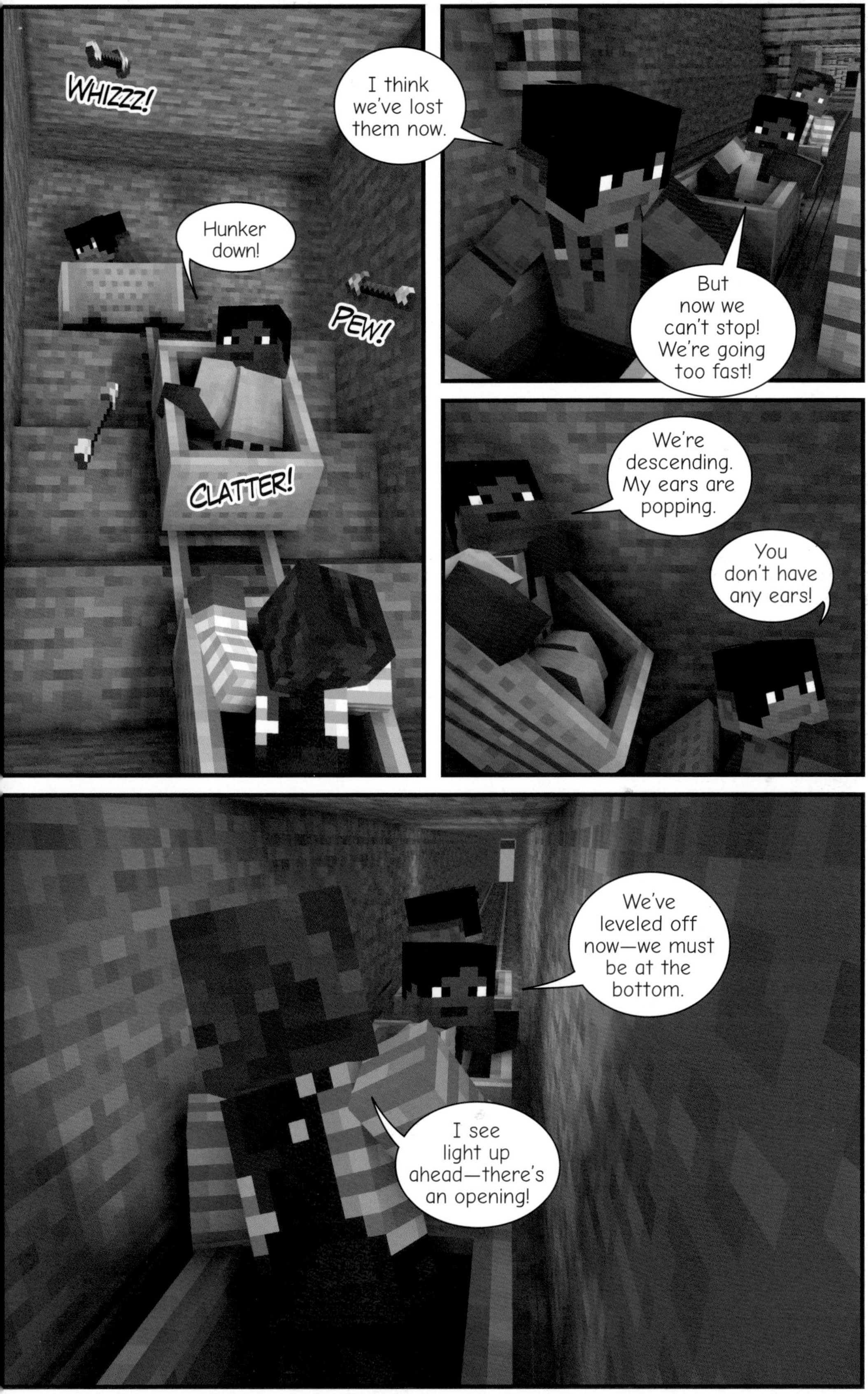
WHIZZZ!
Hunker down!
PEW!
CLATTER!
I think we've lost them now.
But now we can't stop! We're going too fast!
We're descending. My ears are popping.
You don't have any ears!
We've leveled off now—we must be at the bottom.
I see light up ahead—there's an opening!

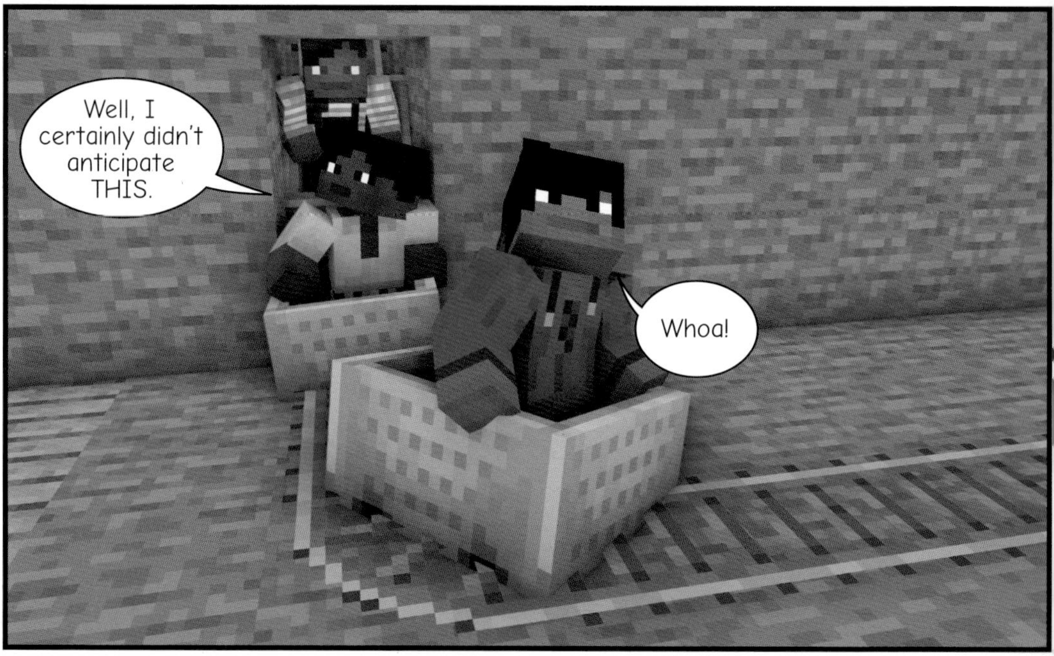
Well, I certainly didn't anticipate THIS.
Whoa!

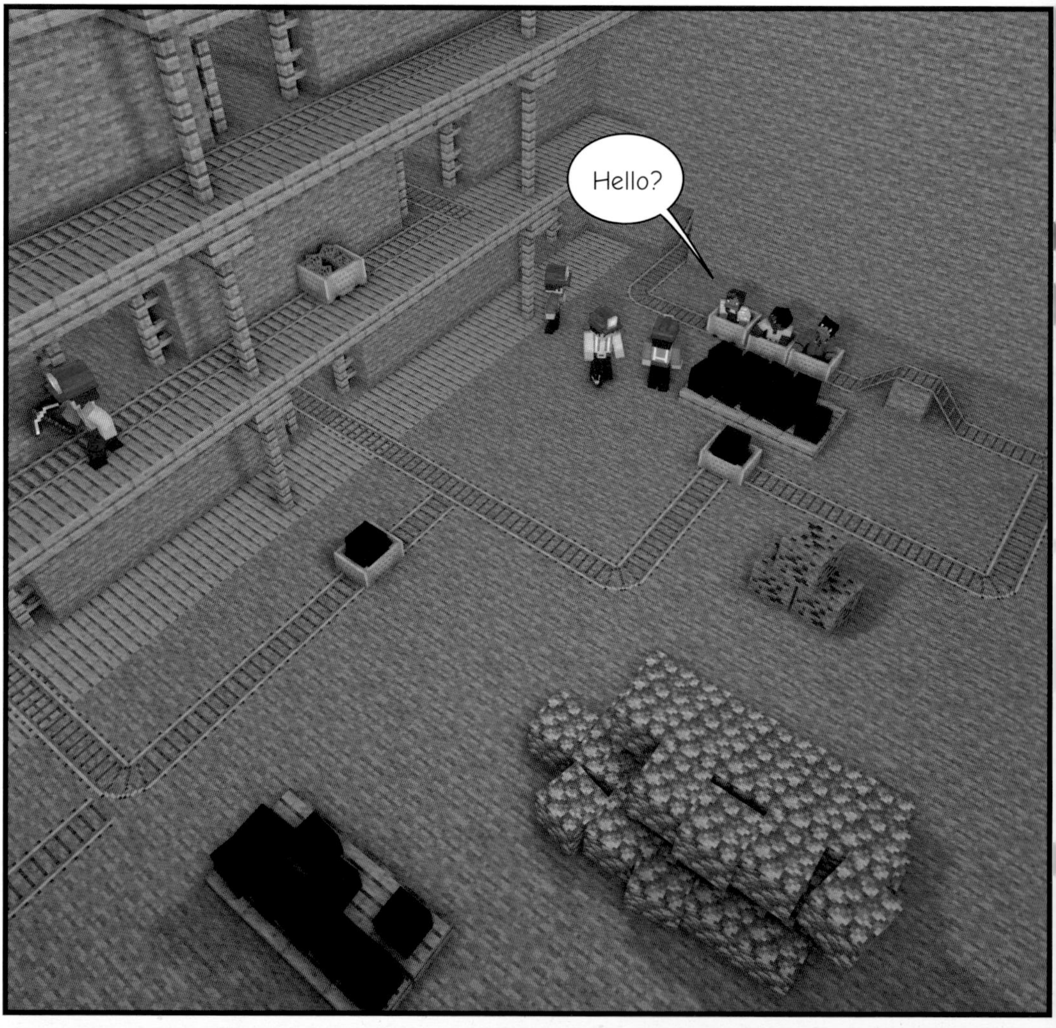
Hello?

Chapter 3

Union
Cobblestone
Camp

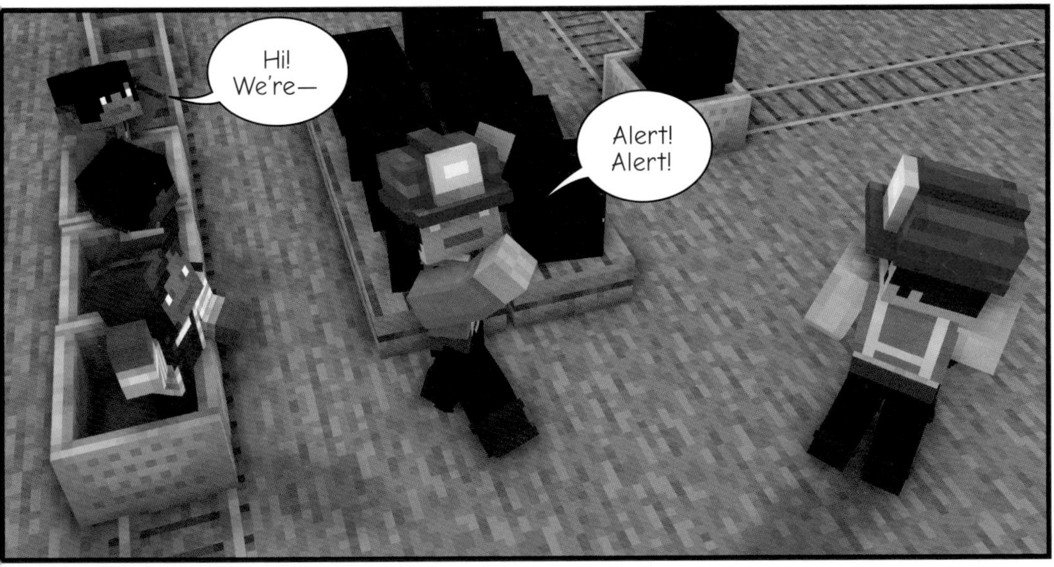
Hi! We're—
Alert! Alert!

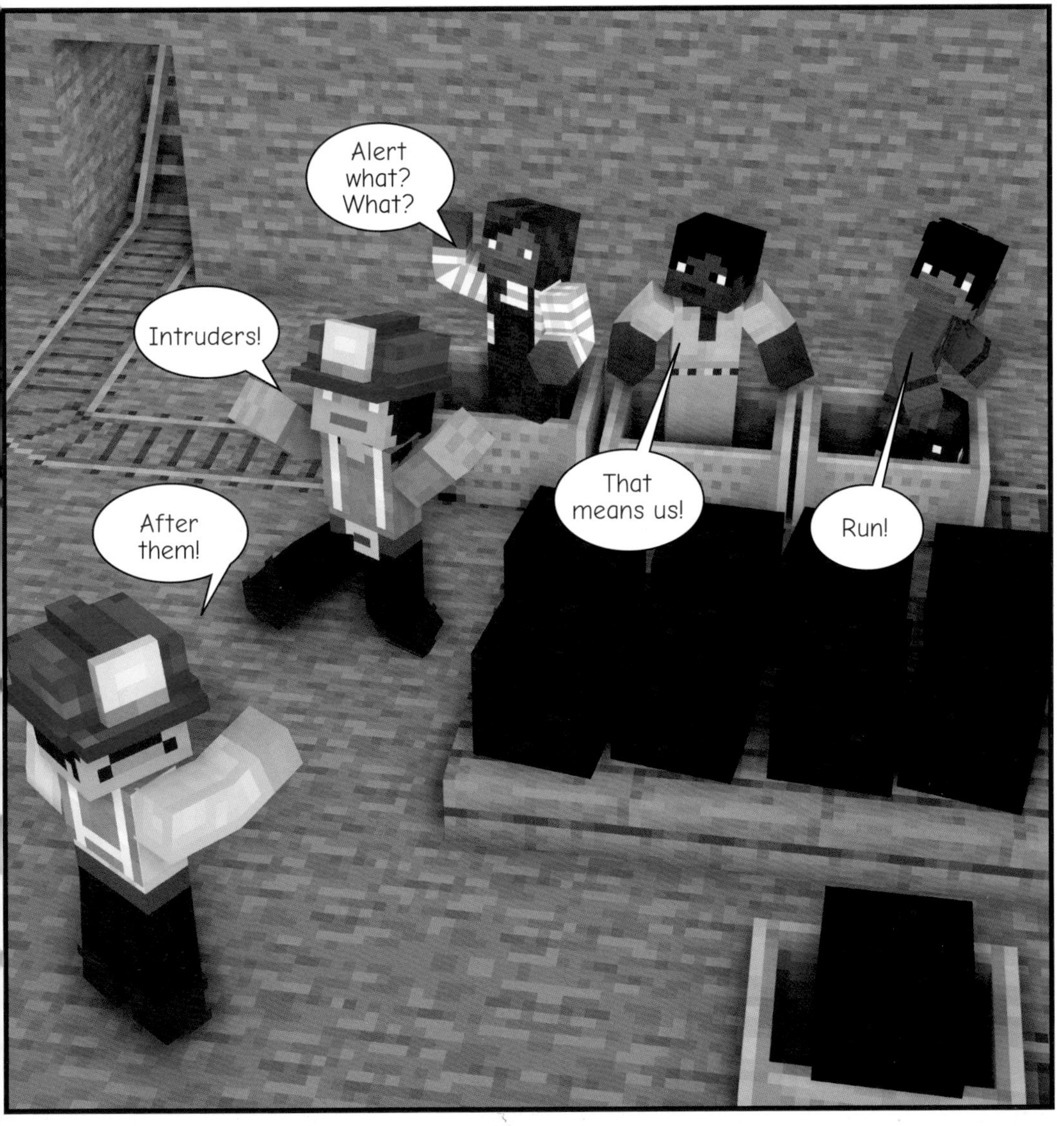
Alert what? What?
Intruders!
After them!
That means us!
Run!

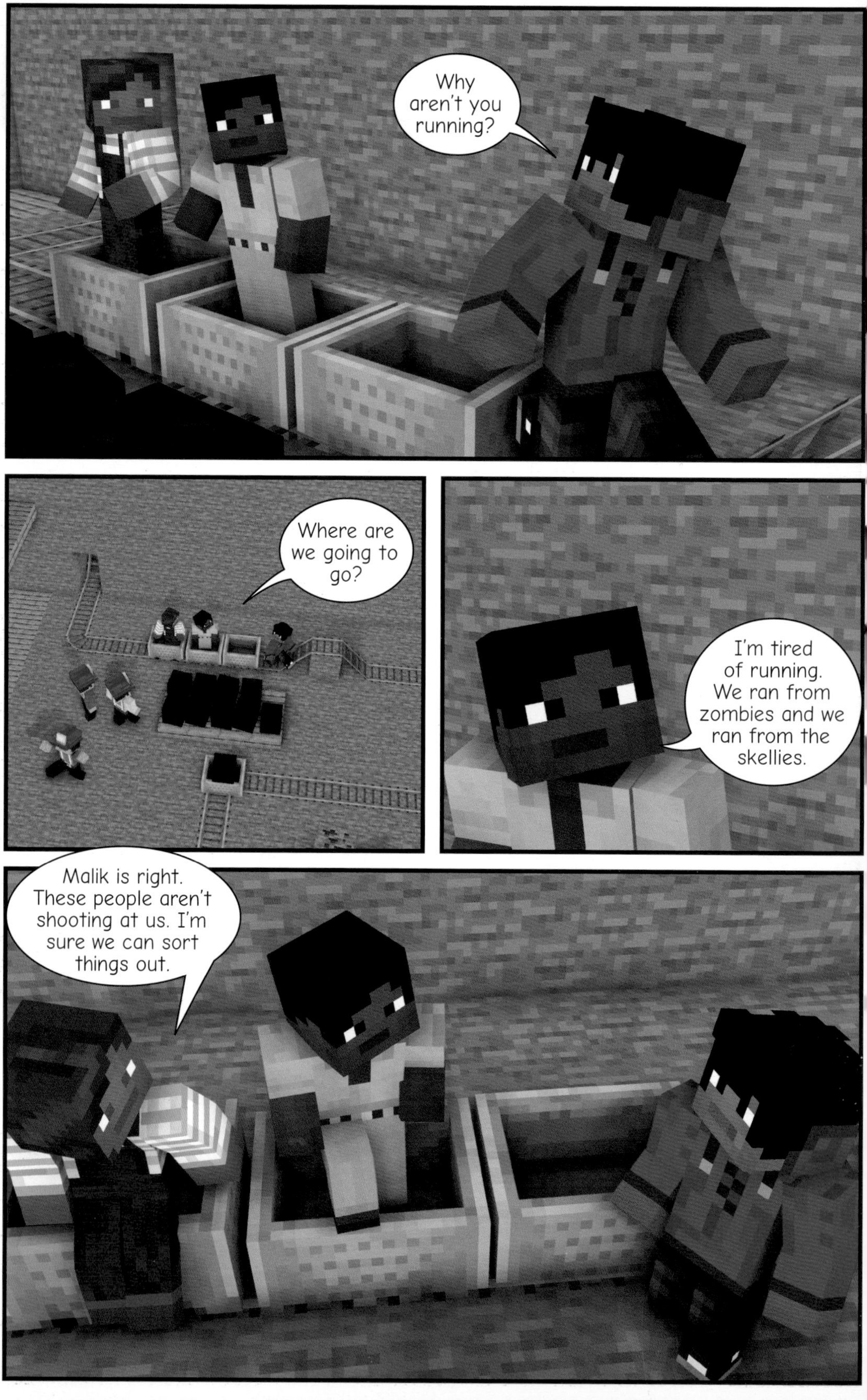
Why aren't you running?
Where are we going to go?
I'm tired of running. We ran from zombies and we ran from the skellies.
Malik is right. These people aren't shooting at us. I'm sure we can sort things out.

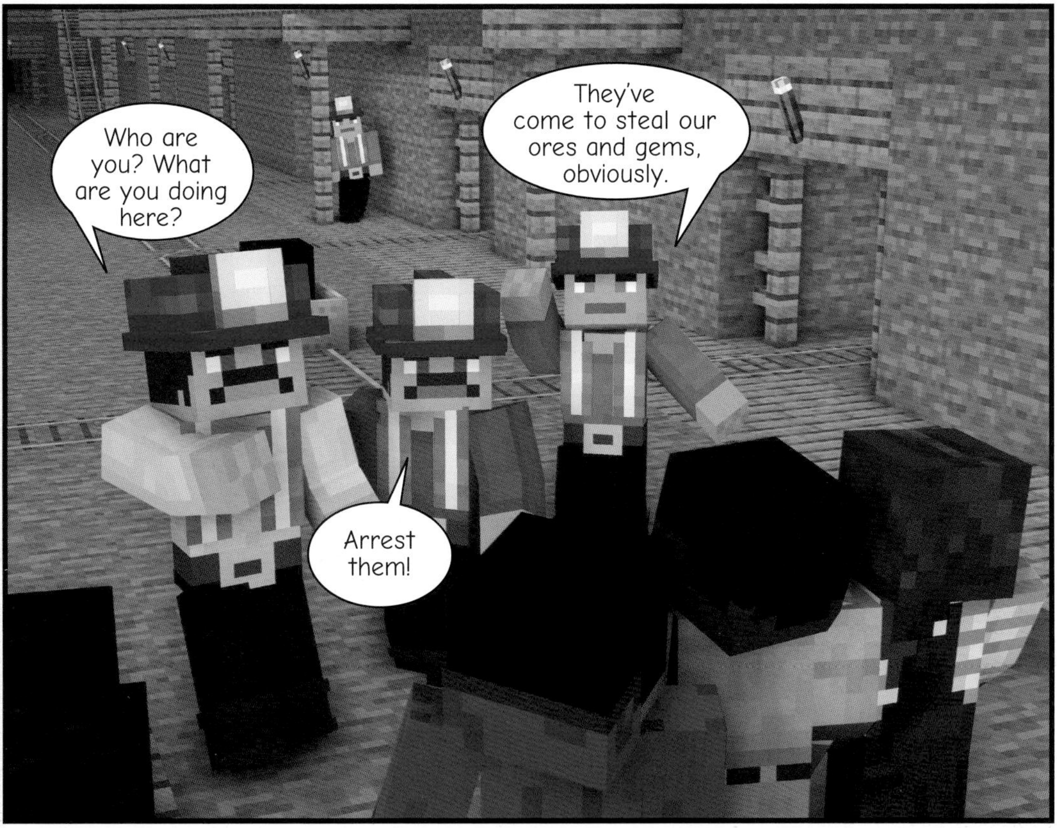
Who are you? What are you doing here?
They've come to steal our ores and gems, obviously.
Arrest them!

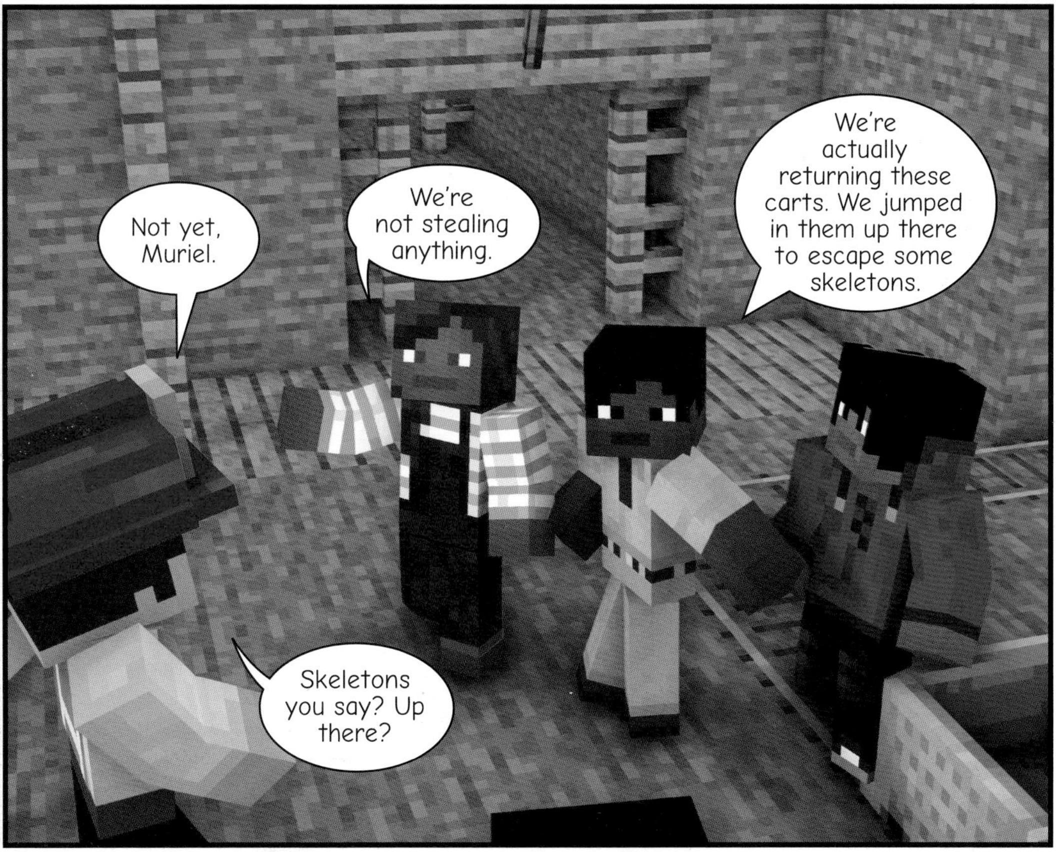
Not yet, Muriel.
We're not stealing anything.
We're actually returning these carts. We jumped in them up there to escape some skeletons.
Skeletons you say? Up there?

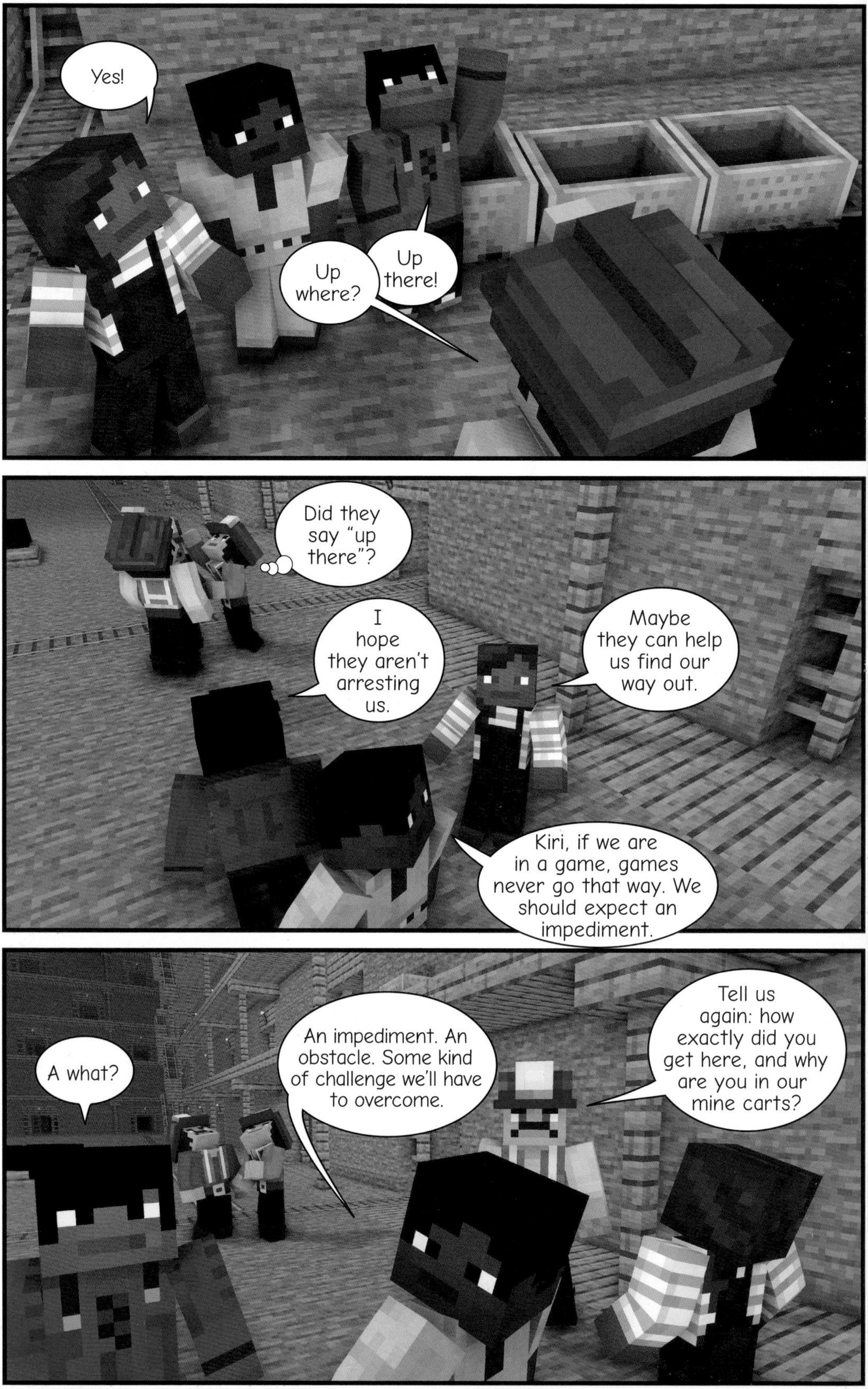
Yes!
Up there!
Up where?
Did they say "up there"?
I hope they aren't arresting us.
Maybe they can help us find our way out.
Kiri, if we are in a game, games never go that way. We should expect an impediment.
A what?
An impediment. An obstacle. Some kind of challenge we'll have to overcome.
Tell us again: how exactly did you get here, and why are you in our mine carts?

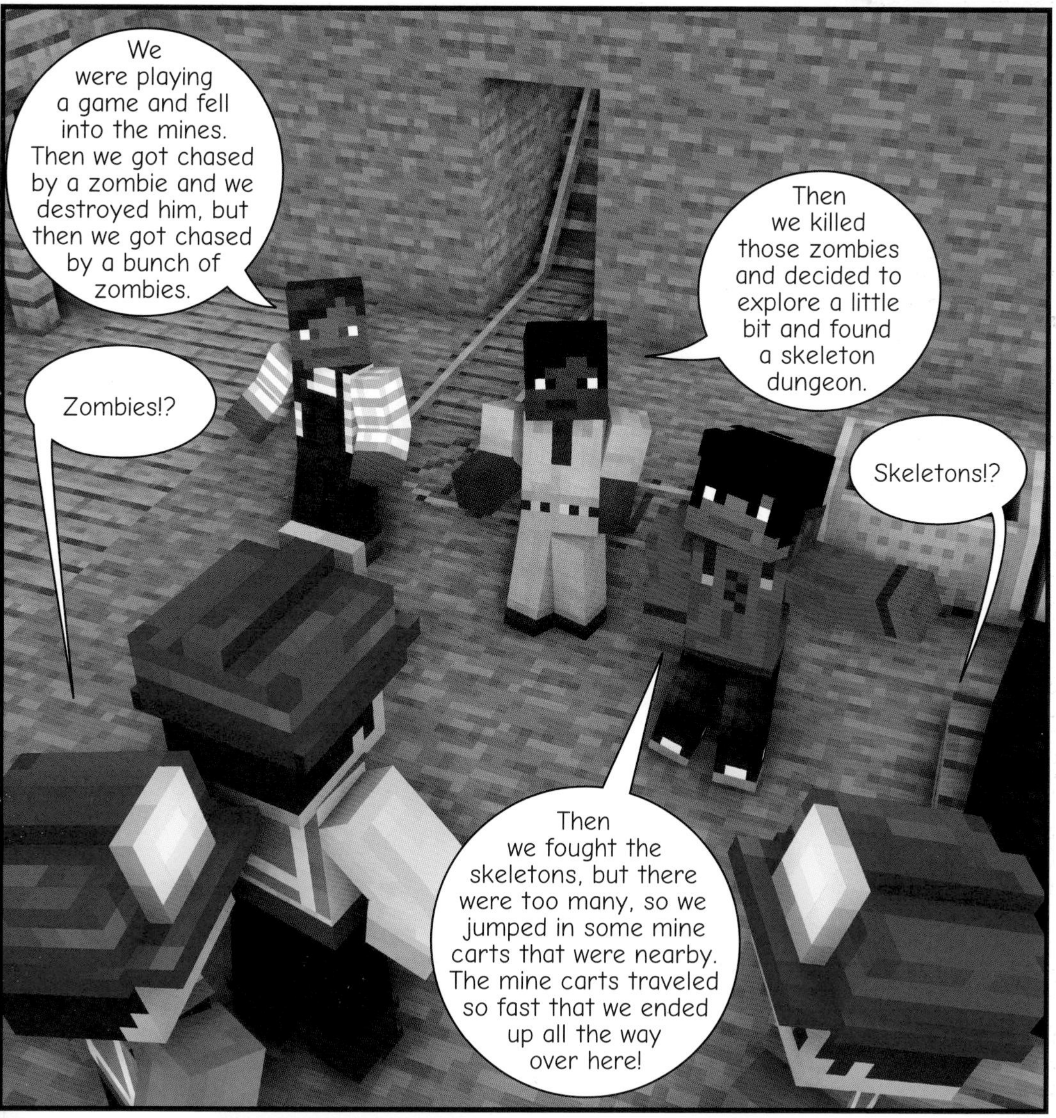
We were playing a game and fell into the mines. Then we got chased by a zombie and we destroyed him, but then we got chased by a bunch of zombies.
Then we killed those zombies and decided to explore a little bit and found a skeleton dungeon.
Zombies!?
Skeletons!?
Then we fought the skeletons, but there were too many, so we jumped in some mine carts that were nearby. The mine carts traveled so fast that we ended up all the way over here!

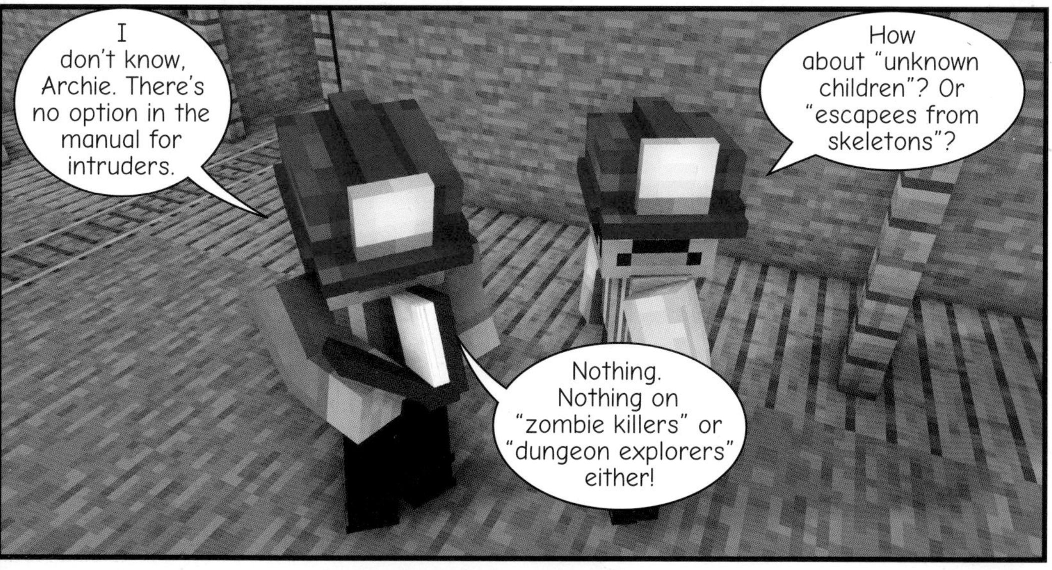
I don't know, Archie. There's no option in the manual for intruders.
How about "unknown children"? Or "escapees from skeletons"?
Nothing. Nothing on "zombie killers" or "dungeon explorers" either!

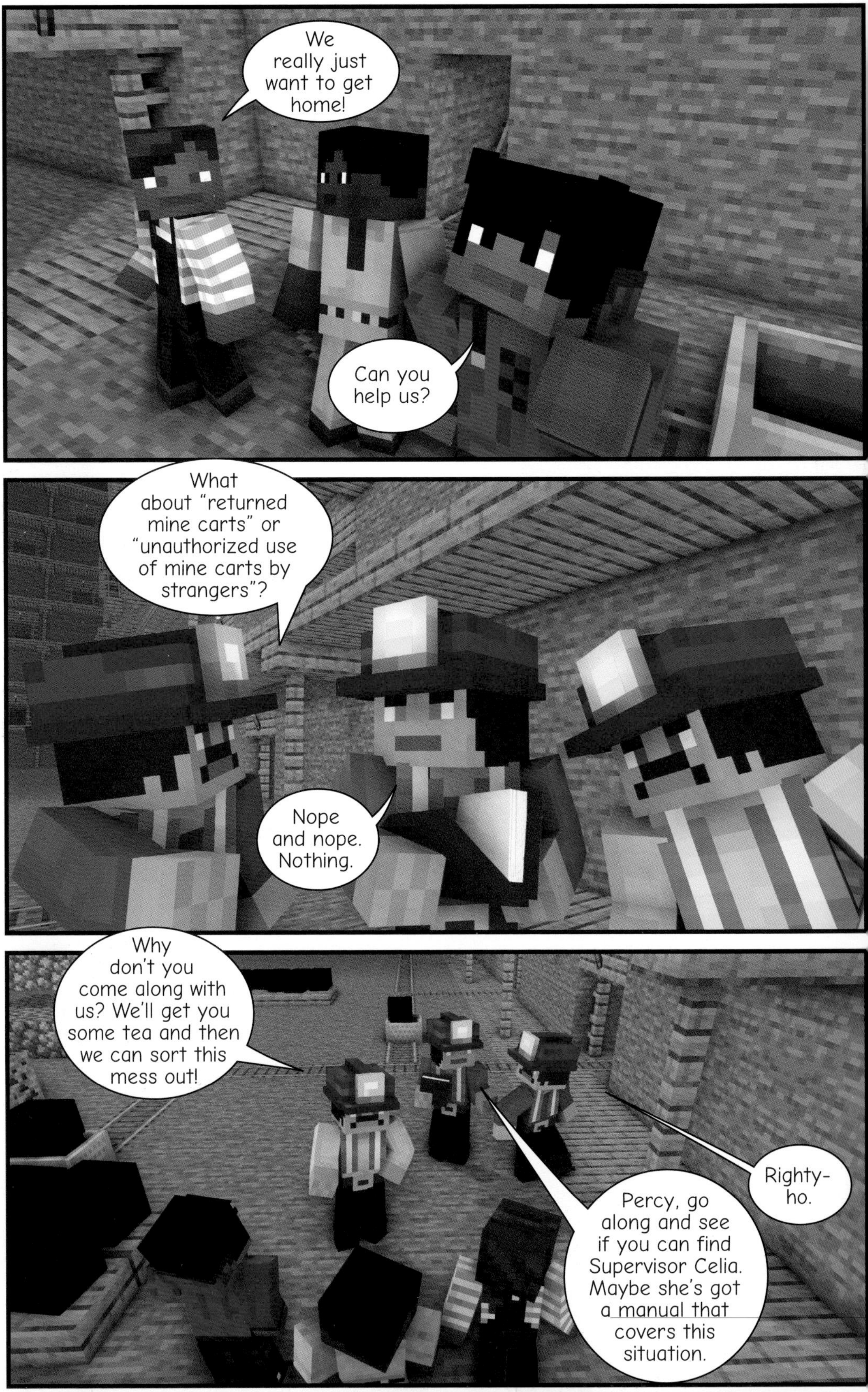

We really just want to get home!
Can you help us?
What about "returned mine carts" or "unauthorized use of mine carts by strangers"?
Nope and nope. Nothing.
Why don't you come along with us? We'll get you some tea and then we can sort this mess out!
Percy, go along and see if you can find Supervisor Celia. Maybe she's got a manual that covers this situation.
Righty-ho.

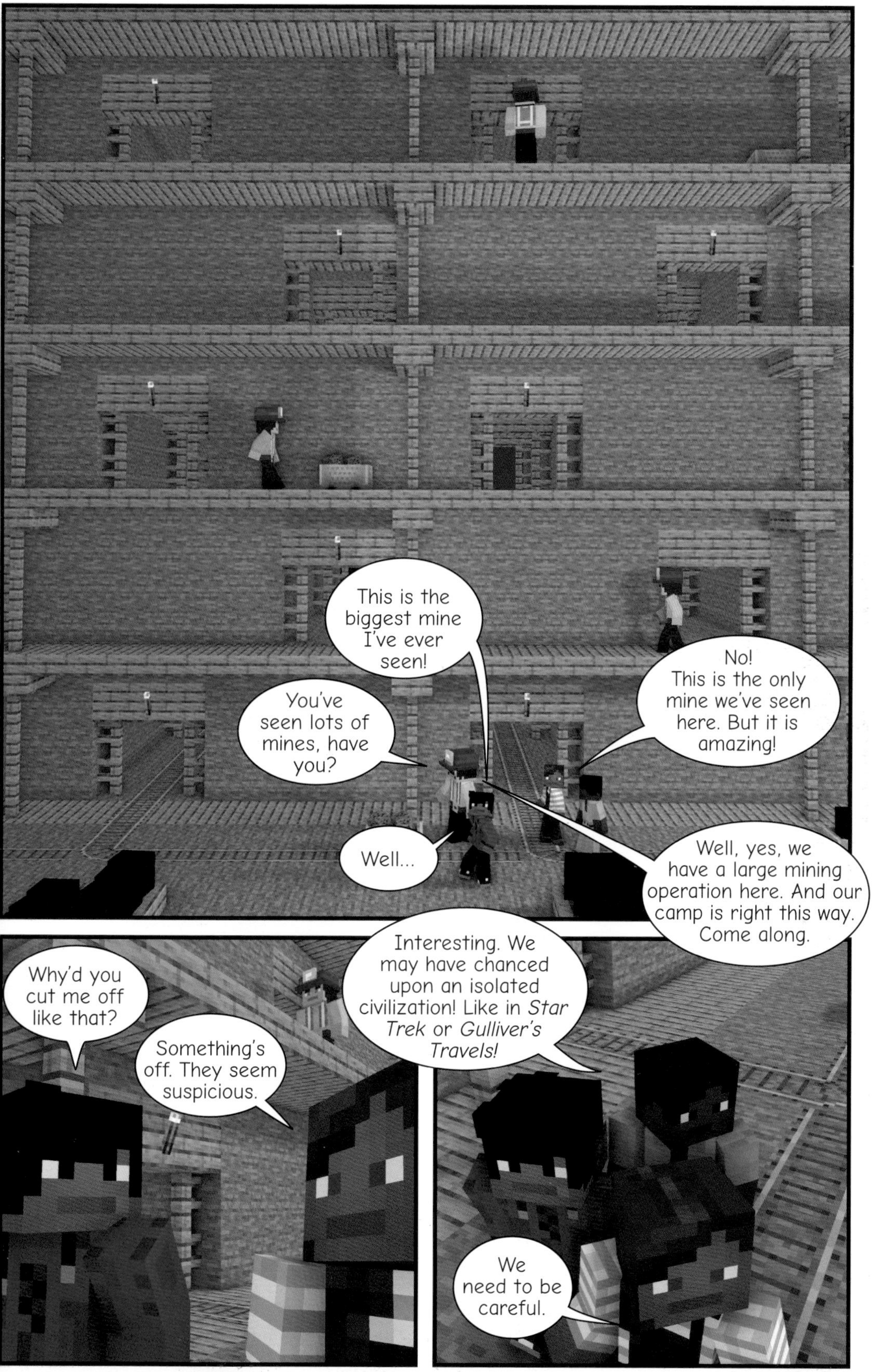
This is the biggest mine I've ever seen!
You've seen lots of mines, have you?
No! This is the only mine we've seen here. But it is amazing!
Well...
Well, yes, we have a large mining operation here. And our camp is right this way. Come along.
Why'd you cut me off like that?
Something's off. They seem suspicious.
Interesting. We may have chanced upon an isolated civilization! Like in *Star Trek* or *Gulliver's Travels!*
We need to be careful.

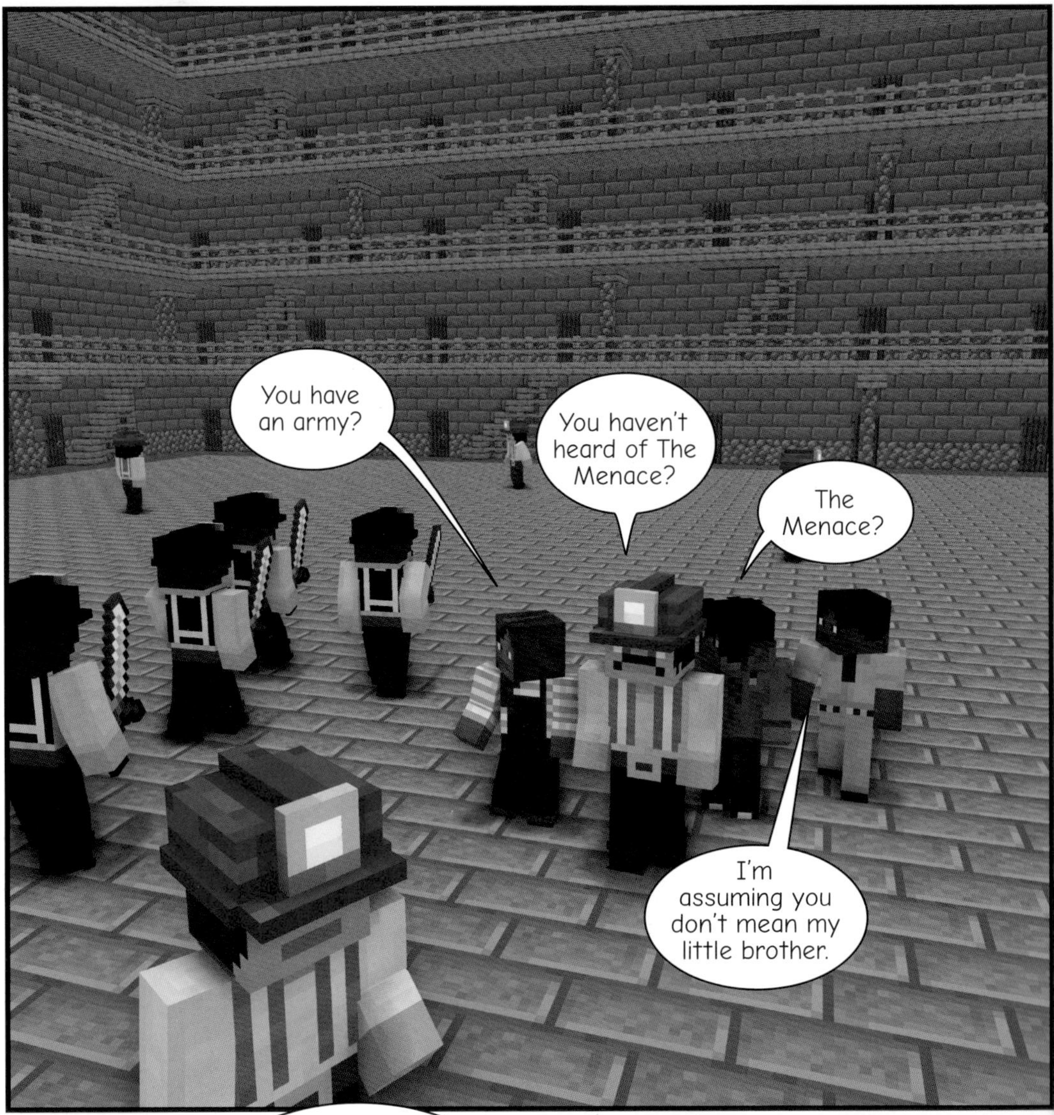
You have an army?
You haven't heard of The Menace?
The Menace?
I'm assuming you don't mean my little brother.

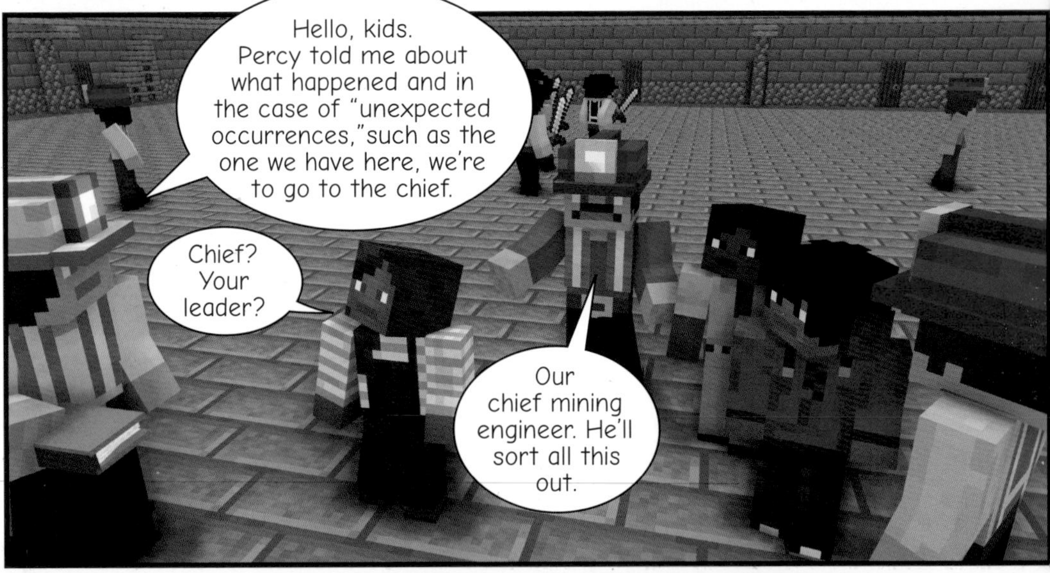
Hello, kids. Percy told me about what happened and in the case of "unexpected occurrences," such as the one we have here, we're to go to the chief.
Chief? Your leader?
Our chief mining engineer. He'll sort all this out.

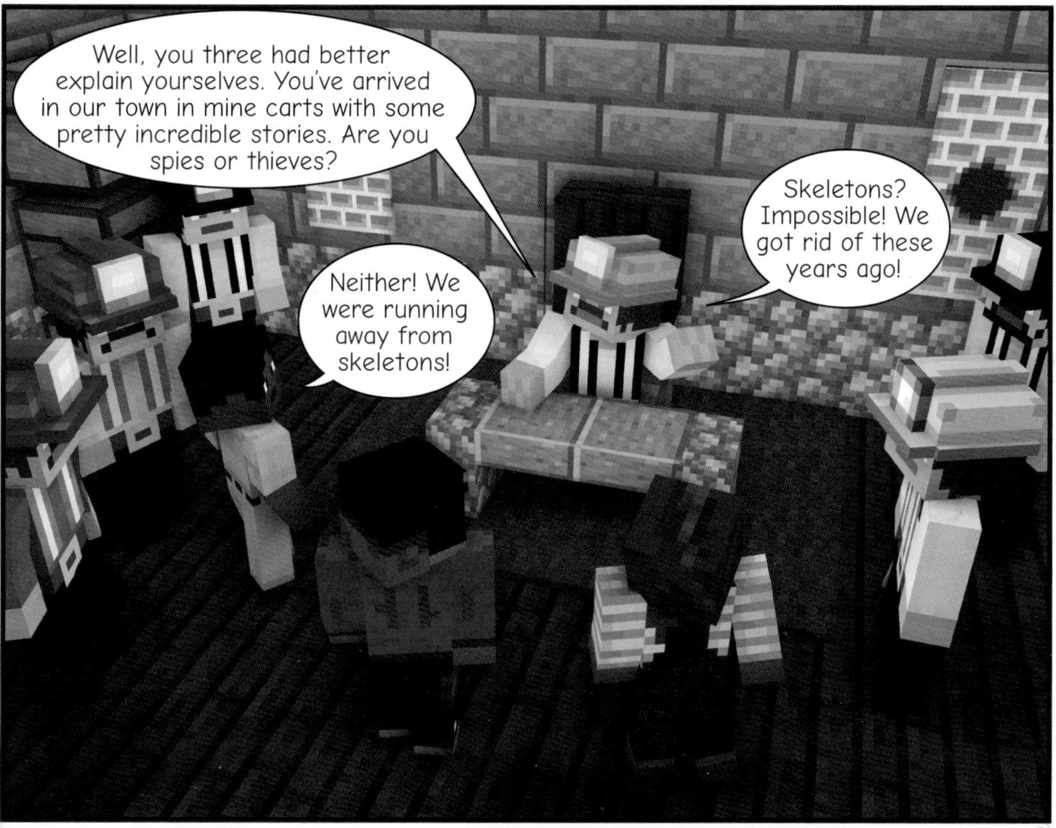
Well, you three had better explain yourselves. You've arrived in our town in mine carts with some pretty incredible stories. Are you spies or thieves?
Neither! We were running away from skeletons!
Skeletons? Impossible! We got rid of these years ago!

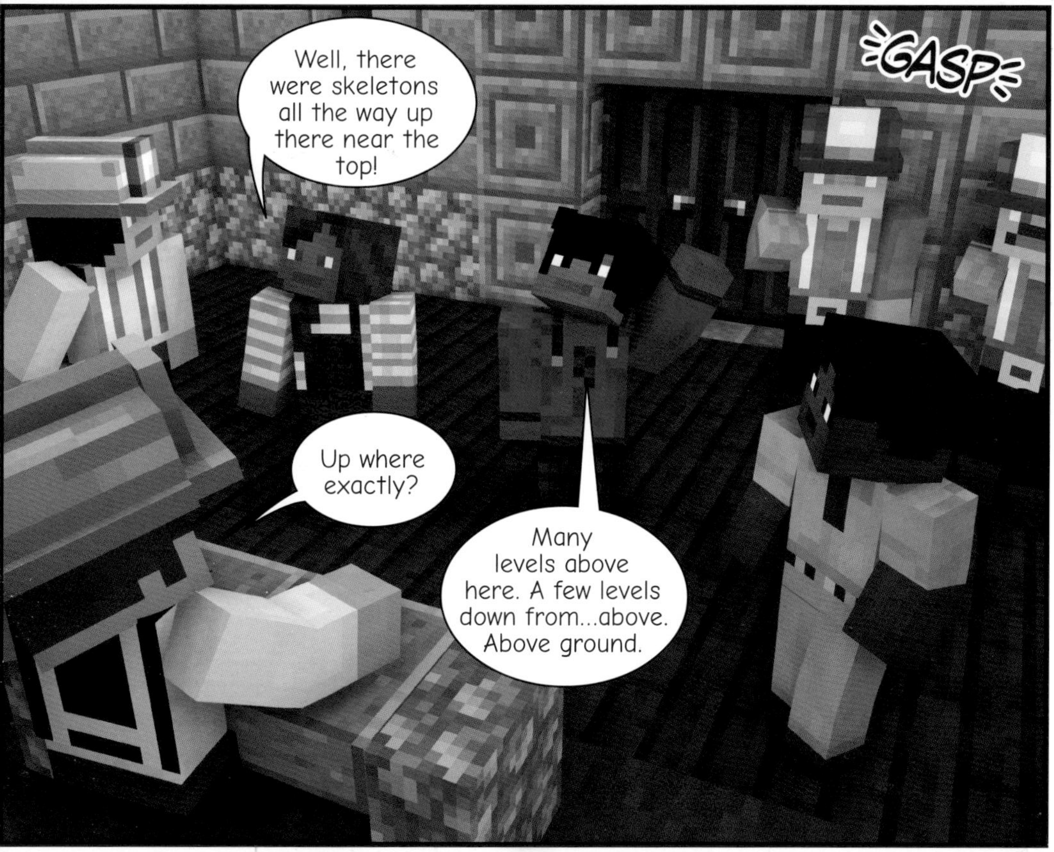
Well, there were skeletons all the way up there near the top!
GASP
Up where exactly?
Many levels above here. A few levels down from...above. Above ground.

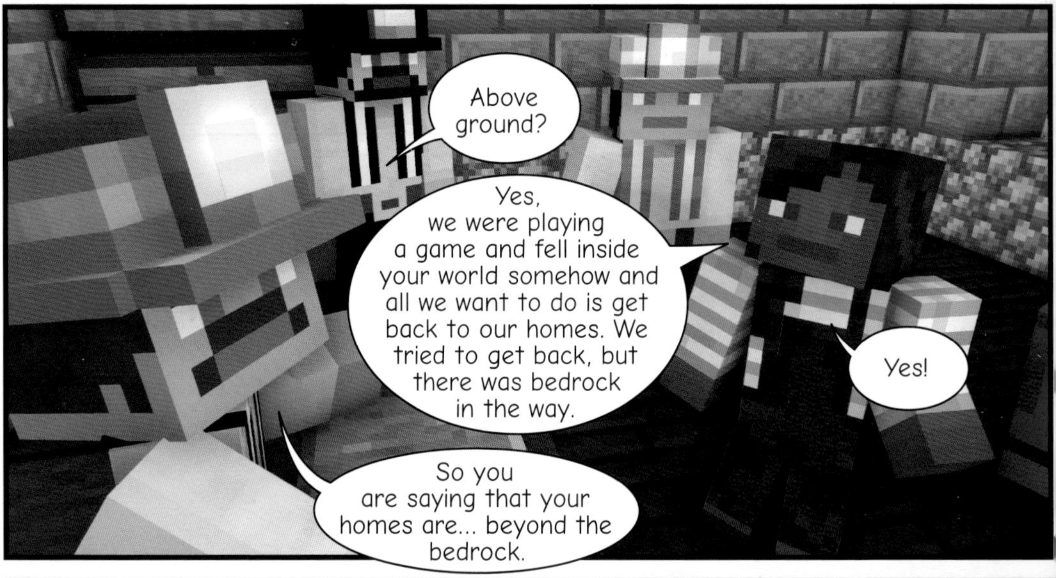
Above ground?
Yes, we were playing a game and fell inside your world somehow and all we want to do is get back to our homes. We tried to get back, but there was bedrock in the way.
Yes!
So you are saying that your homes are... beyond the bedrock.

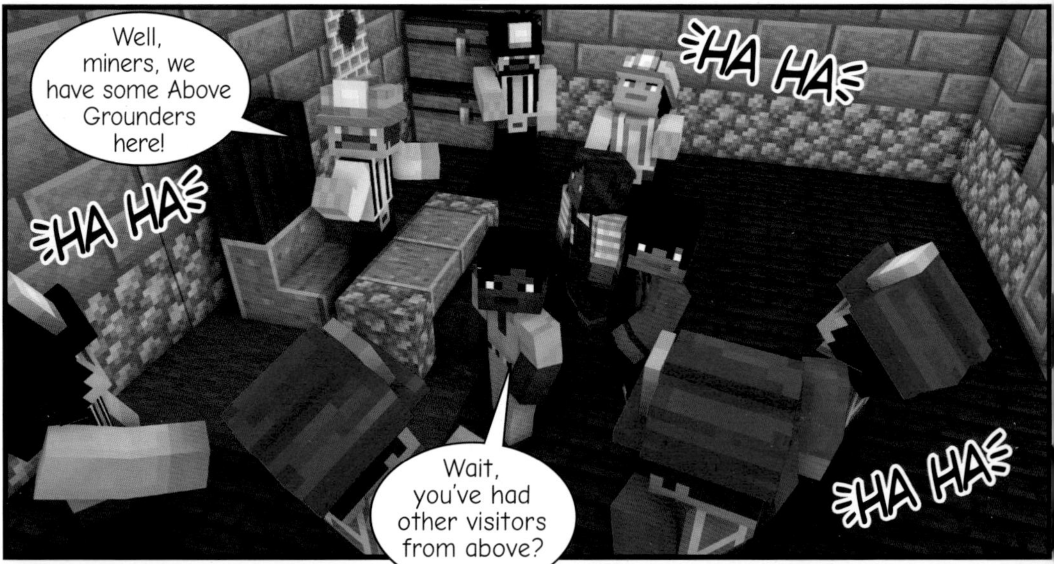
Well, miners, we have some Above Grounders here!
HA HA
HA HA
HA HA
Wait, you've had other visitors from above?

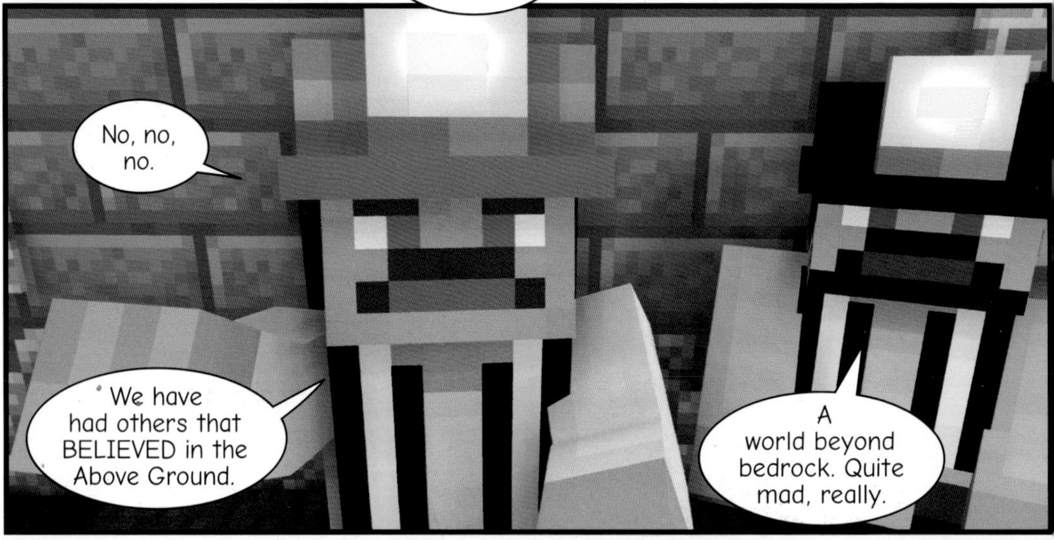
No, no, no.
We have had others that BELIEVED in the Above Ground.
A world beyond bedrock. Quite mad, really.

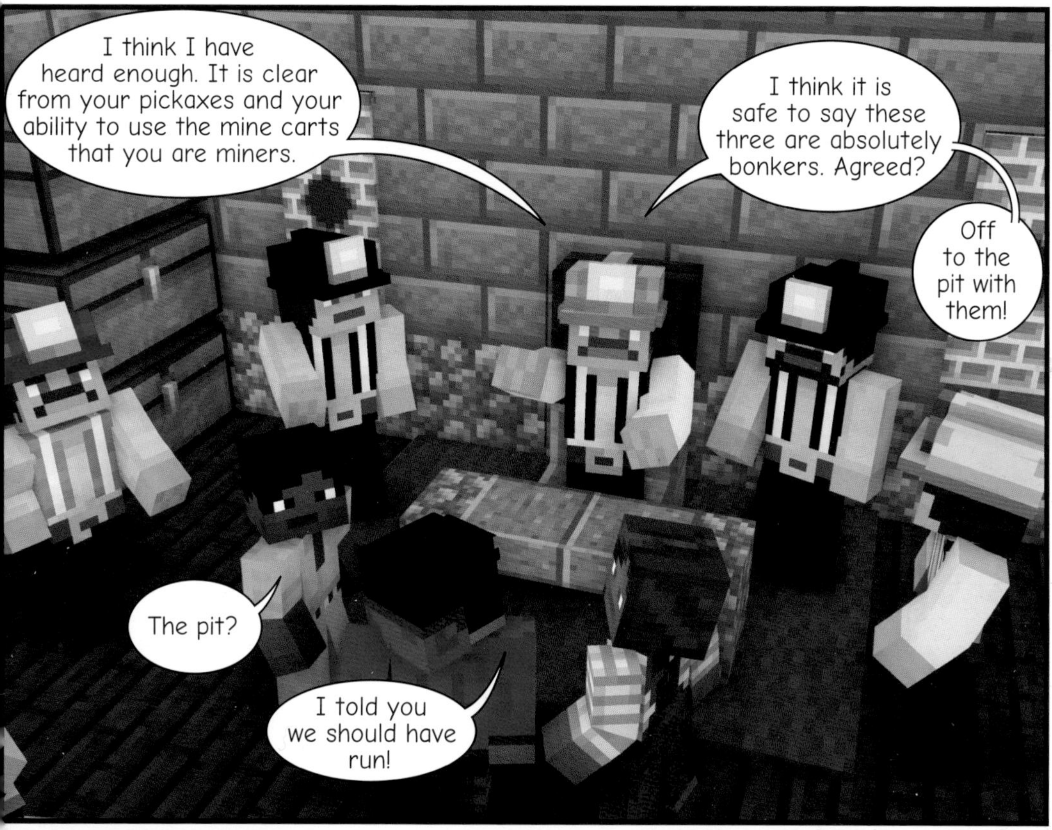
I think I have heard enough. It is clear from your pickaxes and your ability to use the mine carts that you are miners.
I think it is safe to say these three are absolutely bonkers. Agreed?
Off to the pit with them!
The pit?
I told you we should have run!

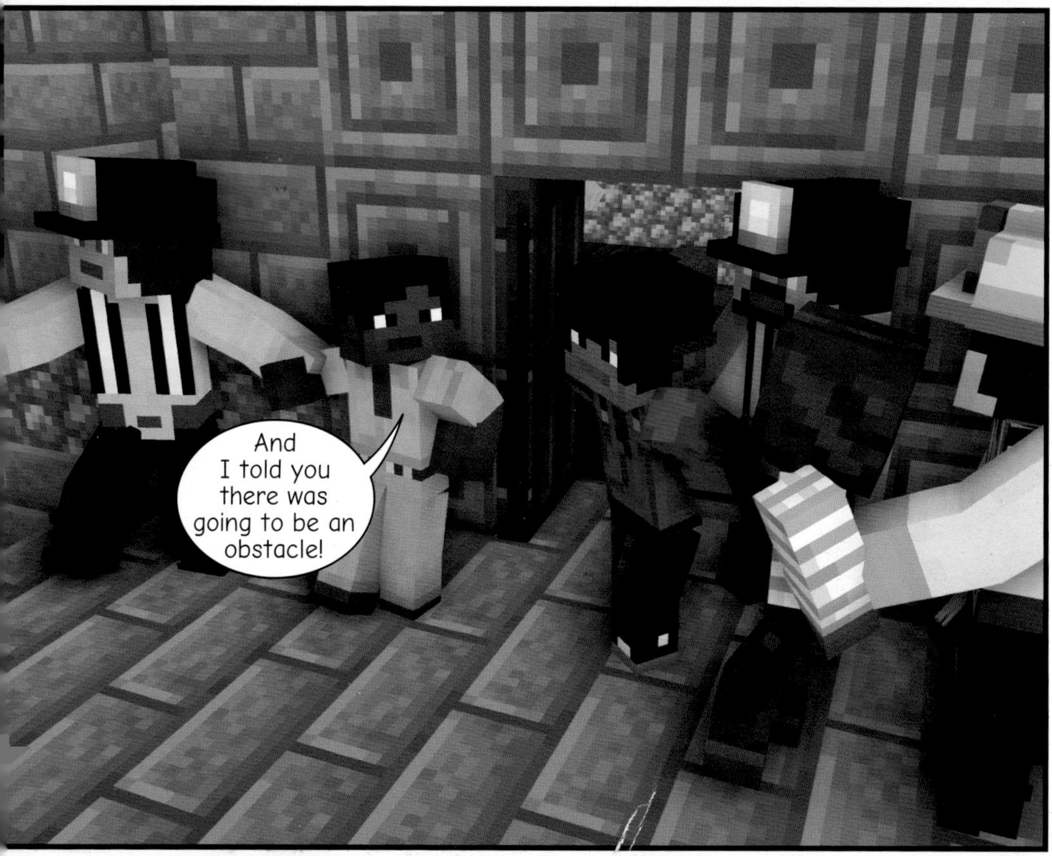
And I told you there was going to be an obstacle!

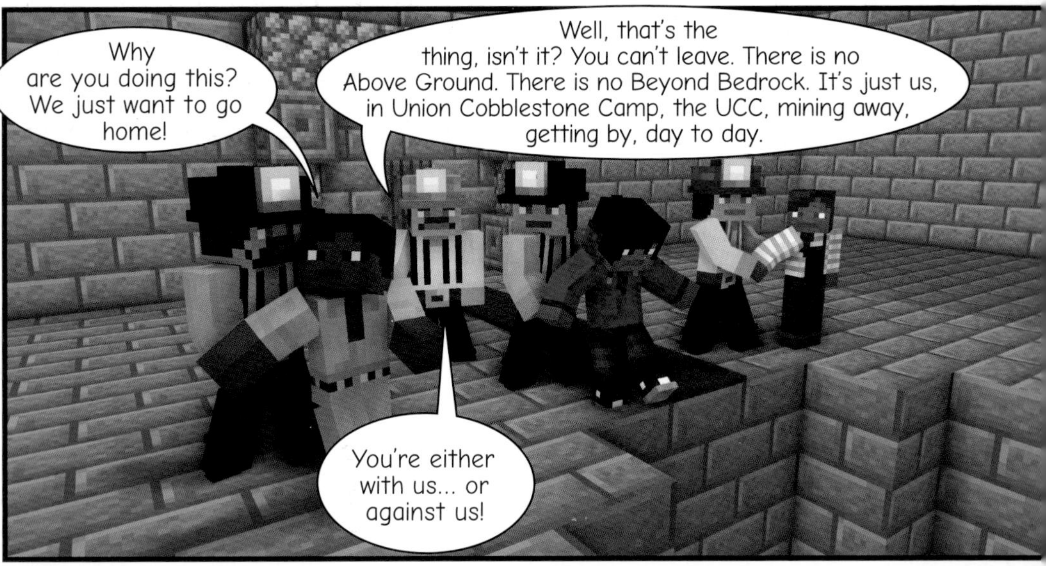
Why are you doing this? We just want to go home!
Well, that's the thing, isn't it? You can't leave. There is no Above Ground. There is no Beyond Bedrock. It's just us, in Union Cobblestone Camp, the UCC, mining away, getting by, day to day.
You're either with us... or against us!

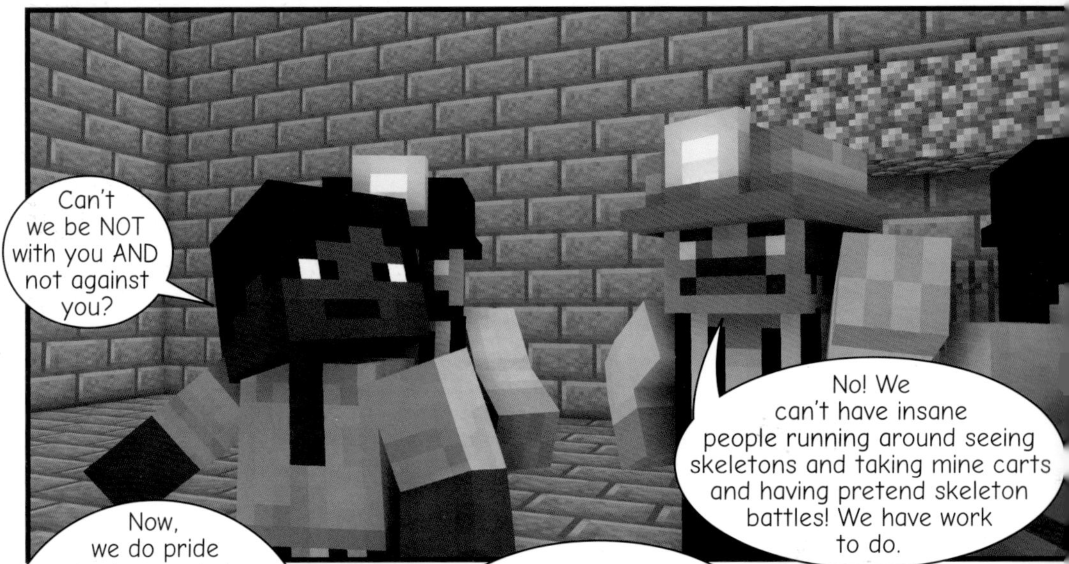
Can't we be NOT with you AND not against you?
No! We can't have insane people running around seeing skeletons and taking mine carts and having pretend skeleton battles! We have work to do.

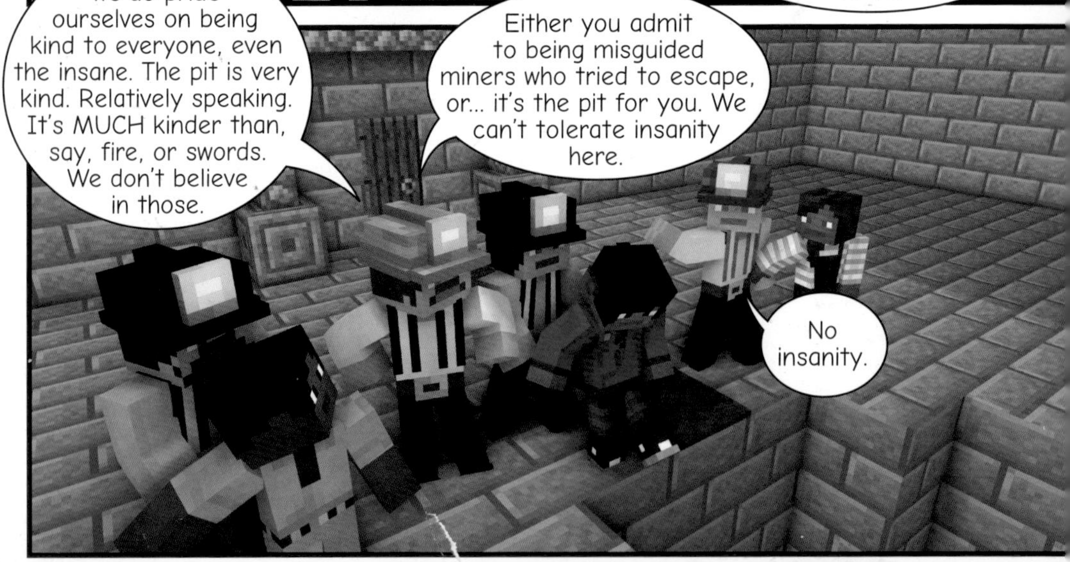
Now, we do pride ourselves on being kind to everyone, even the insane. The pit is very kind. Relatively speaking. It's MUCH kinder than, say, fire, or swords. We don't believe in those.
Either you admit to being misguided miners who tried to escape, or... it's the pit for you. We can't tolerate insanity here.
No insanity.

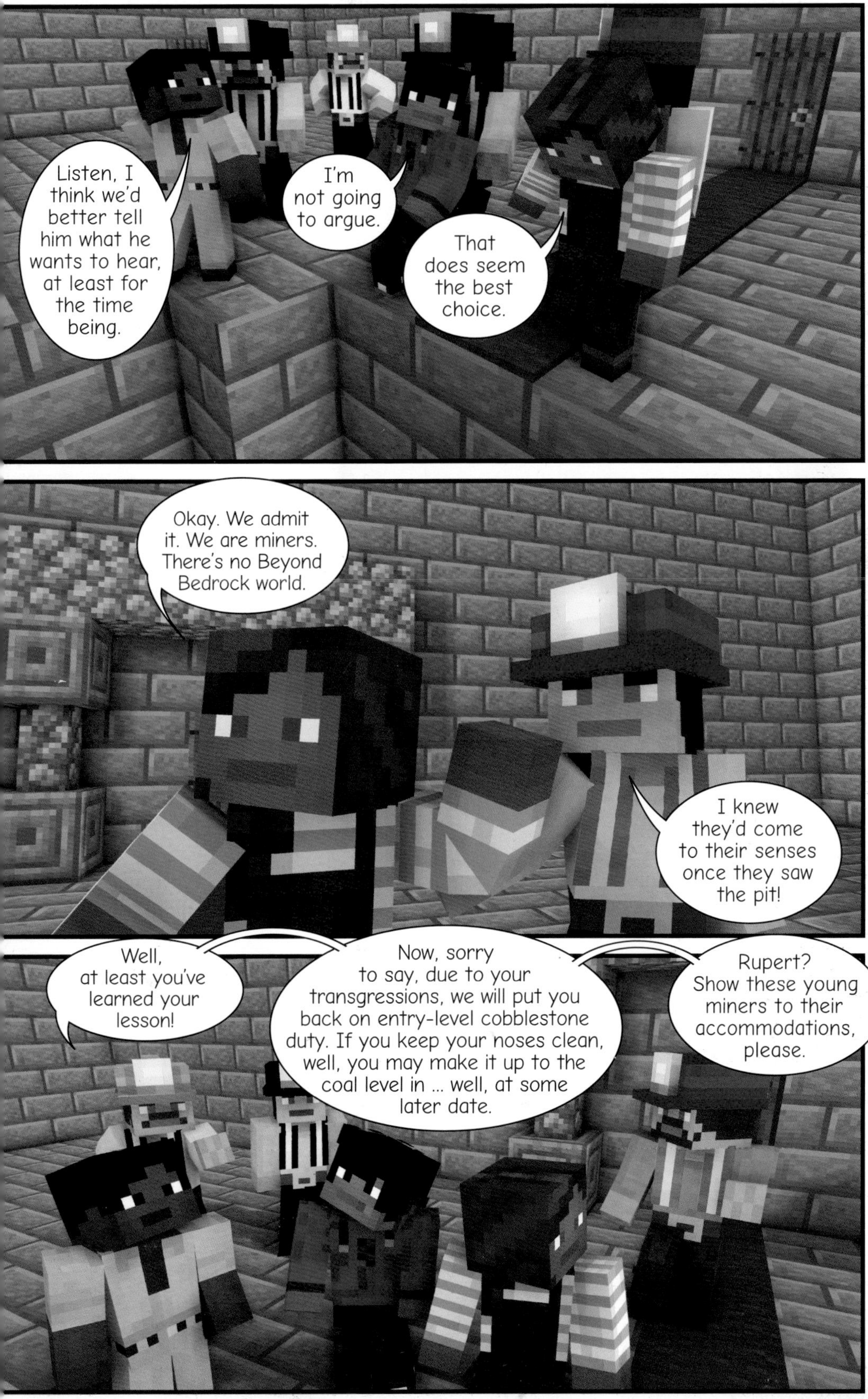

Listen, I think we'd better tell him what he wants to hear, at least for the time being.
I'm not going to argue.
That does seem the best choice.
Okay. We admit it. We are miners. There's no Beyond Bedrock world.
I knew they'd come to their senses once they saw the pit!
Well, at least you've learned your lesson!
Now, sorry to say, due to your transgressions, we will put you back on entry-level cobblestone duty. If you keep your noses clean, well, you may make it up to the coal level in ... well, at some later date.
Rupert? Show these young miners to their accommodations, please.

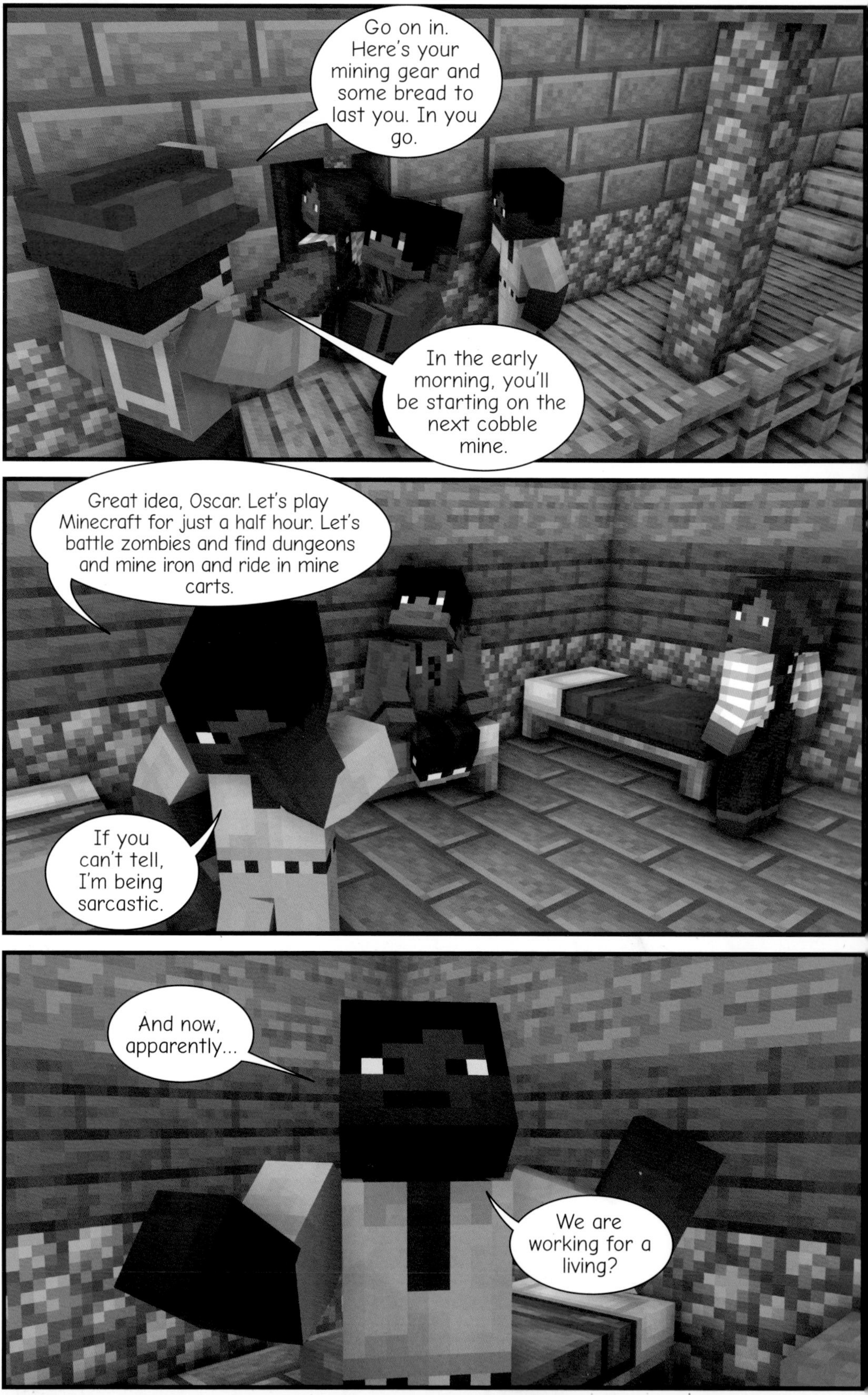
Go on in. Here's your mining gear and some bread to last you. In you go.
In the early morning, you'll be starting on the next cobble mine.
Great idea, Oscar. Let's play Minecraft for just a half hour. Let's battle zombies and find dungeons and mine iron and ride in mine carts.
If you can't tell, I'm being sarcastic.
And now, apparently...
We are working for a living?

Chapter 4

The Mining Life

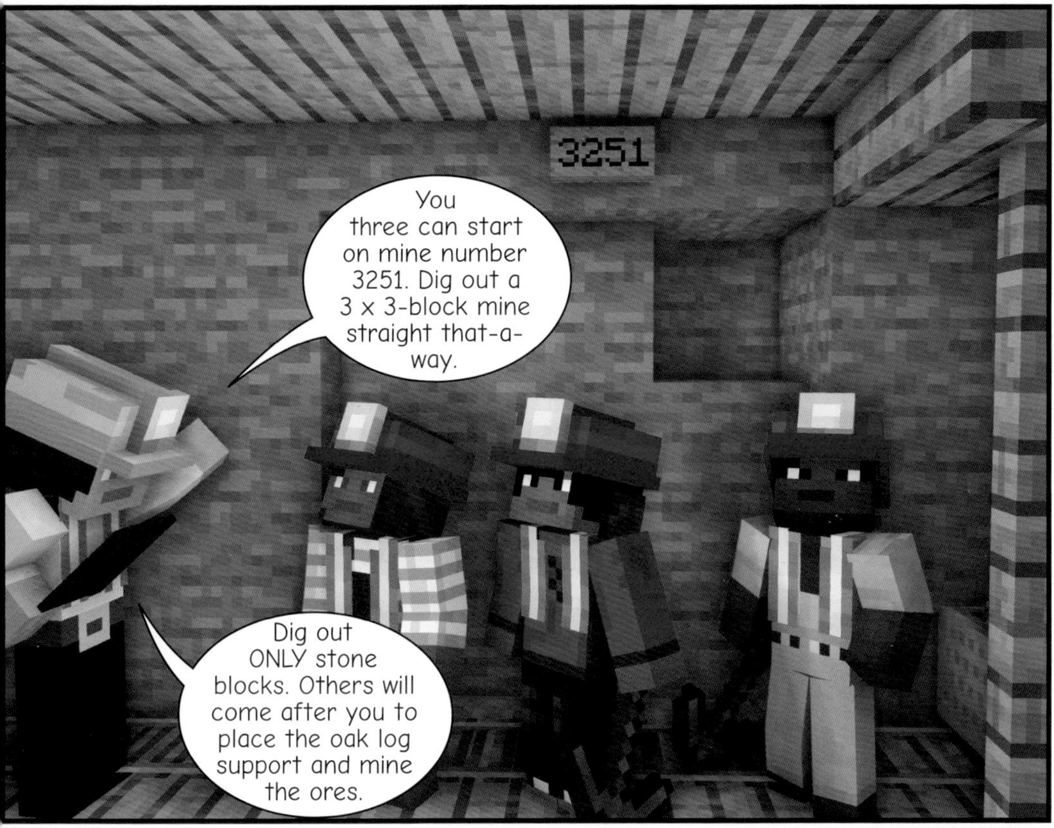

3251
You three can start on mine number 3251. Dig out a 3 x 3-block mine straight that-a-way.
Dig out ONLY stone blocks. Others will come after you to place the oak log support and mine the ores.

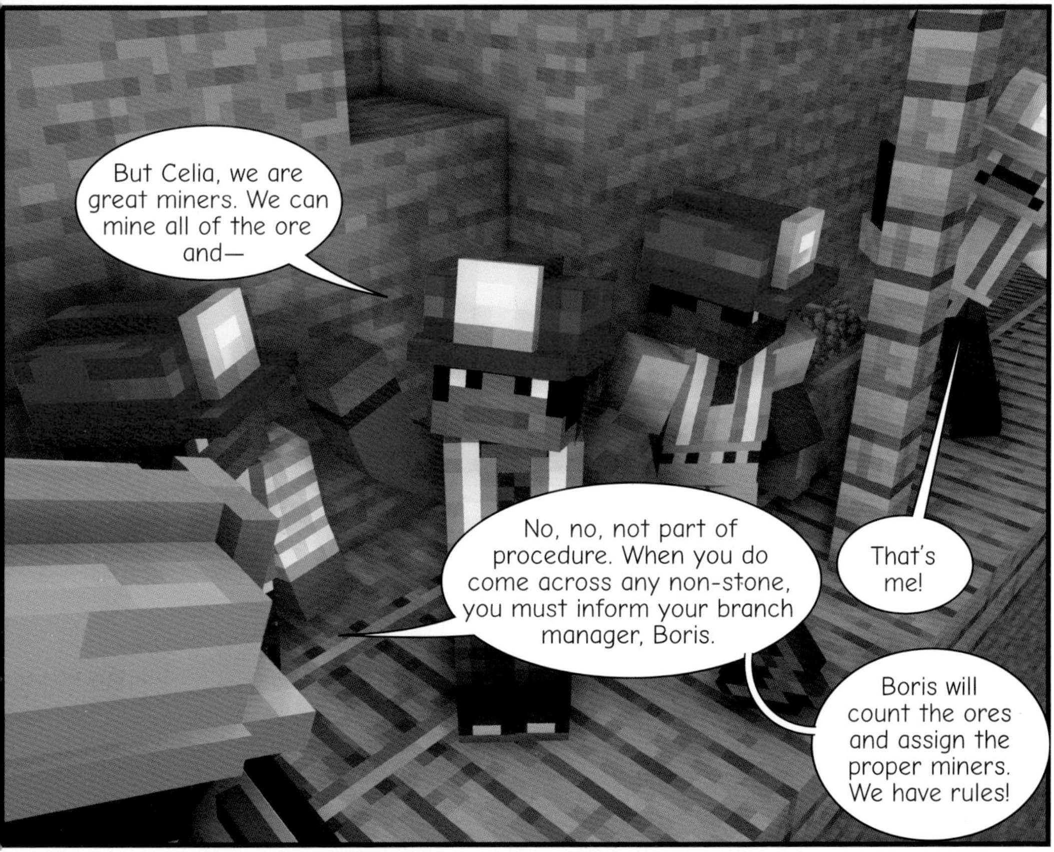

But Celia, we are great miners. We can mine all of the ore and—
No, no, not part of procedure. When you do come across any non-stone, you must inform your branch manager, Boris.
That's me!
Boris will count the ores and assign the proper miners. We have rules!

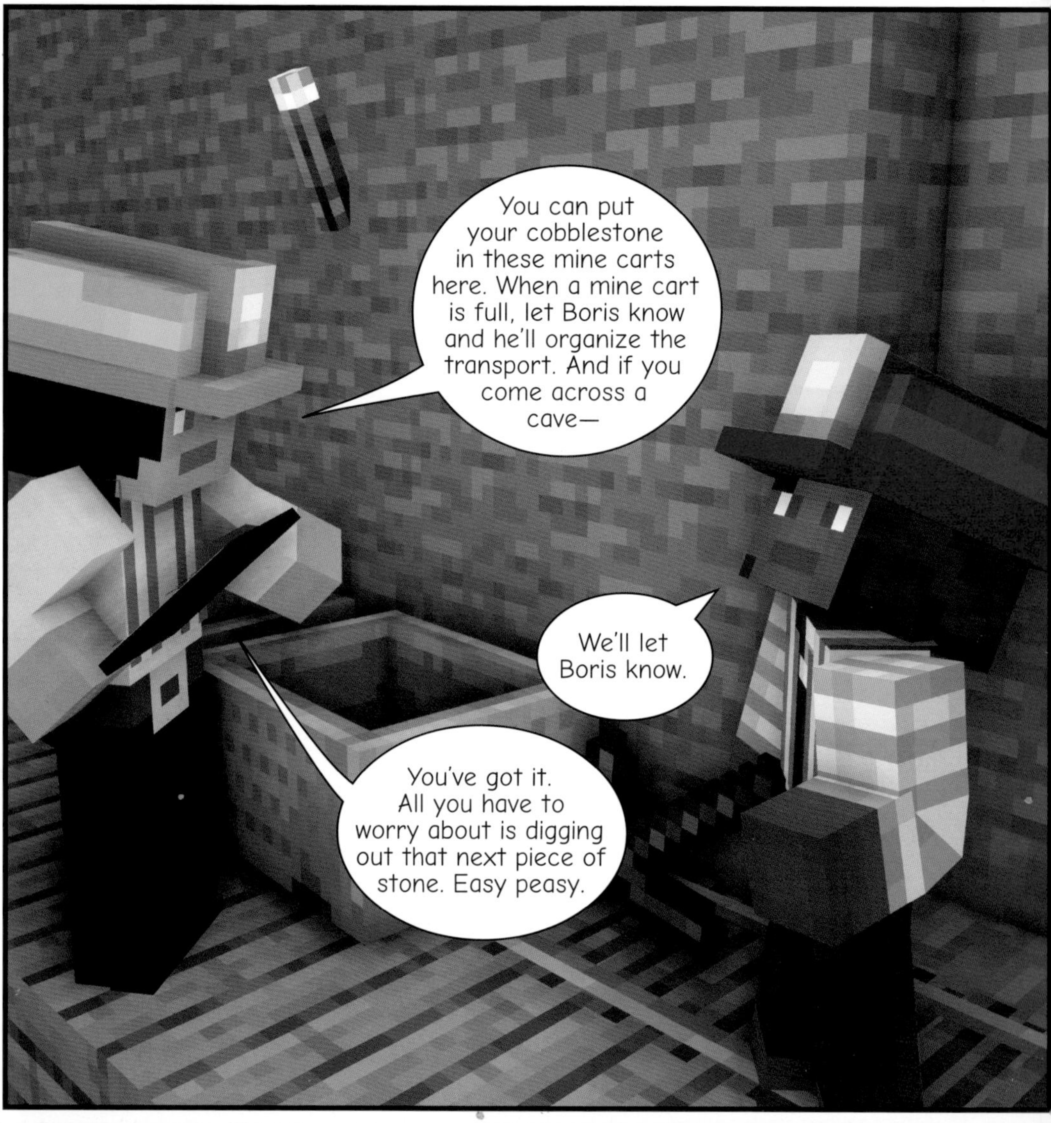
You can put your cobblestone in these mine carts here. When a mine cart is full, let Boris know and he'll organize the transport. And if you come across a cave—
We'll let Boris know.
You've got it. All you have to worry about is digging out that next piece of stone. Easy peasy.

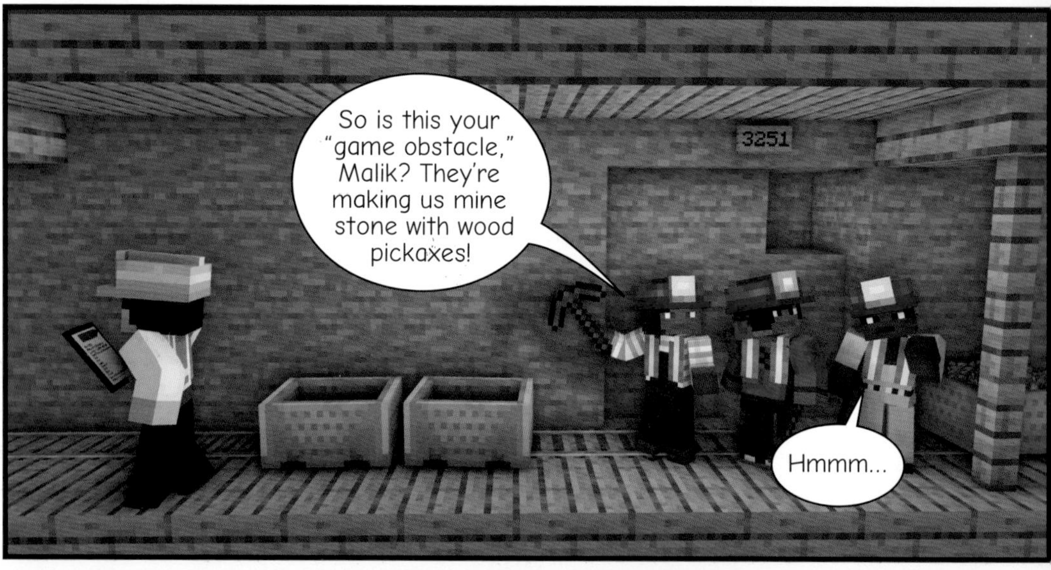
So is this your "game obstacle," Malik? They're making us mine stone with wood pickaxes!
3251
Hmmm...

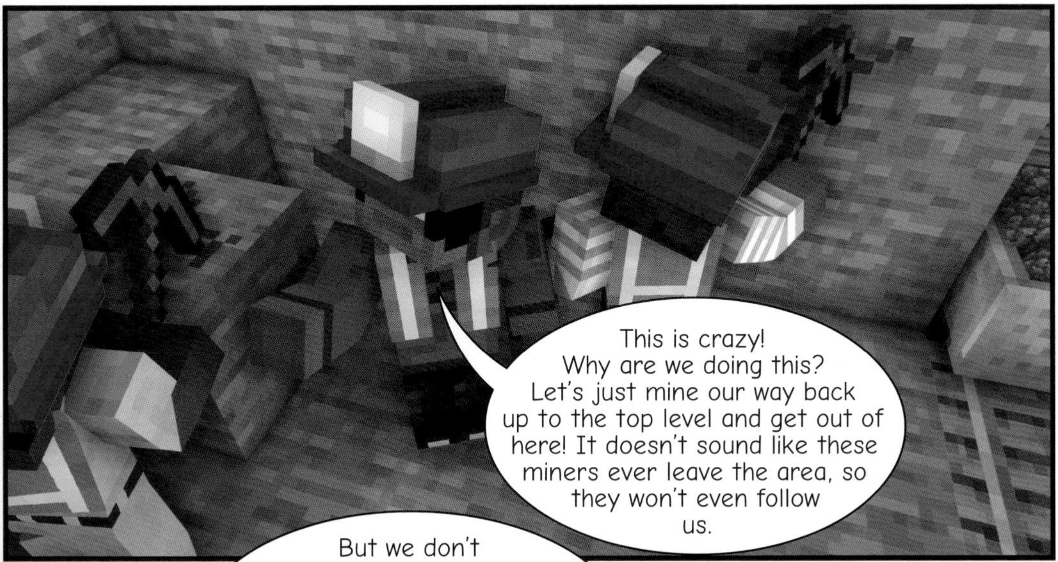
This is crazy! Why are we doing this? Let's just mine our way back up to the top level and get out of here! It doesn't sound like these miners ever leave the area, so they won't even follow us.

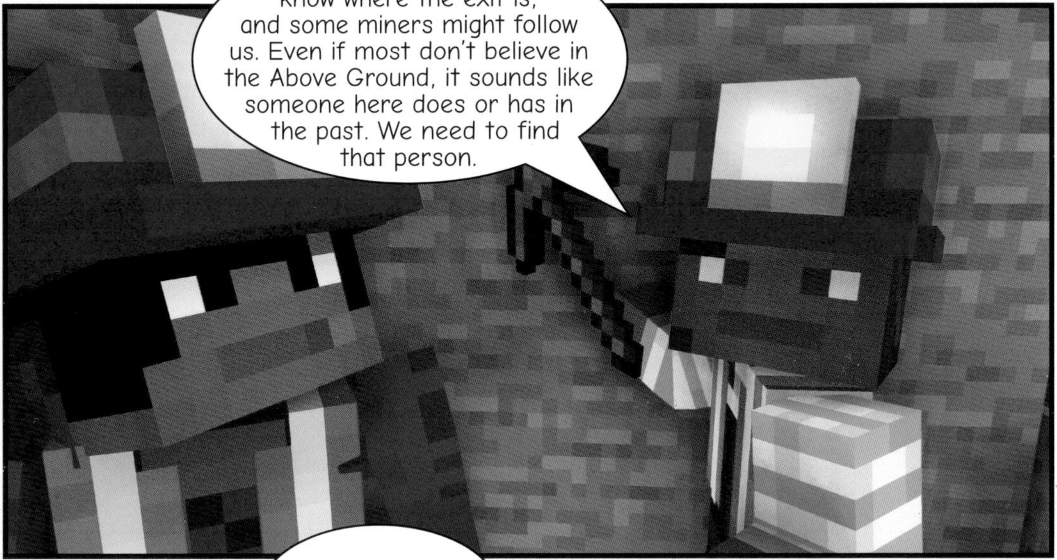
But we don't know where the exit is, and some miners might follow us. Even if most don't believe in the Above Ground, it sounds like someone here does or has in the past. We need to find that person.

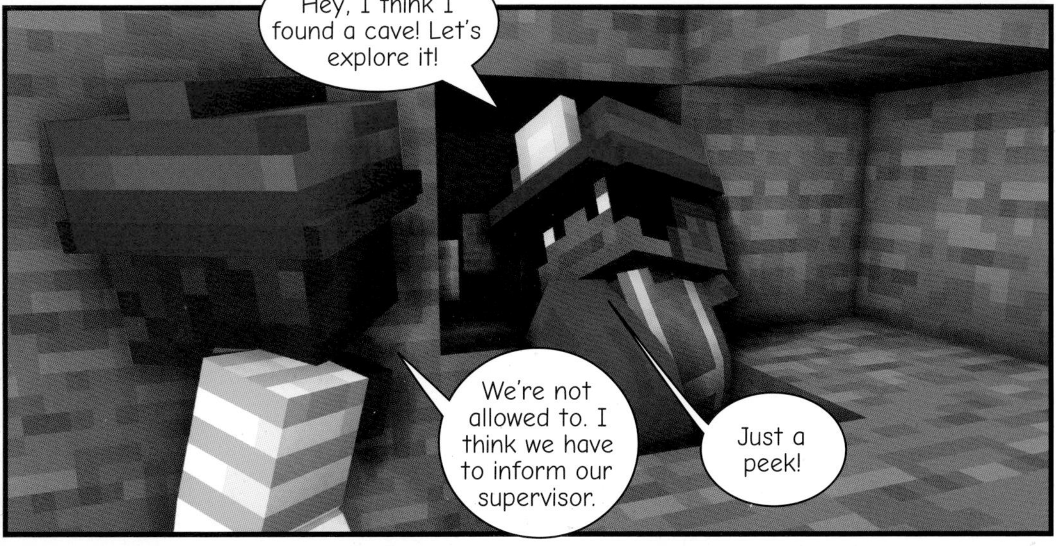
Hey, I think I found a cave! Let's explore it!
We're not allowed to. I think we have to inform our supervisor.
Just a peek!

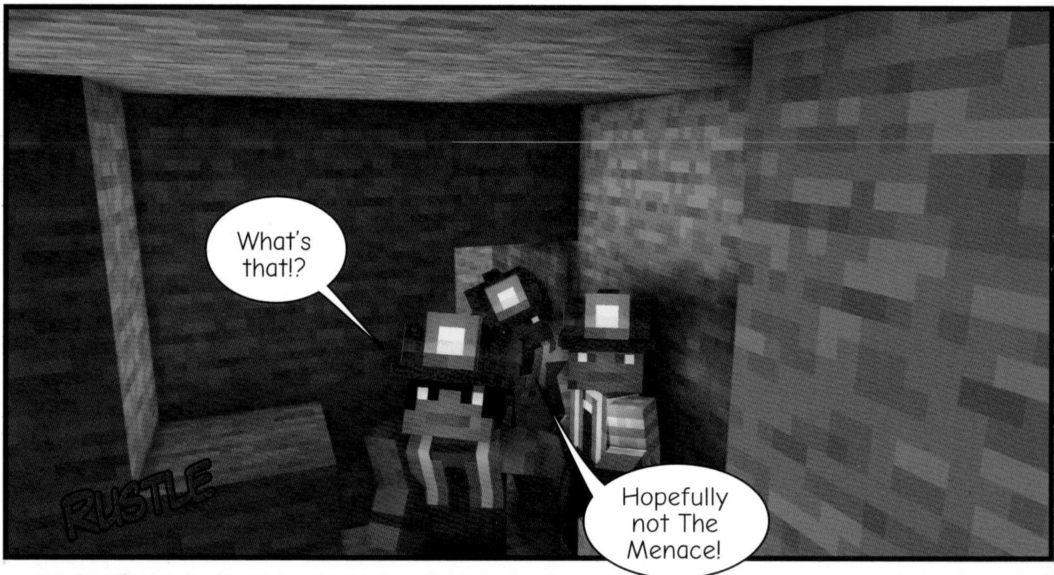
What's that!?
Hopefully not The Menace!
RUSTLE
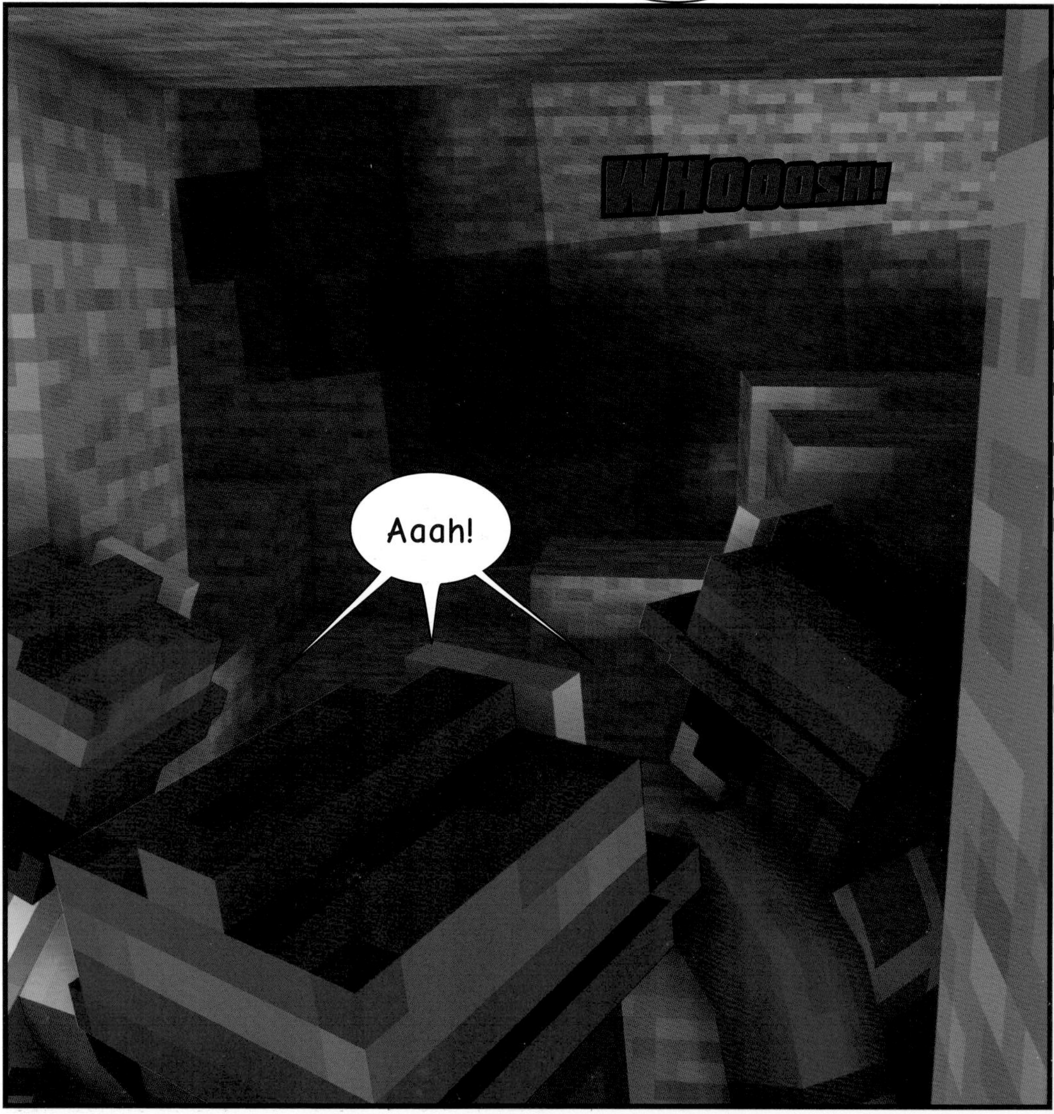
WHOOOSH!
Aaah!

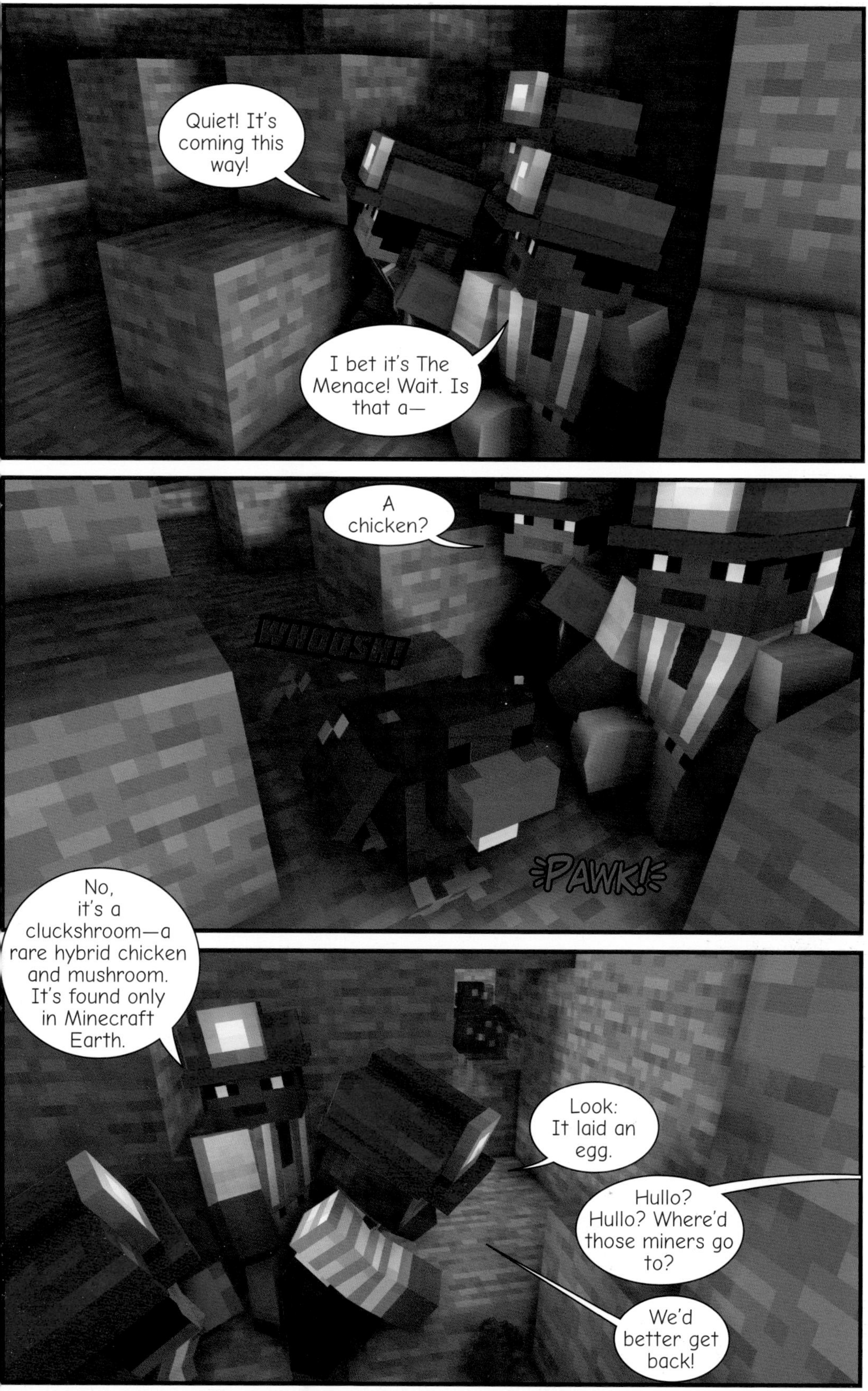
Quiet! It's coming this way!
I bet it's The Menace! Wait. Is that a—
A chicken?
WHOOSH!
PAWK!
No, it's a cluckshroom—a rare hybrid chicken and mushroom. It's found only in Minecraft Earth.
Look: It laid an egg.
Hullo? Hullo? Where'd those miners go to?
We'd better get back!

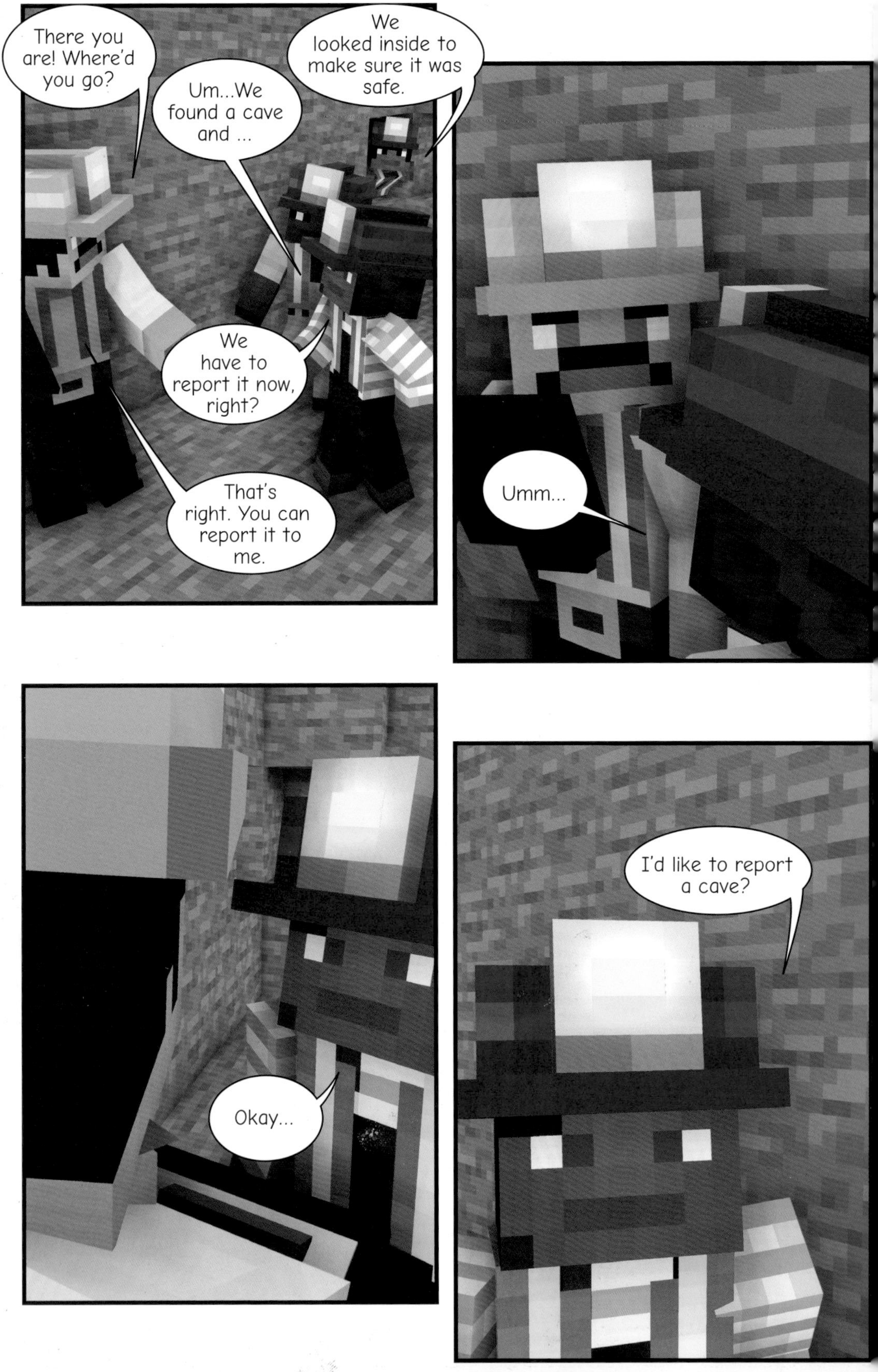
There you are! Where'd you go?
Um...We found a cave and ...
We looked inside to make sure it was safe.
We have to report it now, right?
That's right. You can report it to me.
Umm...
Okay...
I'd like to report a cave?

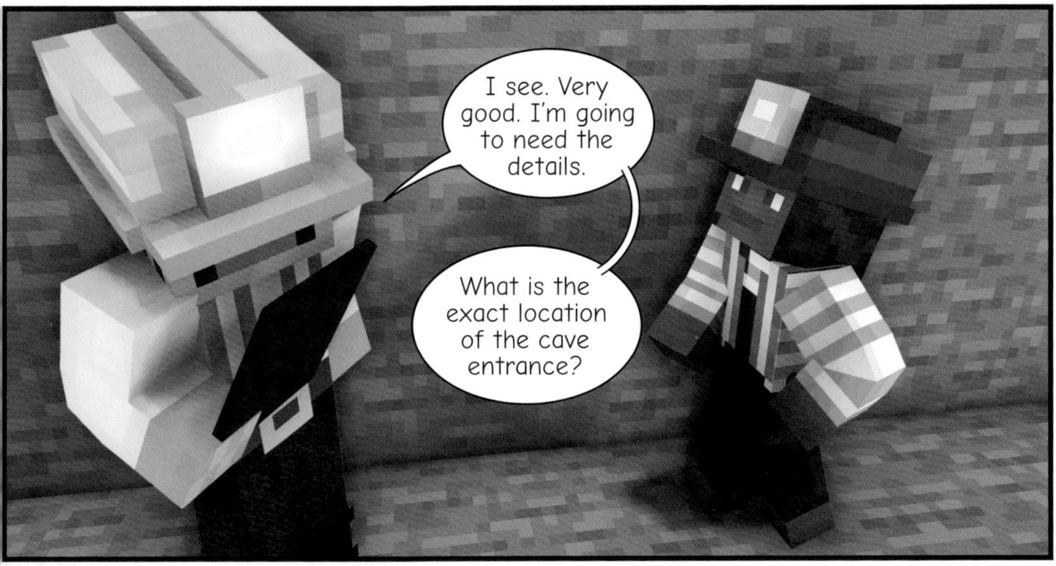
I see. Very good. I'm going to need the details.
What is the exact location of the cave entrance?

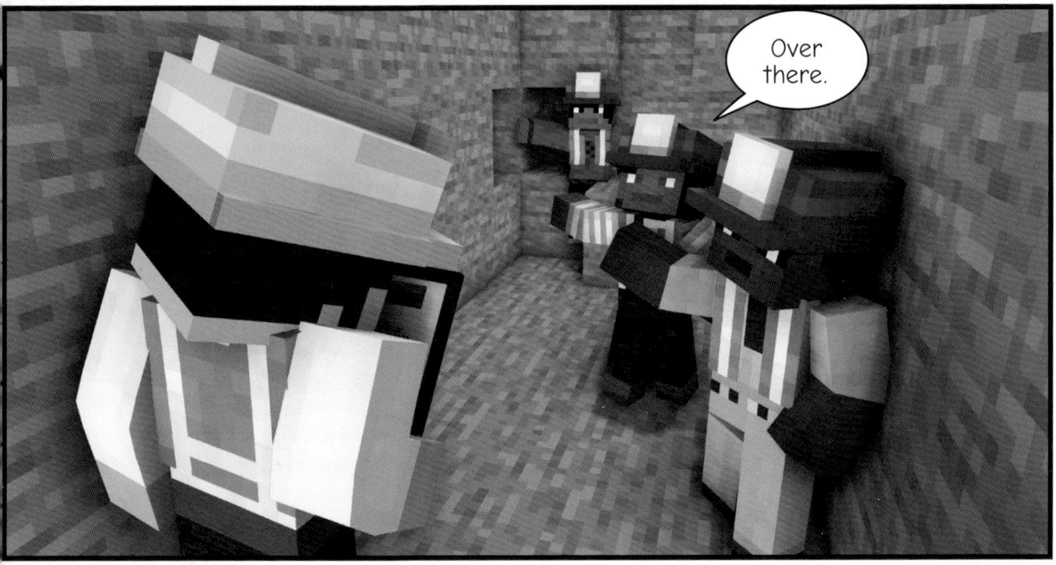
Over there.

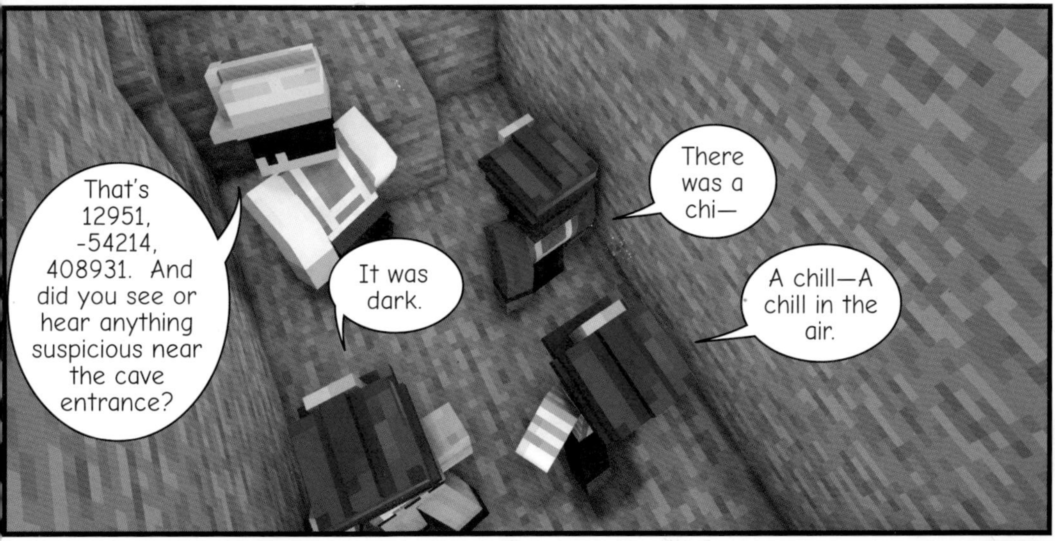
That's 12951, -54214, 408931. And did you see or hear anything suspicious near the cave entrance?
There was a chi—
It was dark.
A chill—A chill in the air.

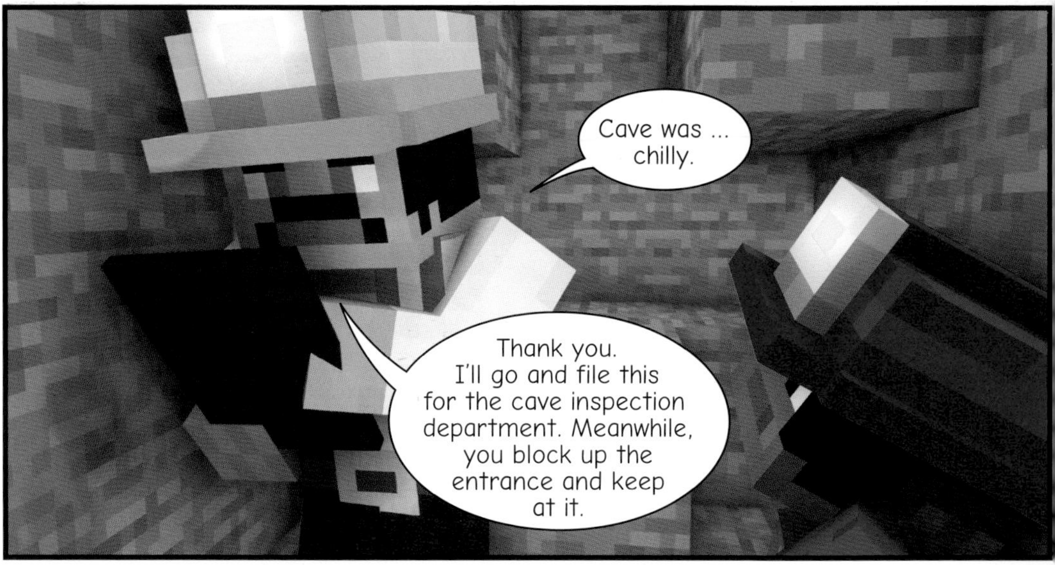
Cave was ... chilly.
Thank you. I'll go and file this for the cave inspection department. Meanwhile, you block up the entrance and keep at it.

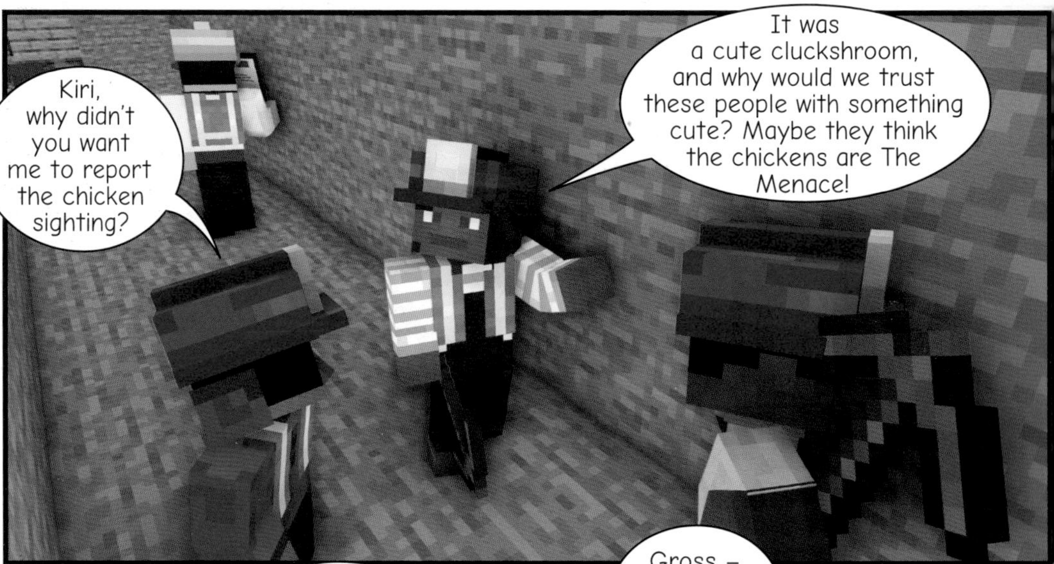
Kiri, why didn't you want me to report the chicken sighting?
It was a cute cluckshroom, and why would we trust these people with something cute? Maybe they think the chickens are The Menace!

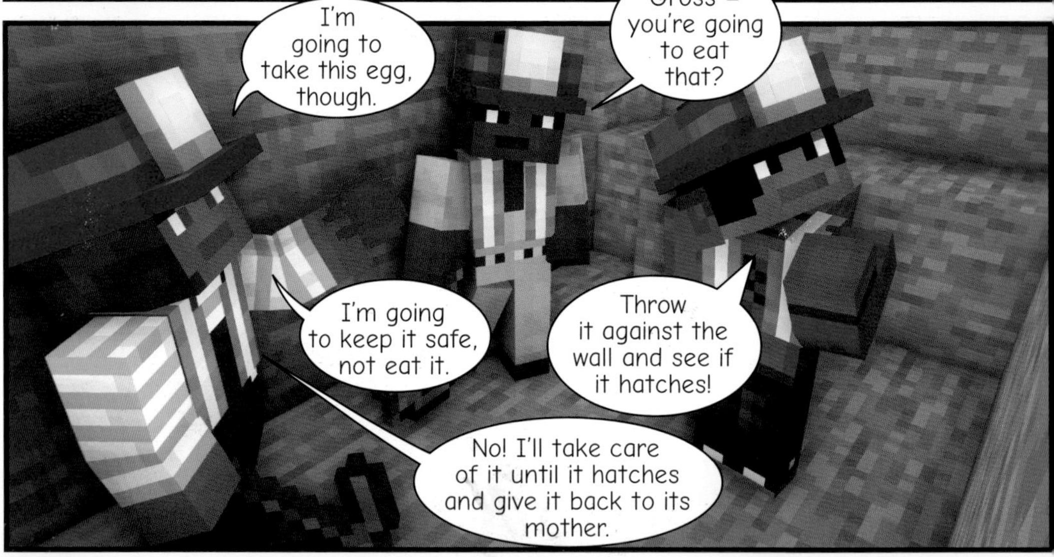
I'm going to take this egg, though.
Gross – you're going to eat that?
I'm going to keep it safe, not eat it.
Throw it against the wall and see if it hatches!
No! I'll take care of it until it hatches and give it back to its mother.

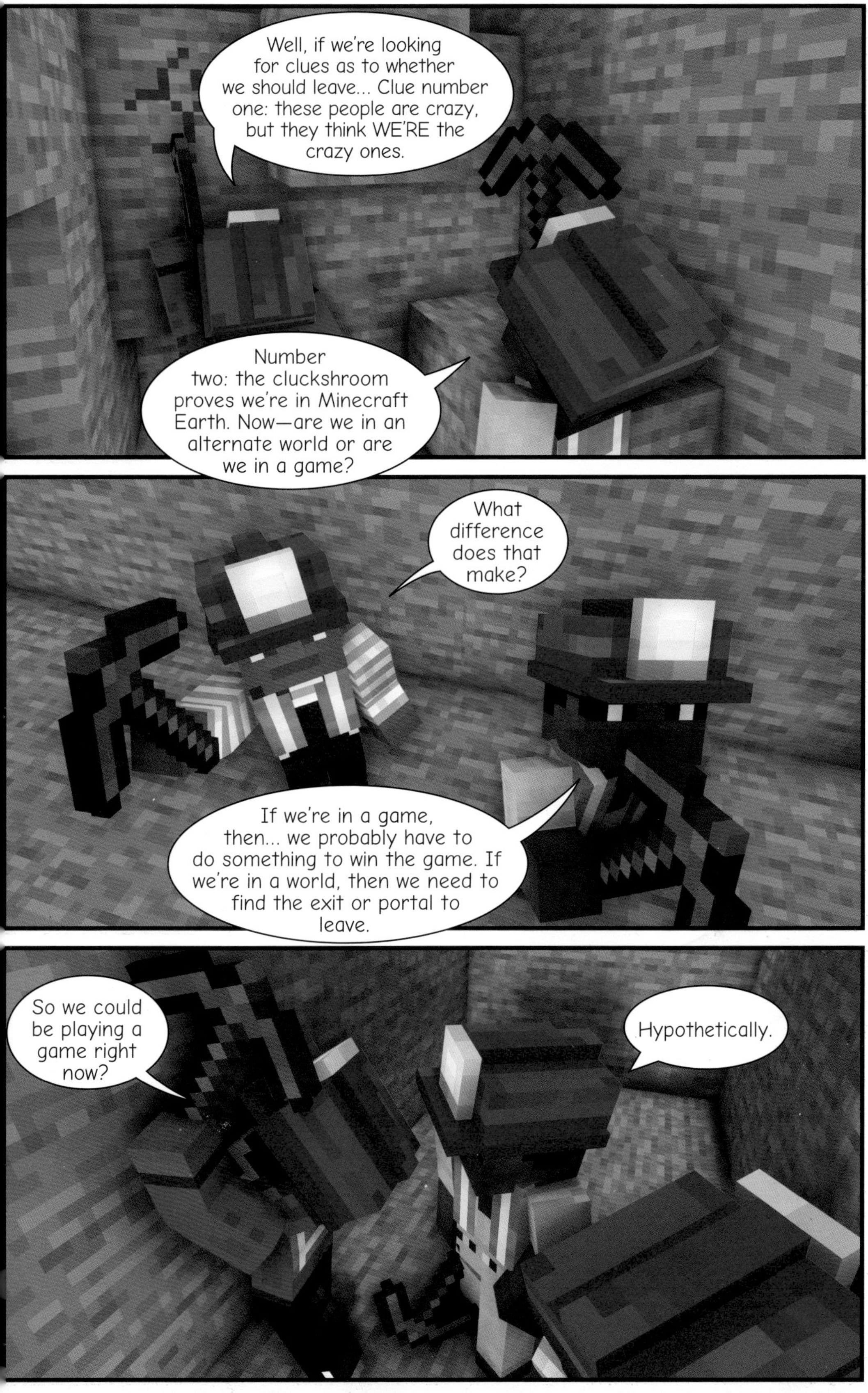
Well, if we're looking for clues as to whether we should leave... Clue number one: these people are crazy, but they think WE'RE the crazy ones.
Number two: the cluckshroom proves we're in Minecraft Earth. Now—are we in an alternate world or are we in a game?
What difference does that make?
If we're in a game, then... we probably have to do something to win the game. If we're in a world, then we need to find the exit or portal to leave.
So we could be playing a game right now?
Hypothetically.

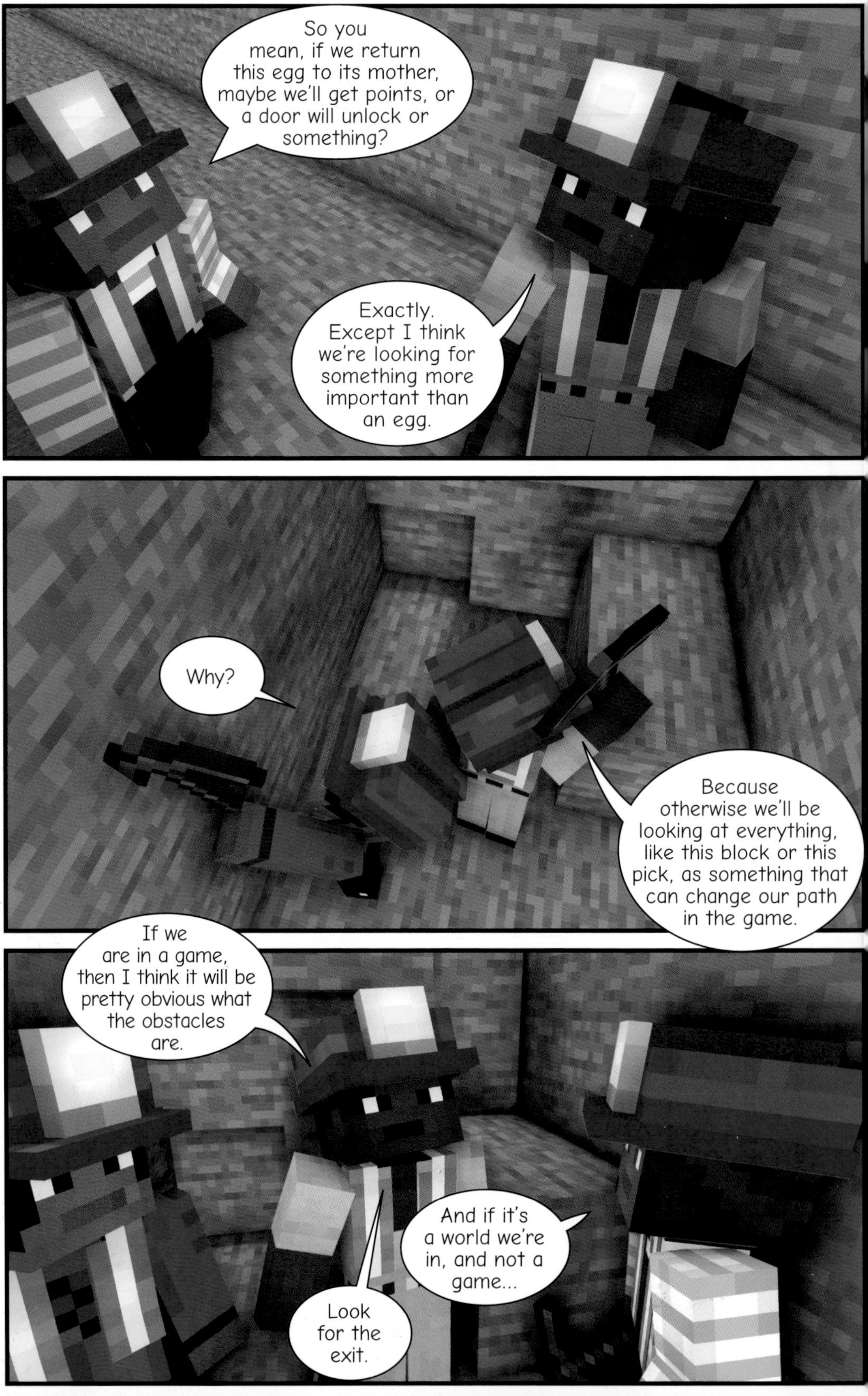
So you mean, if we return this egg to its mother, maybe we'll get points, or a door will unlock or something?
Exactly. Except I think we're looking for something more important than an egg.
Why?
Because otherwise we'll be looking at everything, like this block or this pick, as something that can change our path in the game.
If we are in a game, then I think it will be pretty obvious what the obstacles are.
And if it's a world we're in, and not a game...
Look for the exit.

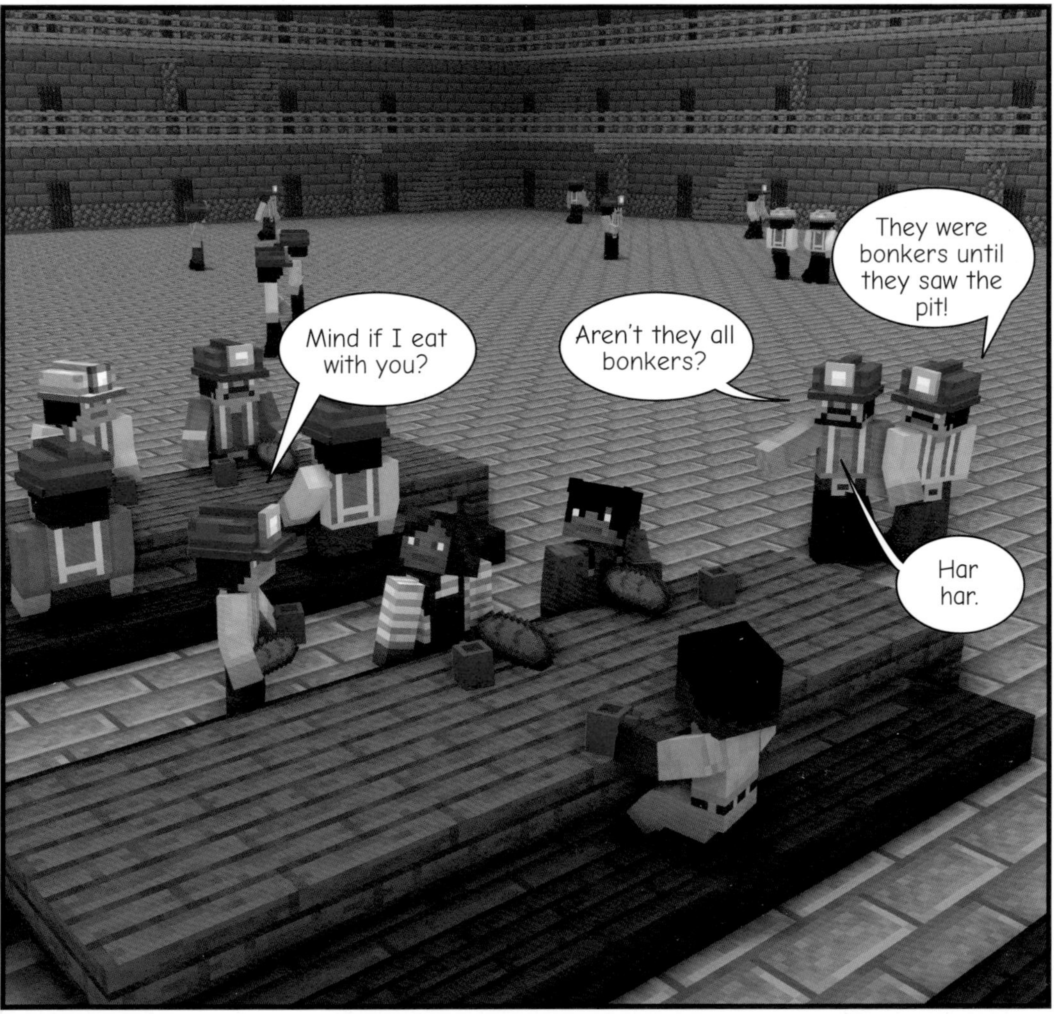
Mind if I eat with you?
Aren't they all bonkers?
They were bonkers until they saw the pit!
Har har.

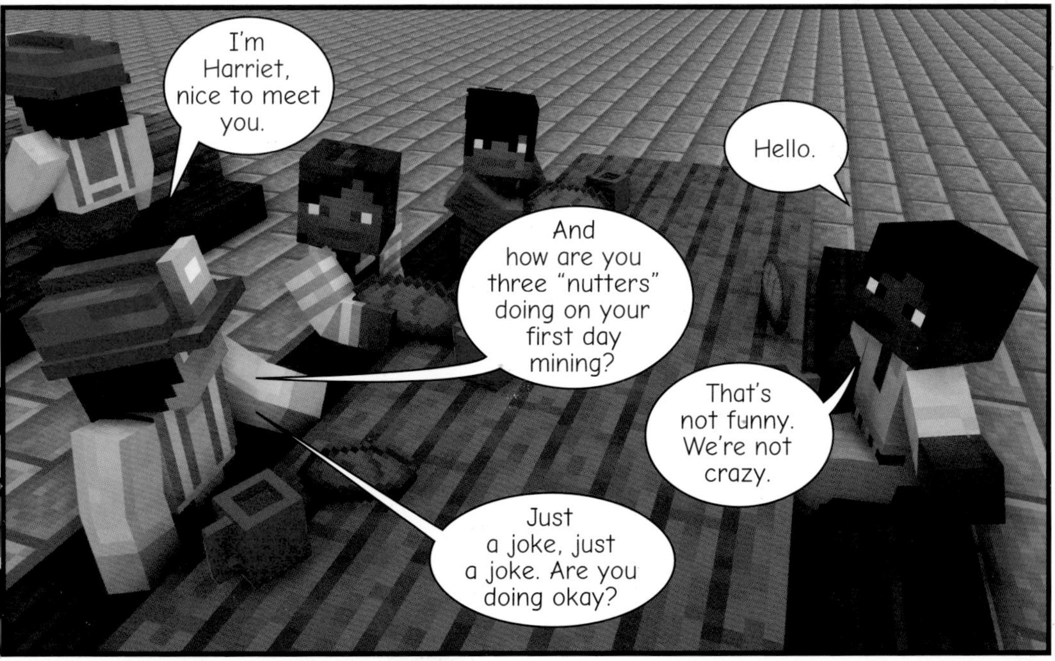
I'm Harriet, nice to meet you.
Hello.
And how are you three "nutters" doing on your first day mining?
That's not funny. We're not crazy.
Just a joke, just a joke. Are you doing okay?

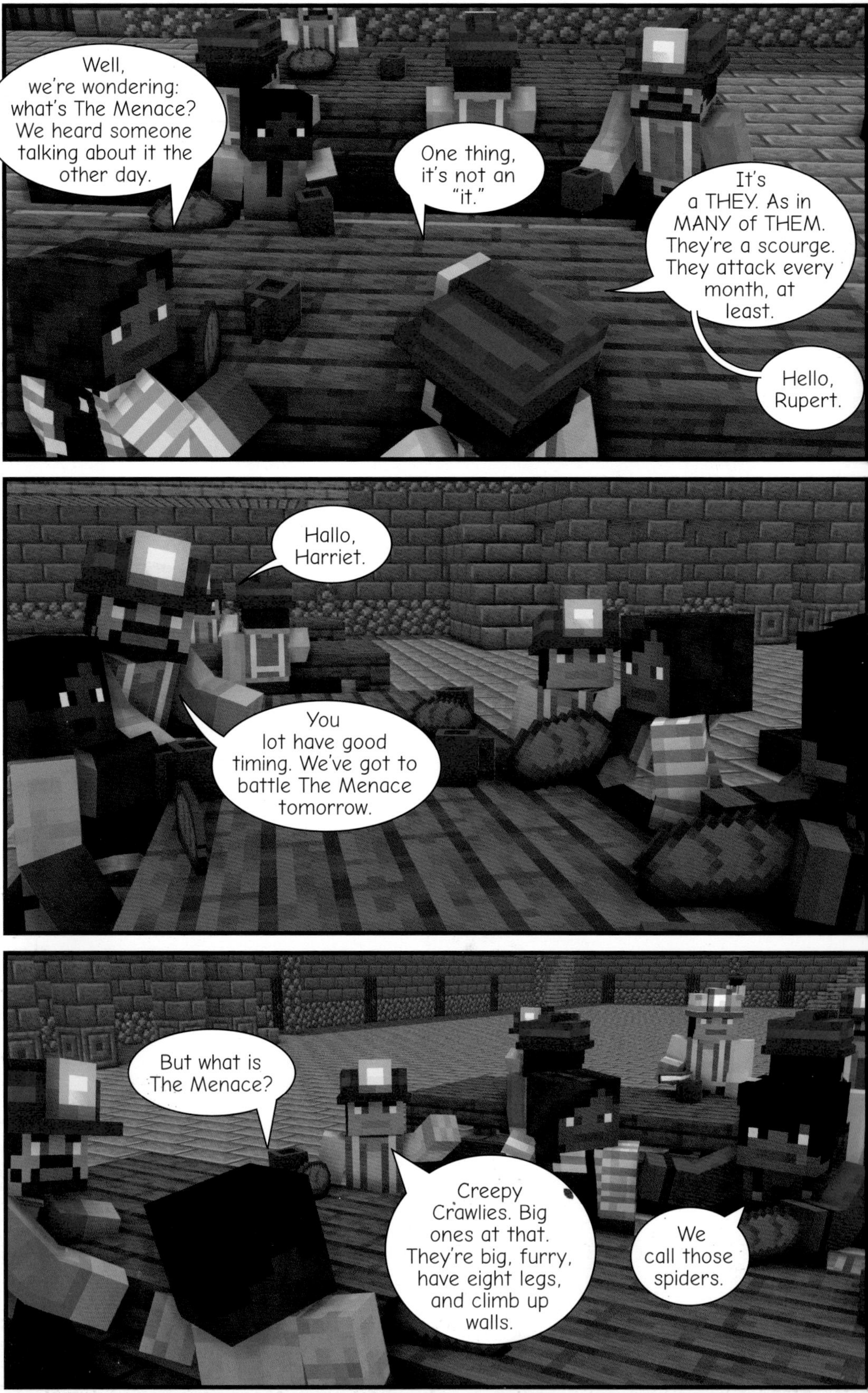

Well, we're wondering: what's The Menace? We heard someone talking about it the other day.
One thing, it's not an "it."
It's a THEY. As in MANY of THEM. They're a scourge. They attack every month, at least.
Hello, Rupert.
Hallo, Harriet.
You lot have good timing. We've got to battle The Menace tomorrow.
But what is The Menace?
Creepy Crawlies. Big ones at that. They're big, furry, have eight legs, and climb up walls.
We call those spiders.

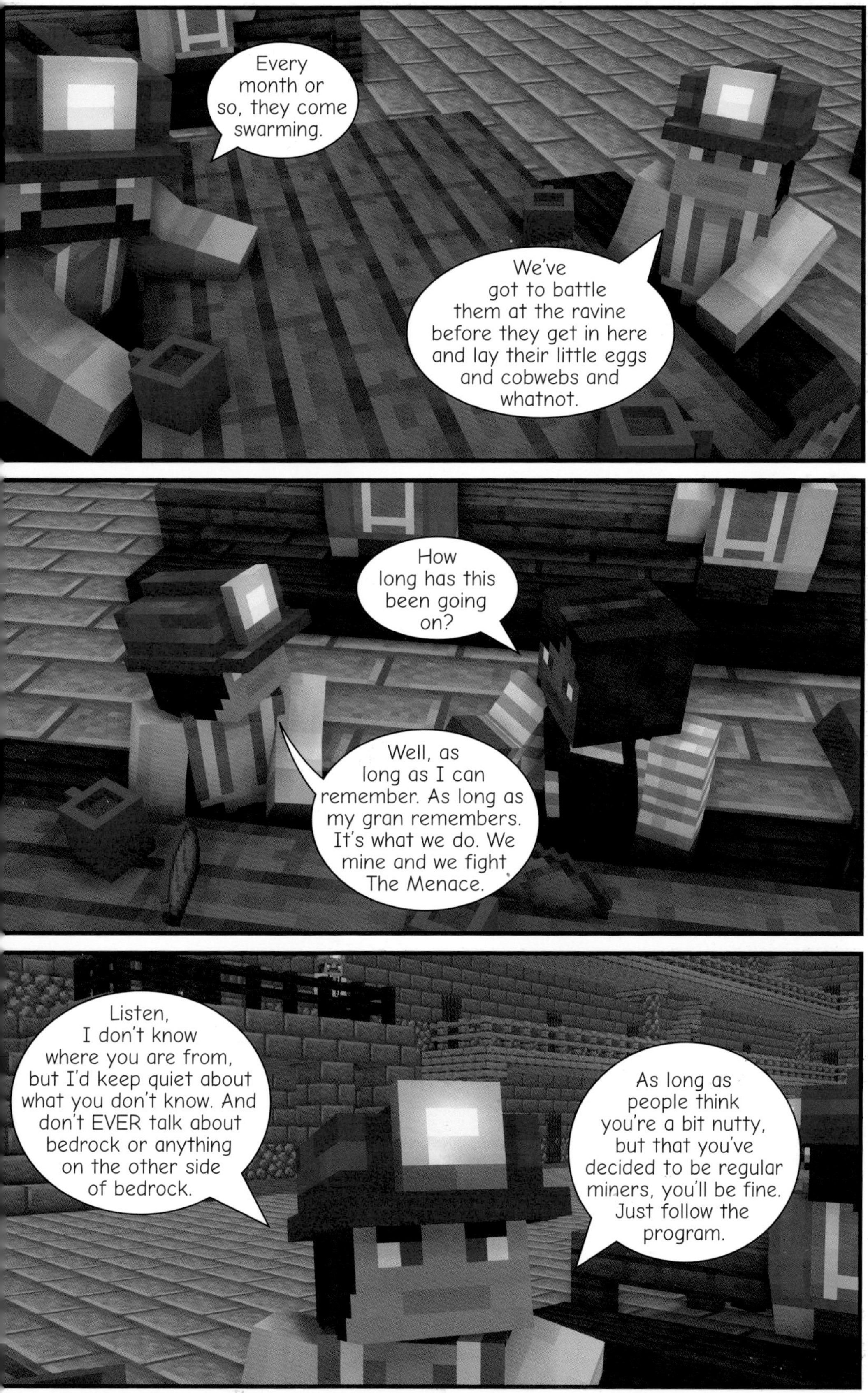
Every month or so, they come swarming.
We've got to battle them at the ravine before they get in here and lay their little eggs and cobwebs and whatnot.
How long has this been going on?
Well, as long as I can remember. As long as my gran remembers. It's what we do. We mine and we fight The Menace.
Listen, I don't know where you are from, but I'd keep quiet about what you don't know. And don't EVER talk about bedrock or anything on the other side of bedrock.
As long as people think you're a bit nutty, but that you've decided to be regular miners, you'll be fine. Just follow the program.

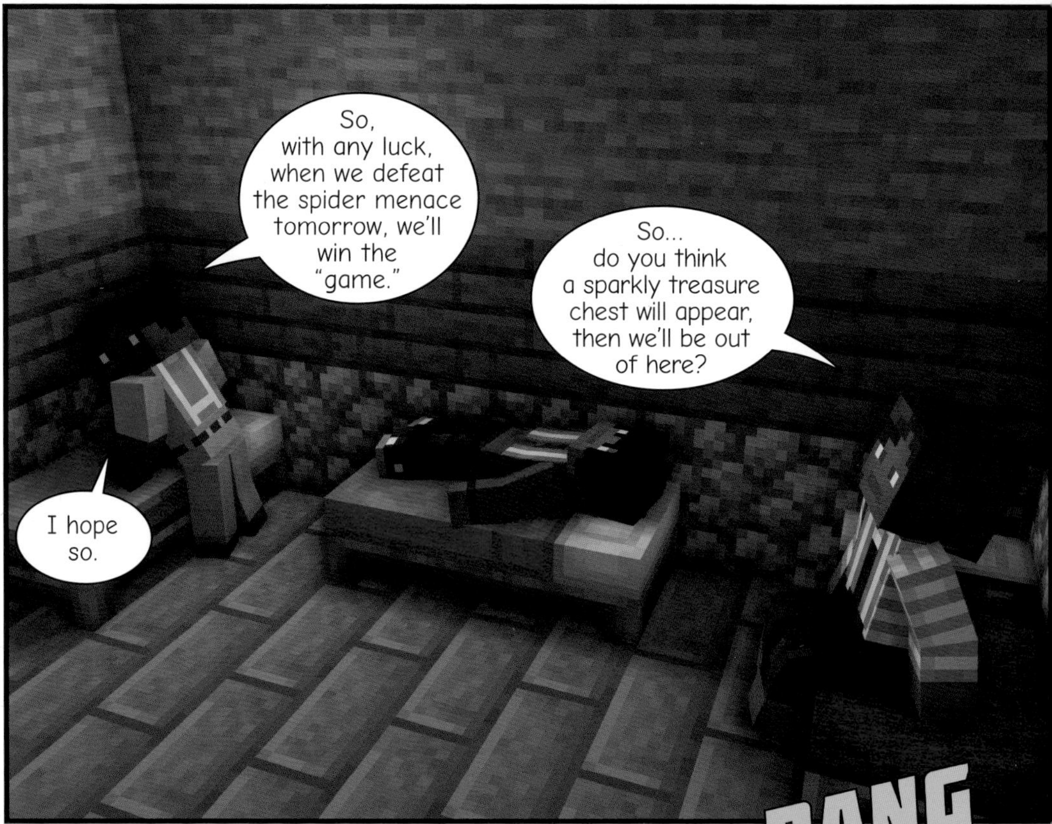
So, with any luck, when we defeat the spider menace tomorrow, we'll win the "game."
So... do you think a sparkly treasure chest will appear, then we'll be out of here?
I hope so.

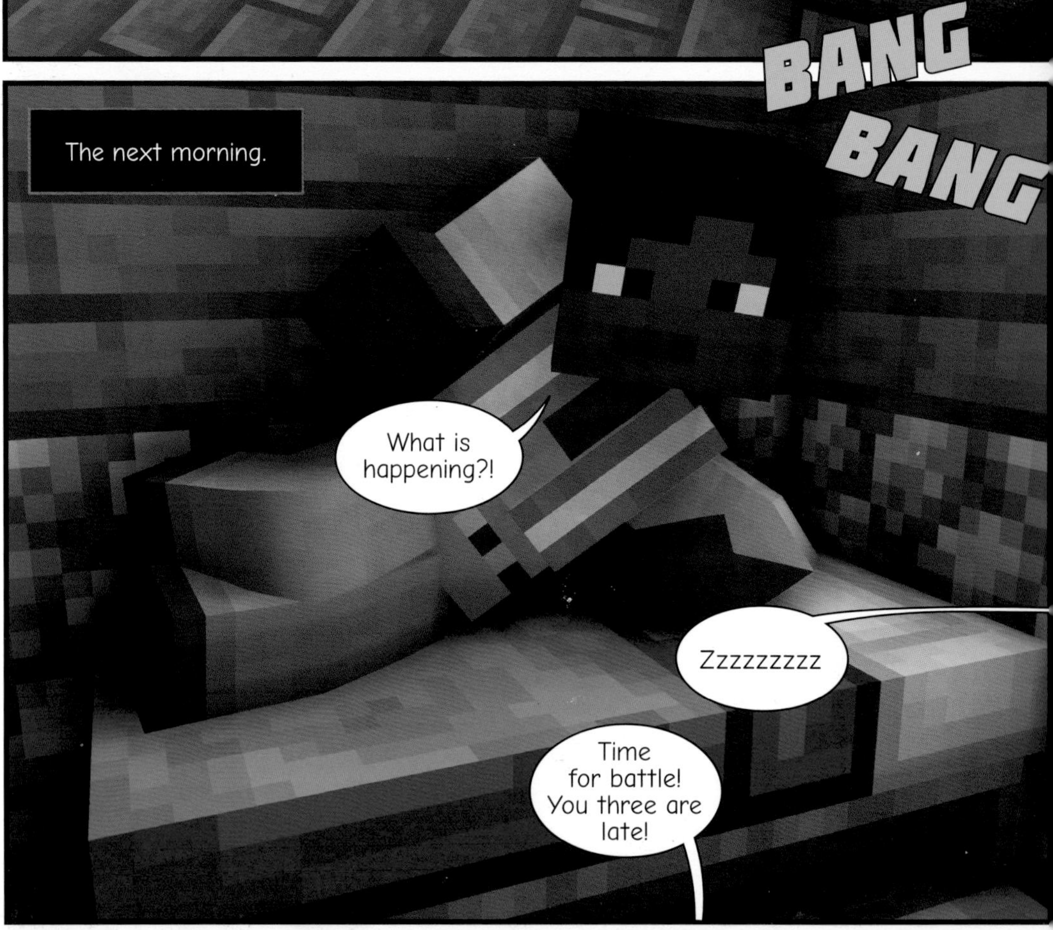
BANG
BANG
The next morning.
What is happening?!
Zzzzzzzzz
Time for battle! You three are late!

Chapter 5

A Wall
of Webs

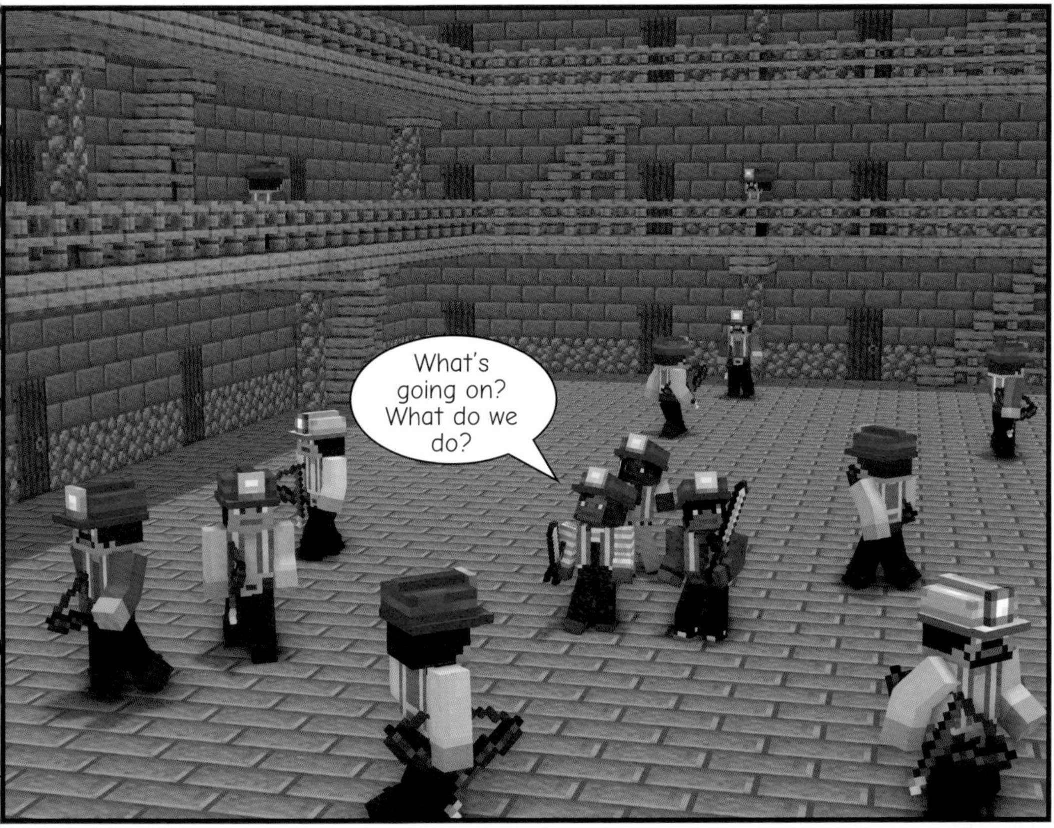
What's going on? What do we do?

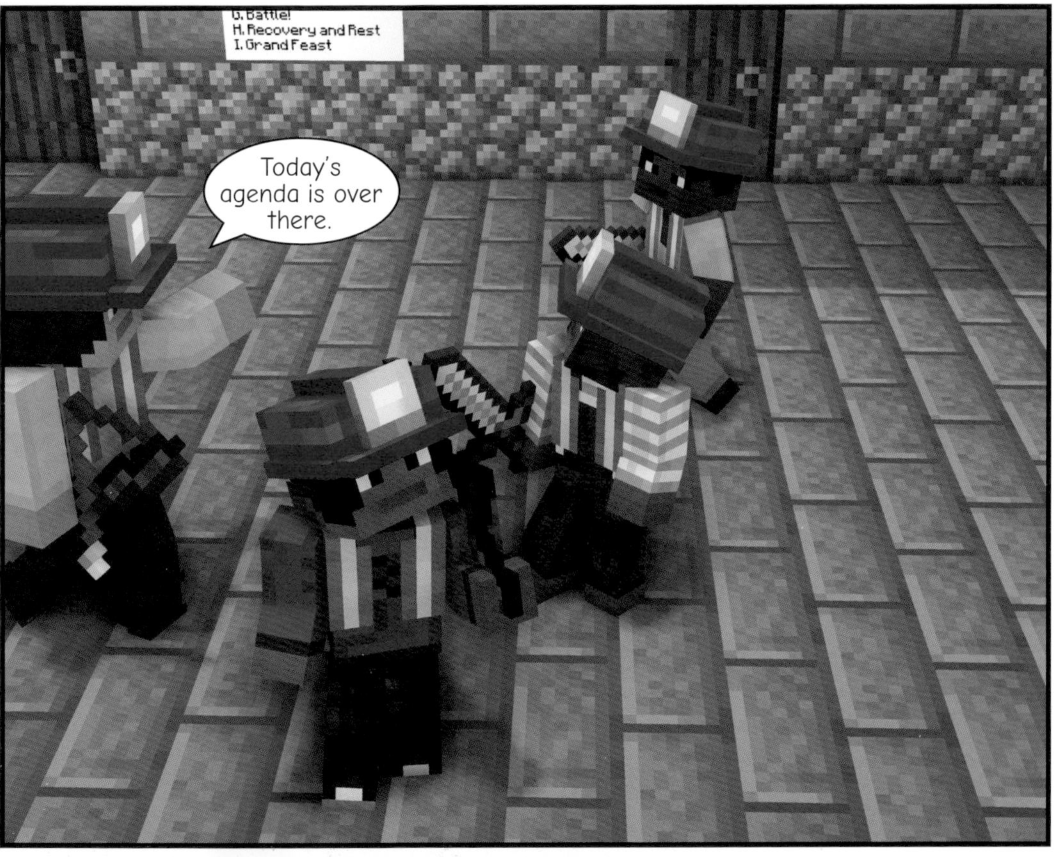
G. Battle!
H. Recovery and Rest
I. Grand Feast
Today's agenda is over there.

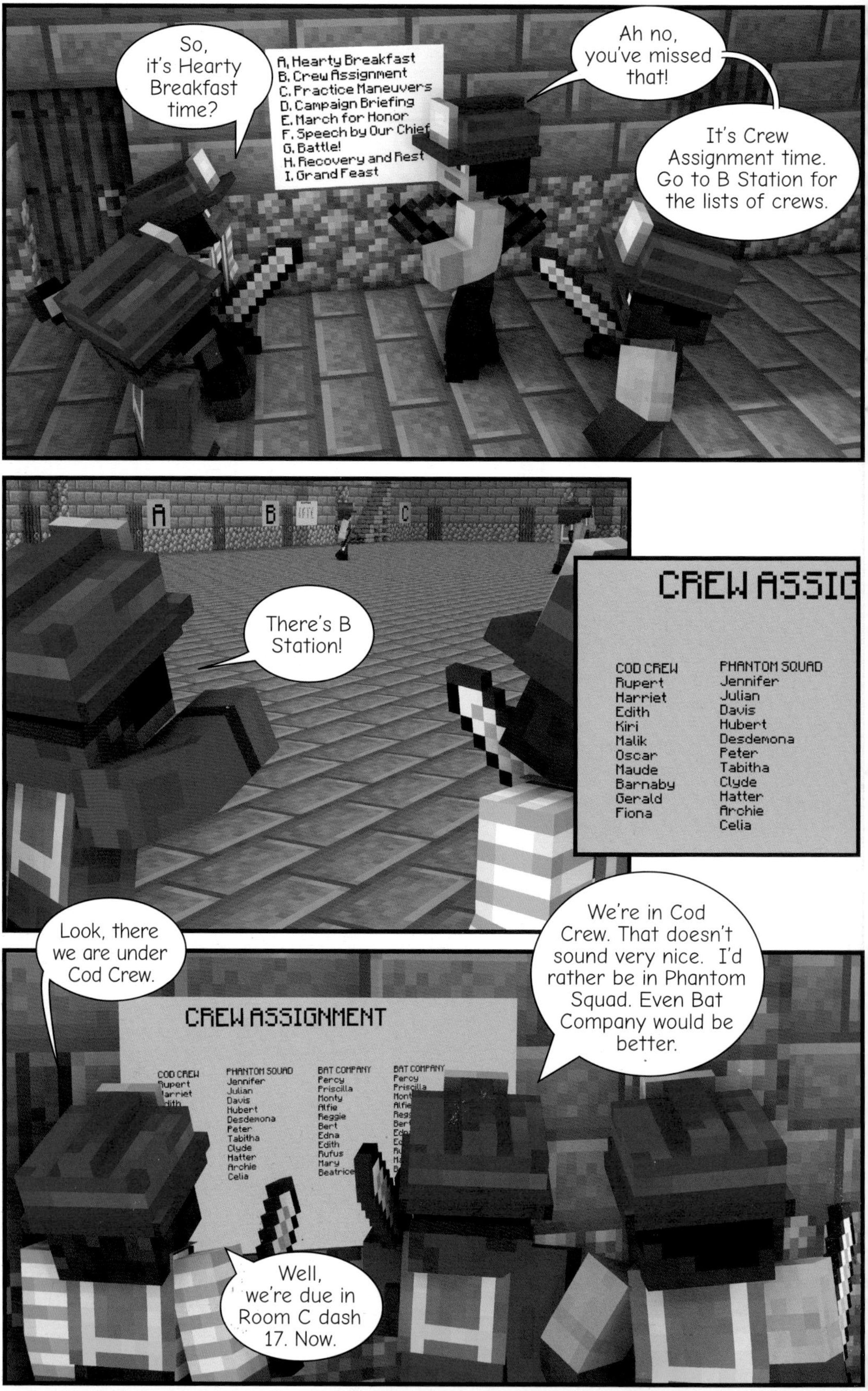
So, it's Hearty Breakfast time?
A. Hearty Breakfast
B. Crew Assignment
C. Practice Maneuvers
D. Campaign Briefing
E. March for Honor
F. Speech by Our Chief
G. Battle!
H. Recovery and Rest
I. Grand Feast
Ah no, you've missed that!
It's Crew Assignment time. Go to B Station for the lists of crews.
A
B
C
There's B Station!
CREW ASSIG
COD CREW
Rupert
Harriet
Edith
Kiri
Malik
Oscar
Maude
Barnaby
Gerald
Fiona
PHANTOM SQUAD
Jennifer
Julian
Davis
Hubert
Desdemona
Peter
Tabitha
Clyde
Hatter
Archie
Celia
Look, there we are under Cod Crew.
CREW ASSIGNMENT
COD CREW
Rupert
PHANTOM SQUAD
Jennifer
Julian
Davis
Hubert
Desdemona
Peter
Tabitha
Clyde
Hatter
Archie
Celia
BAT COMPANY
Percy
Priscilla
Monty
Alfie
Reggie
Bert
Edna
Edith
Rufus
Mary
Beatrice
BAT COMPANY
Percy
Priscilla
We're in Cod Crew. That doesn't sound very nice. I'd rather be in Phantom Squad. Even Bat Company would be better.
Well, we're due in Room C dash 17. Now.

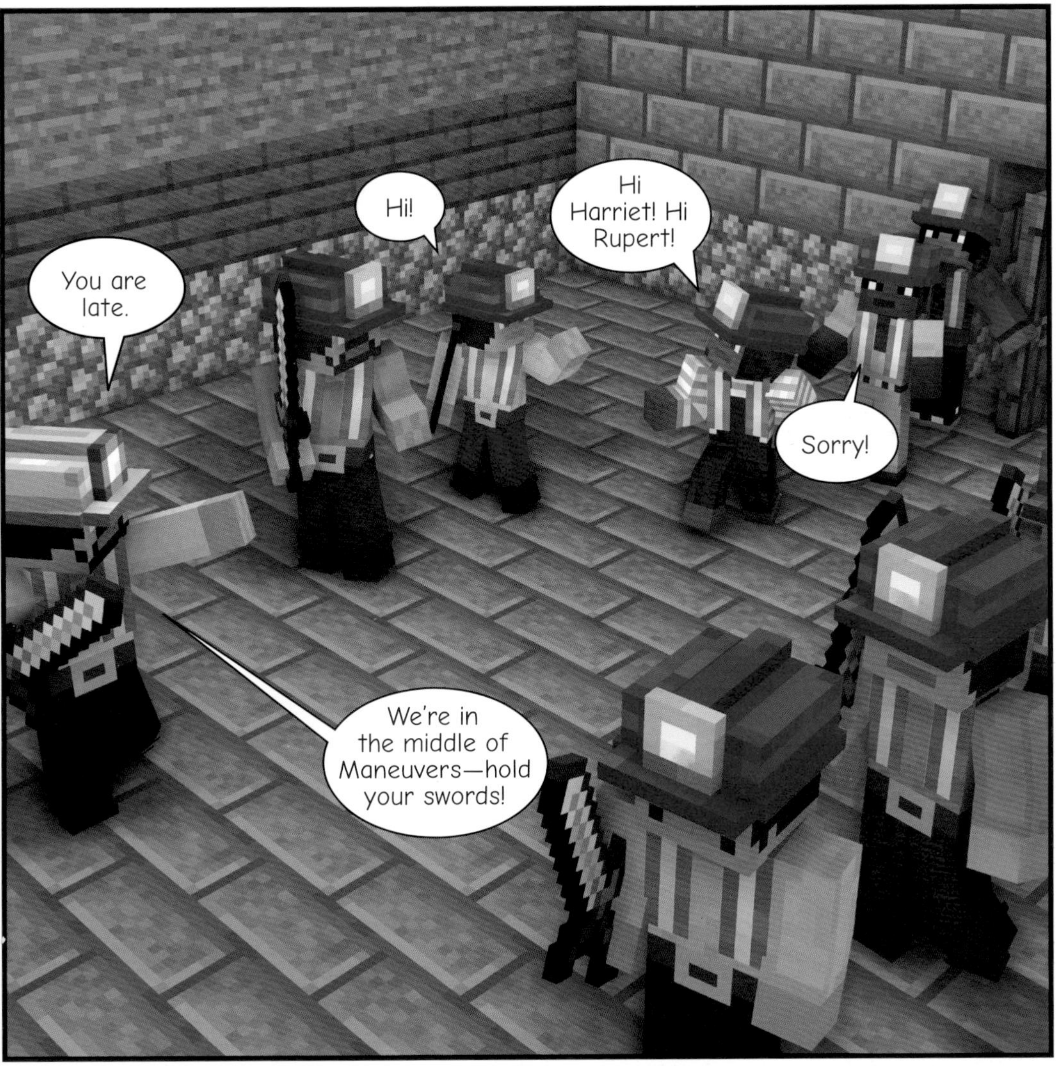
You are late.
Hi!
Hi Harriet! Hi Rupert!
Sorry!
We're in the middle of Maneuvers—hold your swords!

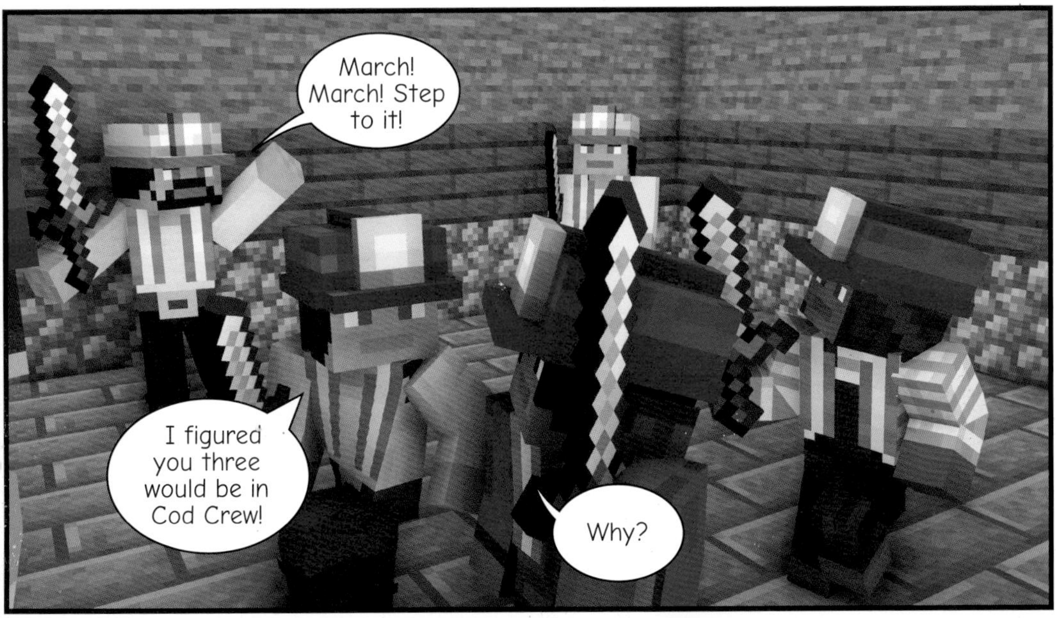
March! March! Step to it!
I figured you three would be in Cod Crew!
Why?

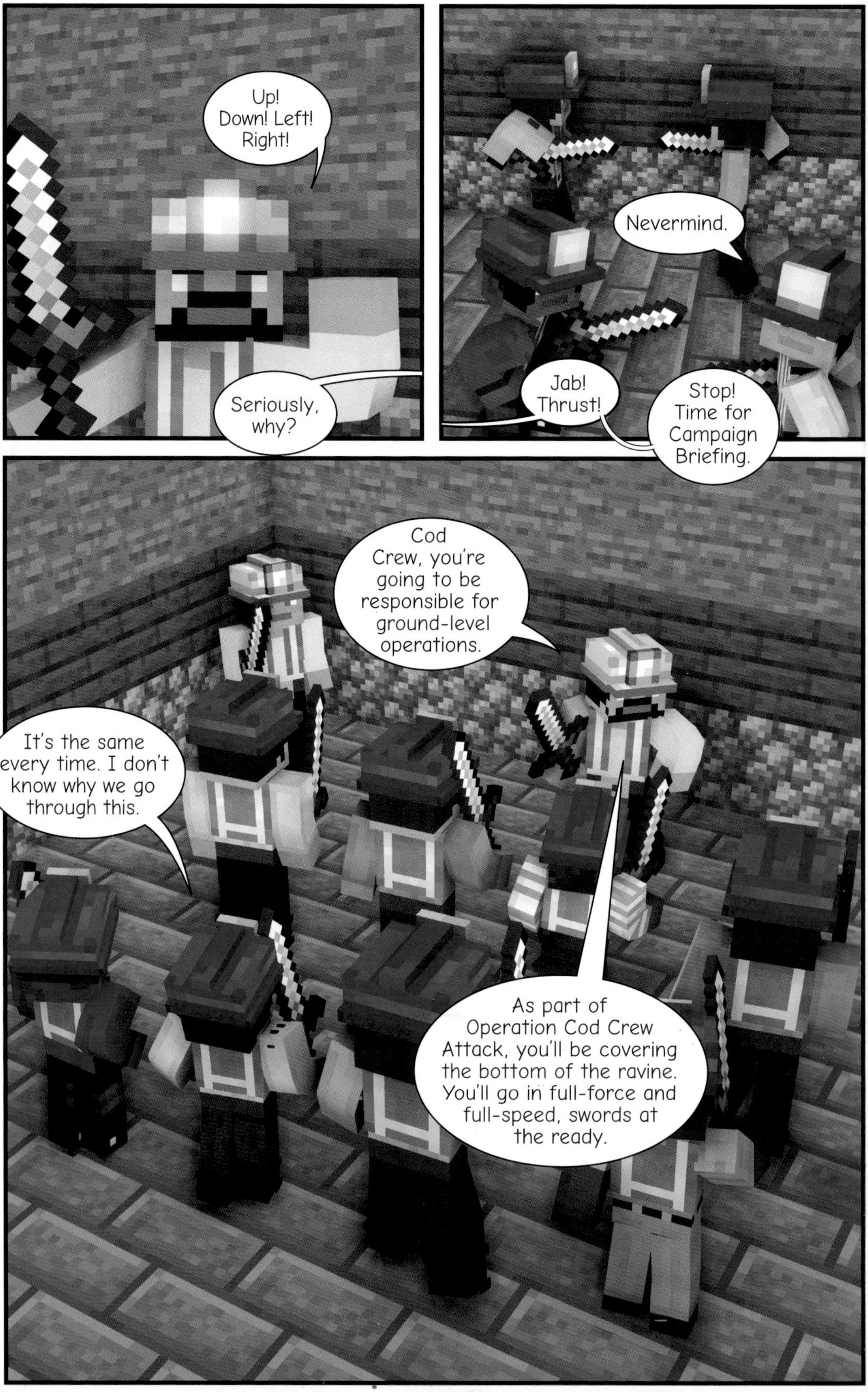
Up! Down! Left! Right!
Seriously, why?
Nevermind.
Jab! Thrust!
Stop! Time for Campaign Briefing.
Cod Crew, you're going to be responsible for ground-level operations.
It's the same every time. I don't know why we go through this.
As part of Operation Cod Crew Attack, you'll be covering the bottom of the ravine. You'll go in full-force and full-speed, swords at the ready.

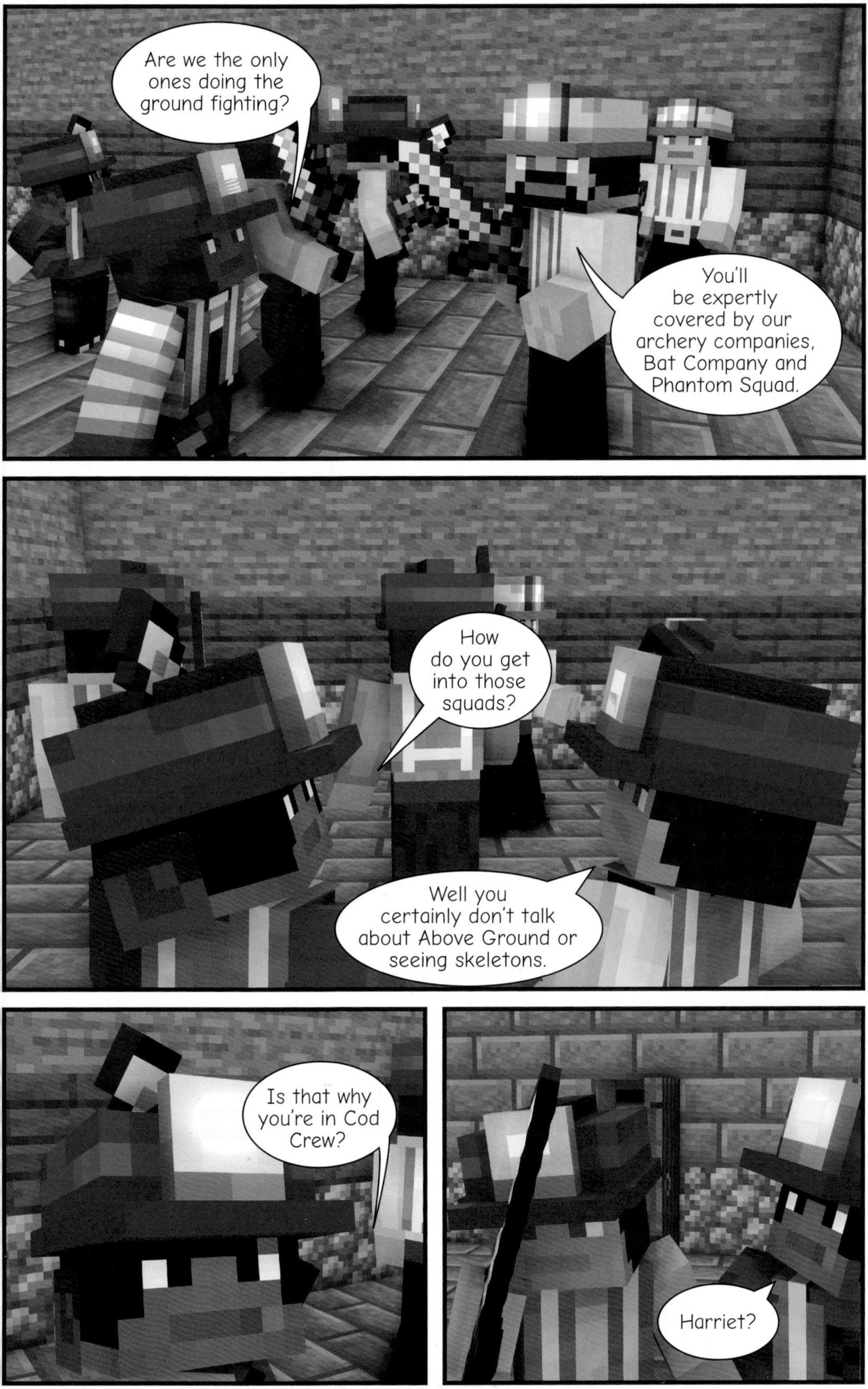
Are we the only ones doing the ground fighting?
You'll be expertly covered by our archery companies, Bat Company and Phantom Squad.
How do you get into those squads?
Well you certainly don't talk about Above Ground or seeing skeletons.
Is that why you're in Cod Crew?
Harriet?

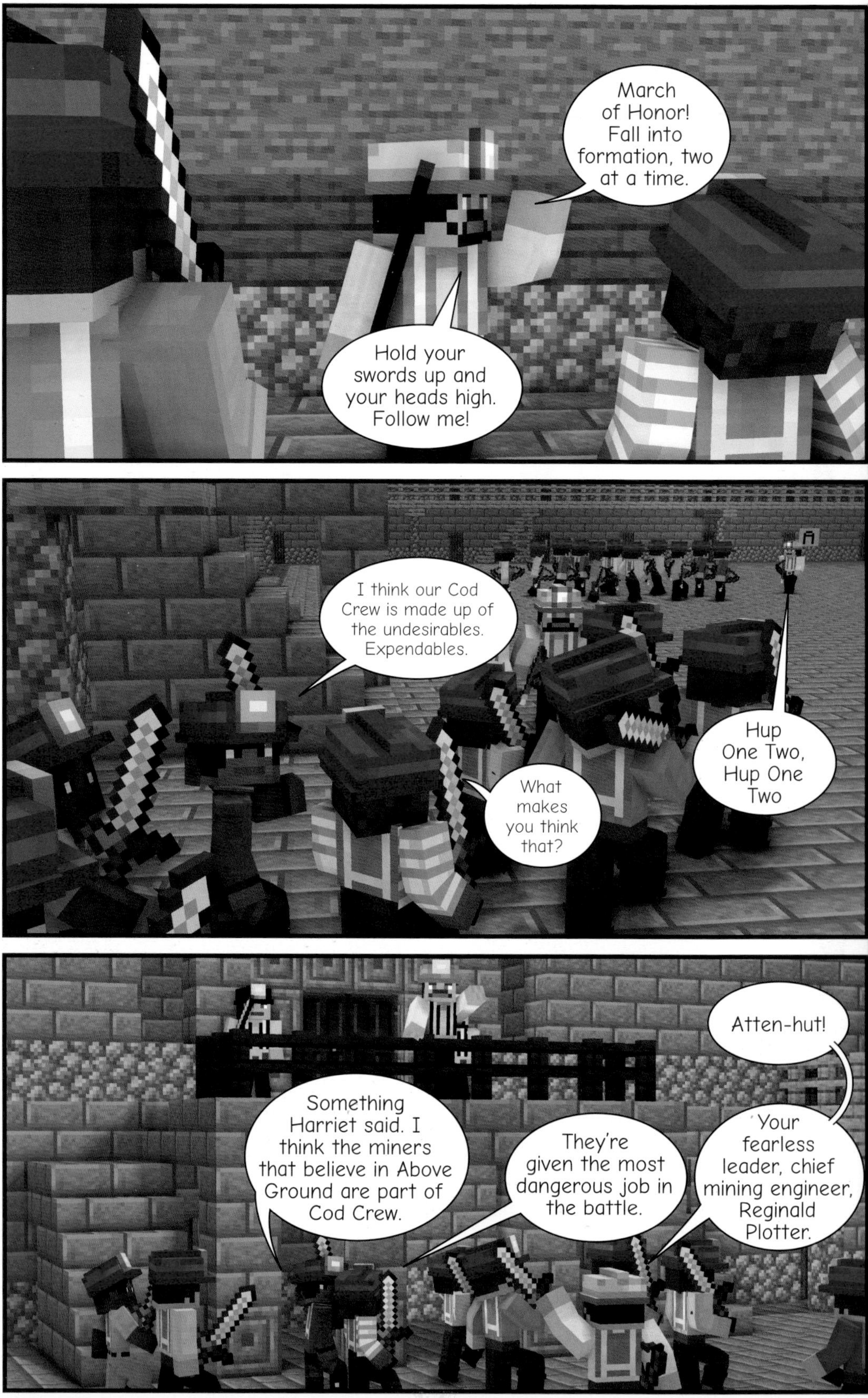
March of Honor! Fall into formation, two at a time.
Hold your swords up and your heads high. Follow me!
I think our Cod Crew is made up of the undesirables. Expendables.
What makes you think that?
Hup One Two, Hup One Two
Atten-hut!
Something Harriet said. I think the miners that believe in Above Ground are part of Cod Crew.
They're given the most dangerous job in the battle.
Your fearless leader, chief mining engineer, Reginald Plotter.

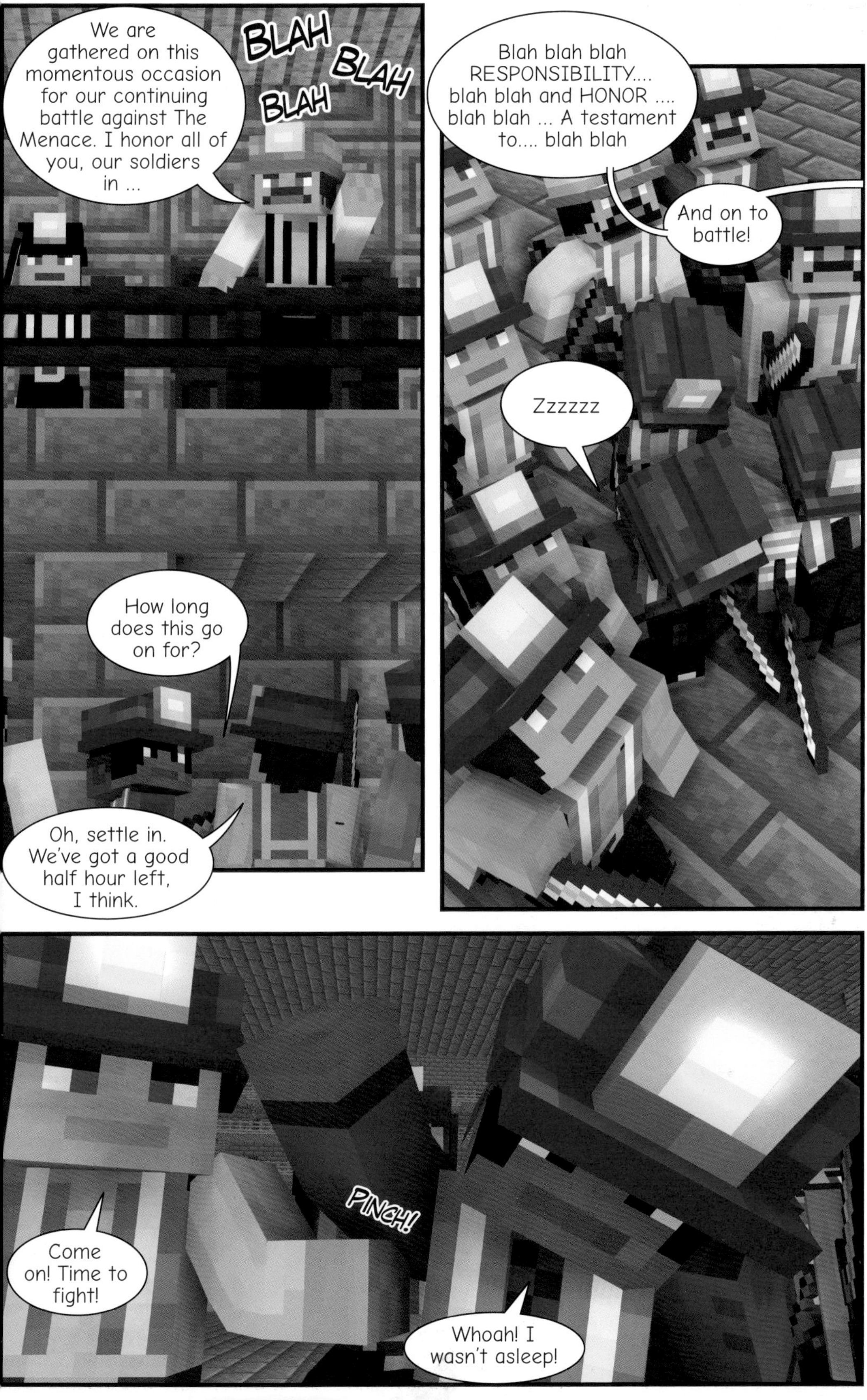
We are gathered on this momentous occasion for our continuing battle against The Menace. I honor all of you, our soldiers in ...
BLAH BLAH BLAH
How long does this go on for?
Oh, settle in. We've got a good half hour left, I think.
Blah blah blah RESPONSIBILITY.... blah blah and HONOR .... blah blah ... A testament to.... blah blah
And on to battle!
Zzzzzz
PINCH!
Come on! Time to fight!
Whoah! I wasn't asleep!

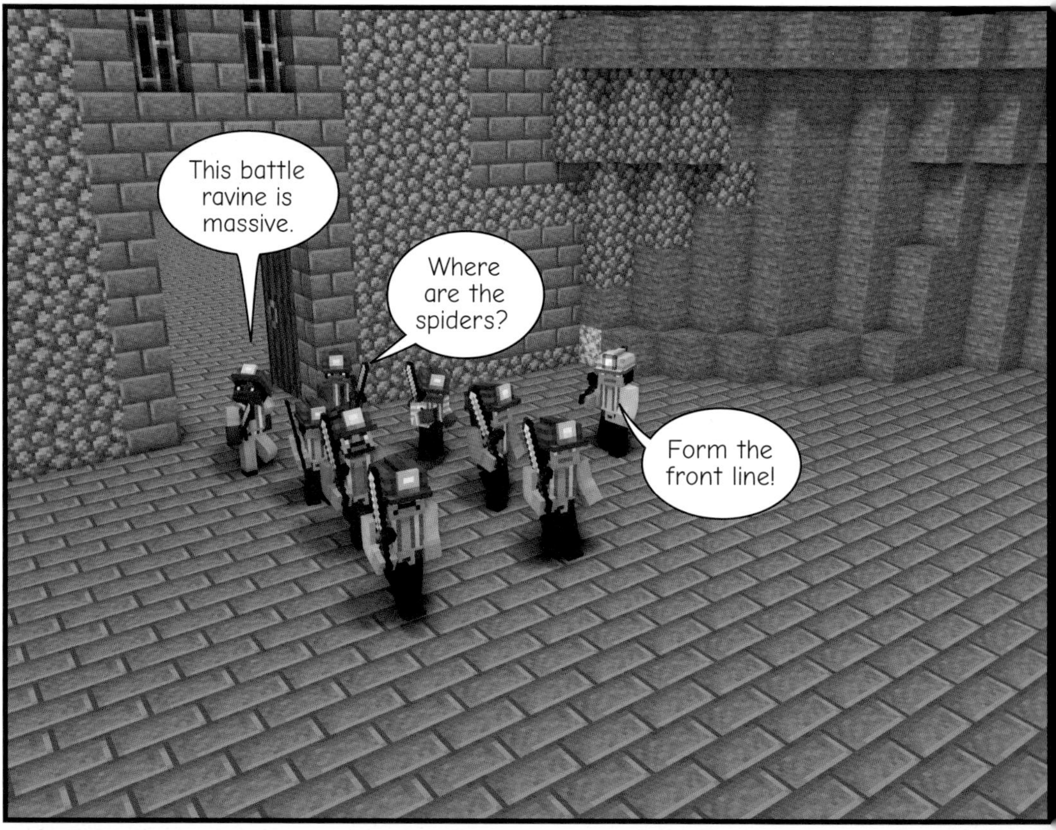
This battle ravine is massive.
Where are the spiders?
Form the front line!

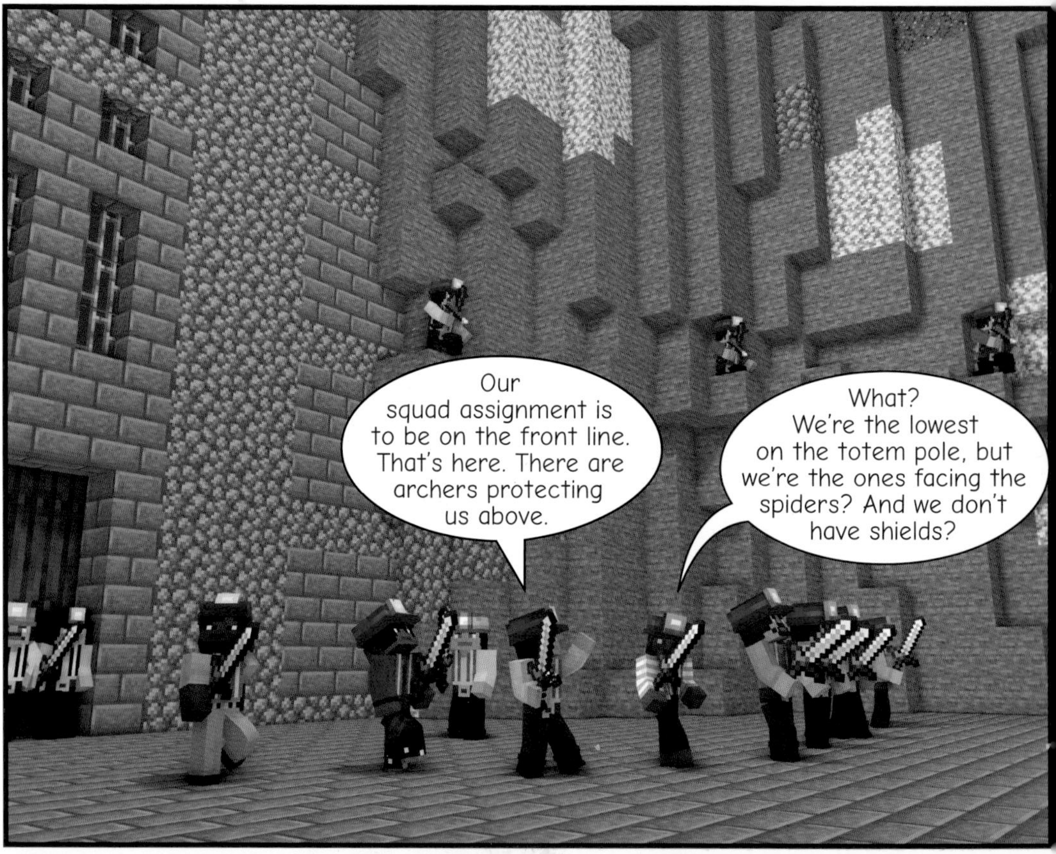
Our squad assignment is to be on the front line. That's here. There are archers protecting us above.
What? We're the lowest on the totem pole, but we're the ones facing the spiders? And we don't have shields?

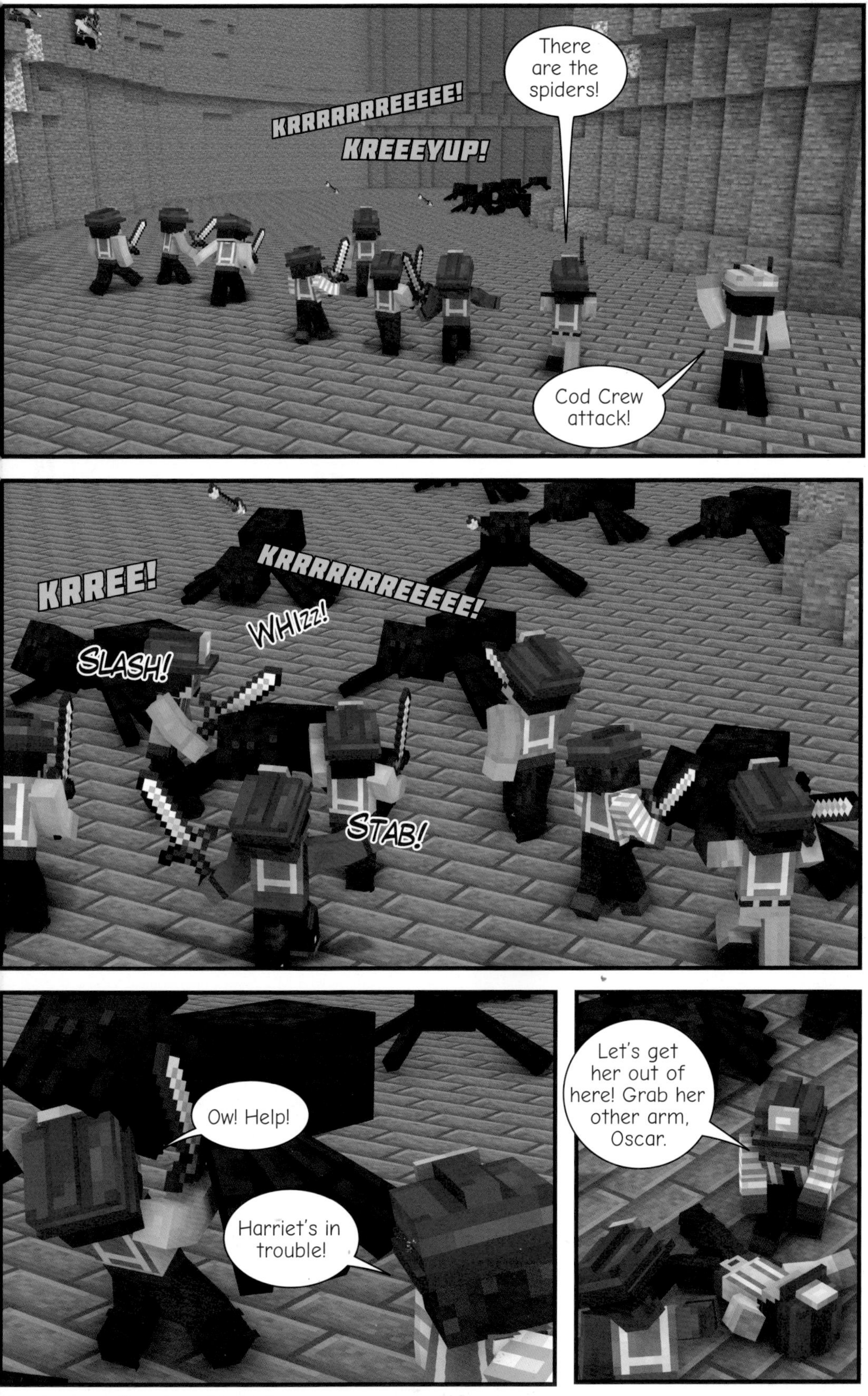
KRRRRRRREEEEE!
KREEEYUP!
There are the spiders!
Cod Crew attack!
KRREE!
KRRRRRRREEEEE!
WHIZZ!
SLASH!
STAB!
Ow! Help!
Harriet's in trouble!
Let's get her out of here! Grab her other arm, Oscar.

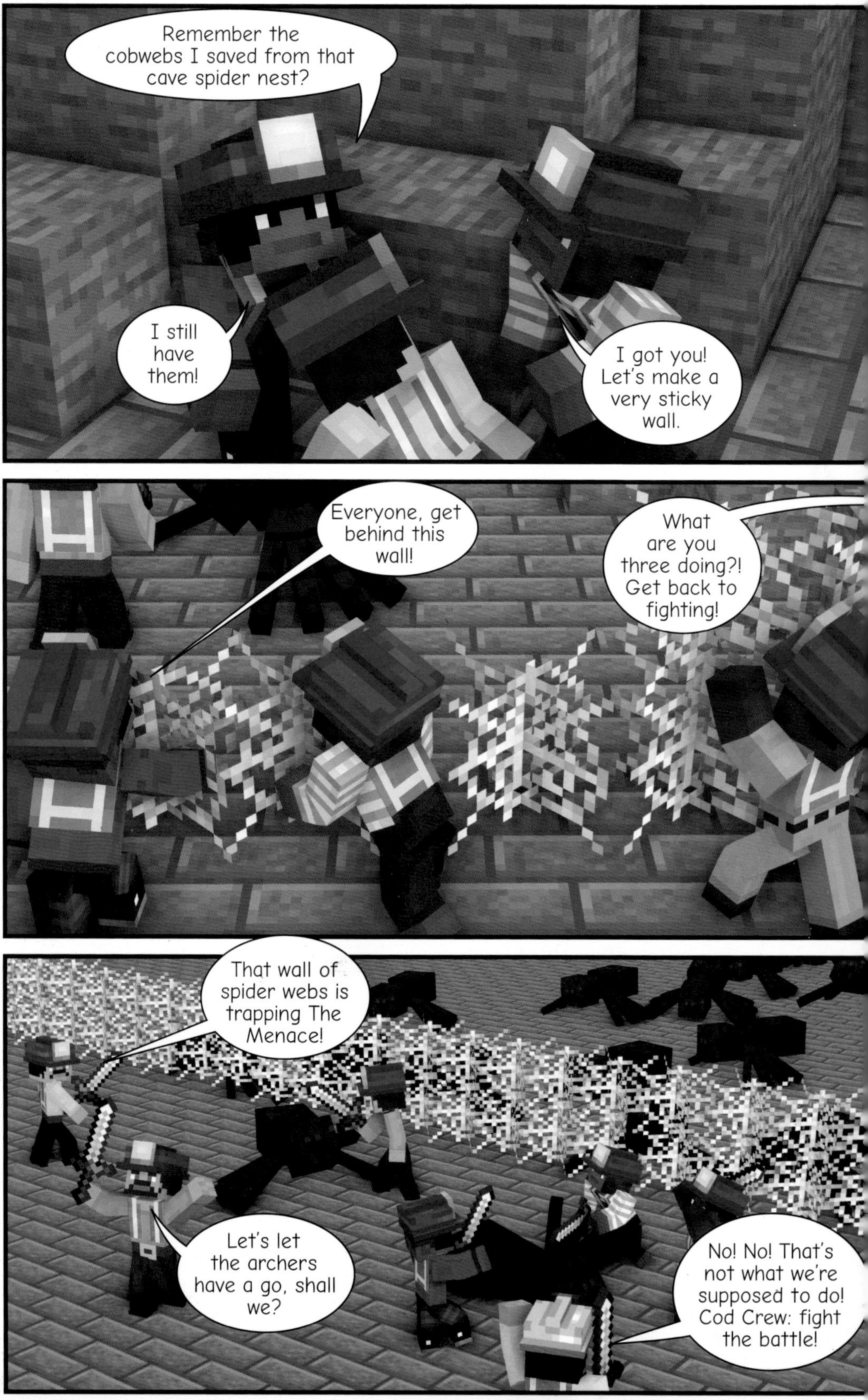
Remember the cobwebs I saved from that cave spider nest?
I still have them!
I got you! Let's make a very sticky wall.
Everyone, get behind this wall!
What are you three doing?! Get back to fighting!
That wall of spider webs is trapping The Menace!
Let's let the archers have a go, shall we?
No! No! That's not what we're supposed to do! Cod Crew: fight the battle!

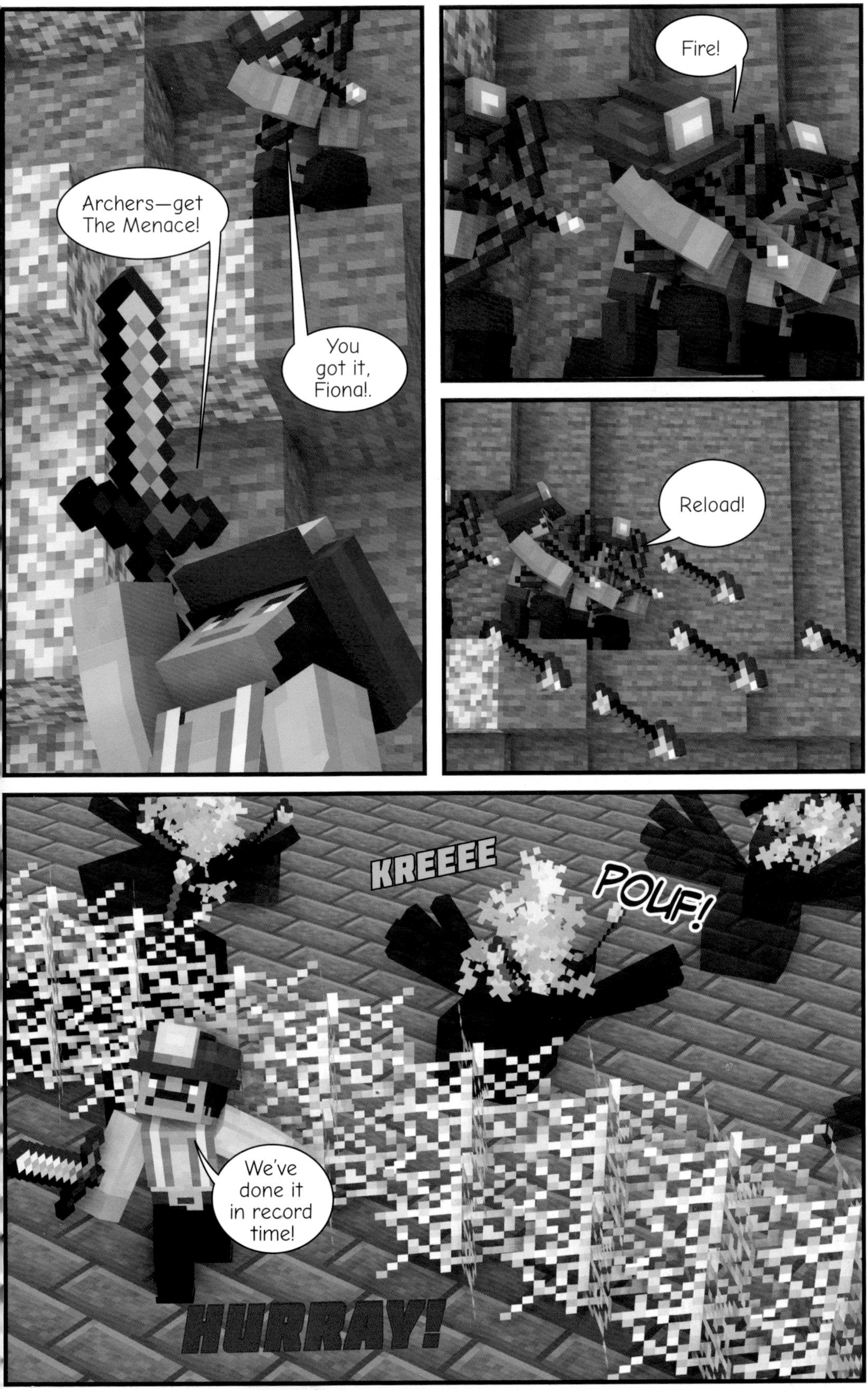
Archers—get The Menace!
You got it, Fiona!.
Fire!
Reload!
KREEEE
POUF!
We've done it in record time!
HURRAY!

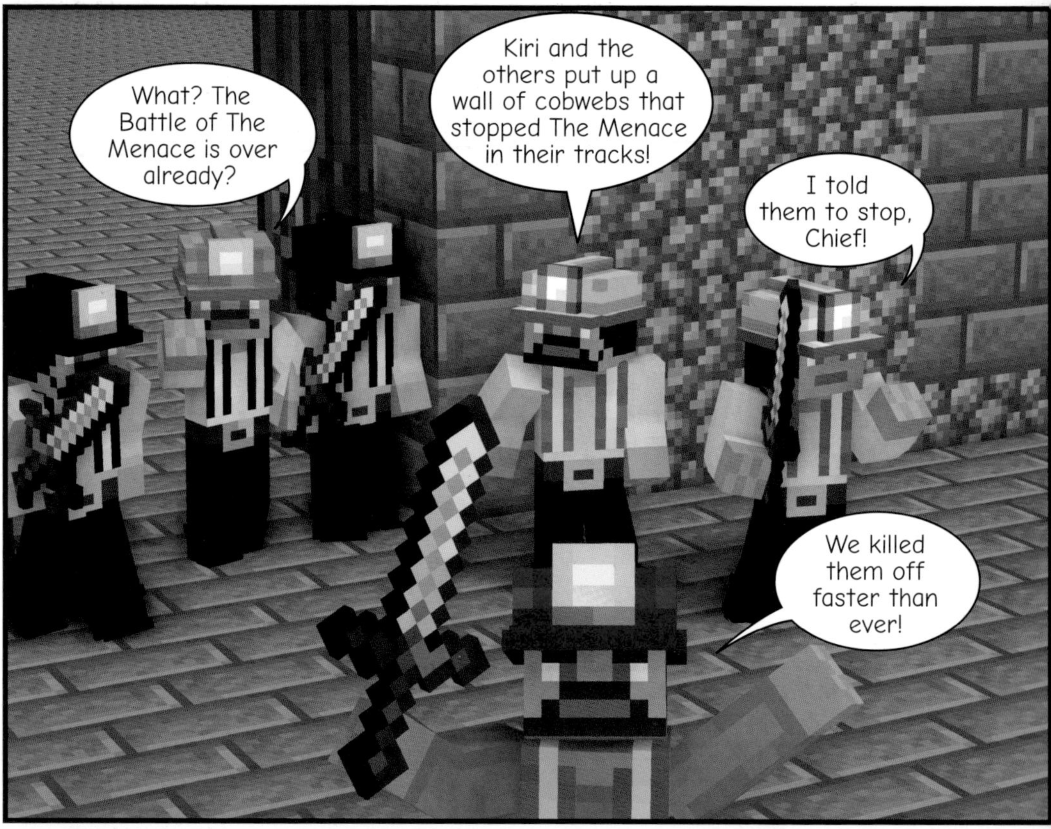
What? The Battle of The Menace is over already?
Kiri and the others put up a wall of cobwebs that stopped The Menace in their tracks!
I told them to stop, Chief!
We killed them off faster than ever!

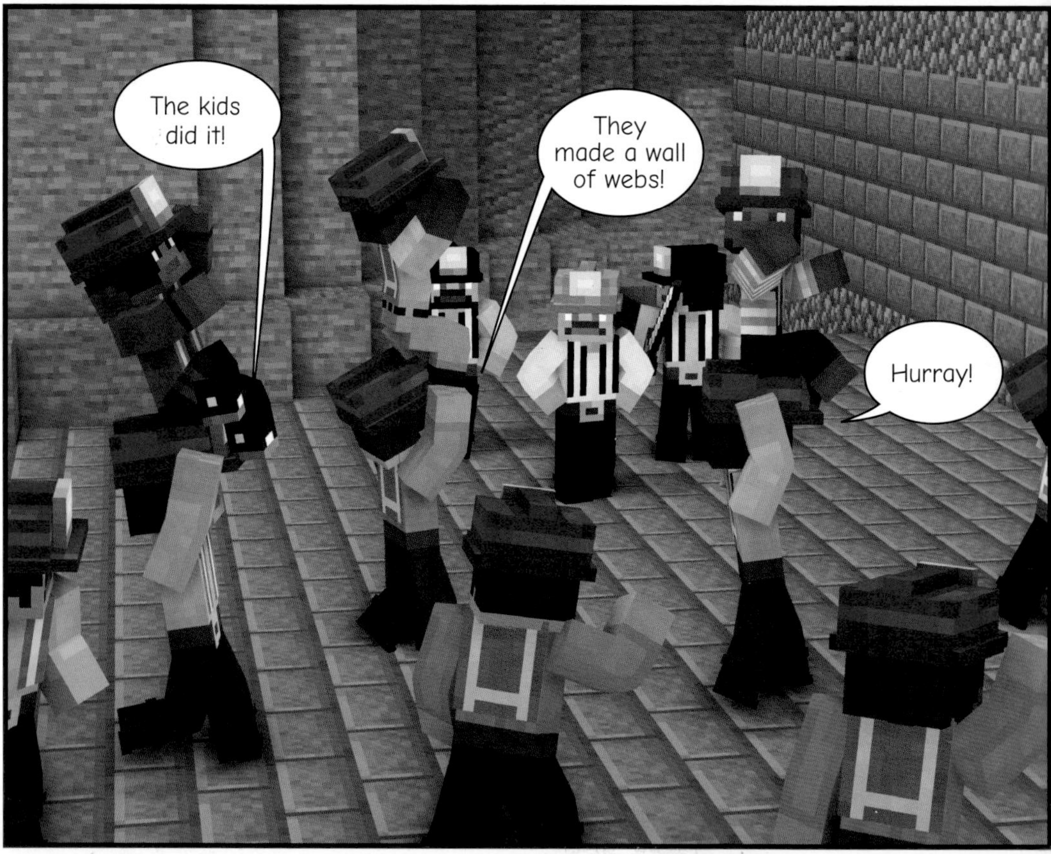
The kids did it!
They made a wall of webs!
Hurray!

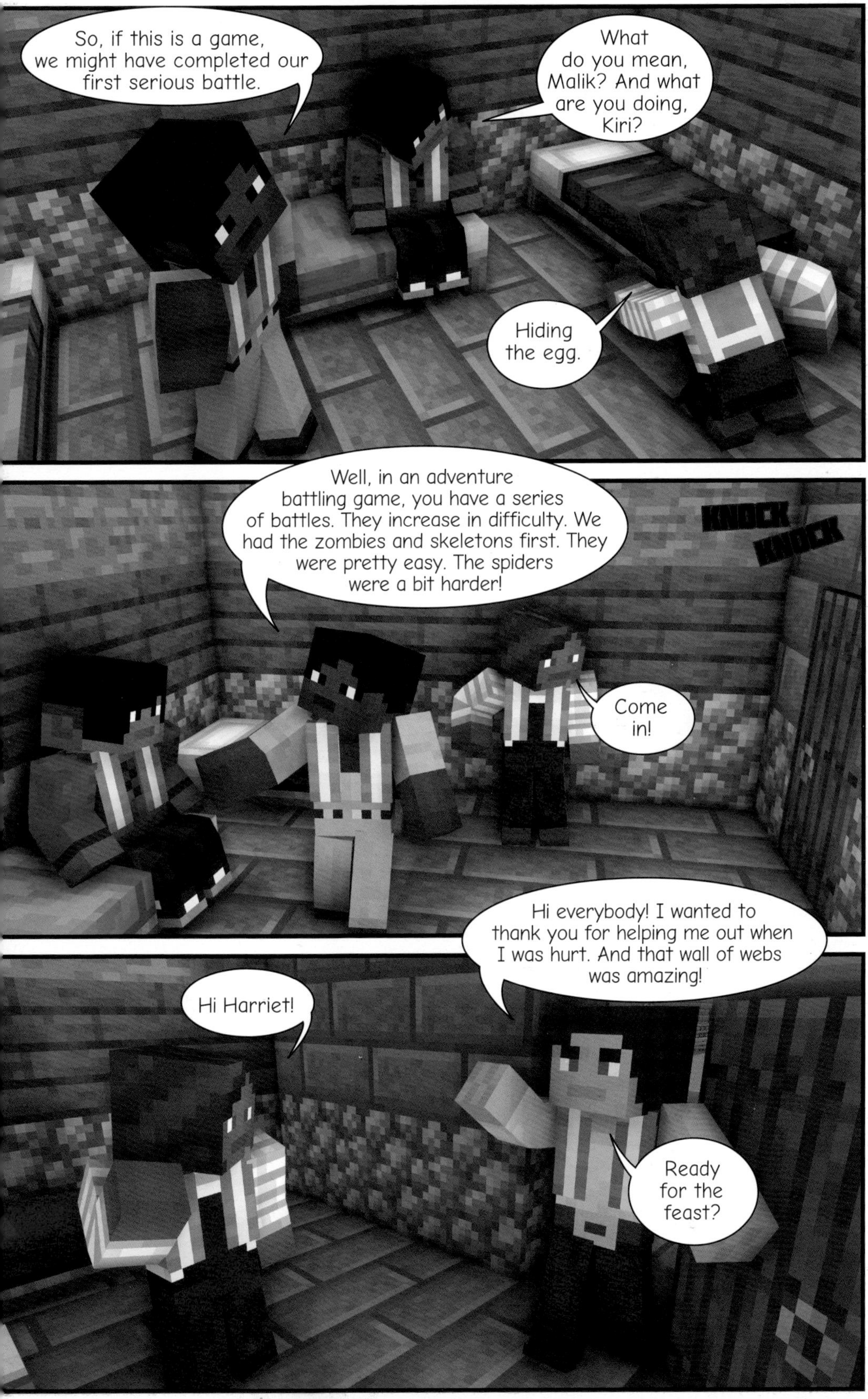
So, if this is a game, we might have completed our first serious battle.
What do you mean, Malik? And what are you doing, Kiri?
Hiding the egg.
Well, in an adventure battling game, you have a series of battles. They increase in difficulty. We had the zombies and skeletons first. They were pretty easy. The spiders were a bit harder!
KNOCK KNOCK
Come in!
Hi everybody! I wanted to thank you for helping me out when I was hurt. And that wall of webs was amazing!
Hi Harriet!
Ready for the feast?

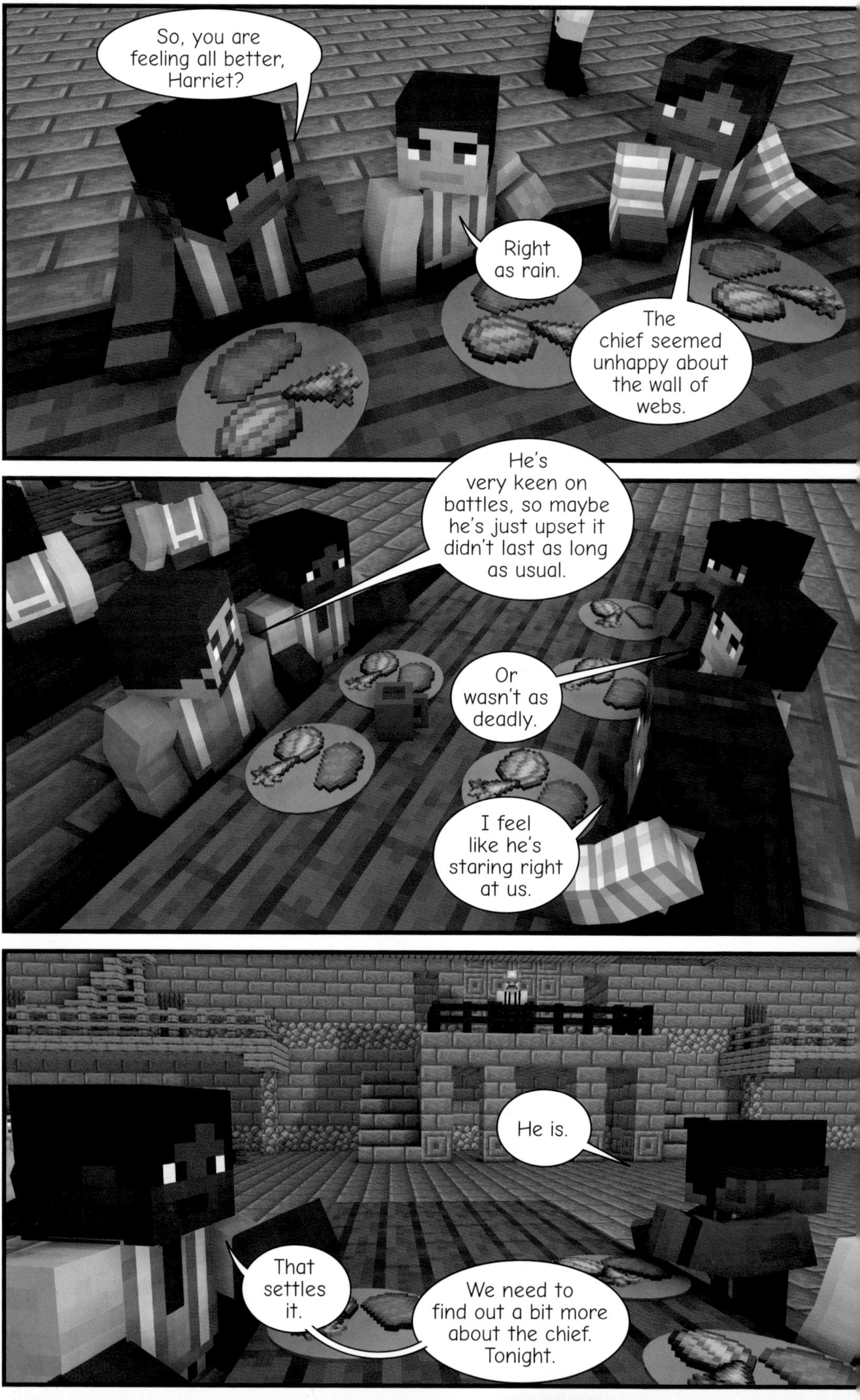
So, you are feeling all better, Harriet?
Right as rain.
The chief seemed unhappy about the wall of webs.
He's very keen on battles, so maybe he's just upset it didn't last as long as usual.
Or wasn't as deadly.
I feel like he's staring right at us.
He is.
That settles it.
We need to find out a bit more about the chief. Tonight.

Chapter 6

Egg Hunt

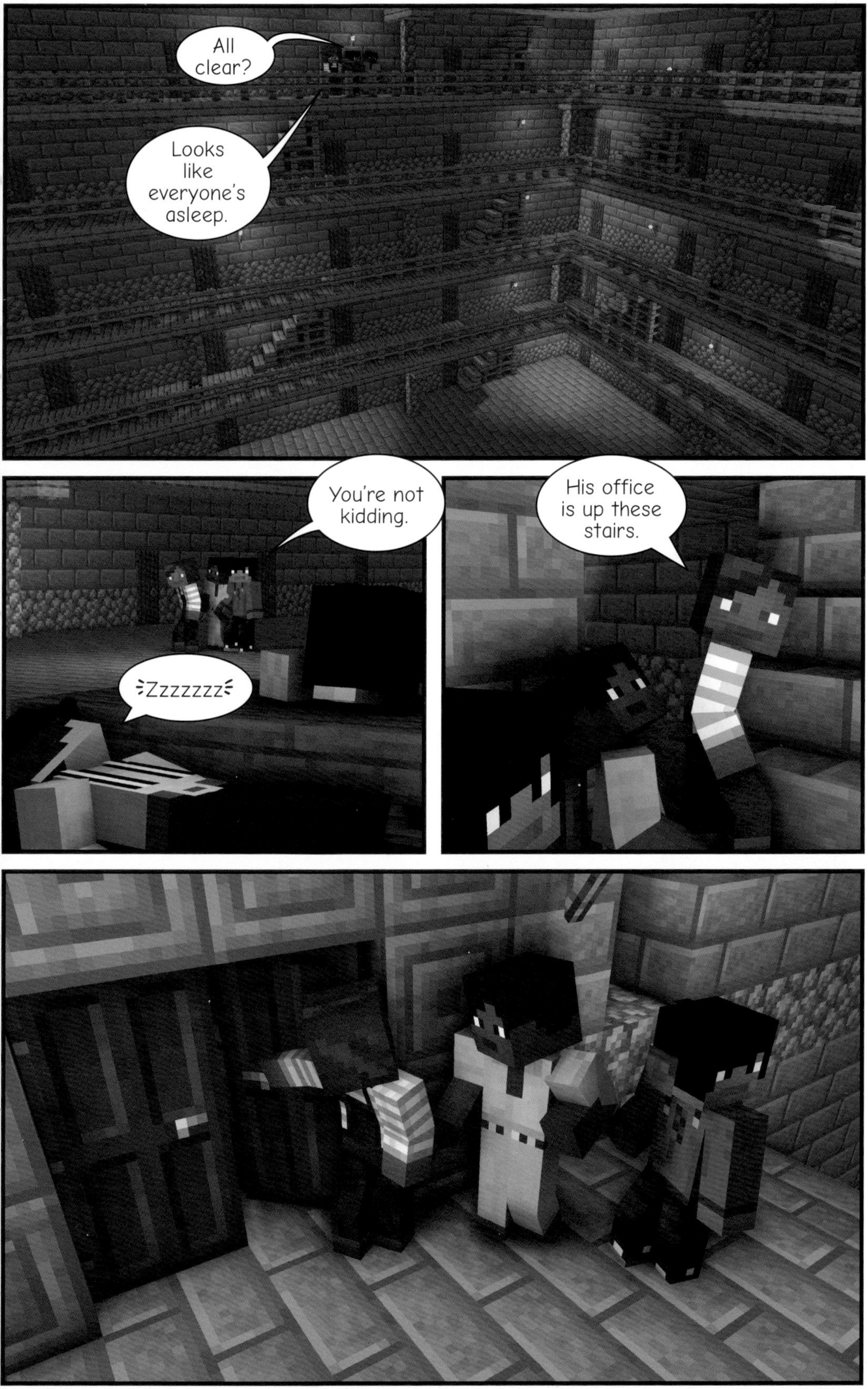
All clear?
Looks like everyone's asleep.
You're not kidding.
Zzzzzzz
His office is up these stairs.

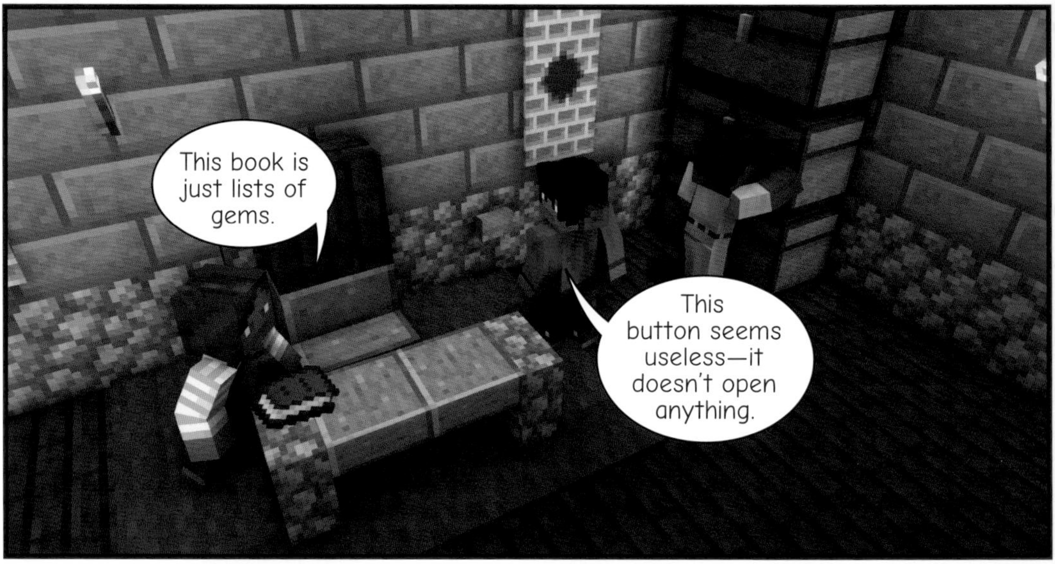
This book is just lists of gems.
This button seems useless—it doesn't open anything.

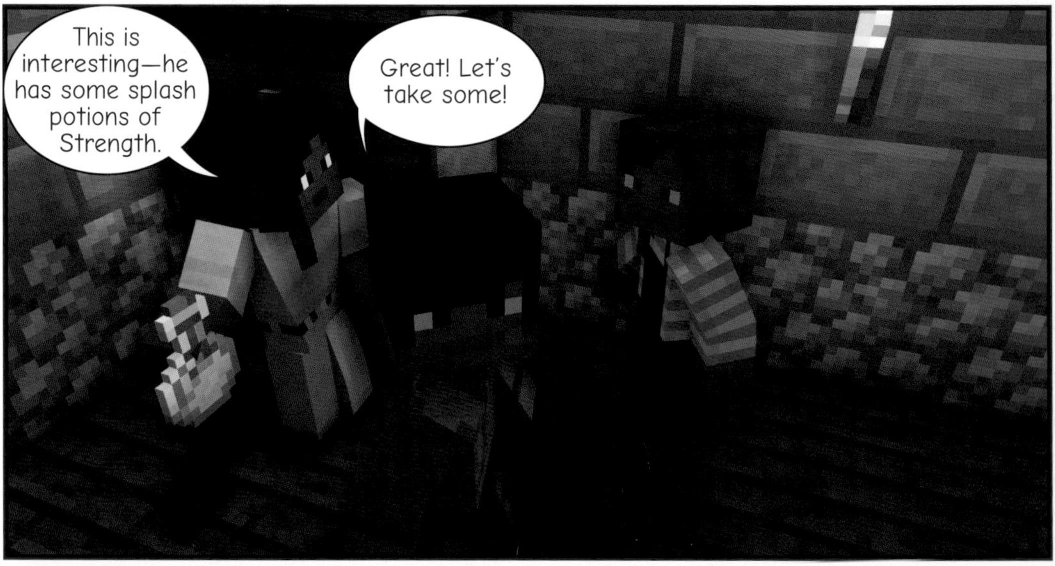
This is interesting—he has some splash potions of Strength.
Great! Let's take some!

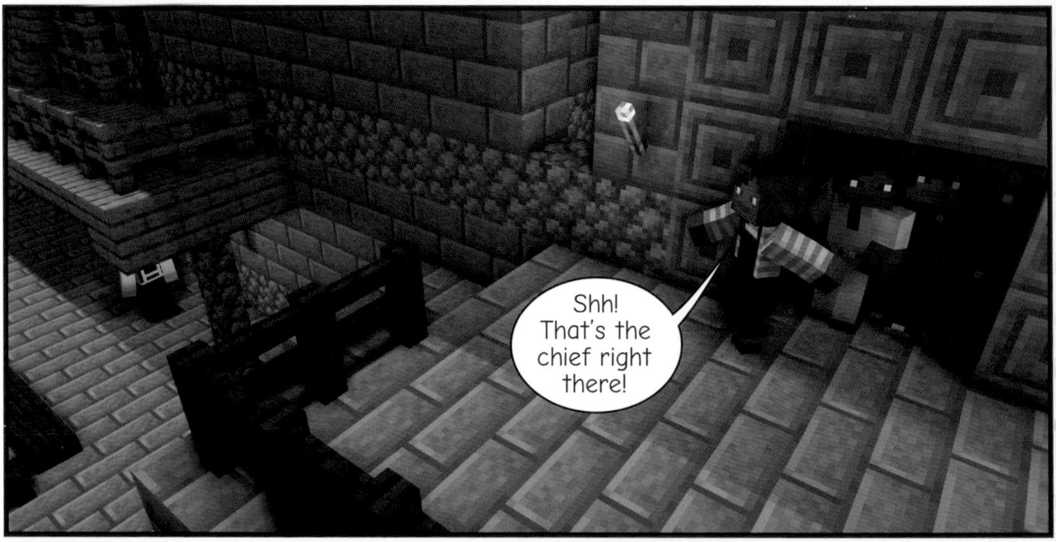
Shh! That's the chief right there!

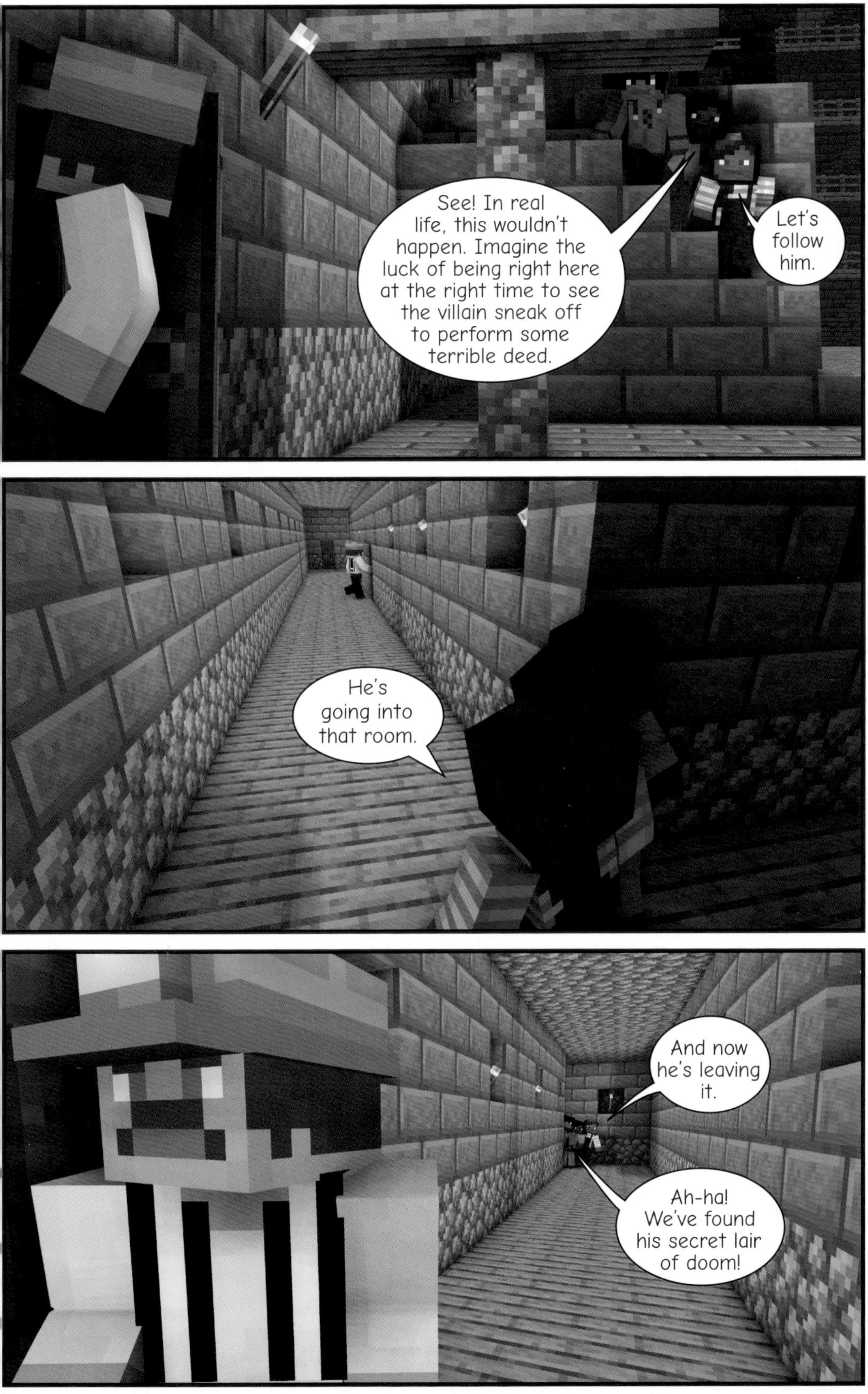
See! In real life, this wouldn't happen. Imagine the luck of being right here at the right time to see the villain sneak off to perform some terrible deed.
Let's follow him.
He's going into that room.
And now he's leaving it.
Ah-ha! We've found his secret lair of doom!

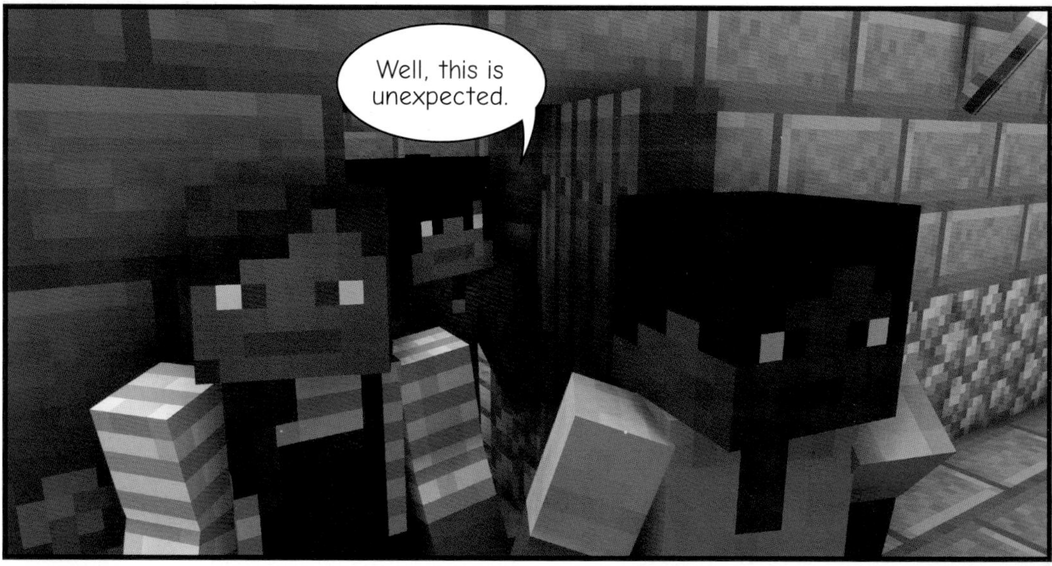
Well, this is unexpected.

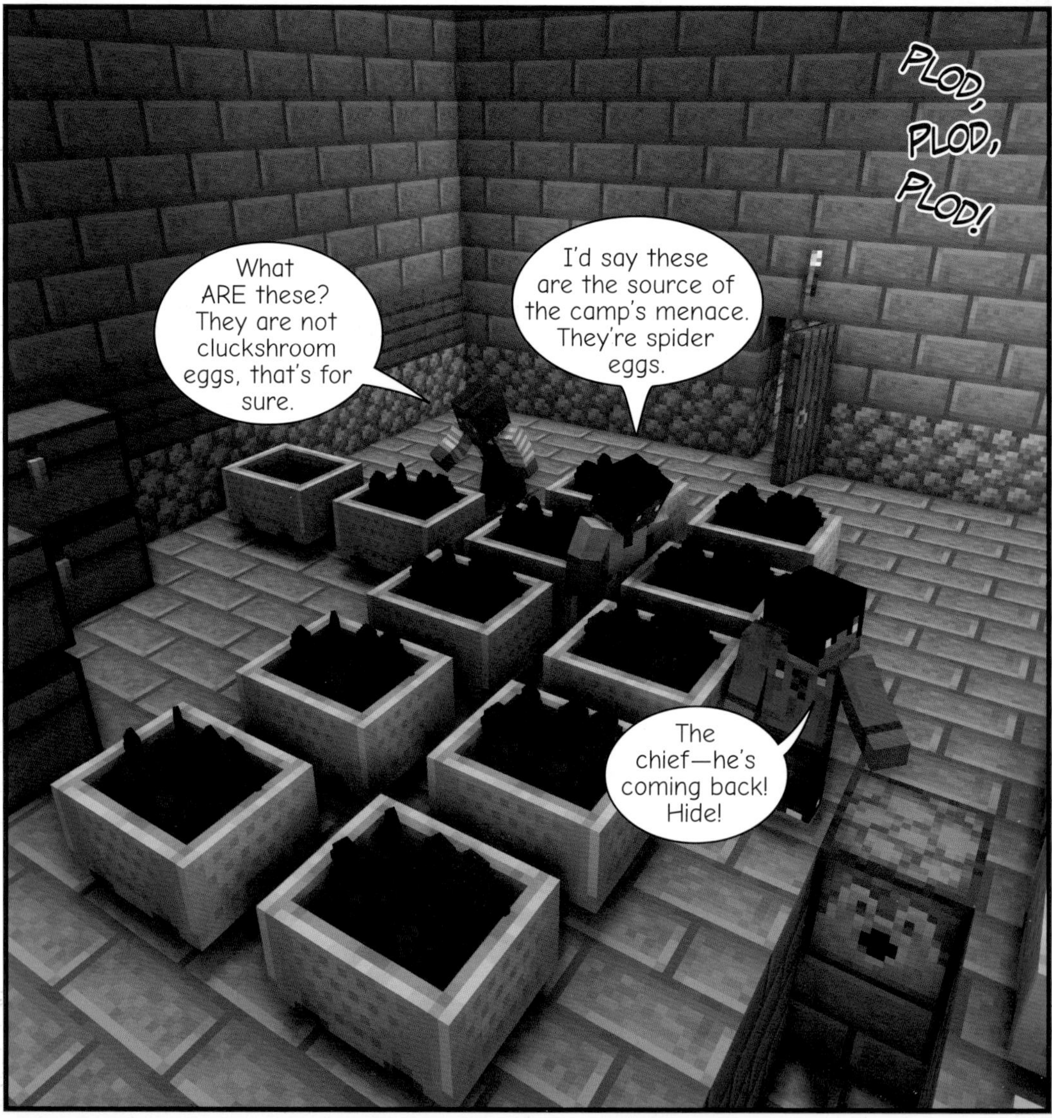
PLOD, PLOD, PLOD!
What ARE these? They are not cluckshroom eggs, that's for sure.
I'd say these are the source of the camp's menace. They're spider eggs.
The chief—he's coming back! Hide!

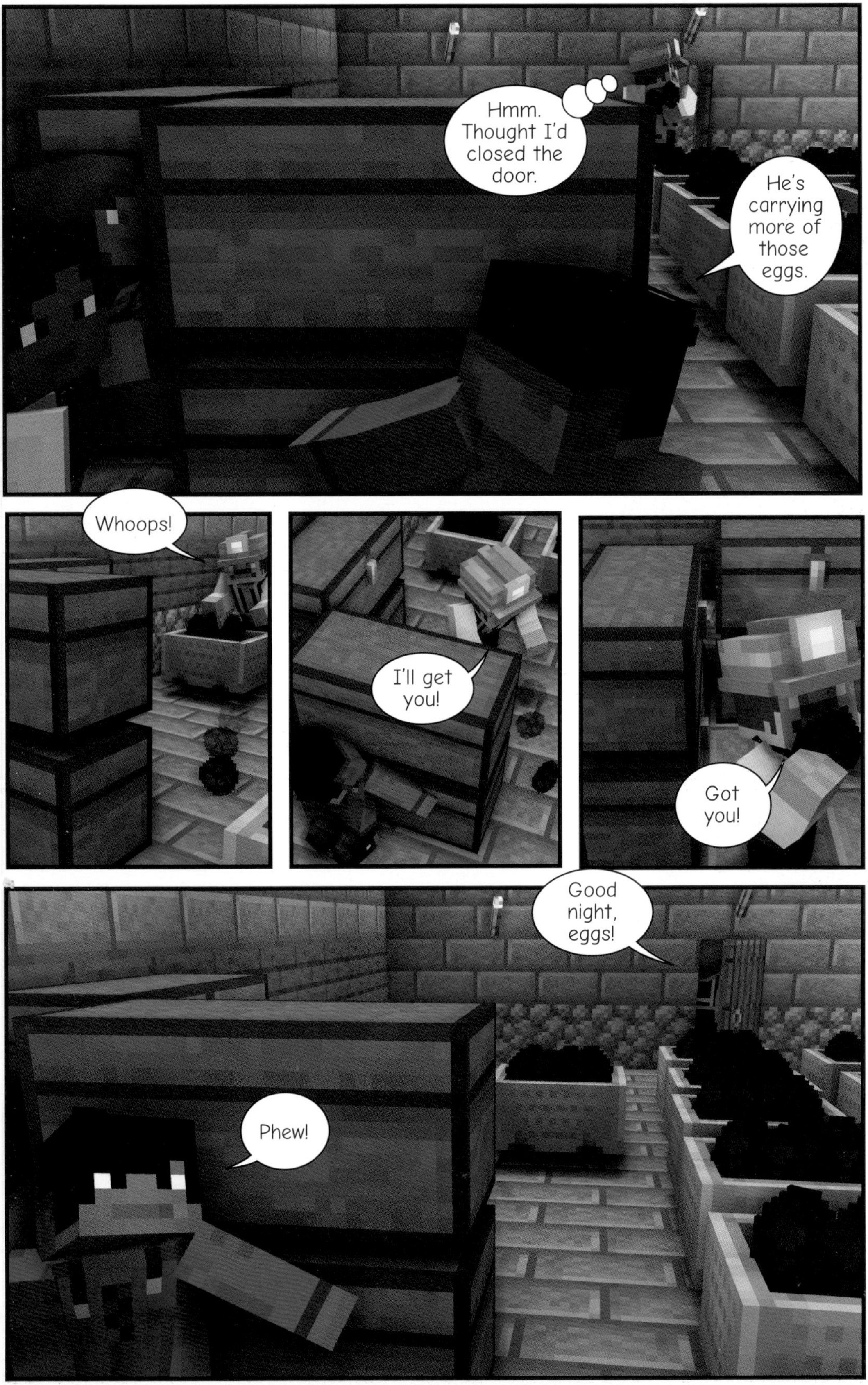
Hmm. Thought I'd closed the door.
He's carrying more of those eggs.
Whoops!
I'll get you!
Got you!
Good night, eggs!
Phew!

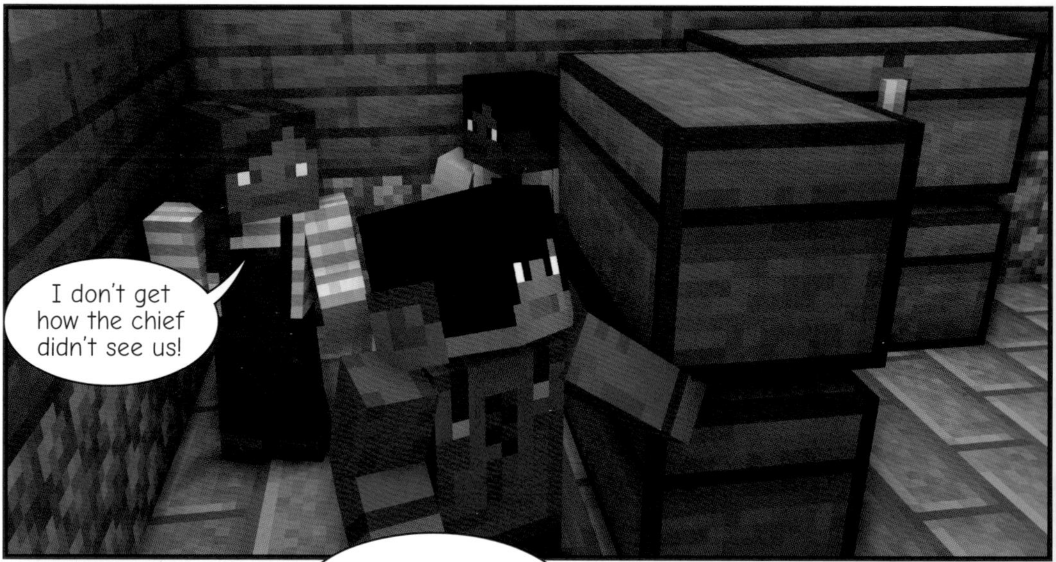
I don't get how the chief didn't see us!

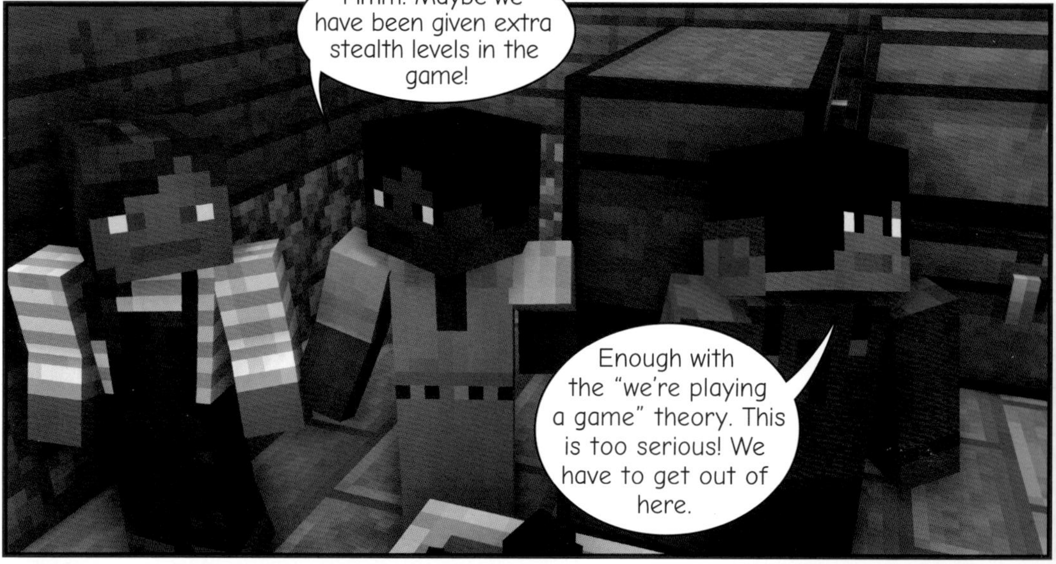
Hmm. Maybe we have been given extra stealth levels in the game!
Enough with the "we're playing a game" theory. This is too serious! We have to get out of here.

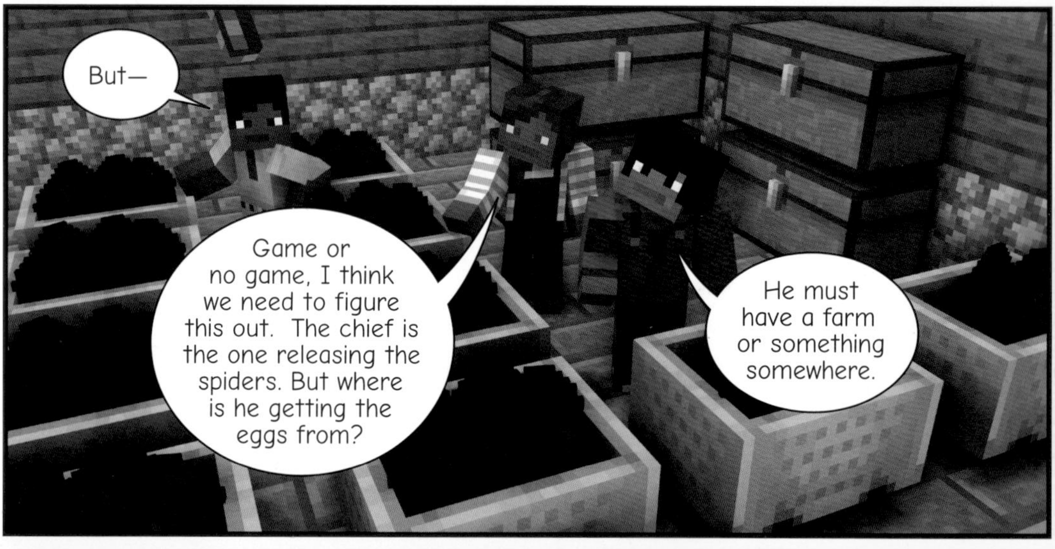
But—
Game or no game, I think we need to figure this out. The chief is the one releasing the spiders. But where is he getting the eggs from?
He must have a farm or something somewhere.

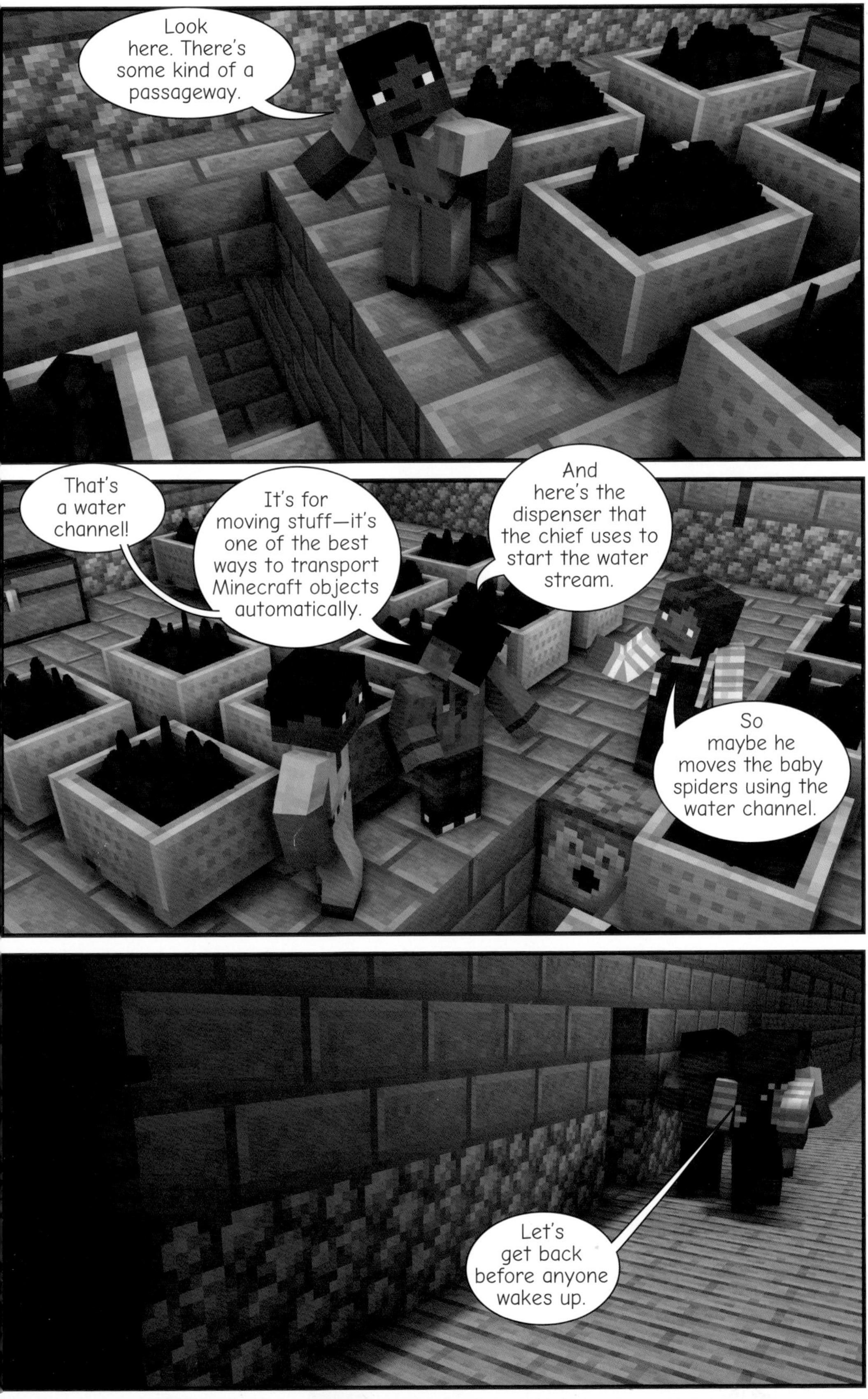
Look here. There's some kind of a passageway.
That's a water channel!
It's for moving stuff—it's one of the best ways to transport Minecraft objects automatically.
And here's the dispenser that the chief uses to start the water stream.
So maybe he moves the baby spiders using the water channel.
Let's get back before anyone wakes up.

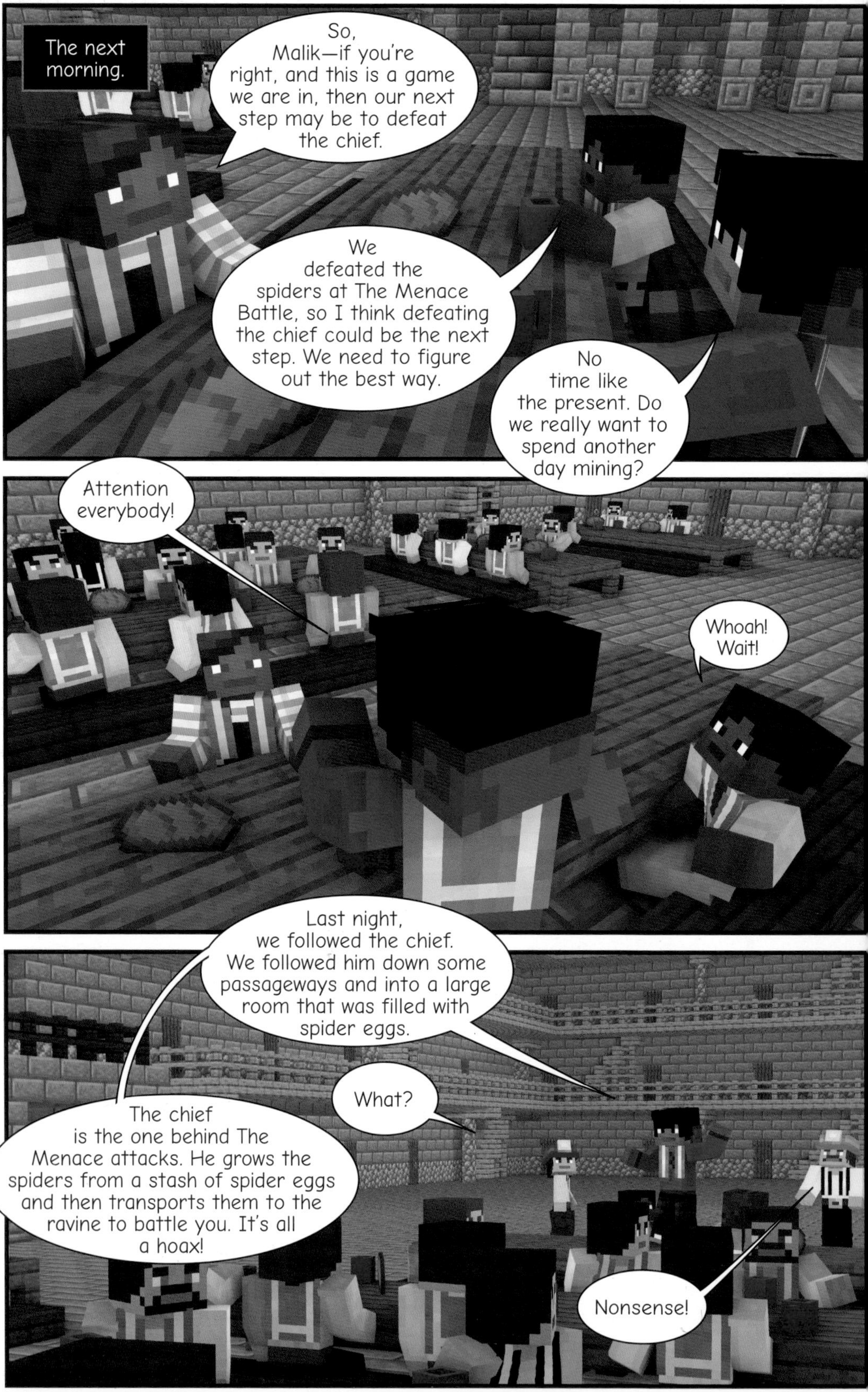
The next morning.
So, Malik—if you're right, and this is a game we are in, then our next step may be to defeat the chief.
We defeated the spiders at The Menace Battle, so I think defeating the chief could be the next step. We need to figure out the best way.
No time like the present. Do we really want to spend another day mining?
Attention everybody!
Whoah! Wait!
Last night, we followed the chief. We followed him down some passageways and into a large room that was filled with spider eggs.
What?
The chief is the one behind The Menace attacks. He grows the spiders from a stash of spider eggs and then transports them to the ravine to battle you. It's all a hoax!
Nonsense!

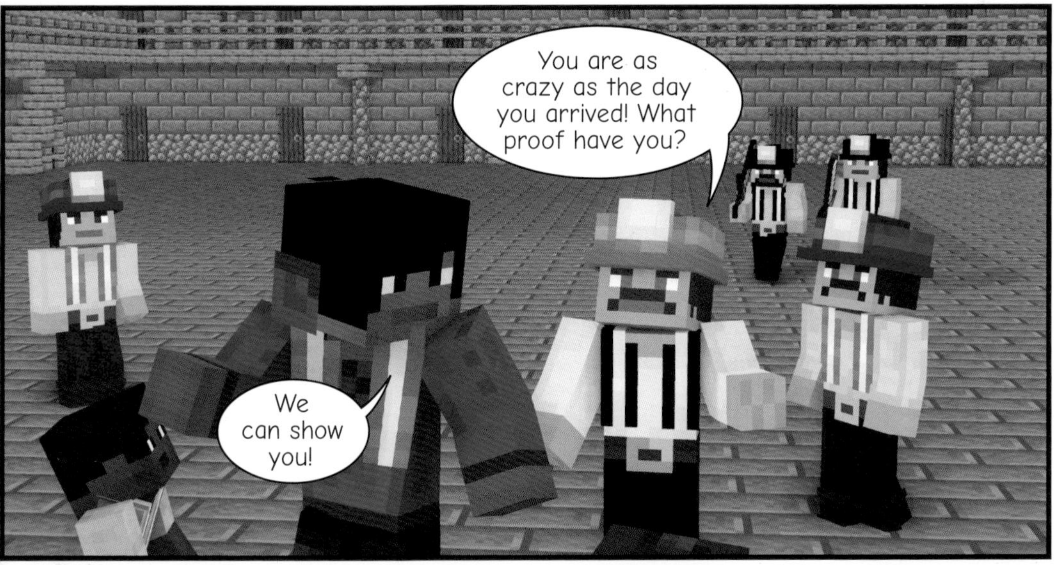
You are as crazy as the day you arrived! What proof have you?
We can show you!

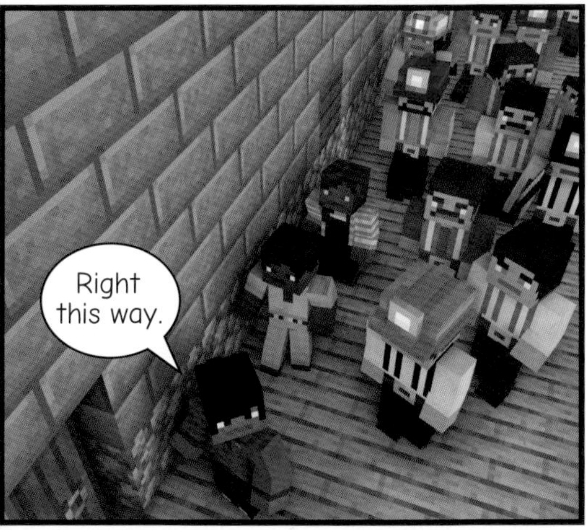
Right this way.

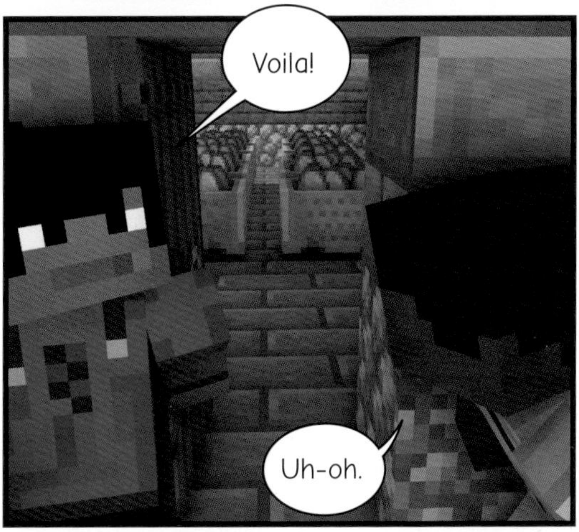
Voila!
Uh-oh.

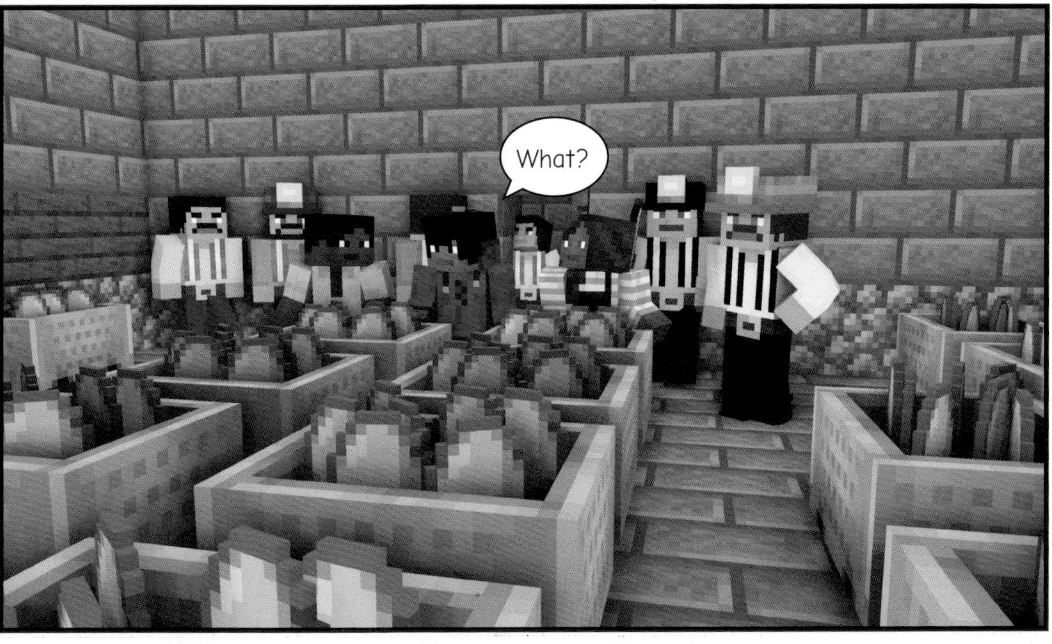
What?

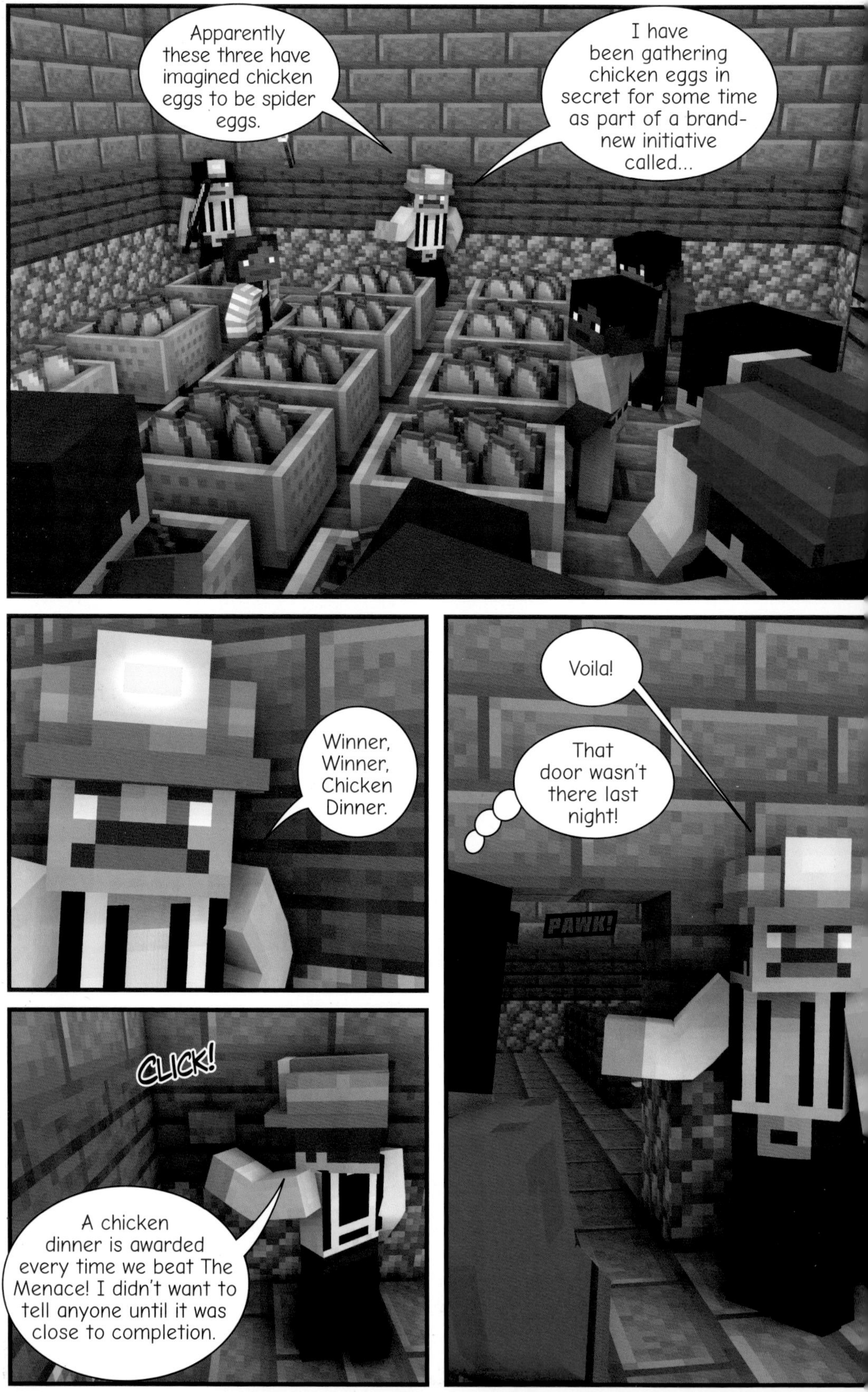
Apparently these three have imagined chicken eggs to be spider eggs.
I have been gathering chicken eggs in secret for some time as part of a brand-new initiative called...
Winner, Winner, Chicken Dinner.
CLICK!
A chicken dinner is awarded every time we beat The Menace! I didn't want to tell anyone until it was close to completion.
Voila!
That door wasn't there last night!
PAWK!

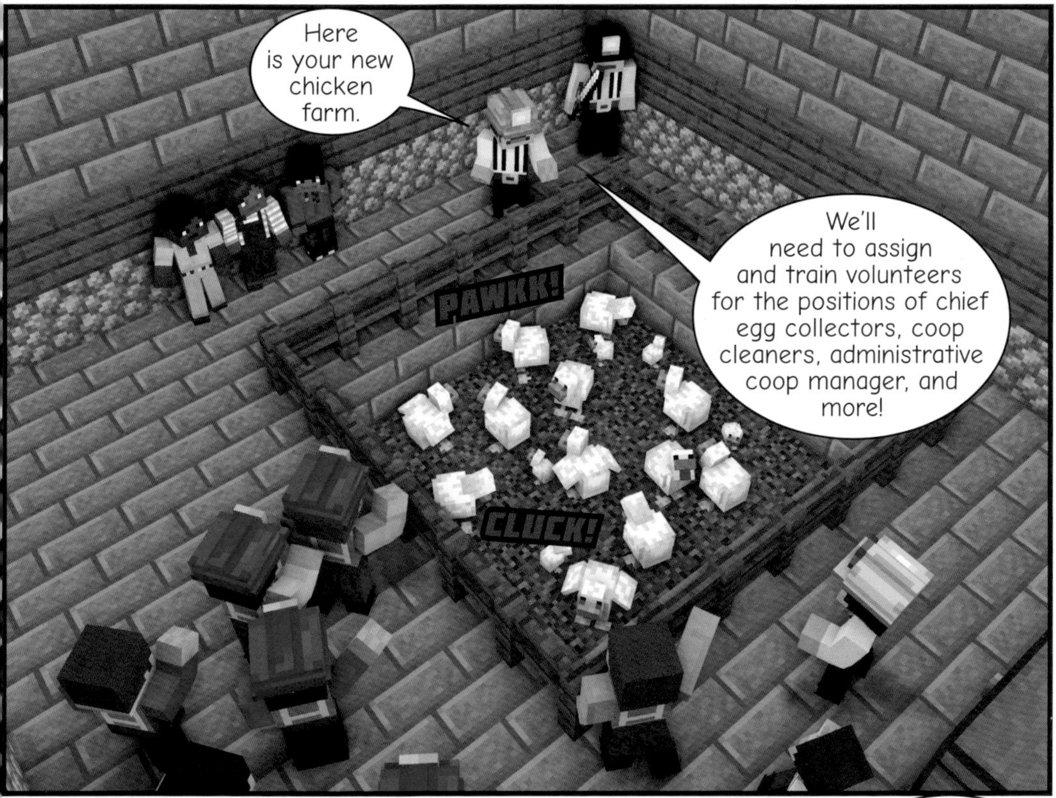
Here is your new chicken farm.
We'll need to assign and train volunteers for the positions of chief egg collectors, coop cleaners, administrative coop manager, and more!
PAWKK!
CLUCK!

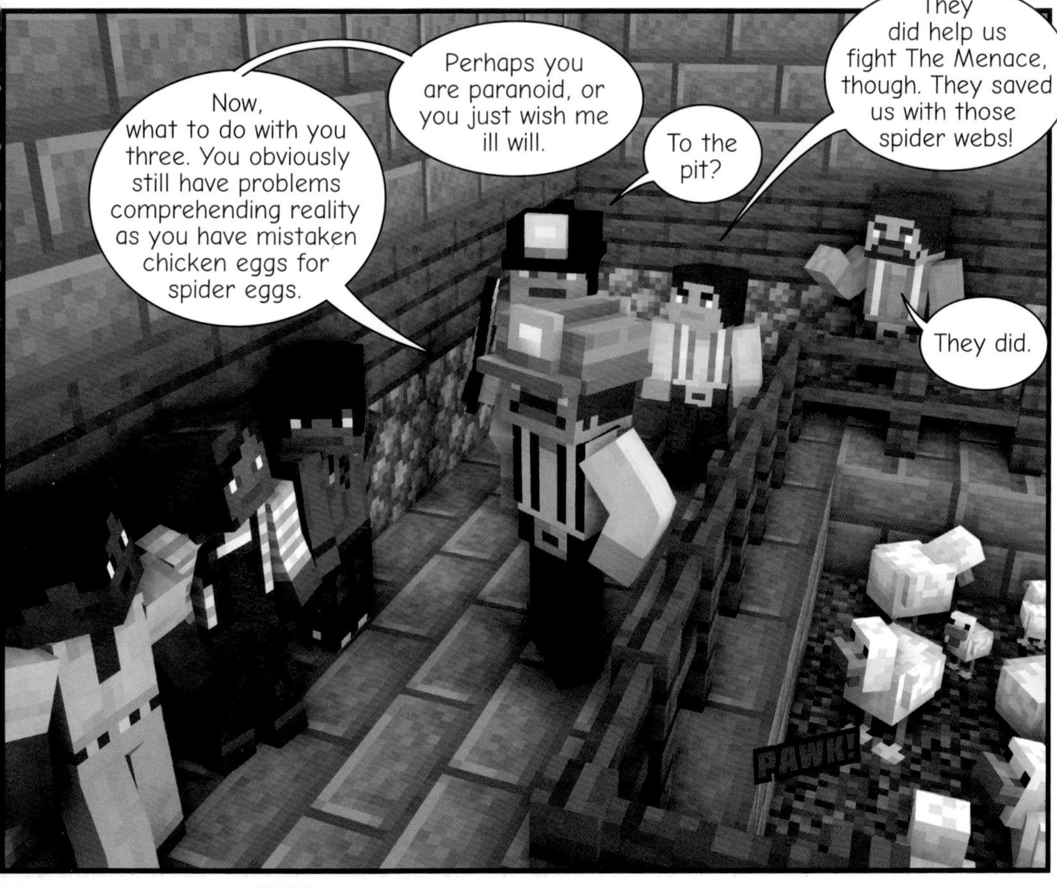
Now, what to do with you three. You obviously still have problems comprehending reality as you have mistaken chicken eggs for spider eggs.
Perhaps you are paranoid, or you just wish me ill will.
To the pit?
They did help us fight The Menace, though. They saved us with those spider webs!
They did.
PAWK!

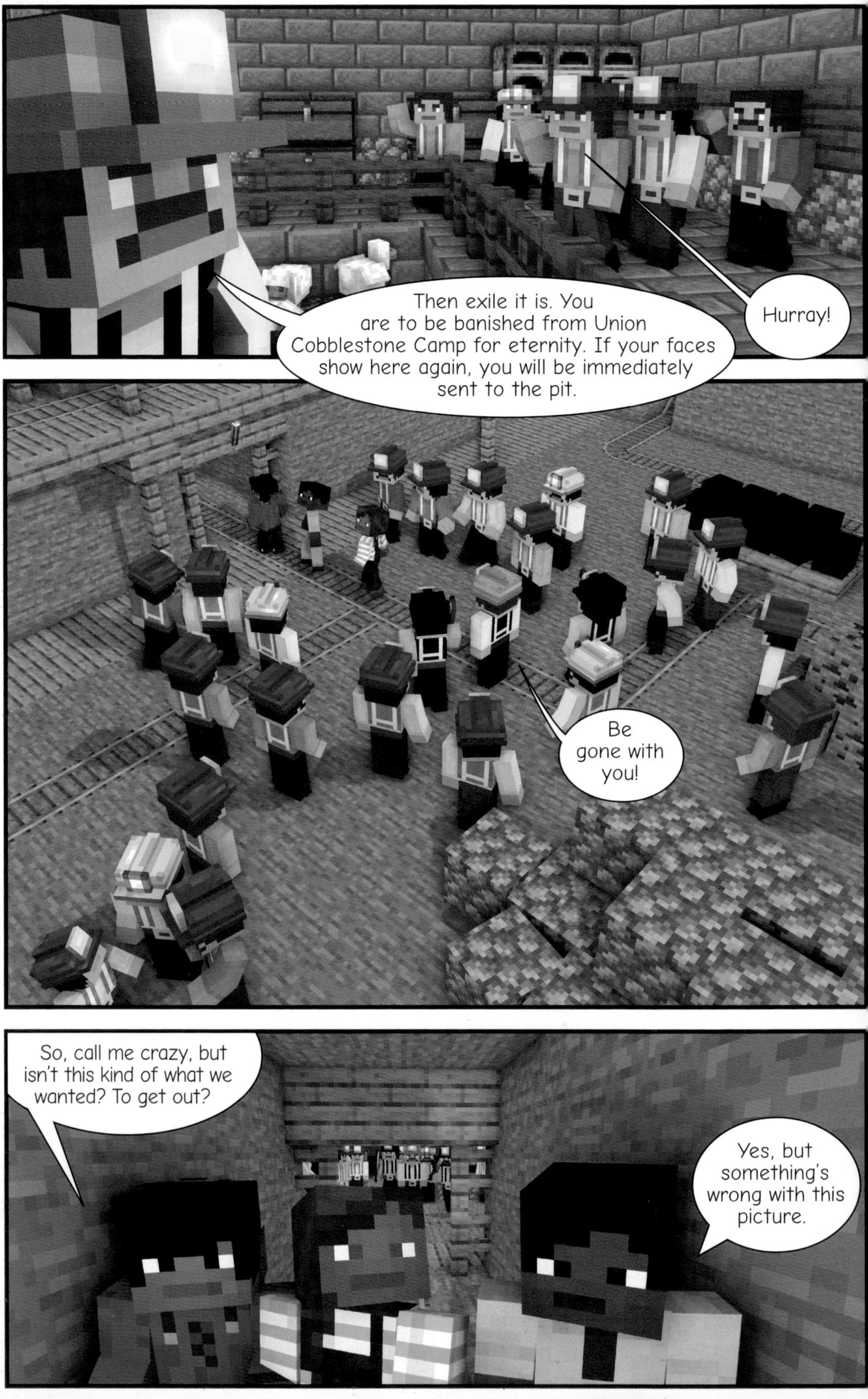
Then exile it is. You are to be banished from Union Cobblestone Camp for eternity. If your faces show here again, you will be immediately sent to the pit.
Hurray!
Be gone with you!
So, call me crazy, but isn't this kind of what we wanted? To get out?
Yes, but something's wrong with this picture.

Chapter 7

Egg—sile

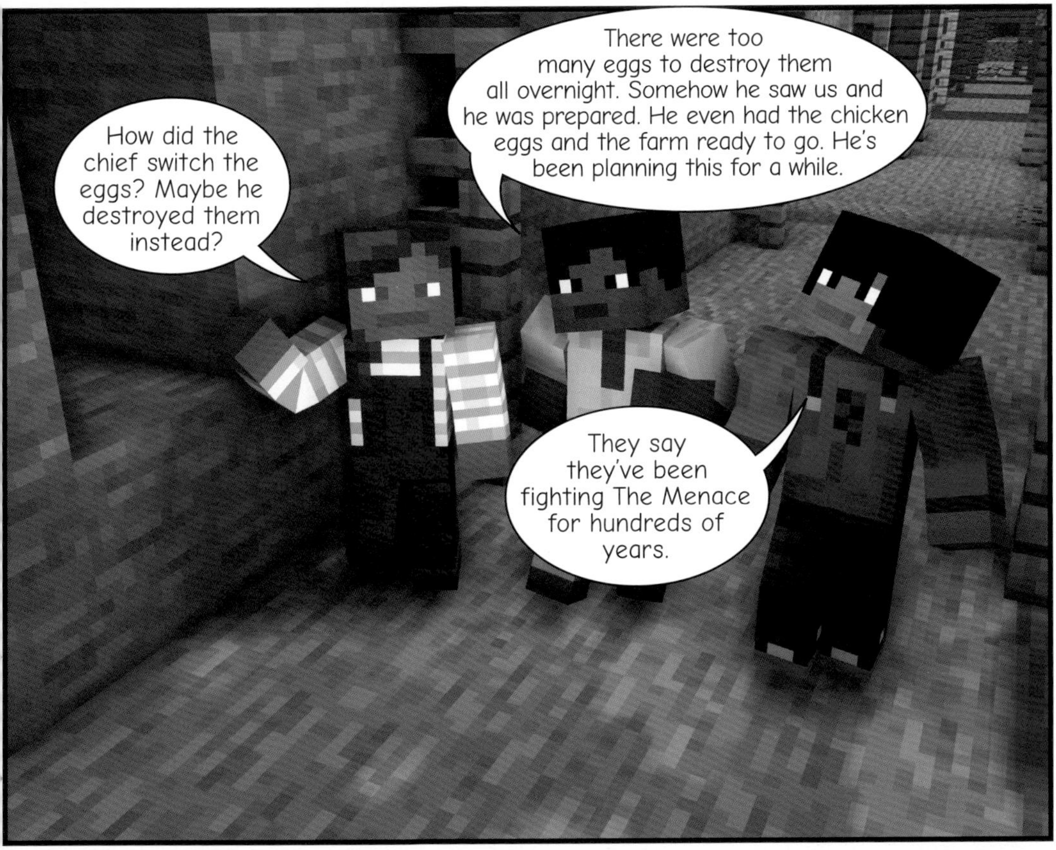
How did the chief switch the eggs? Maybe he destroyed them instead?
There were too many eggs to destroy them all overnight. Somehow he saw us and he was prepared. He even had the chicken eggs and the farm ready to go. He's been planning this for a while.
They say they've been fighting The Menace for hundreds of years.

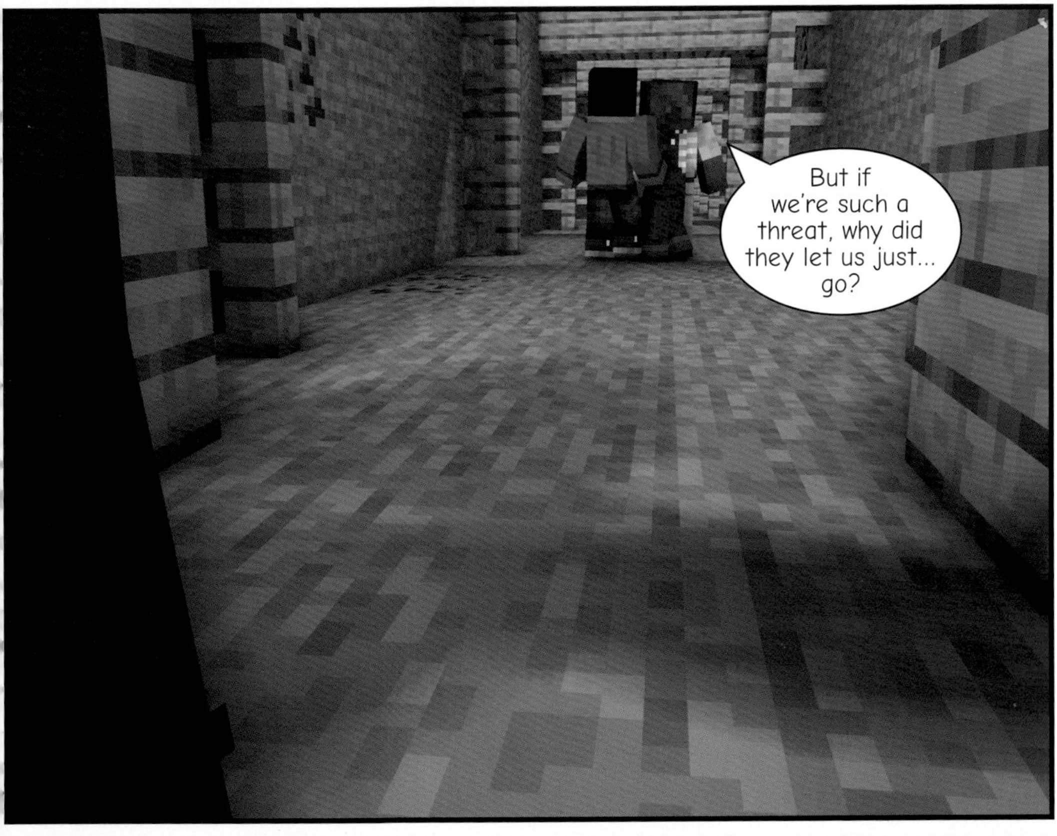
But if we're such a threat, why did they let us just... go?

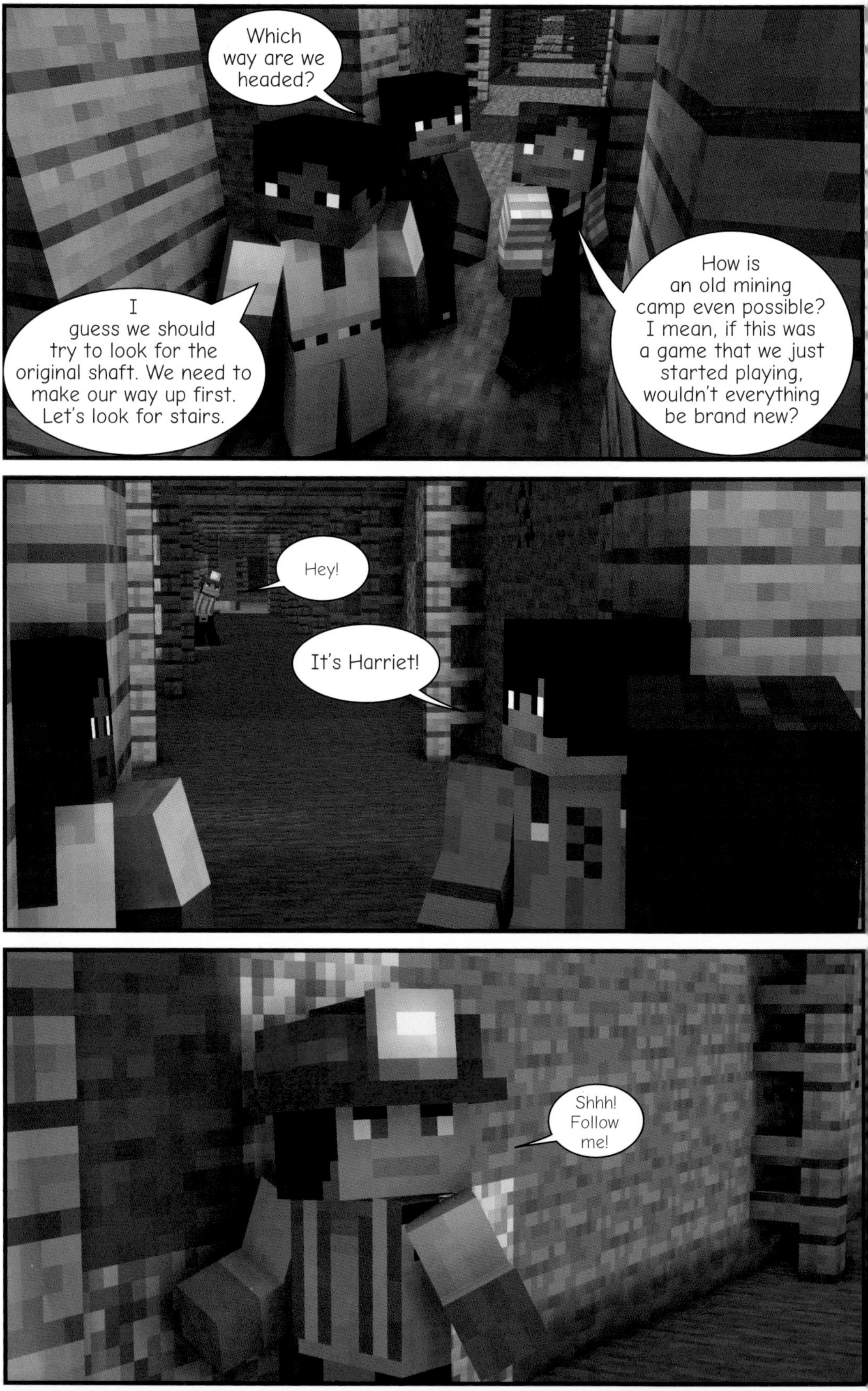
Which way are we headed?
I guess we should try to look for the original shaft. We need to make our way up first. Let's look for stairs.
How is an old mining camp even possible? I mean, if this was a game that we just started playing, wouldn't everything be brand new?
Hey!
It's Harriet!
Shhh! Follow me!

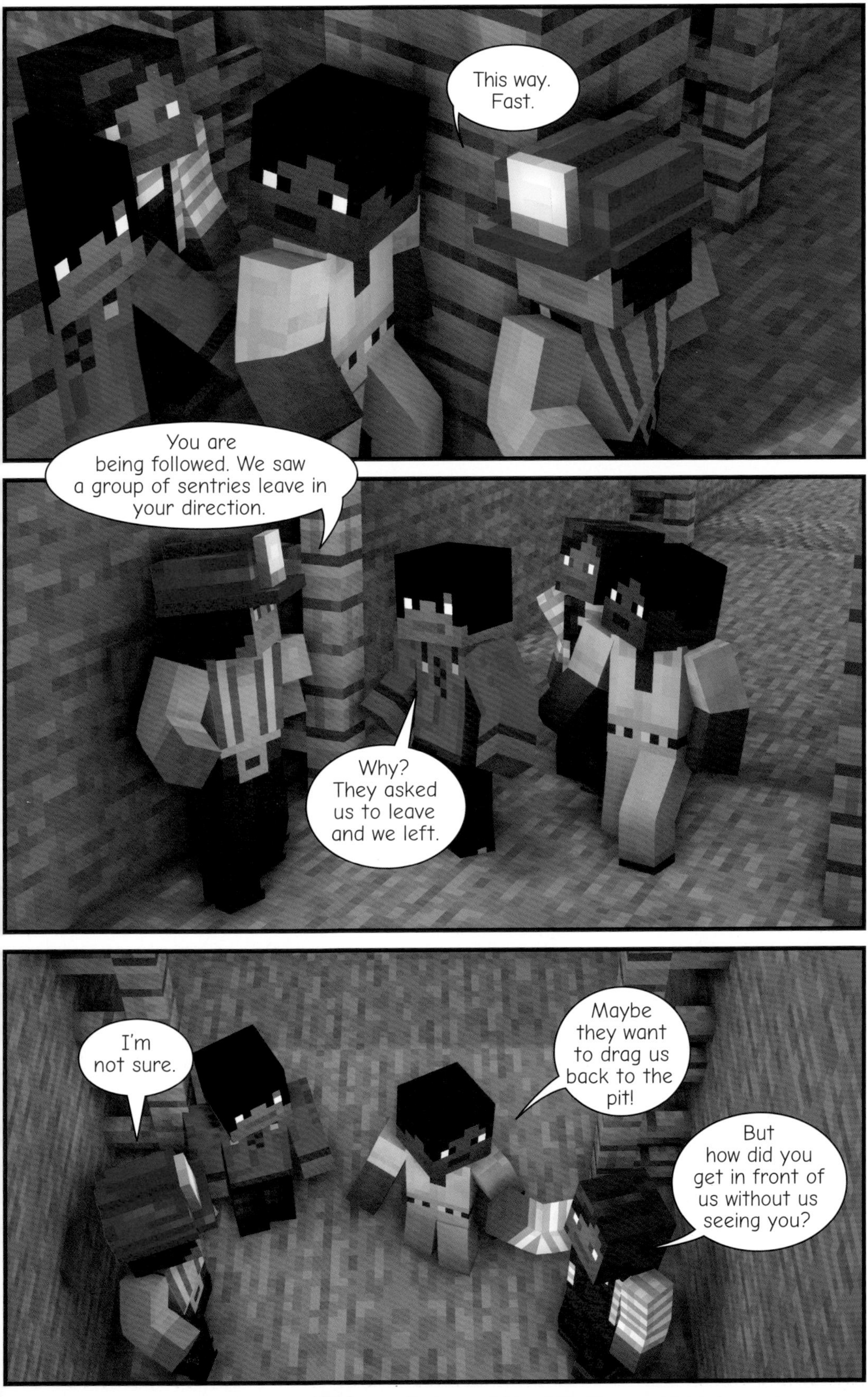
This way. Fast.
You are being followed. We saw a group of sentries leave in your direction.
Why? They asked us to leave and we left.
I'm not sure.
Maybe they want to drag us back to the pit!
But how did you get in front of us without us seeing you?

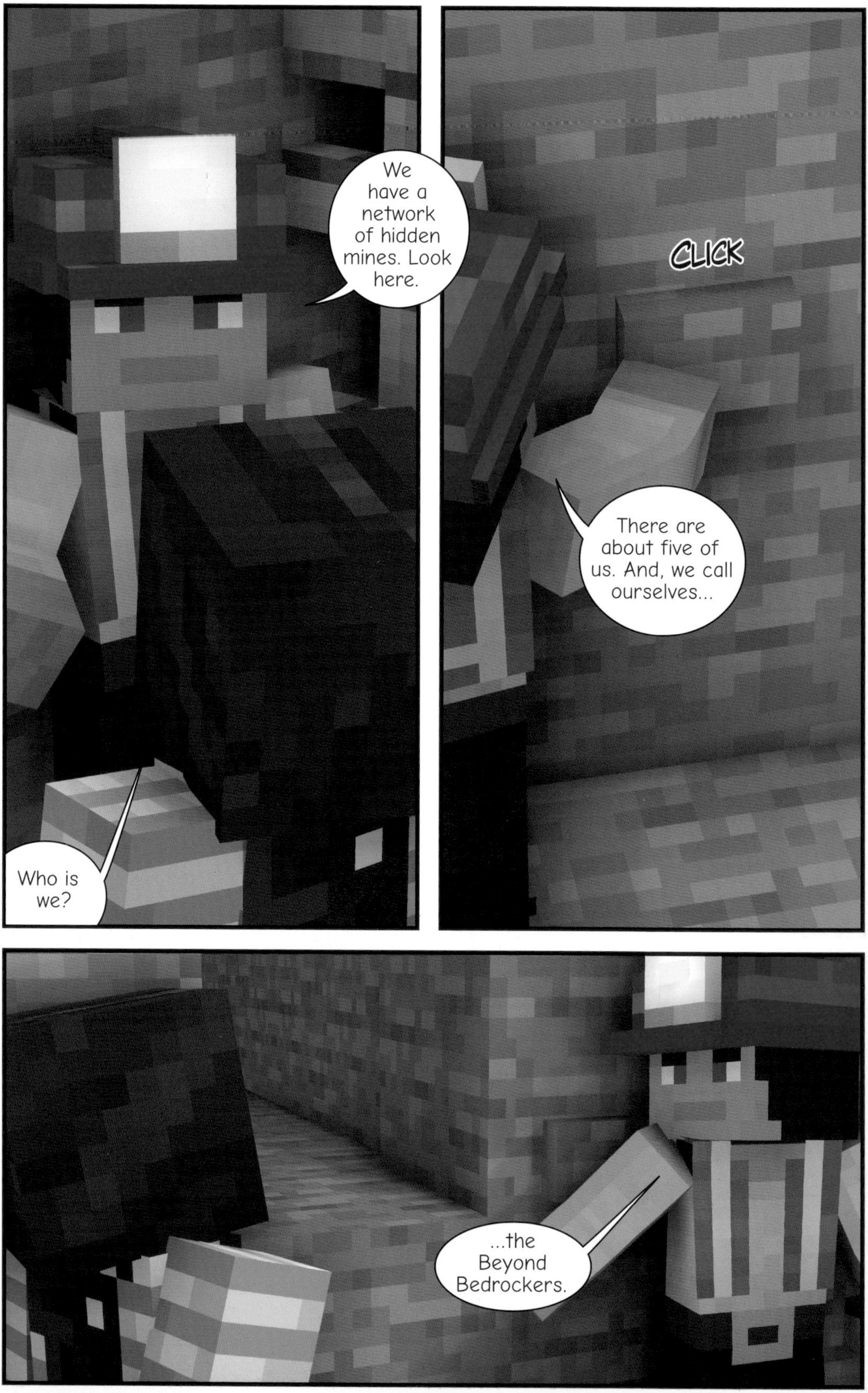
We have a network of hidden mines. Look here.
Who is we?
CLICK
There are about five of us. And, we call ourselves...
...the Beyond Bedrockers.

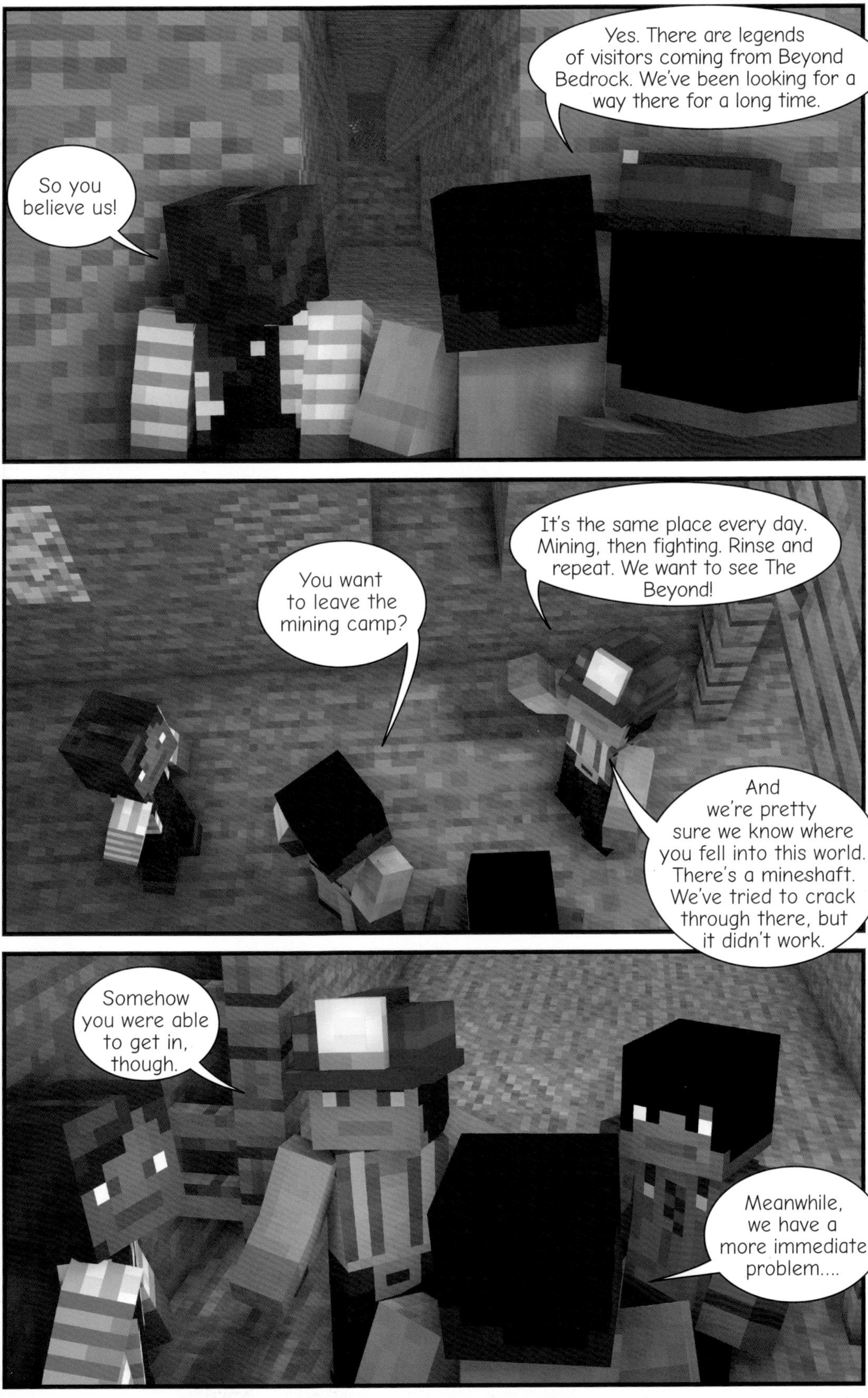
So you believe us!
Yes. There are legends of visitors coming from Beyond Bedrock. We've been looking for a way there for a long time.
You want to leave the mining camp?
It's the same place every day. Mining, then fighting. Rinse and repeat. We want to see The Beyond!
And we're pretty sure we know where you fell into this world. There's a mineshaft. We've tried to crack through there, but it didn't work.
Somehow you were able to get in, though.
Meanwhile, we have a more immediate problem....

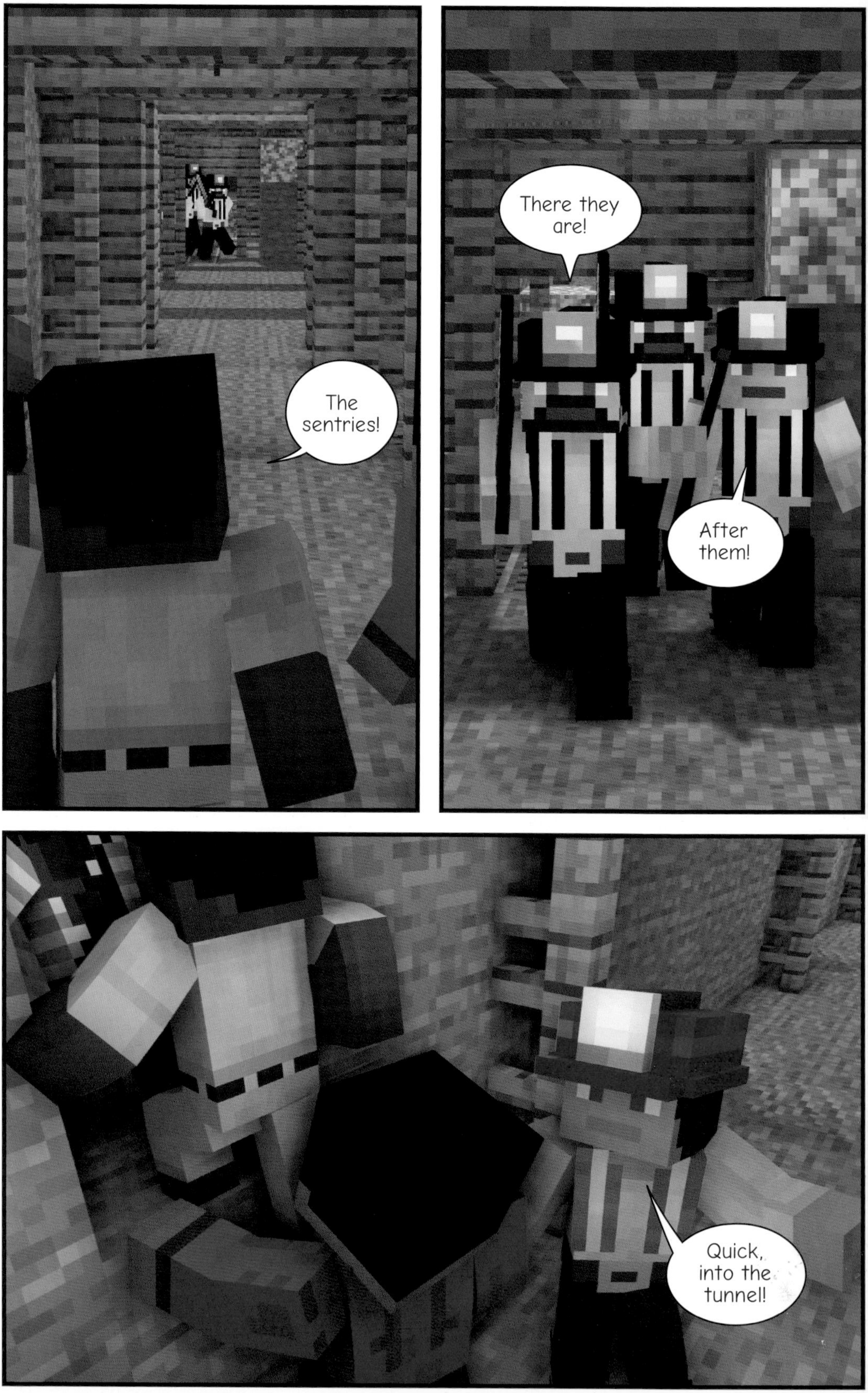
The sentries!
There they are!
After them!
Quick, into the tunnel!

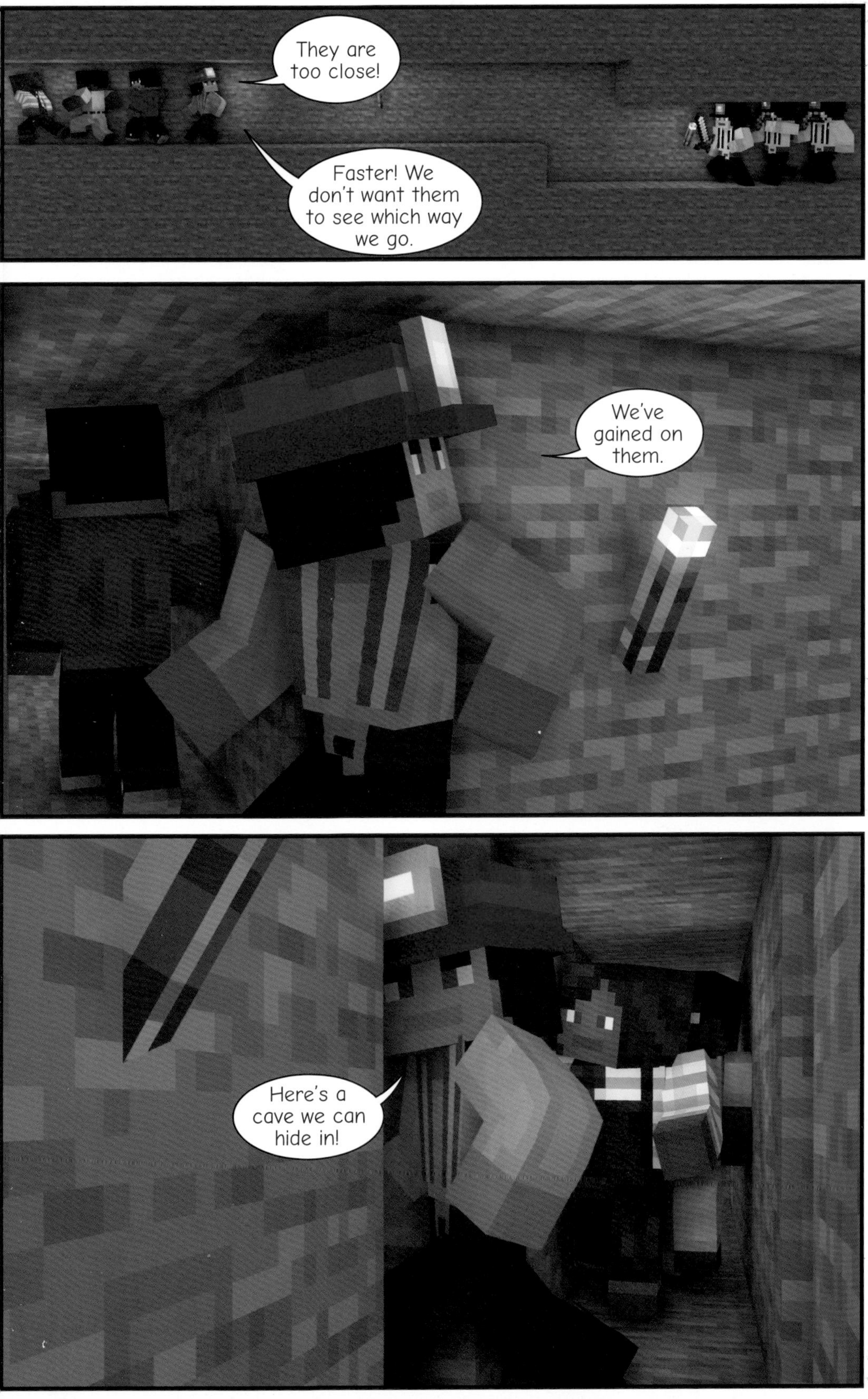
They are too close!
Faster! We don't want them to see which way we go.
We've gained on them.
Here's a cave we can hide in!

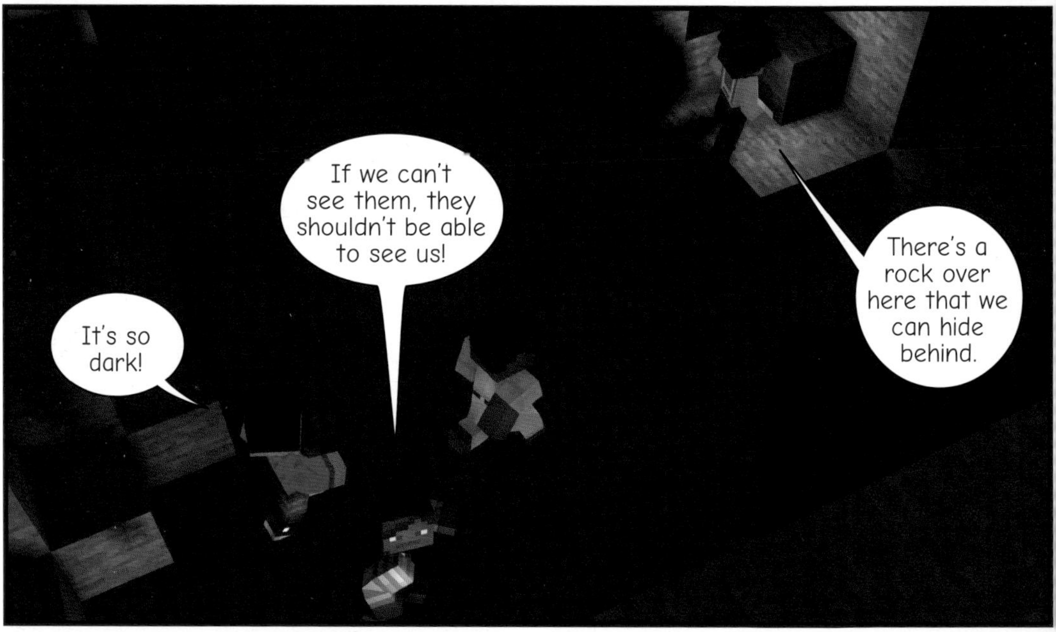
It's so dark!
If we can't see them, they shouldn't be able to see us!
There's a rock over here that we can hide behind.

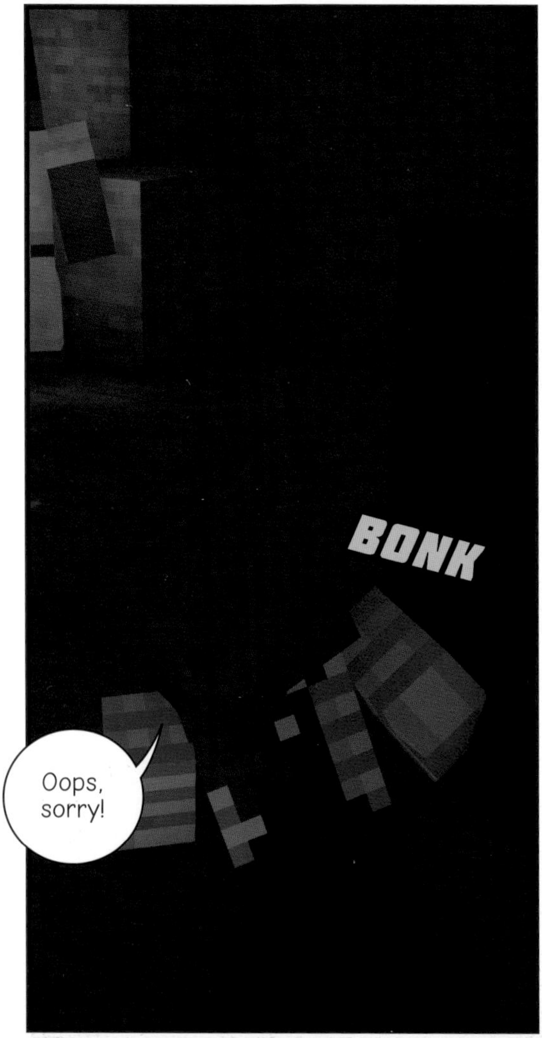
BONK
Oops, sorry!

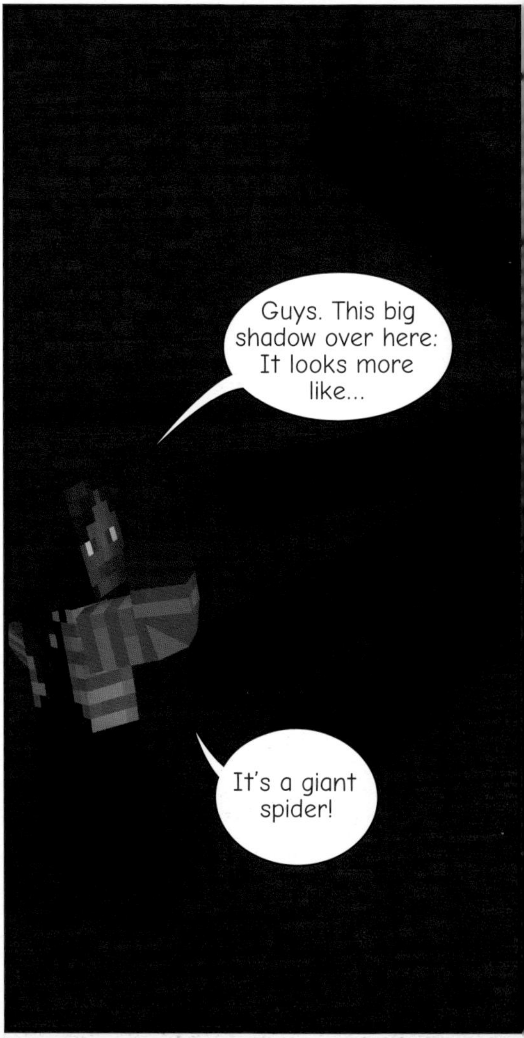
Guys. This big shadow over here: It looks more like...
It's a giant spider!

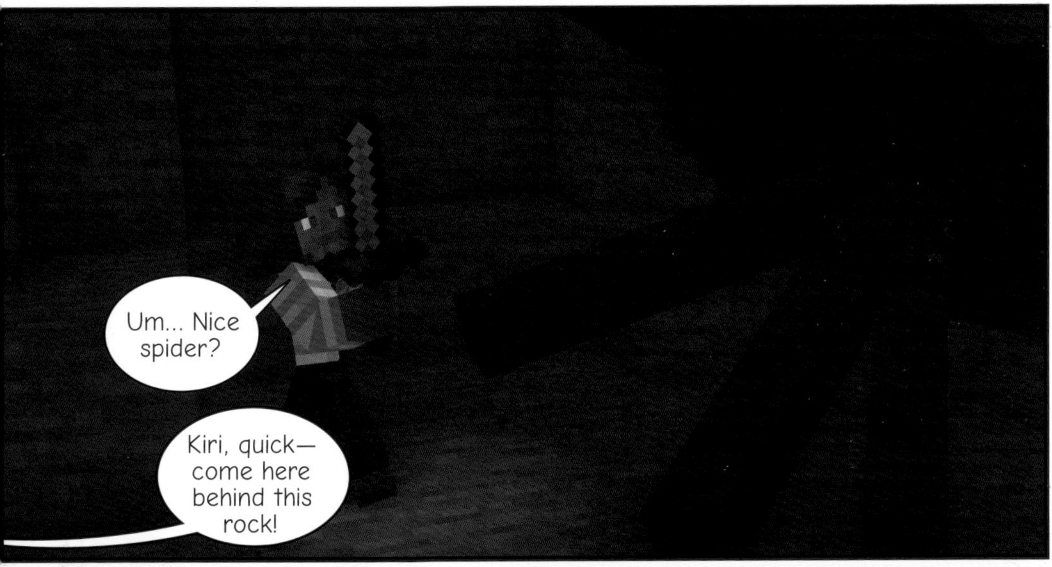
Um... Nice spider?
Kiri, quick—come here behind this rock!

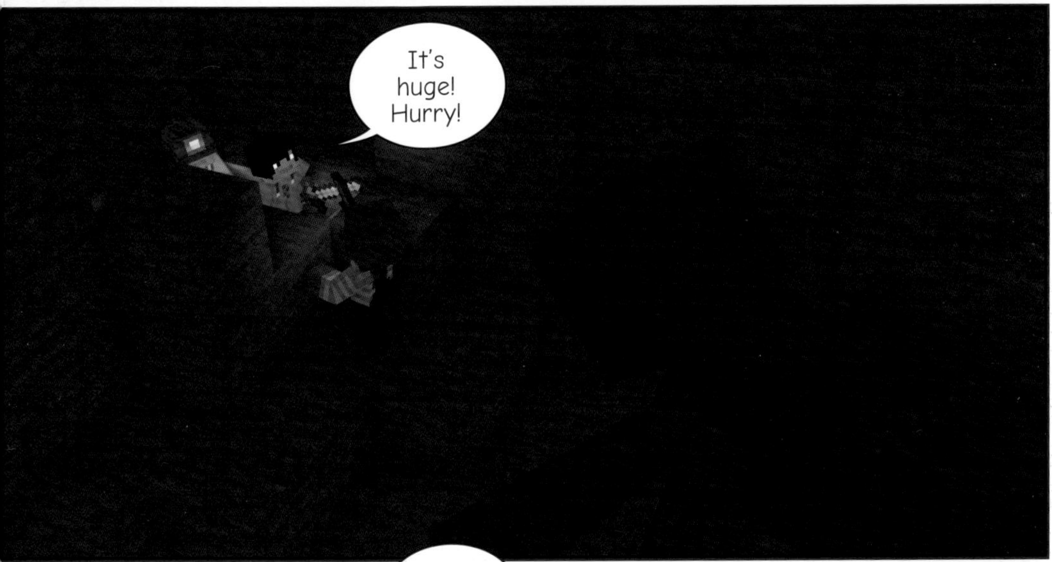
It's huge! Hurry!

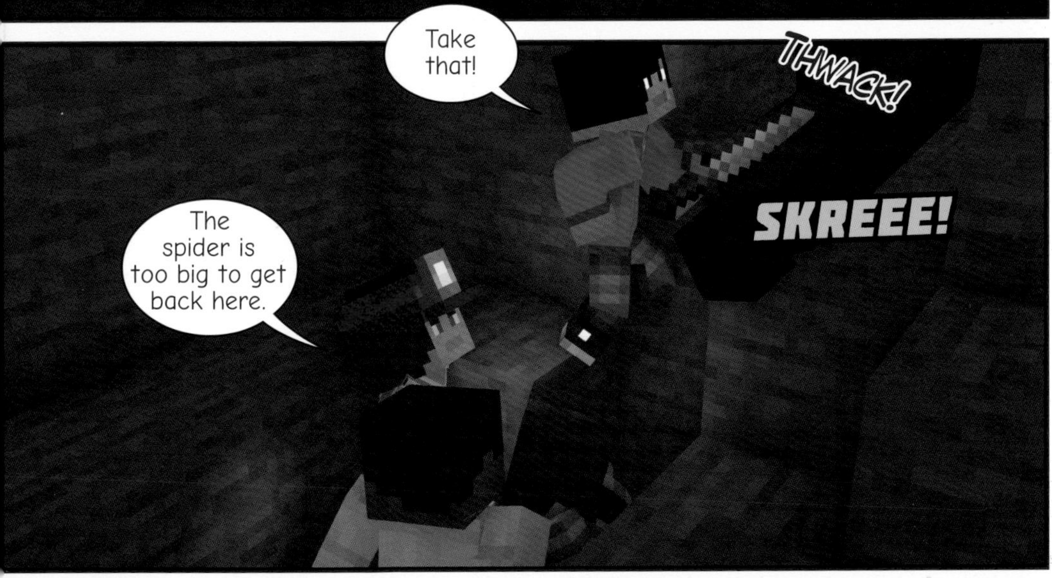
Take that!
THWACK!
SKREEE!
The spider is too big to get back here.

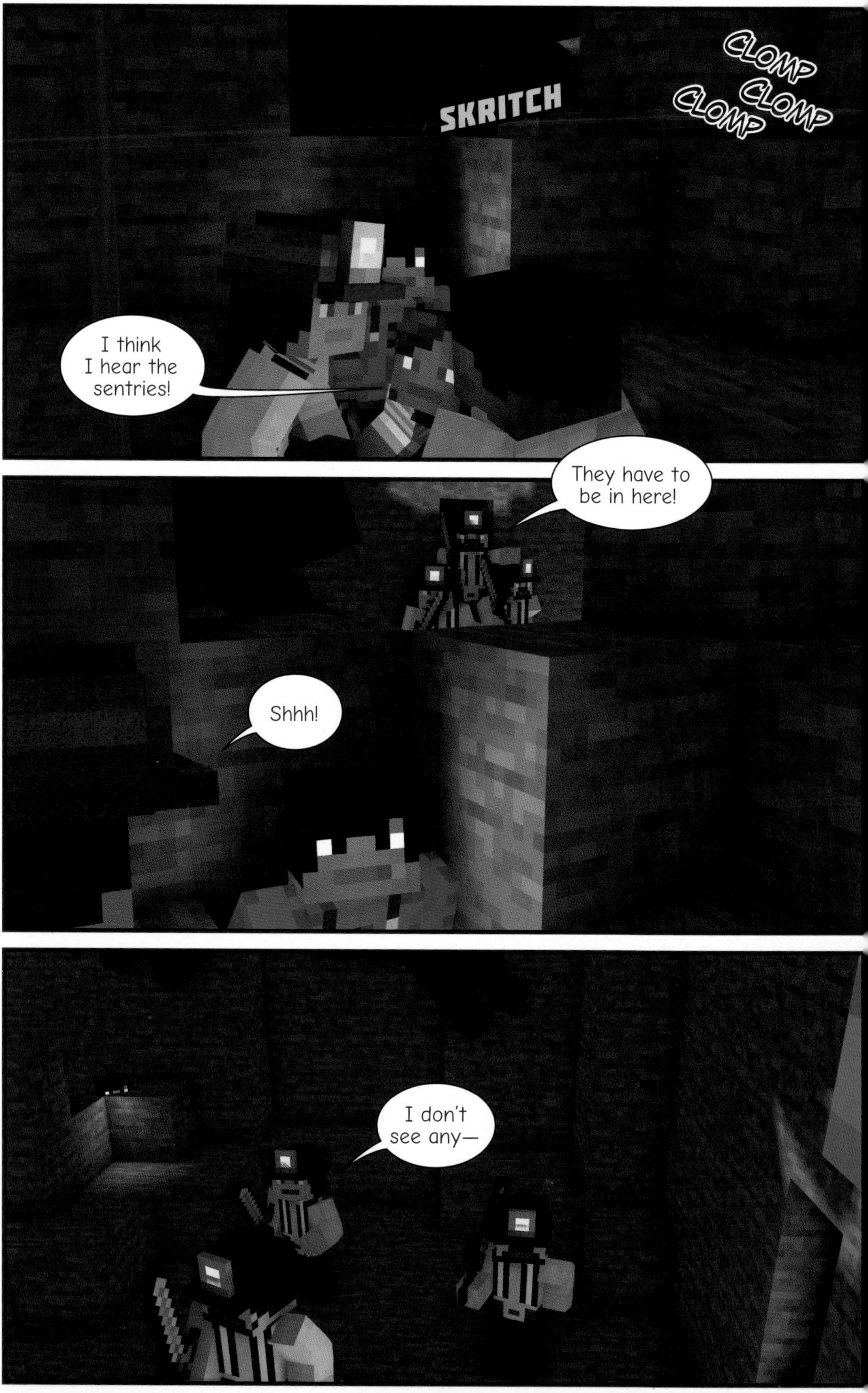
SKRITCH
CLOMP CLOMP CLOMP
I think I hear the sentries!
They have to be in here!
Shhh!
I don't see any—

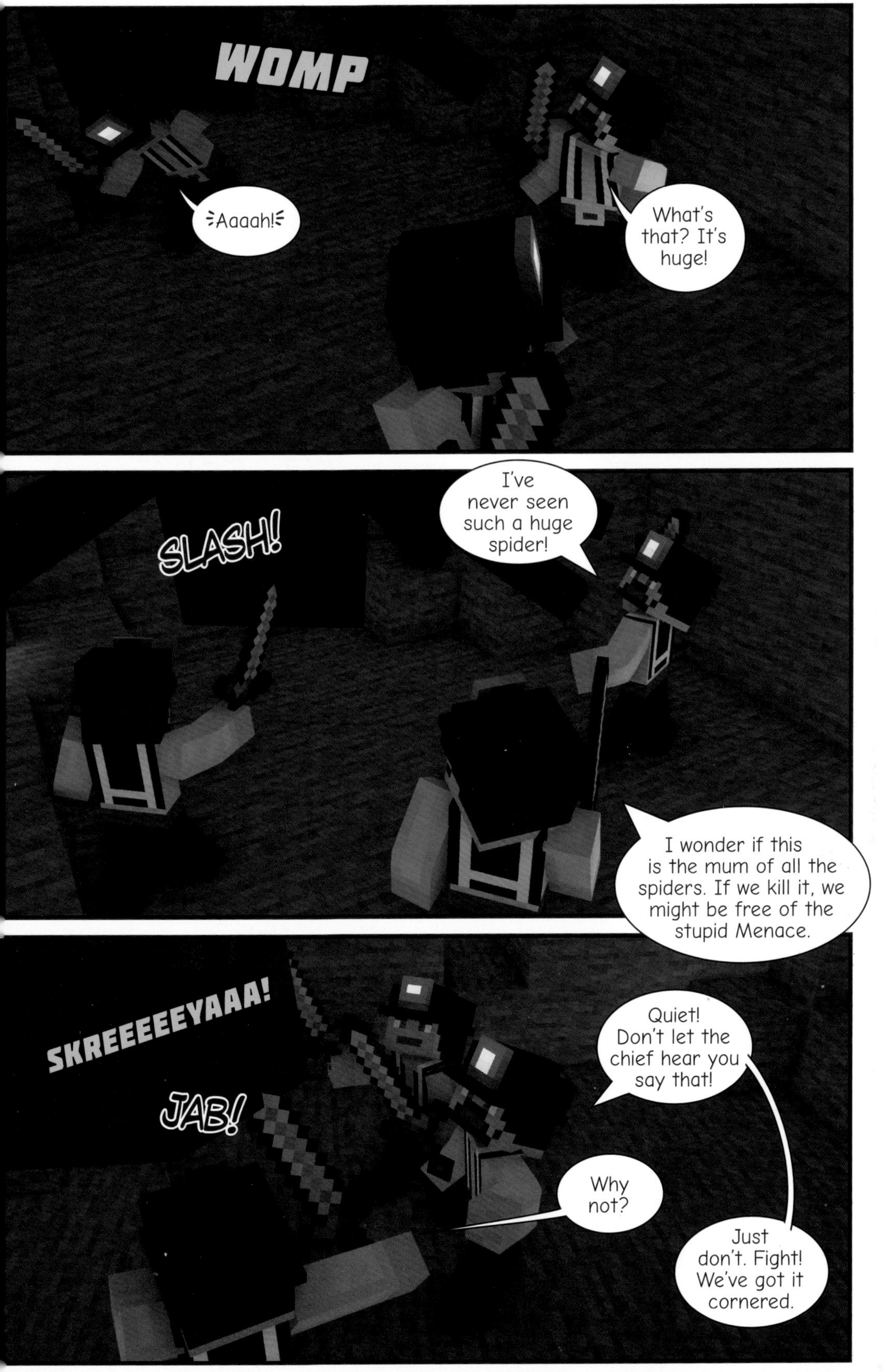
WOMP
Aaaah!
What's that? It's huge!
SLASH!
I've never seen such a huge spider!
I wonder if this is the mum of all the spiders. If we kill it, we might be free of the stupid Menace.
SKREEEEEEYAAA!
JAB!
Quiet! Don't let the chief hear you say that!
Why not?
Just don't. Fight! We've got it cornered.

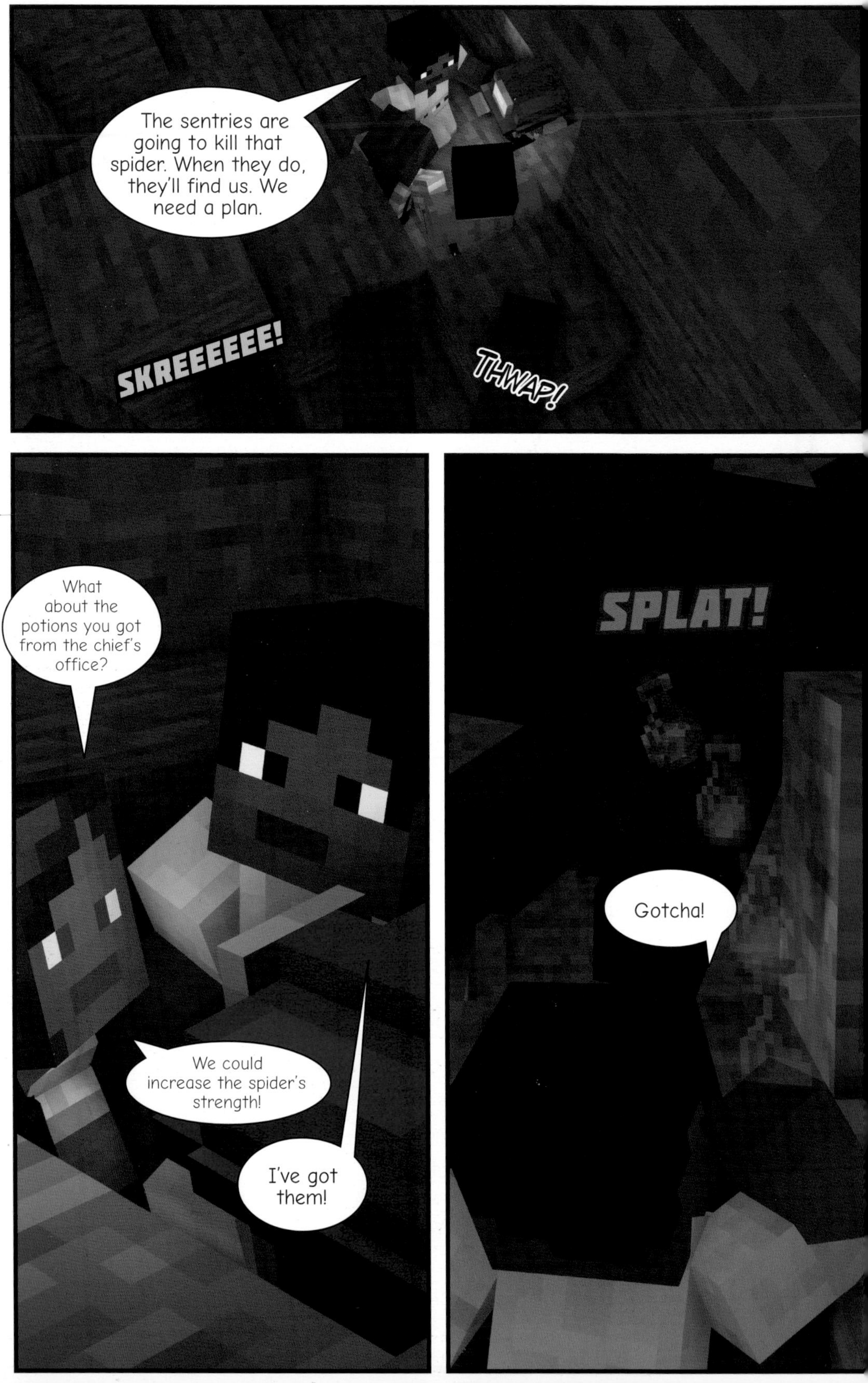
The sentries are going to kill that spider. When they do, they'll find us. We need a plan.
SKREEEEEEE!
THWAP!
What about the potions you got from the chief's office?
We could increase the spider's strength!
I've got them!
SPLAT!
Gotcha!

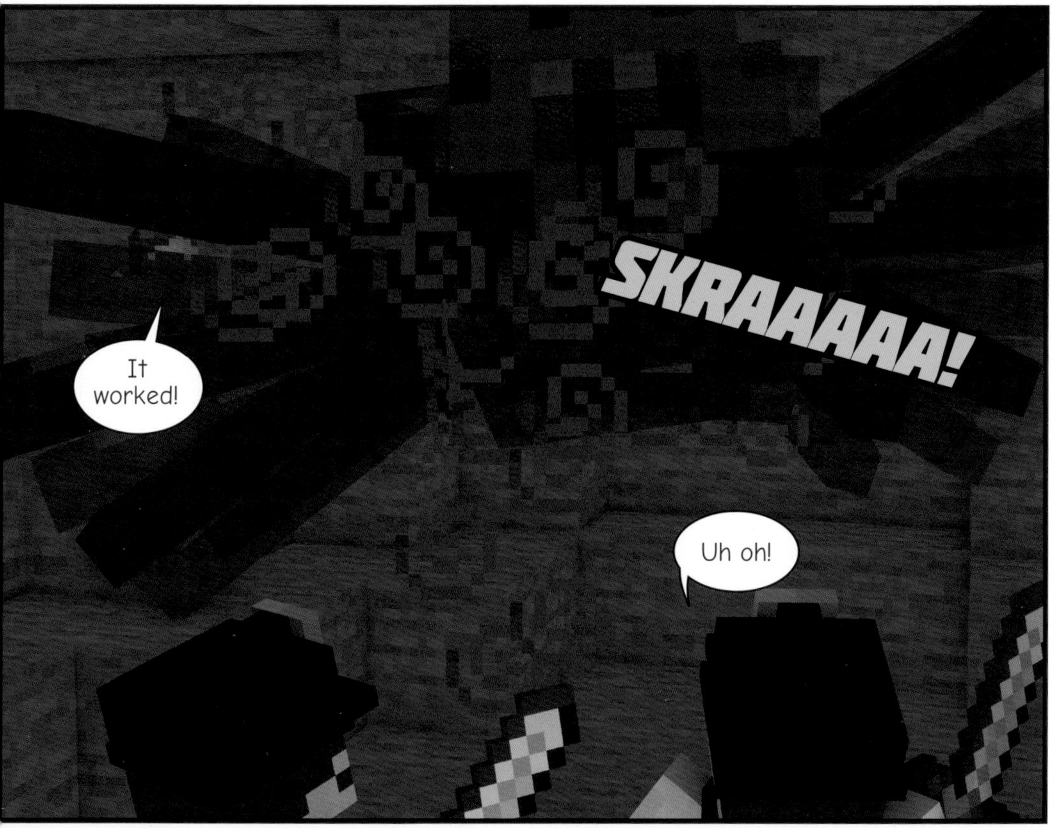
It worked!
SKRAAAAAA!
Uh oh!

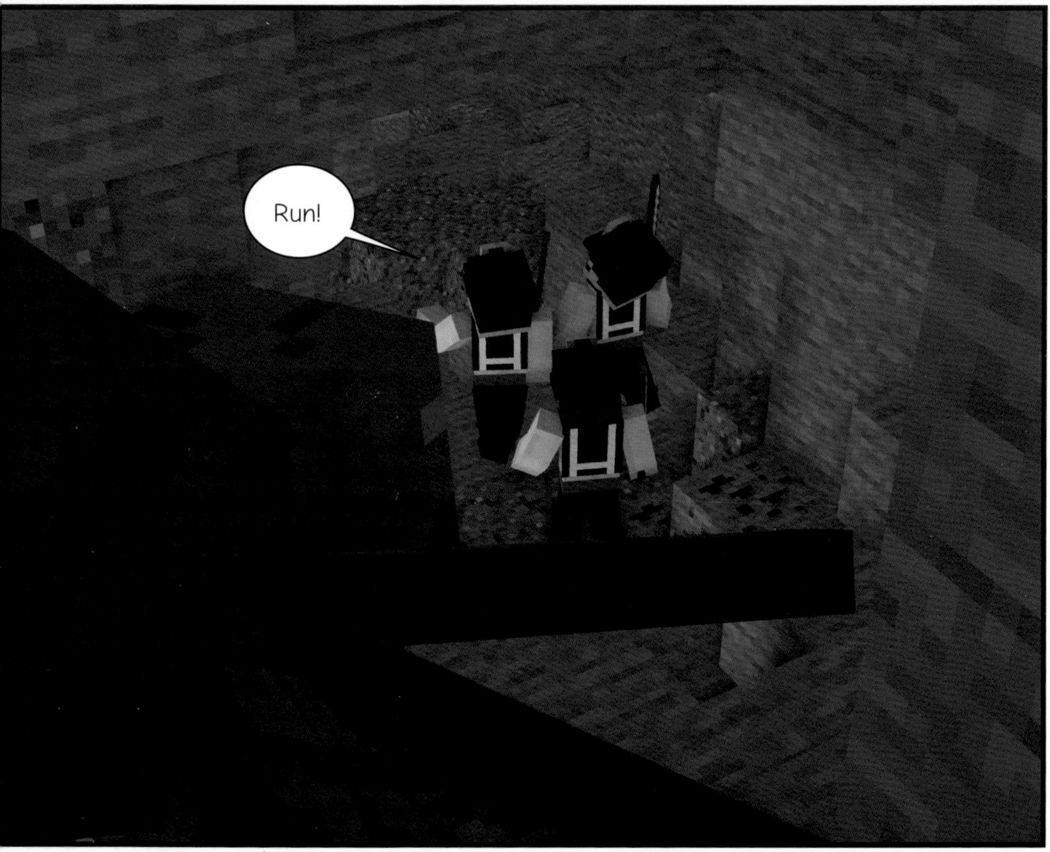
Run!

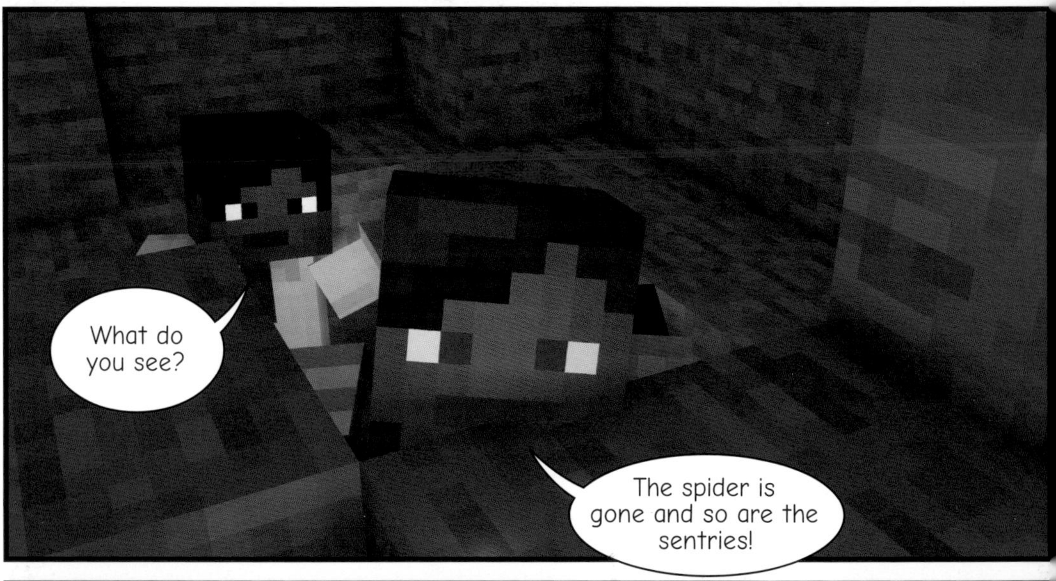
What do you see?
The spider is gone and so are the sentries!

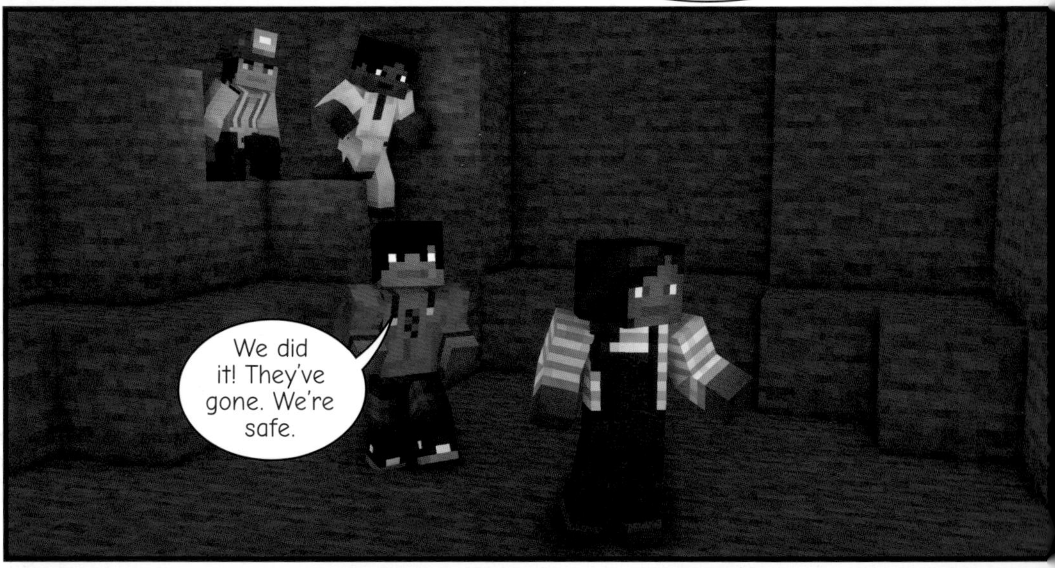
We did it! They've gone. We're safe.

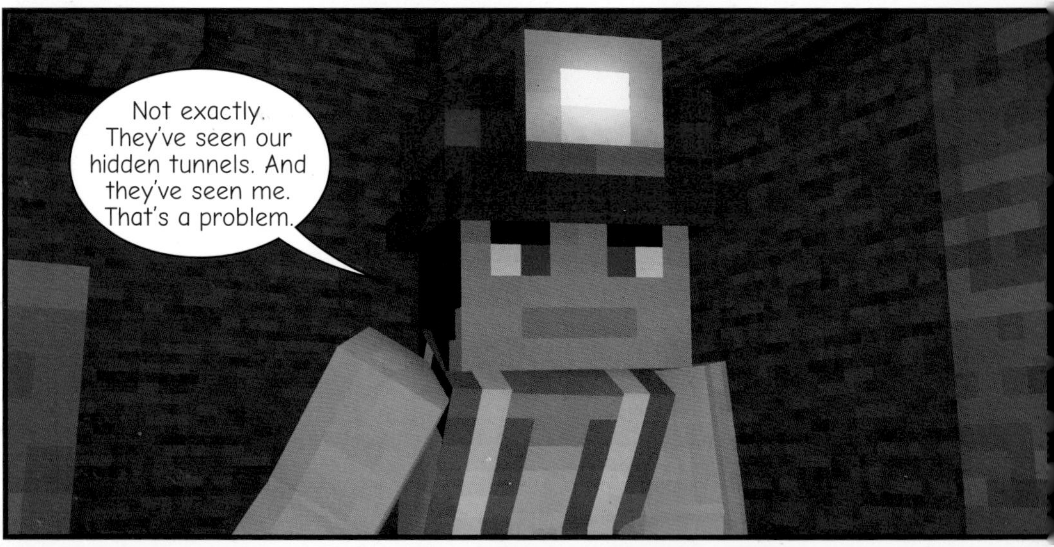
Not exactly. They've seen our hidden tunnels. And they've seen me. That's a problem.

Chapter 8

Geems and Sneepers

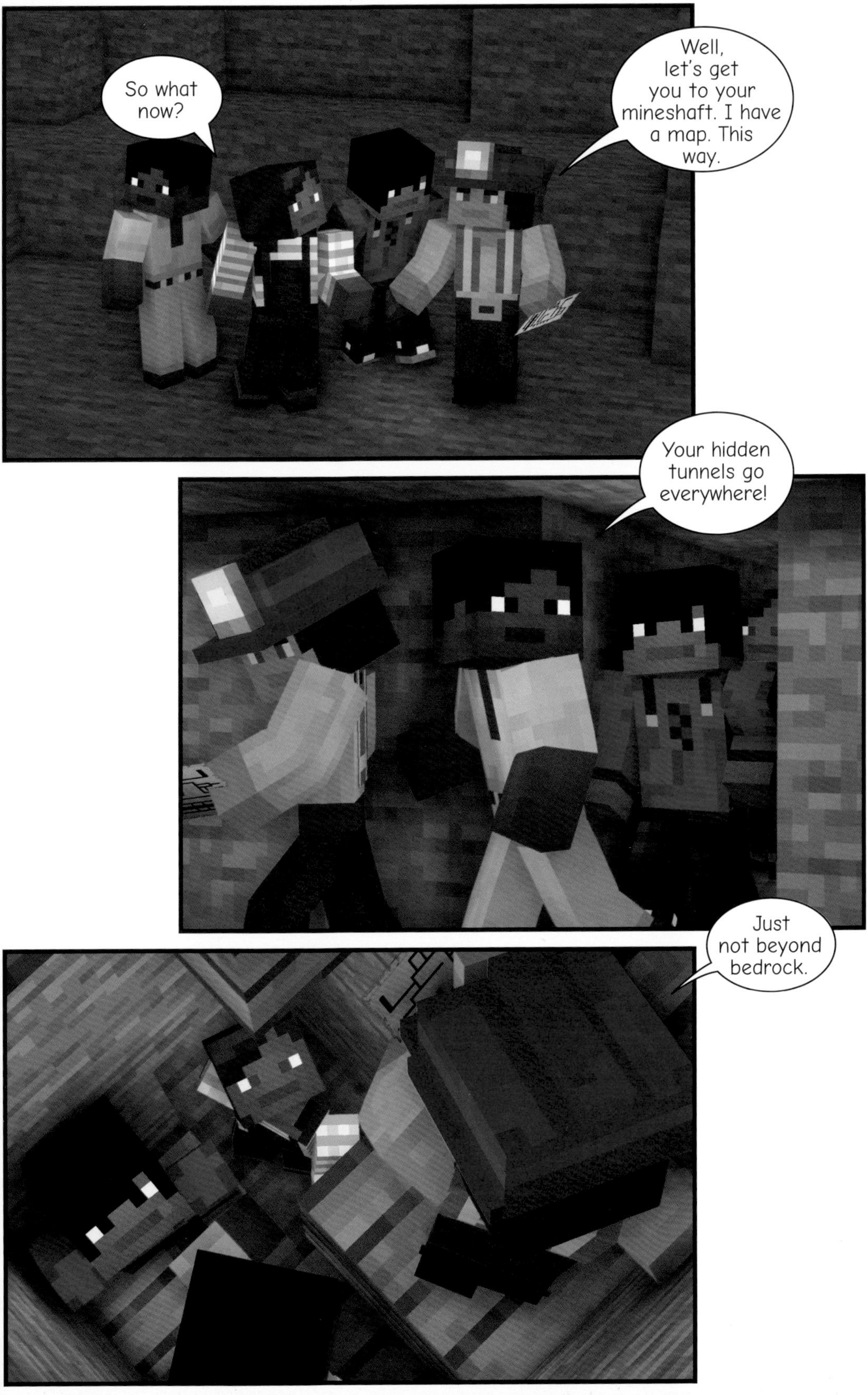
So what now?
Well, let's get you to your mineshaft. I have a map. This way.
Your hidden tunnels go everywhere!
Just not beyond bedrock.

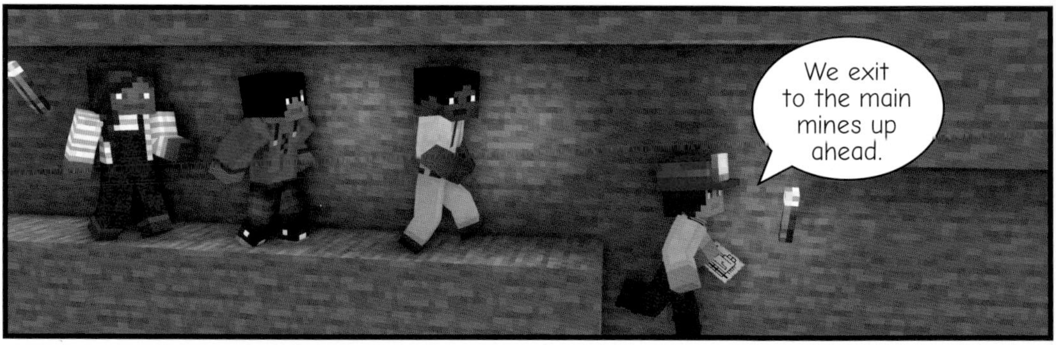

We exit to the main mines up ahead.

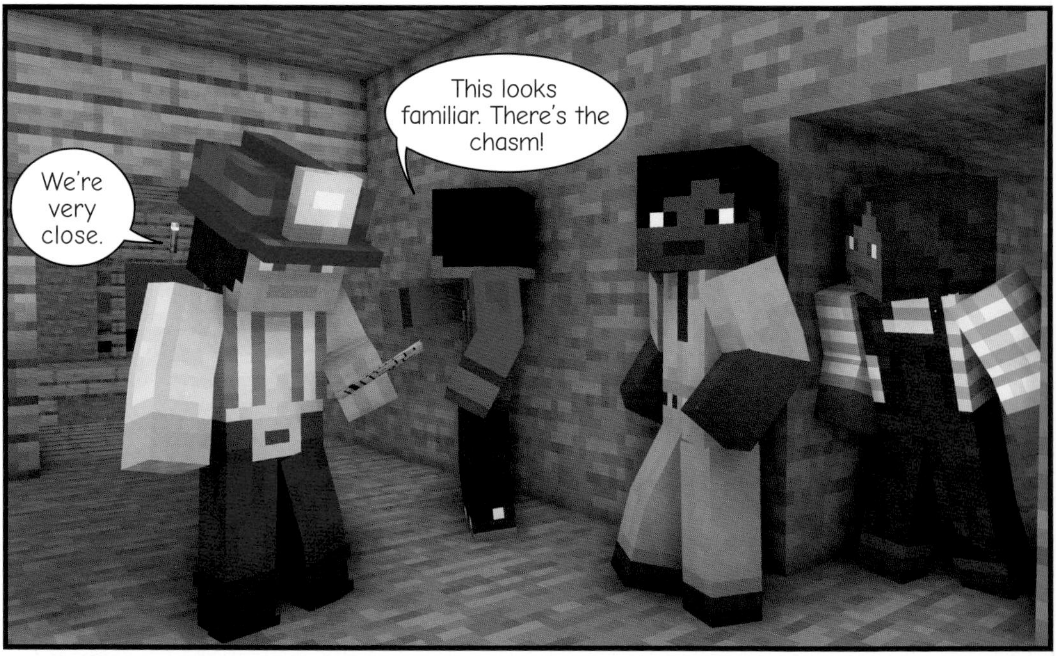

We're very close.
This looks familiar. There's the chasm!

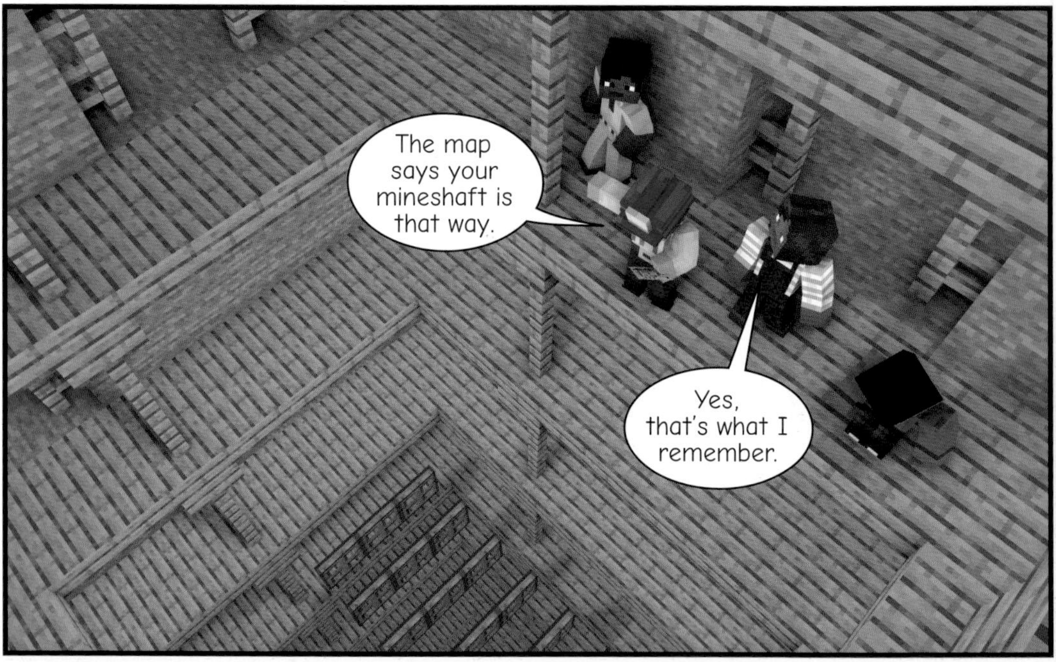

The map says your mineshaft is that way.
Yes, that's what I remember.

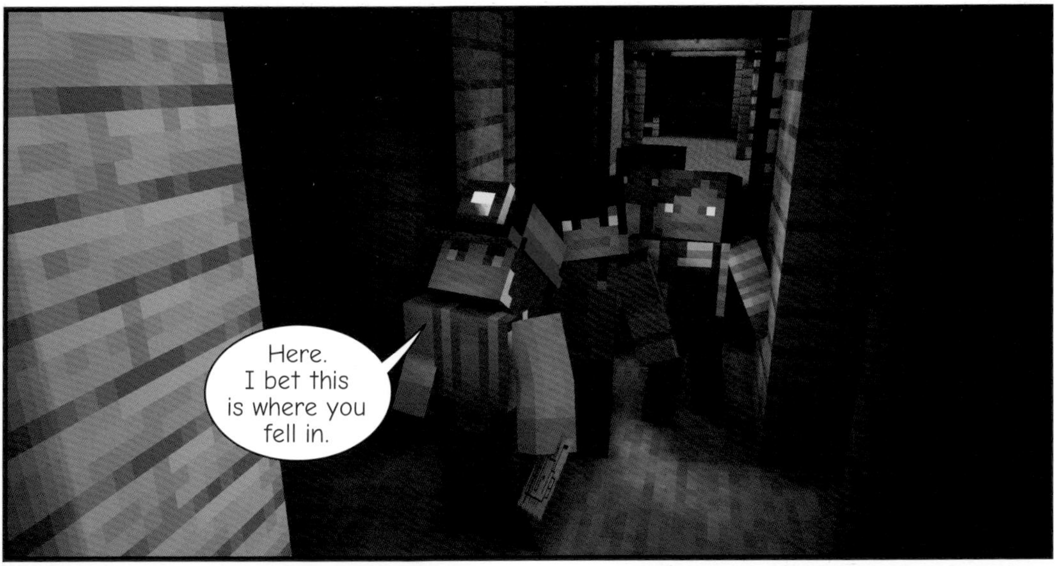
Here. I bet this is where you fell in.

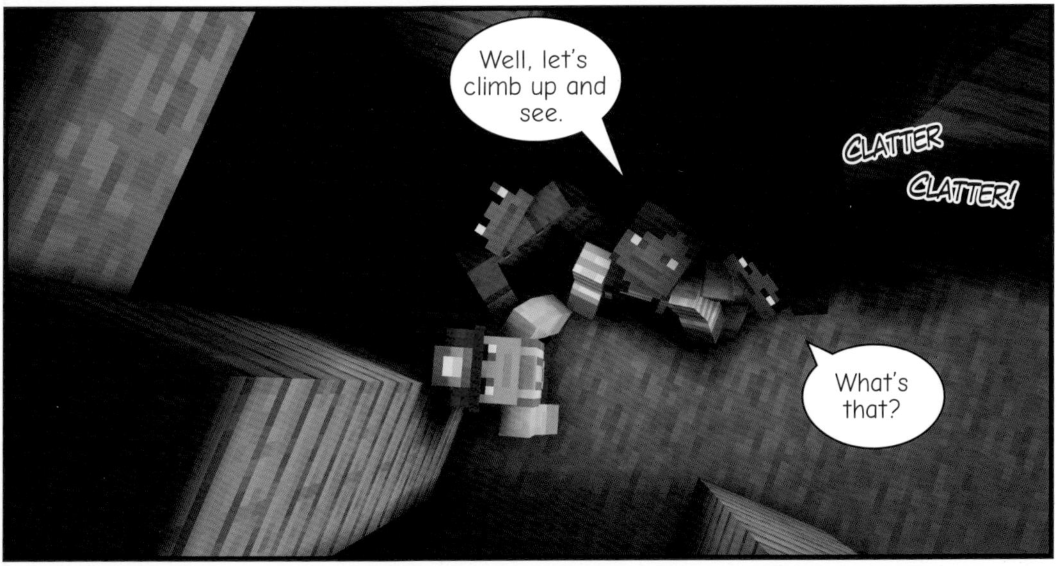
Well, let's climb up and see.
CLATTER
CLATTER!
What's that?

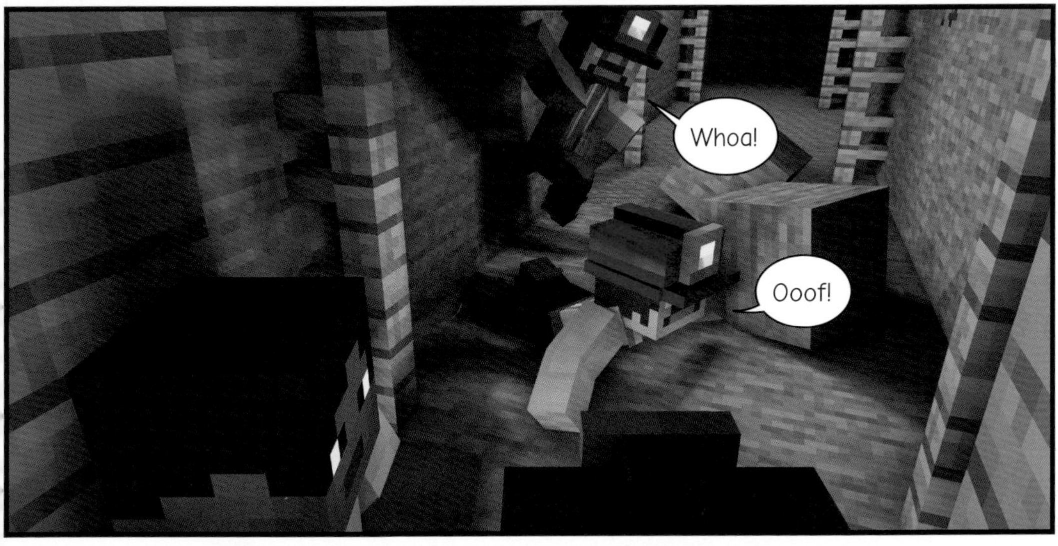
Whoa!
Ooof!

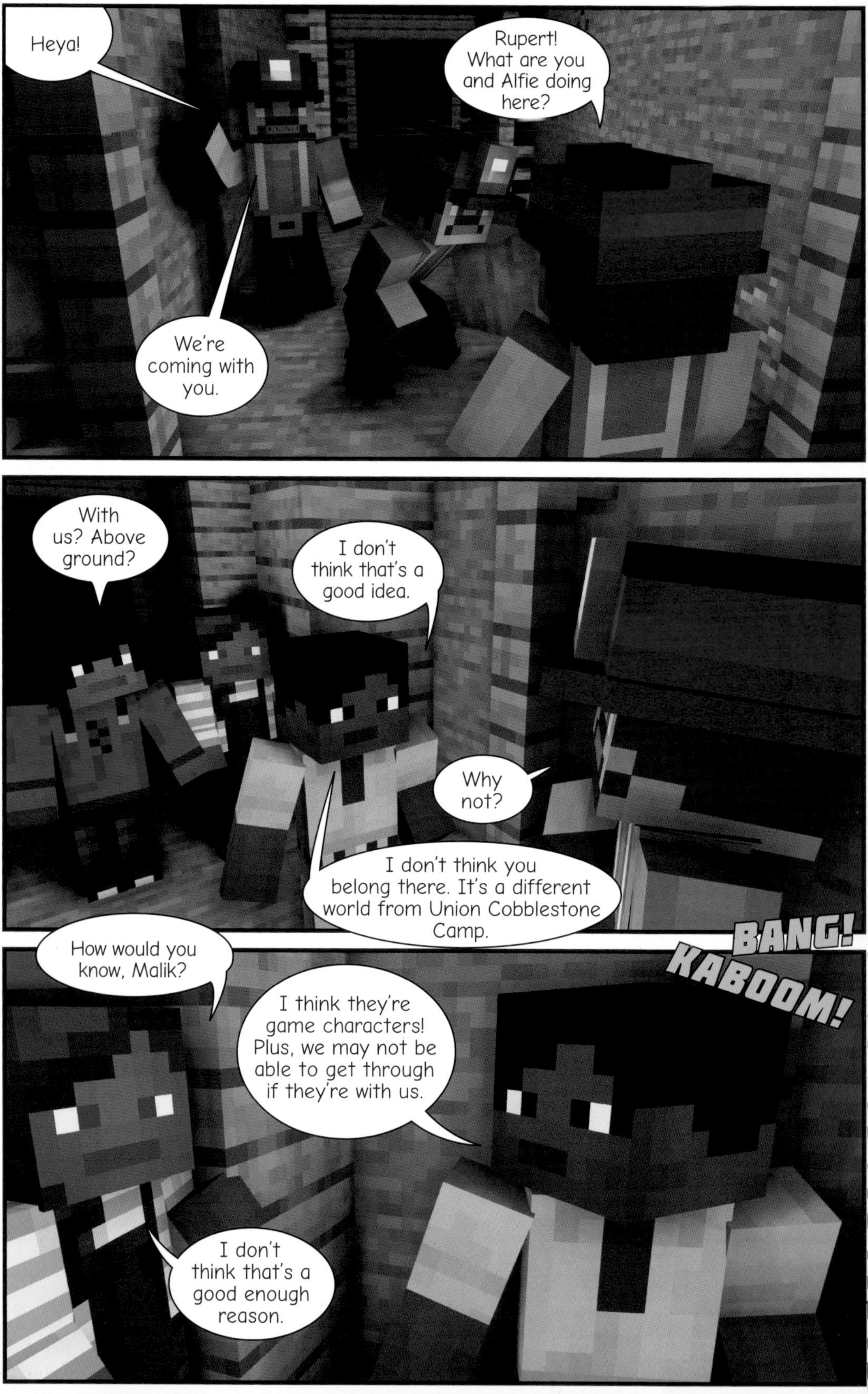

Heya!
Rupert! What are you and Alfie doing here?
We're coming with you.
With us? Above ground?
I don't think that's a good idea.
Why not?
I don't think you belong there. It's a different world from Union Cobblestone Camp.
How would you know, Malik?
BANG! KABOOM!
I think they're game characters! Plus, we may not be able to get through if they're with us.
I don't think that's a good enough reason.

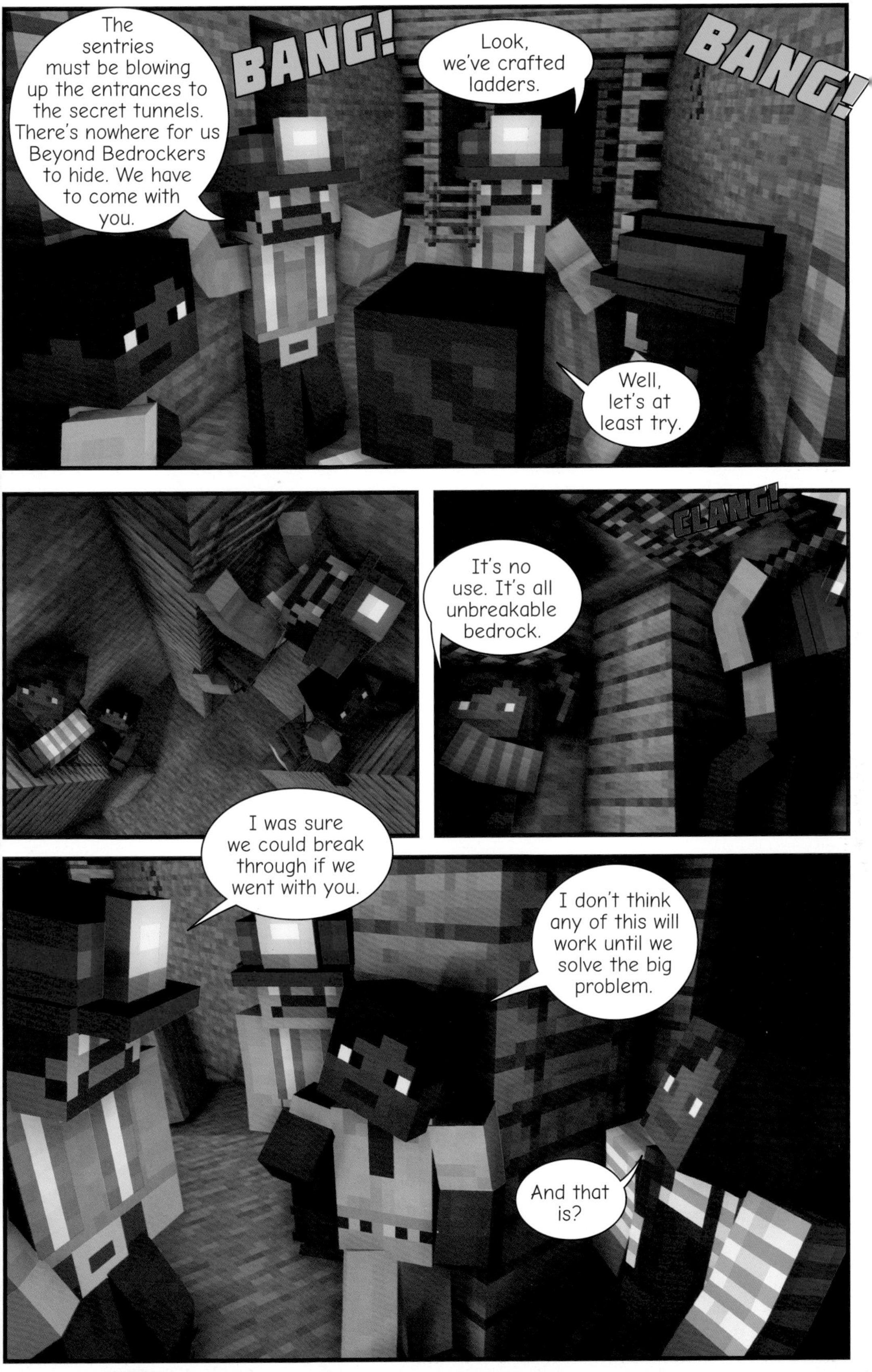
The sentries must be blowing up the entrances to the secret tunnels. There's nowhere for us Beyond Bedrockers to hide. We have to come with you.
BANG!
Look, we've crafted ladders.
BANG!
Well, let's at least try.
CLANG!
It's no use. It's all unbreakable bedrock.
I was sure we could break through if we went with you.
I don't think any of this will work until we solve the big problem.
And that is?

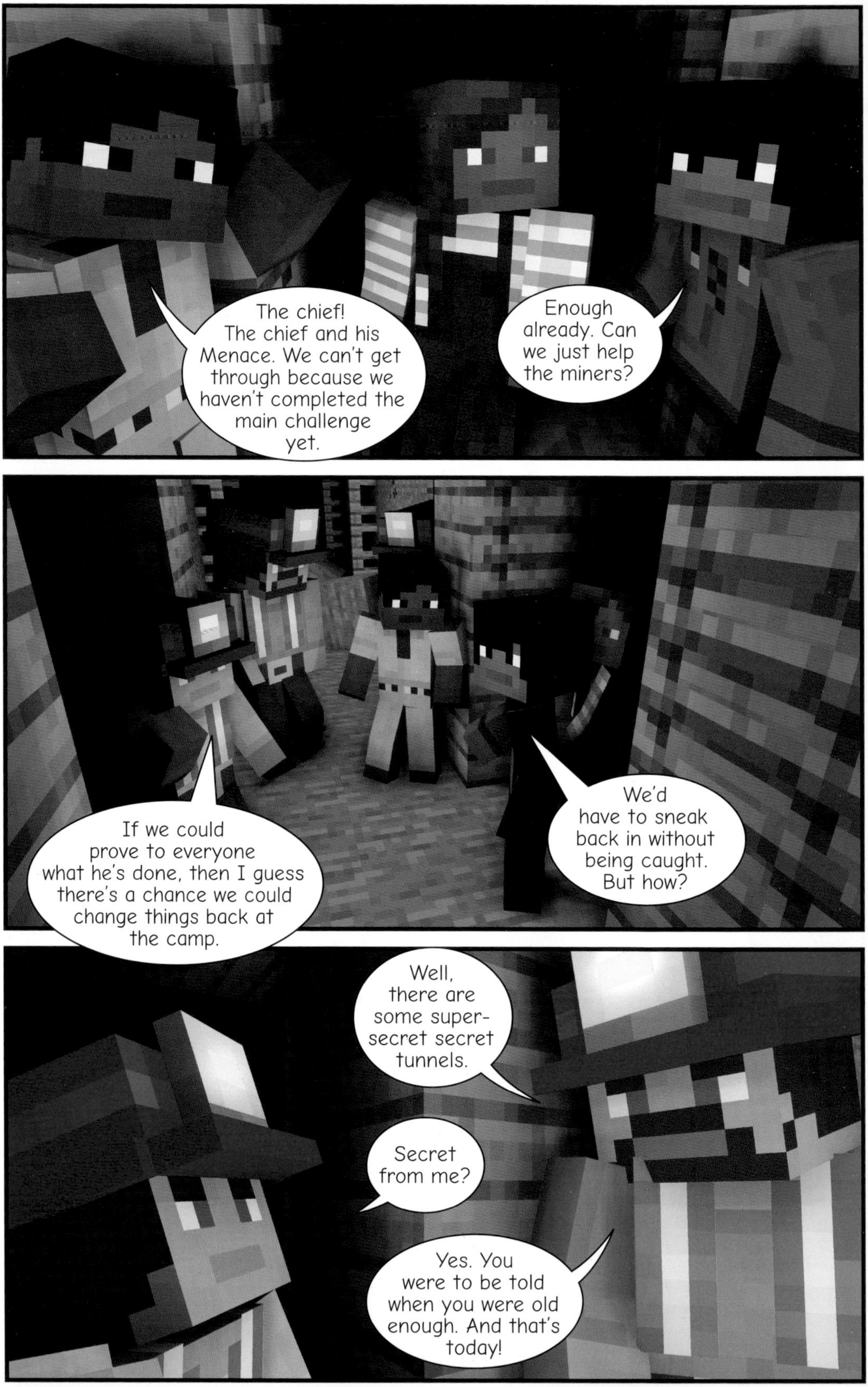
The chief! The chief and his Menace. We can't get through because we haven't completed the main challenge yet.
Enough already. Can we just help the miners?
If we could prove to everyone what he's done, then I guess there's a chance we could change things back at the camp.
We'd have to sneak back in without being caught. But how?
Well, there are some super-secret secret tunnels.
Secret from me?
Yes. You were to be told when you were old enough. And that's today!

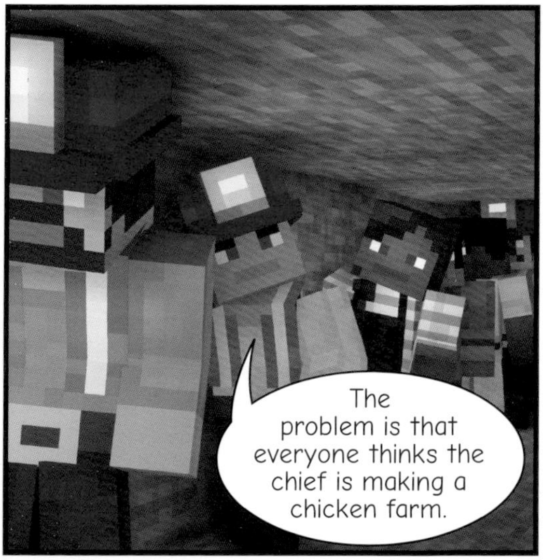
The problem is that everyone thinks the chief is making a chicken farm.

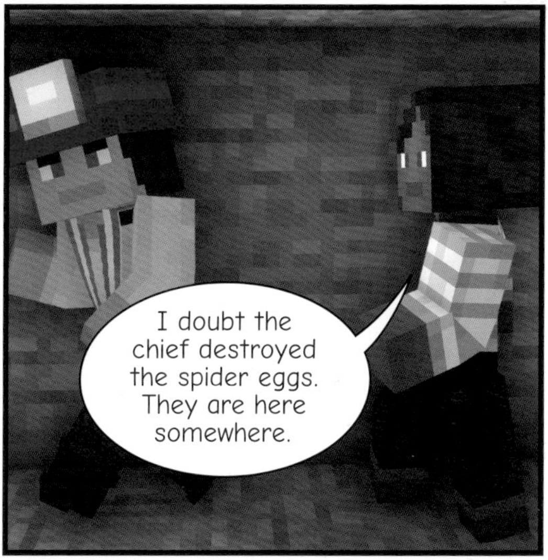
I doubt the chief destroyed the spider eggs. They are here somewhere.

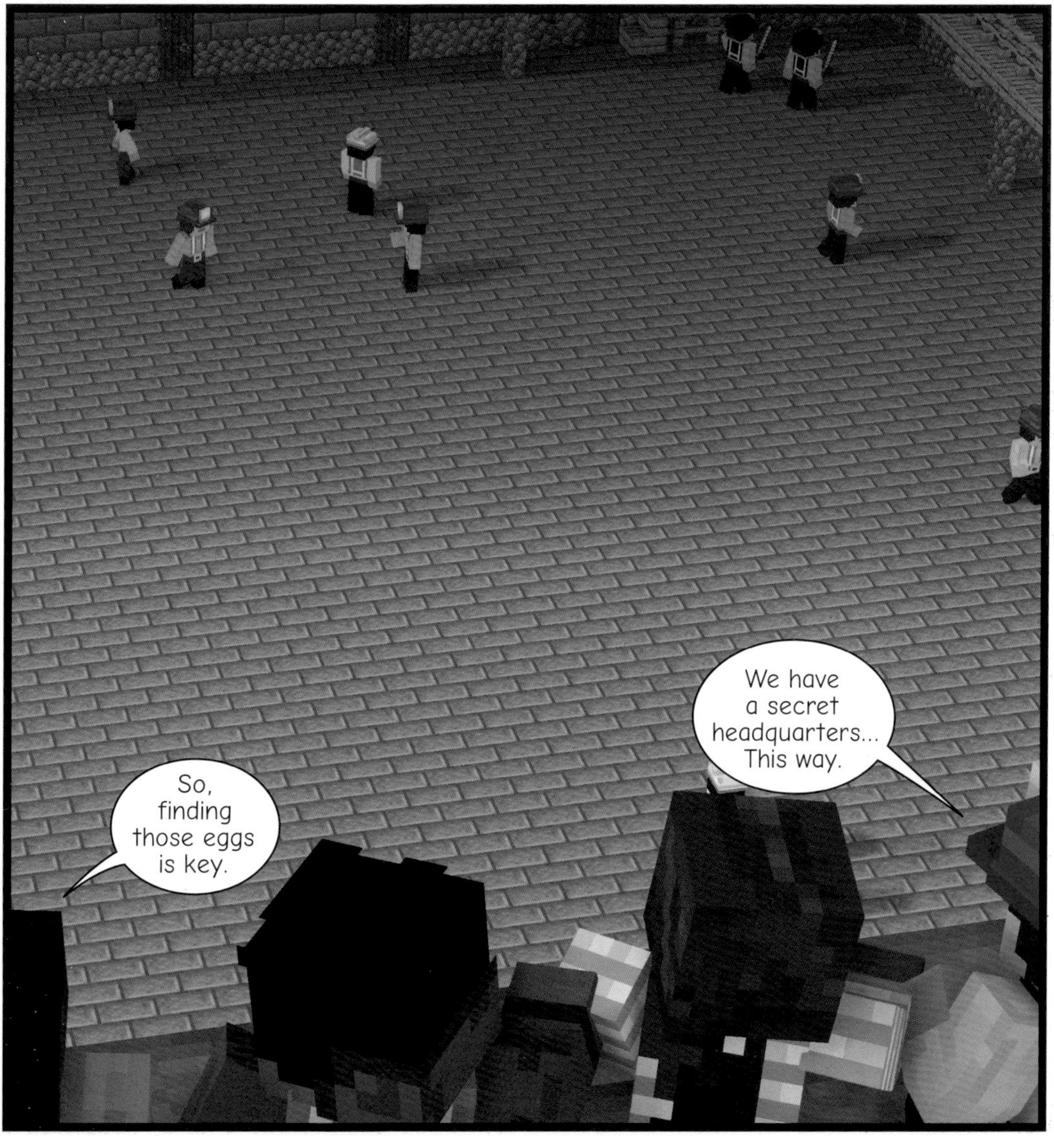
So, finding those eggs is key.
We have a secret headquarters... This way.

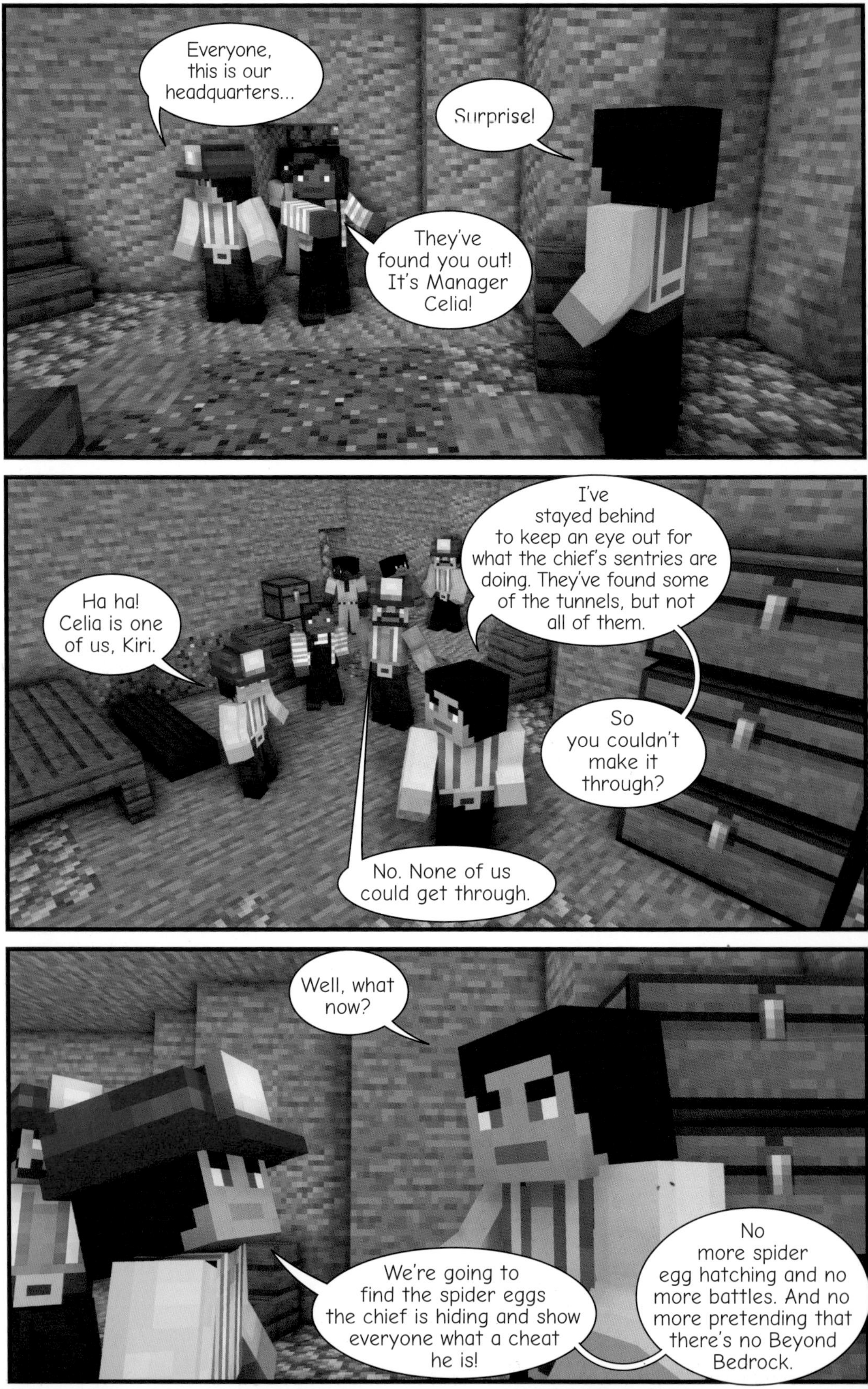
Everyone, this is our headquarters...
Surprise!
They've found you out! It's Manager Celia!
Ha ha! Celia is one of us, Kiri.
I've stayed behind to keep an eye out for what the chief's sentries are doing. They've found some of the tunnels, but not all of them.
So you couldn't make it through?
No. None of us could get through.
Well, what now?
We're going to find the spider eggs the chief is hiding and show everyone what a cheat he is!
No more spider egg hatching and no more battles. And no more pretending that there's no Beyond Bedrock.

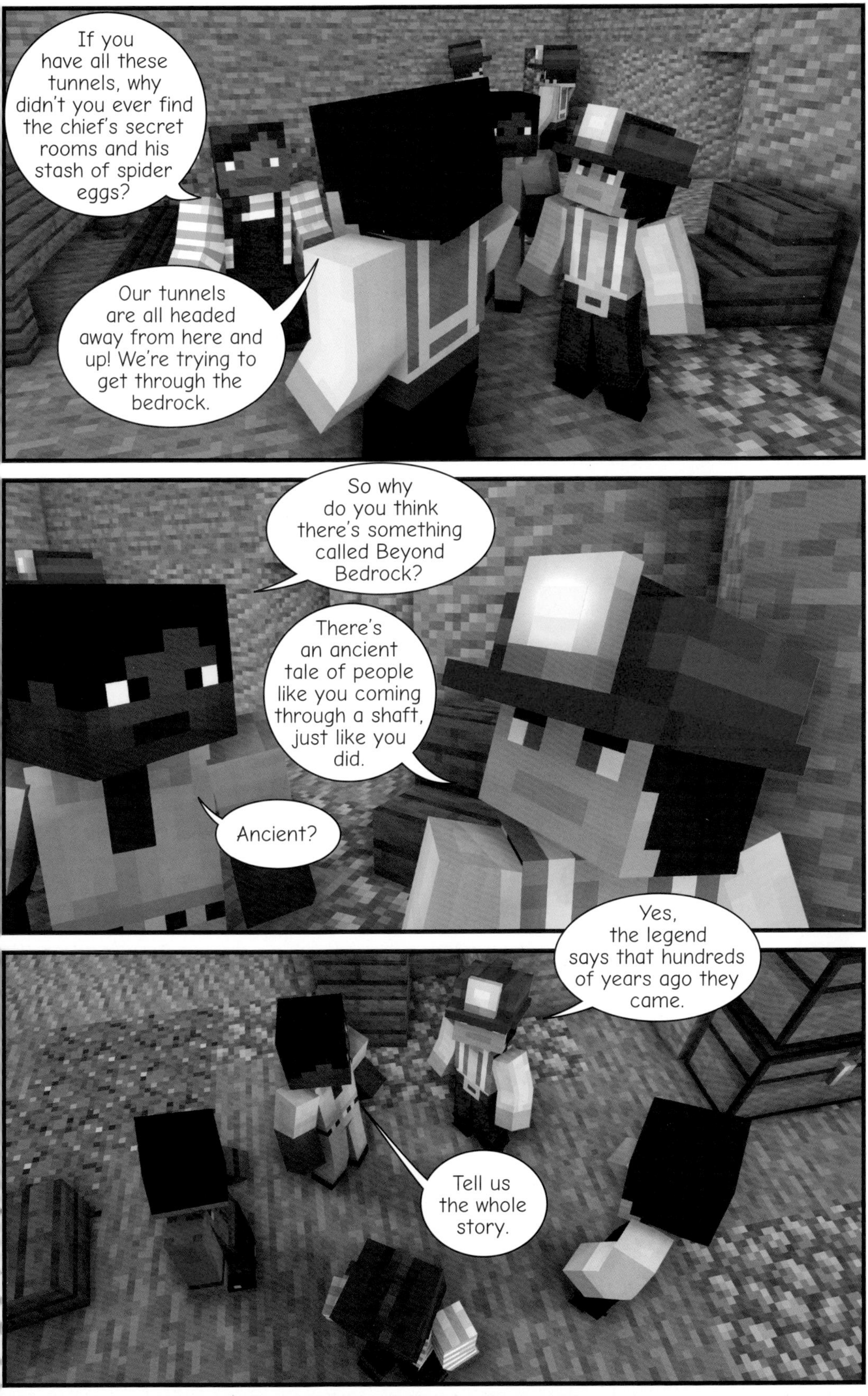
If you have all these tunnels, why didn't you ever find the chief's secret rooms and his stash of spider eggs?
Our tunnels are all headed away from here and up! We're trying to get through the bedrock.
So why do you think there's something called Beyond Bedrock?
There's an ancient tale of people like you coming through a shaft, just like you did.
Ancient?
Yes, the legend says that hundreds of years ago they came.
Tell us the whole story.

This is the story of the ancient miners. Long ago, before our grandparent's grandparents were small children, there were terrible times. Miners lived in a small, dark camp mining coal, and killing zombies for food that sometimes poisoned them. In the center of their little village was a stone pillar that they lit and danced around, but that was their only pleasure.

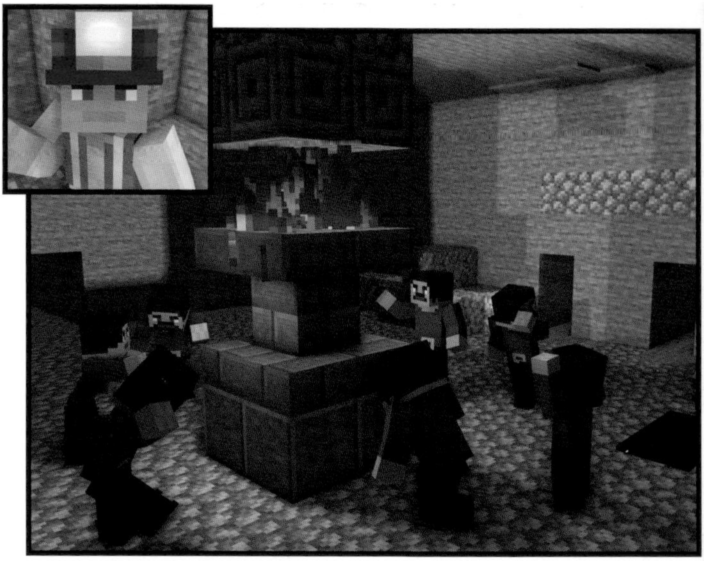

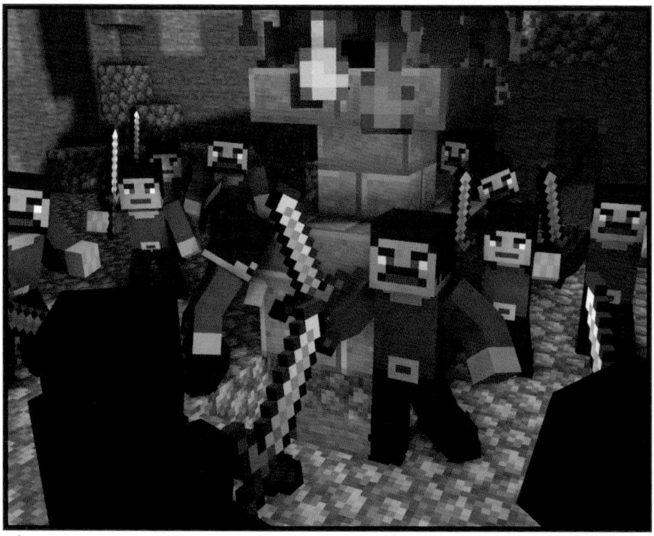

One day, two strangers came into this world swinging from spider webs and vines that grew from above. They saw the pillar and started taking it apart, so the miners fought them. Our ancestors eventually found out why they were trying to dismantle the pillar: the stone pillar was part of a puzzle they were unlocking. If they managed to unlock it, they could go home. They were very sad, so our people helped them.

The puzzle was unlocked, and not only did it allow the strangers to go home; it also opened up a vast network of mineshafts! The miners were able to mine metals and diamonds and find ways to defeat the monsters that lived here and to create this amazing mining camp we now call home. Those strangers were eventually hailed as heroes.

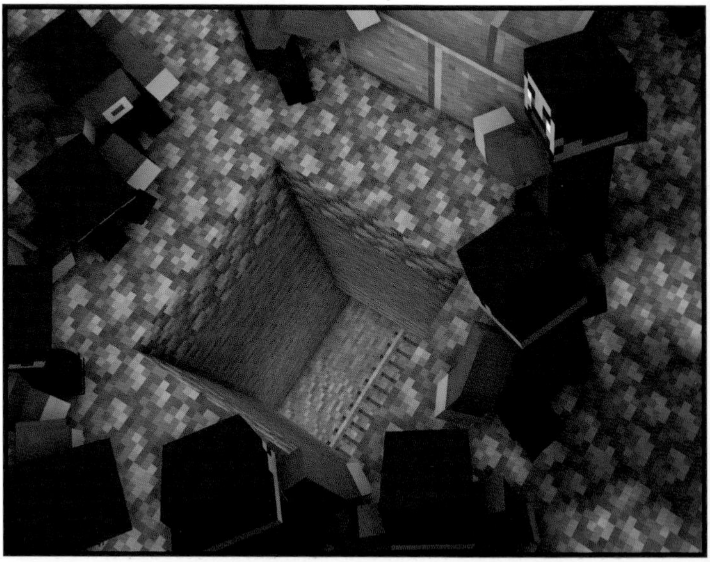

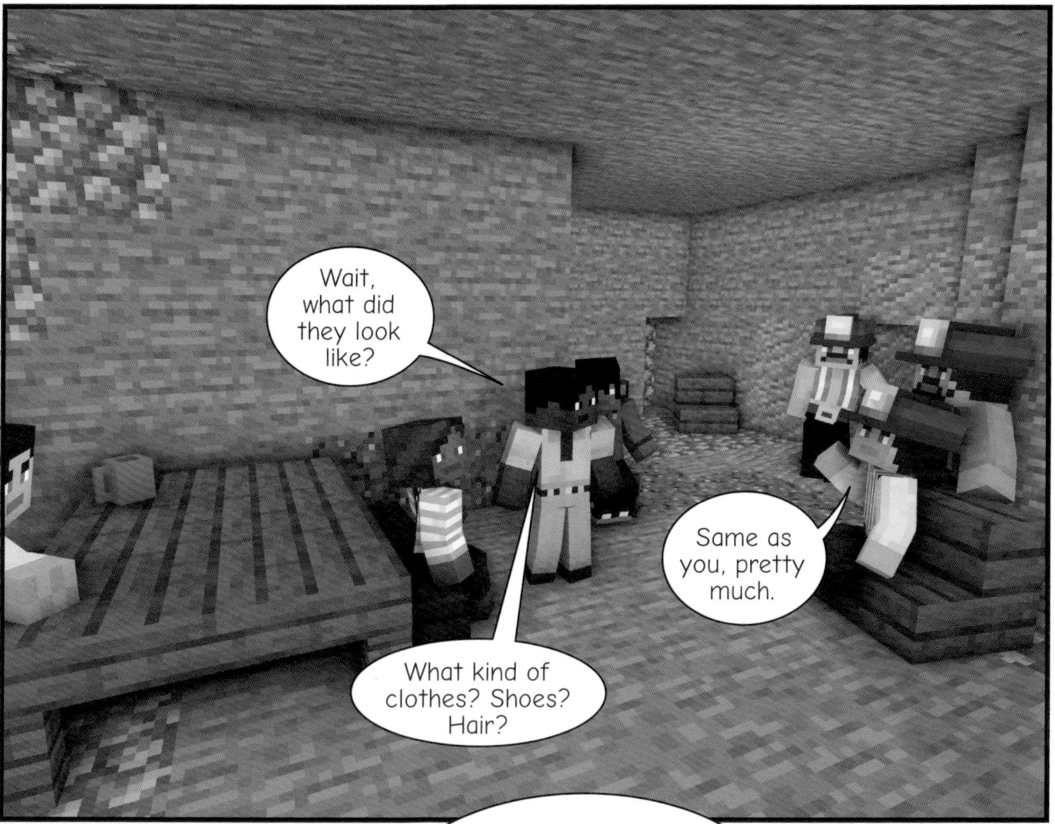
Wait, what did they look like?
Same as you, pretty much.
What kind of clothes? Shoes? Hair?

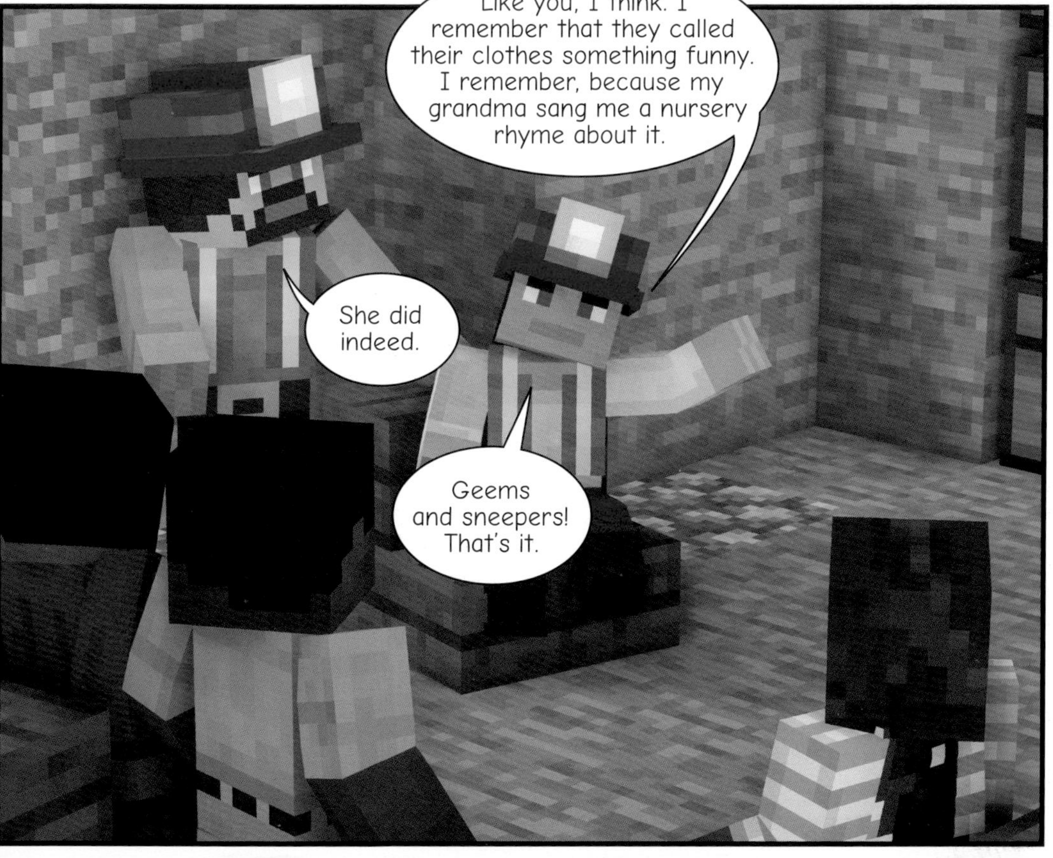
Like you, I think. I remember that they called their clothes something funny. I remember, because my grandma sang me a nursery rhyme about it.
She did indeed.
Geems and sneepers! That's it.

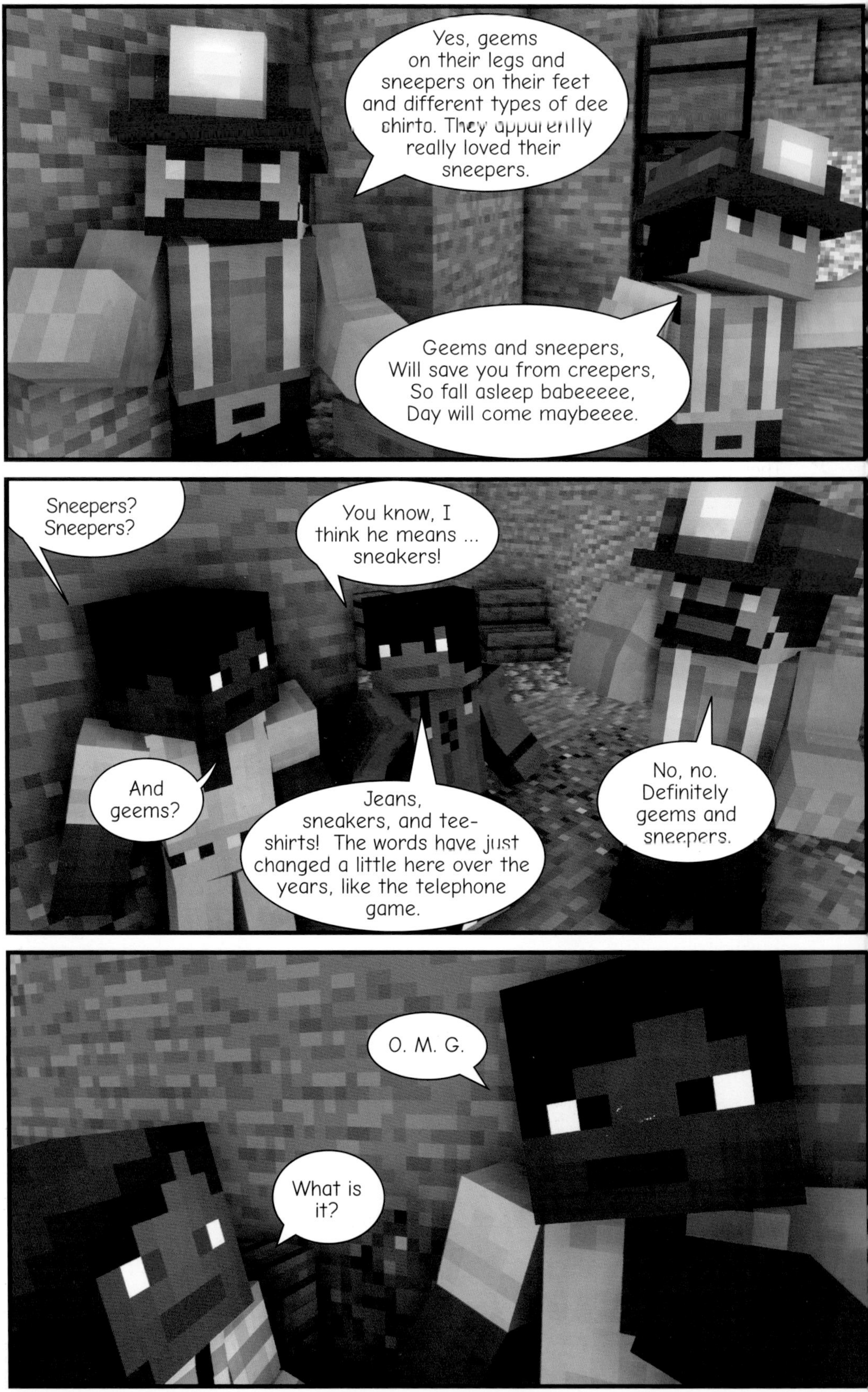
Yes, geems on their legs and sneepers on their feet and different types of dee shirts. They apparently really loved their sneepers.
Geems and sneepers, Will save you from creepers, So fall asleep babeeeee, Day will come maybeeee.
Sneepers? Sneepers?
You know, I think he means ... sneakers!
And geems?
Jeans, sneakers, and tee-shirts! The words have just changed a little here over the years, like the telephone game.
No, no. Definitely geems and sneepers.
O. M. G.
What is it?

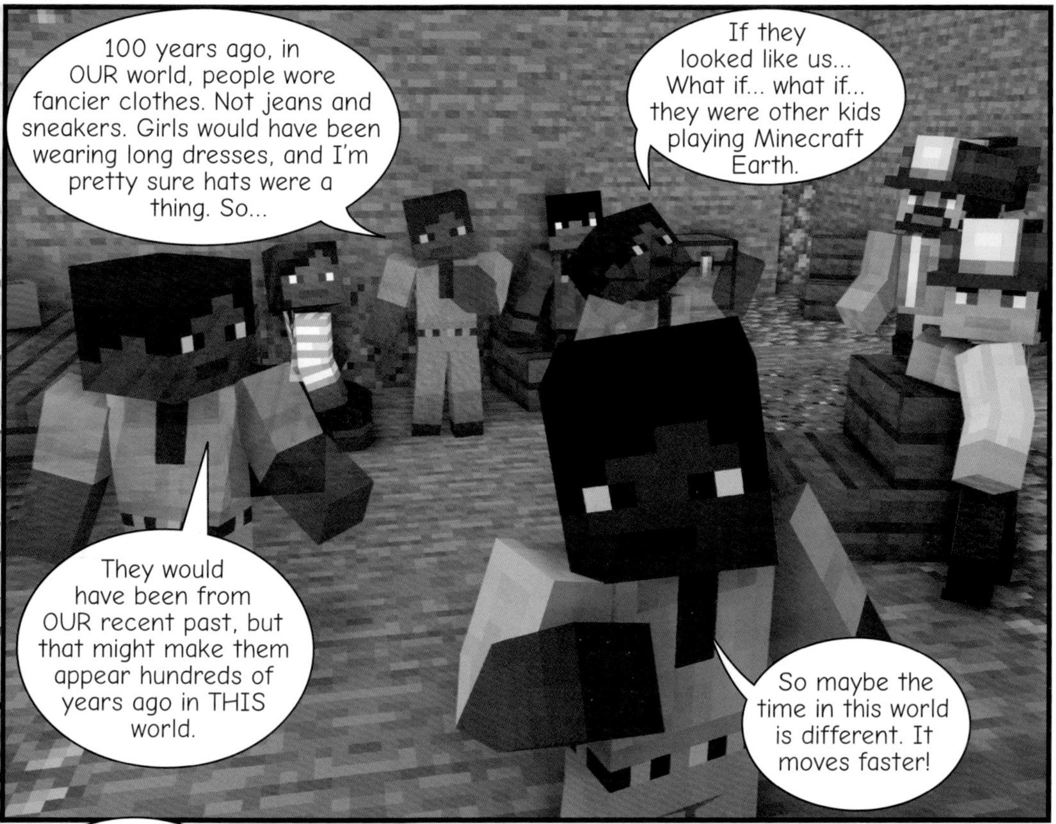
100 years ago, in OUR world, people wore fancier clothes. Not jeans and sneakers. Girls would have been wearing long dresses, and I'm pretty sure hats were a thing. So...
If they looked like us... What if... what if... they were other kids playing Minecraft Earth.
They would have been from OUR recent past, but that might make them appear hundreds of years ago in THIS world.
So maybe the time in this world is different. It moves faster!

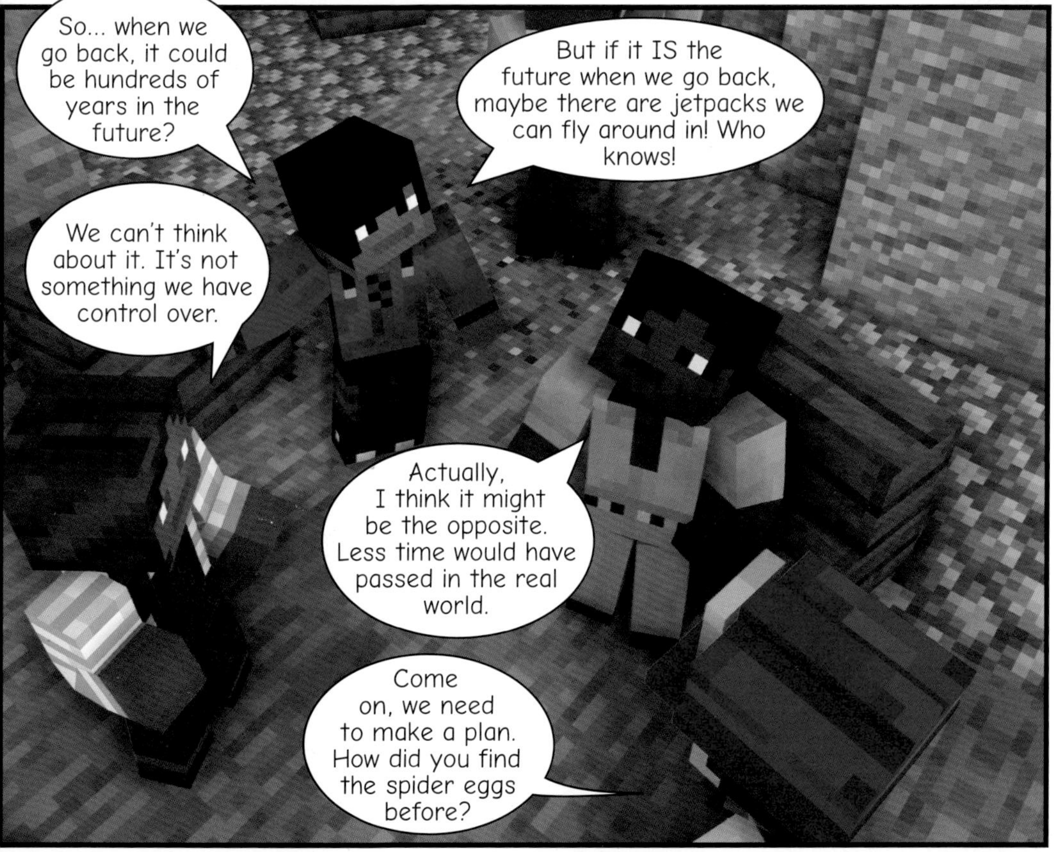
So... when we go back, it could be hundreds of years in the future?
But if it IS the future when we go back, maybe there are jetpacks we can fly around in! Who knows!
We can't think about it. It's not something we have control over.
Actually, I think it might be the opposite. Less time would have passed in the real world.
Come on, we need to make a plan. How did you find the spider eggs before?

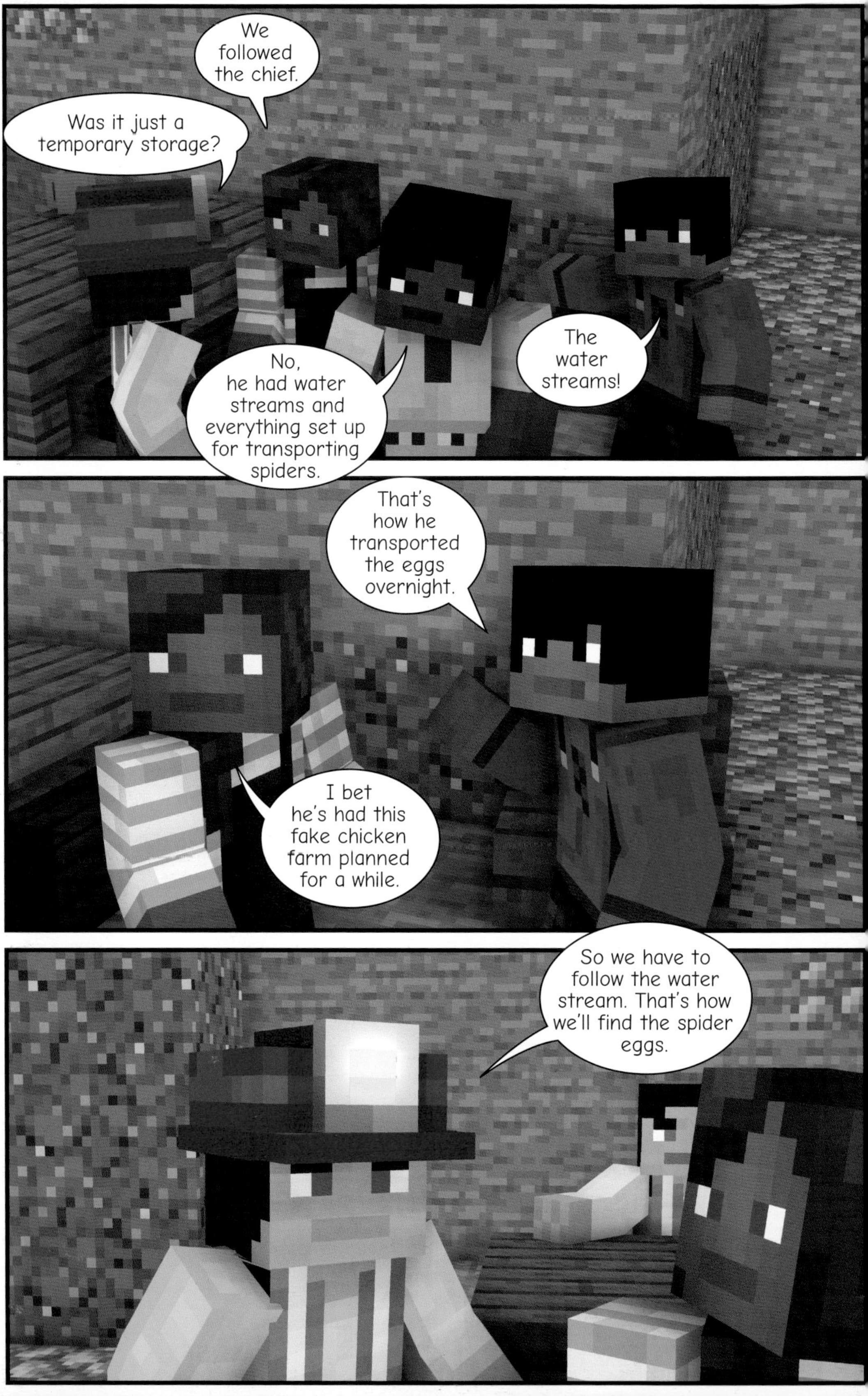
Was it just a temporary storage?
We followed the chief.
No, he had water streams and everything set up for transporting spiders.
The water streams!
That's how he transported the eggs overnight.
I bet he's had this fake chicken farm planned for a while.
So we have to follow the water stream. That's how we'll find the spider eggs.

Chapter 9

Eggs-posure

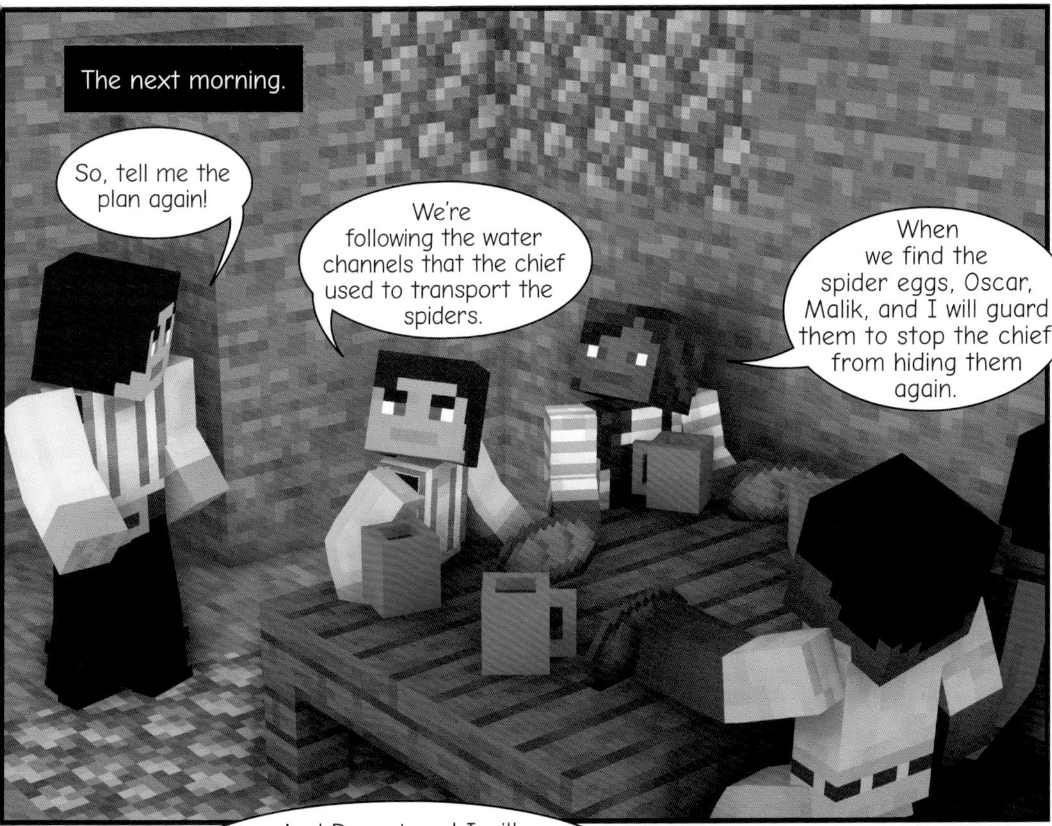
The next morning.
So, tell me the plan again!
We're following the water channels that the chief used to transport the spiders.
When we find the spider eggs, Oscar, Malik, and I will guard them to stop the chief from hiding them again.

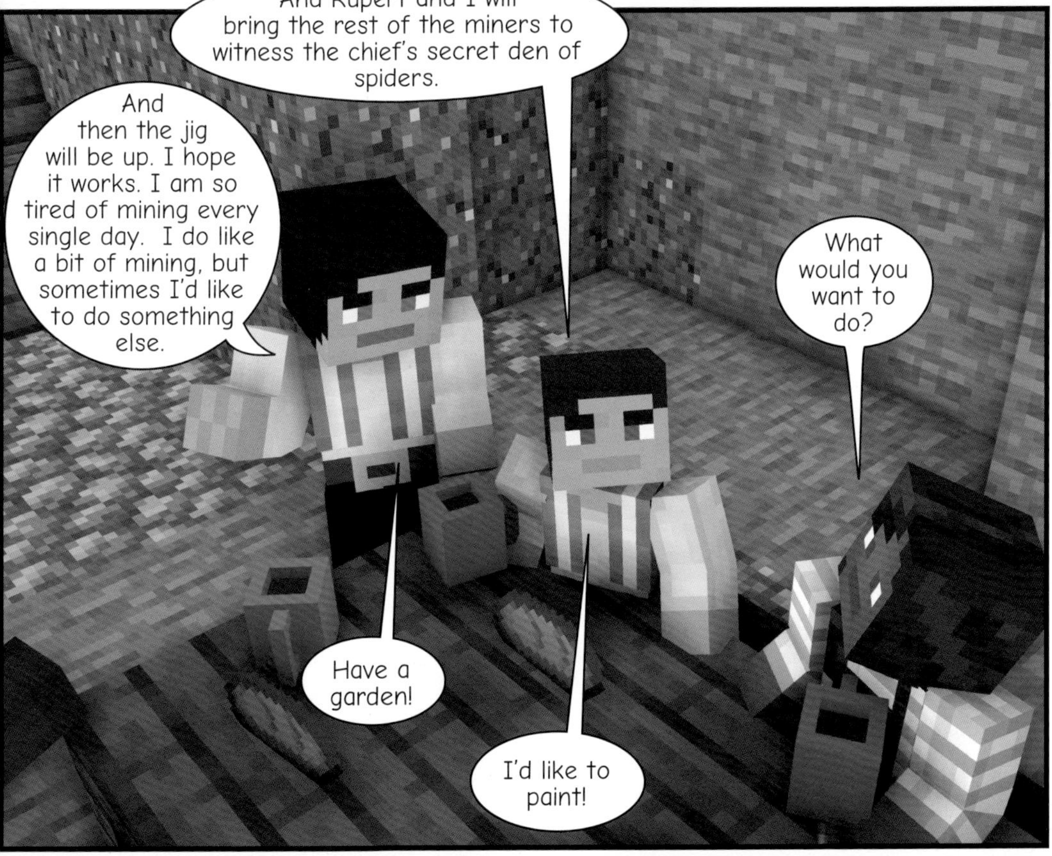
And Rupert and I will bring the rest of the miners to witness the chief's secret den of spiders.
And then the jig will be up. I hope it works. I am so tired of mining every single day. I do like a bit of mining, but sometimes I'd like to do something else.
What would you want to do?
Have a garden!
I'd like to paint!

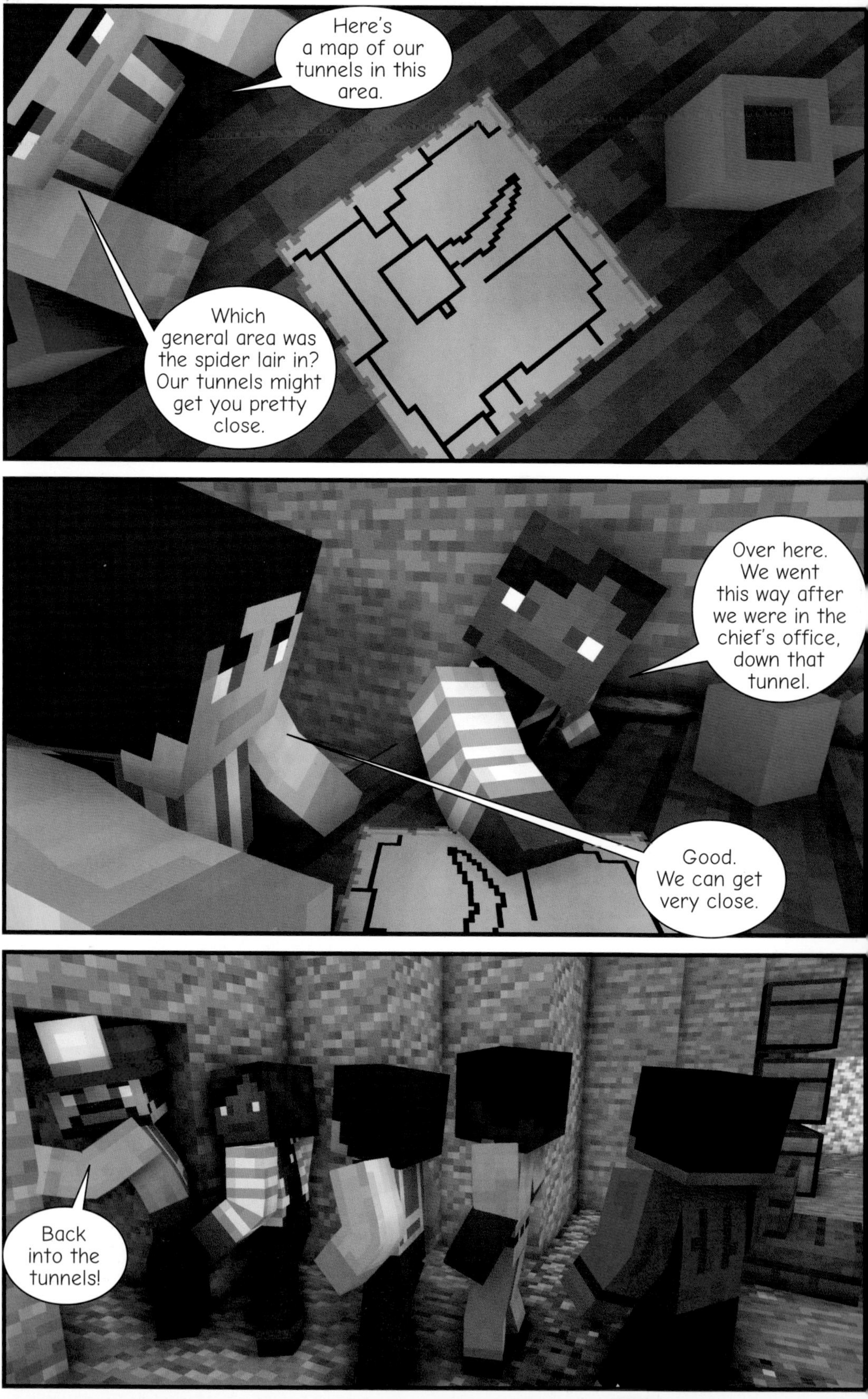
Here's a map of our tunnels in this area.
Which general area was the spider lair in? Our tunnels might get you pretty close.
Over here. We went this way after we were in the chief's office, down that tunnel.
Good. We can get very close.
Back into the tunnels!

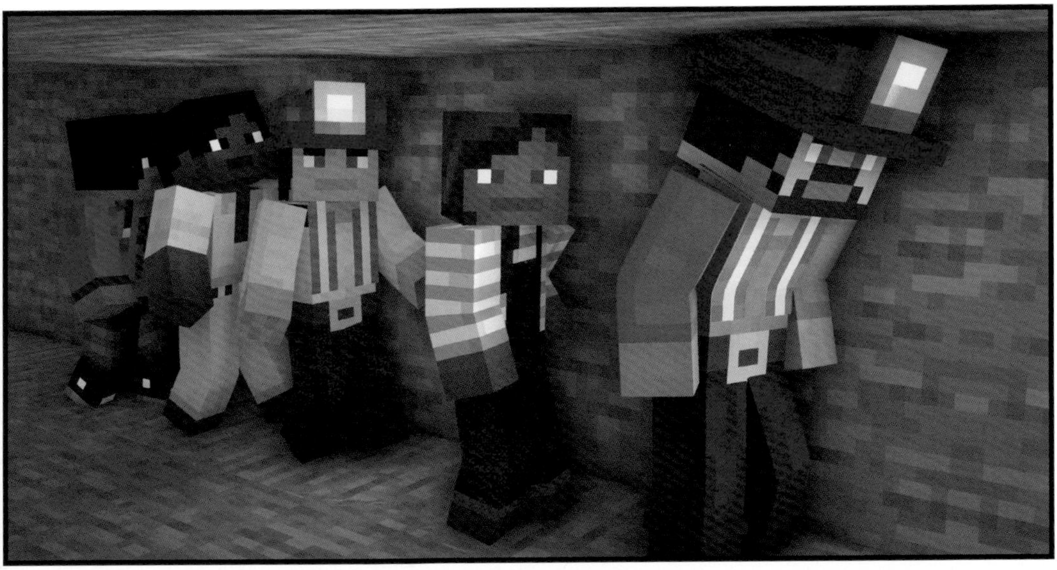

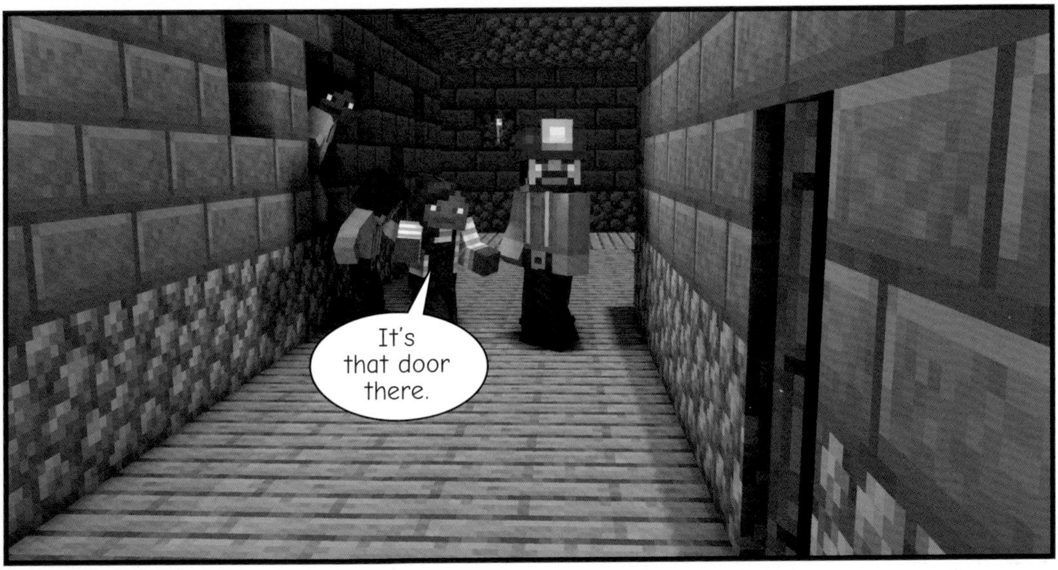
It's that door there.

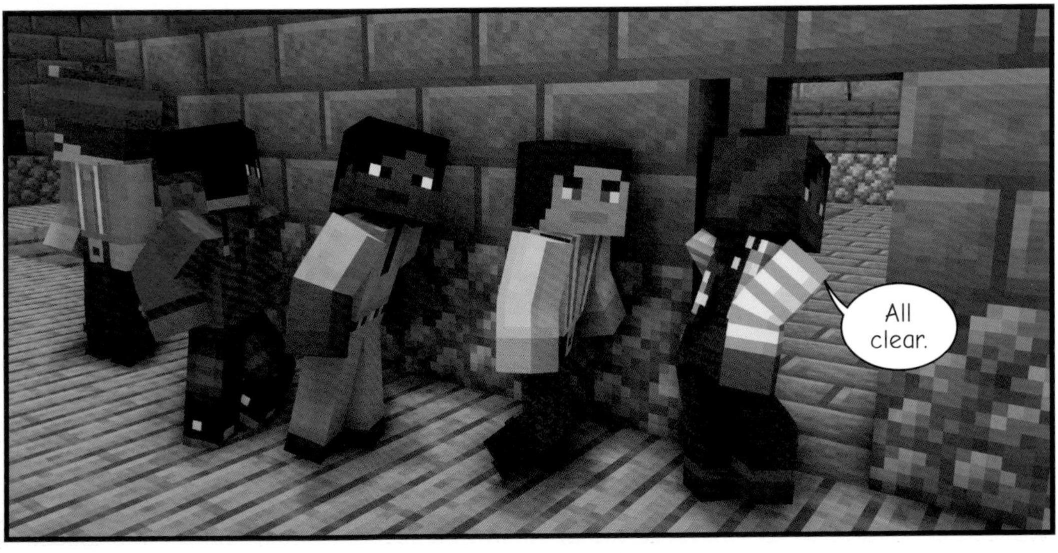
All clear.

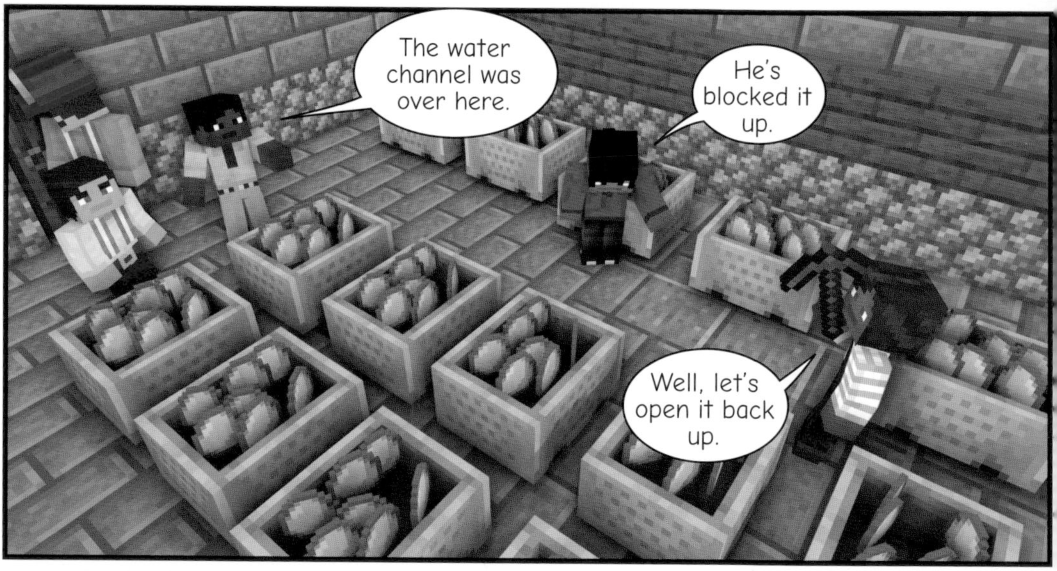
The water channel was over here.
He's blocked it up.
Well, let's open it back up.

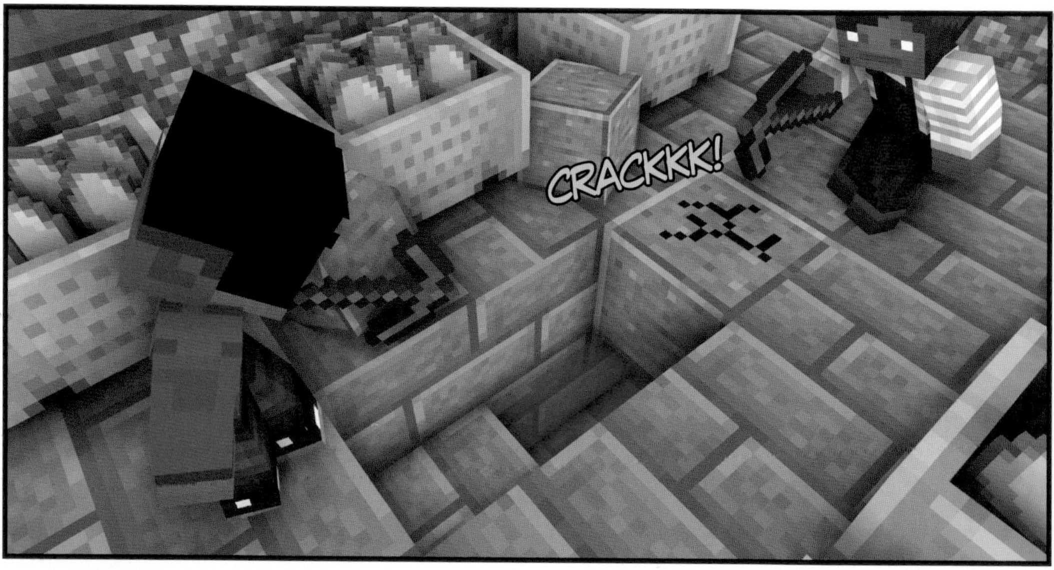
CRACKKK!

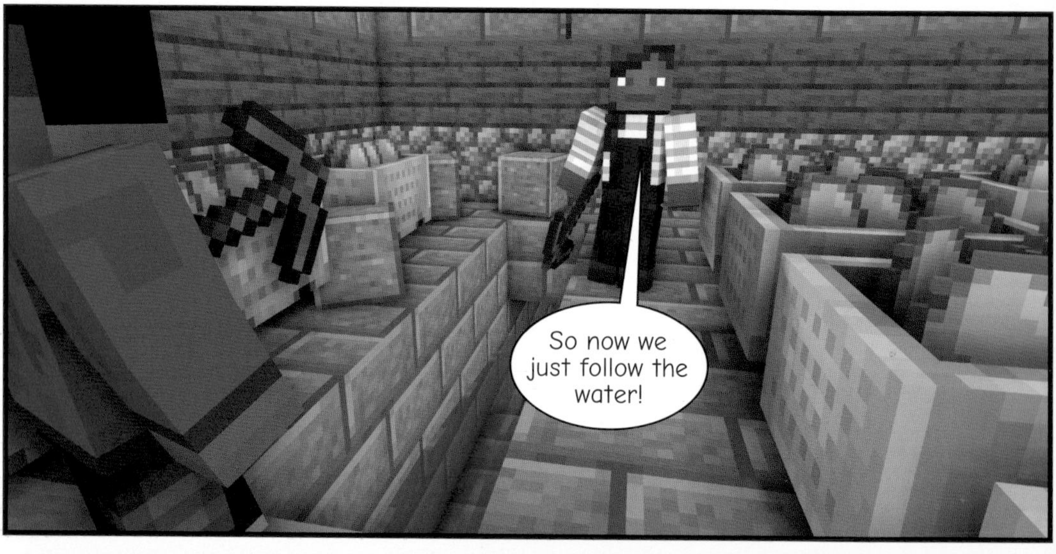
So now we just follow the water!

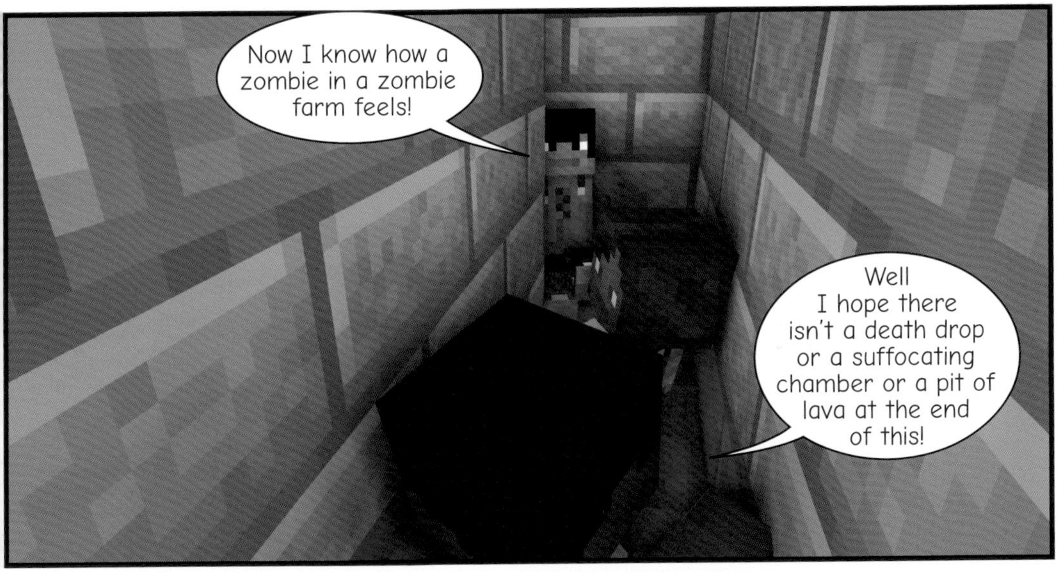
Now I know how a zombie in a zombie farm feels!
Well I hope there isn't a death drop or a suffocating chamber or a pit of lava at the end of this!

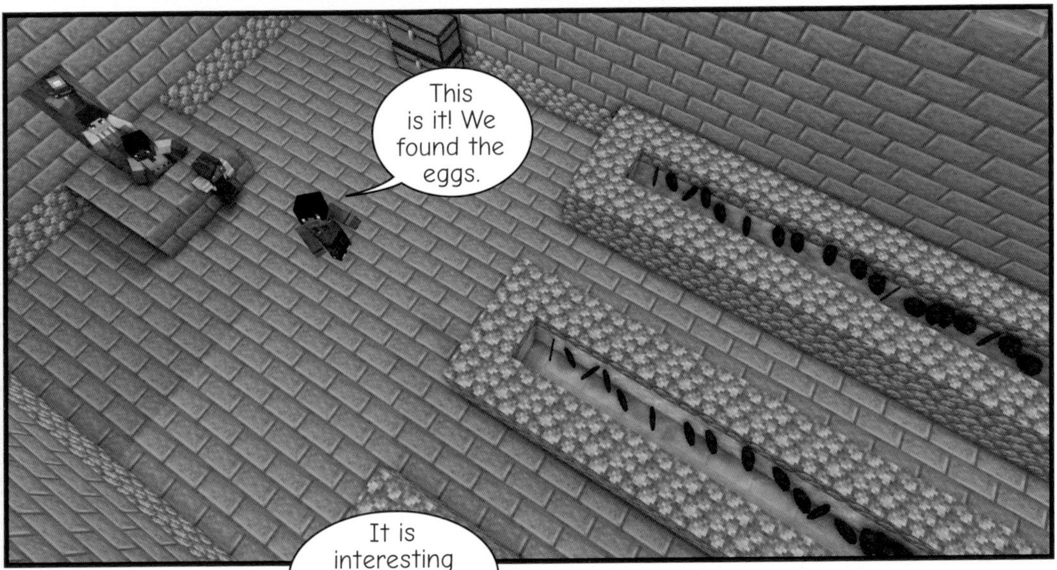
This is it! We found the eggs.

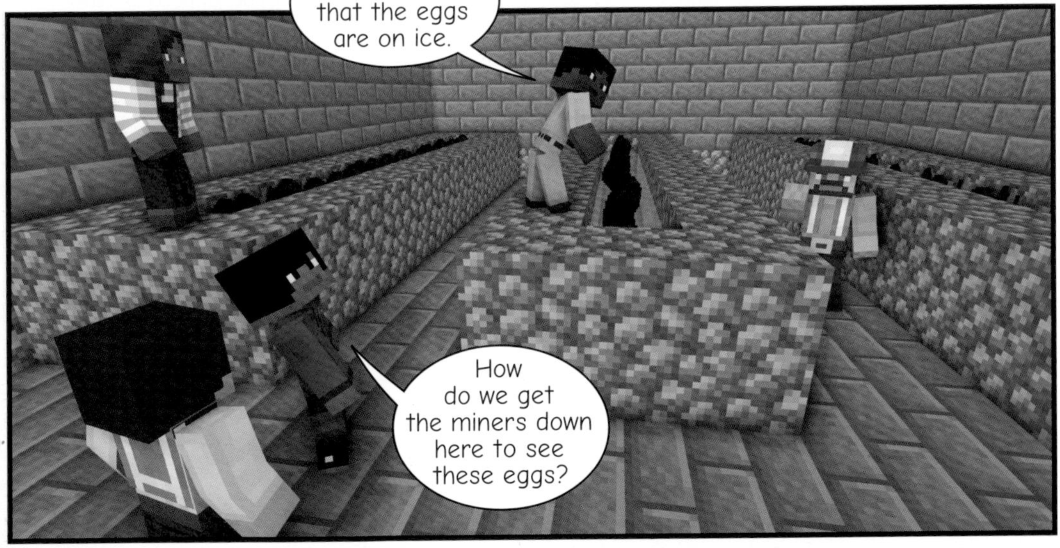
It is interesting that the eggs are on ice.
How do we get the miners down here to see these eggs?

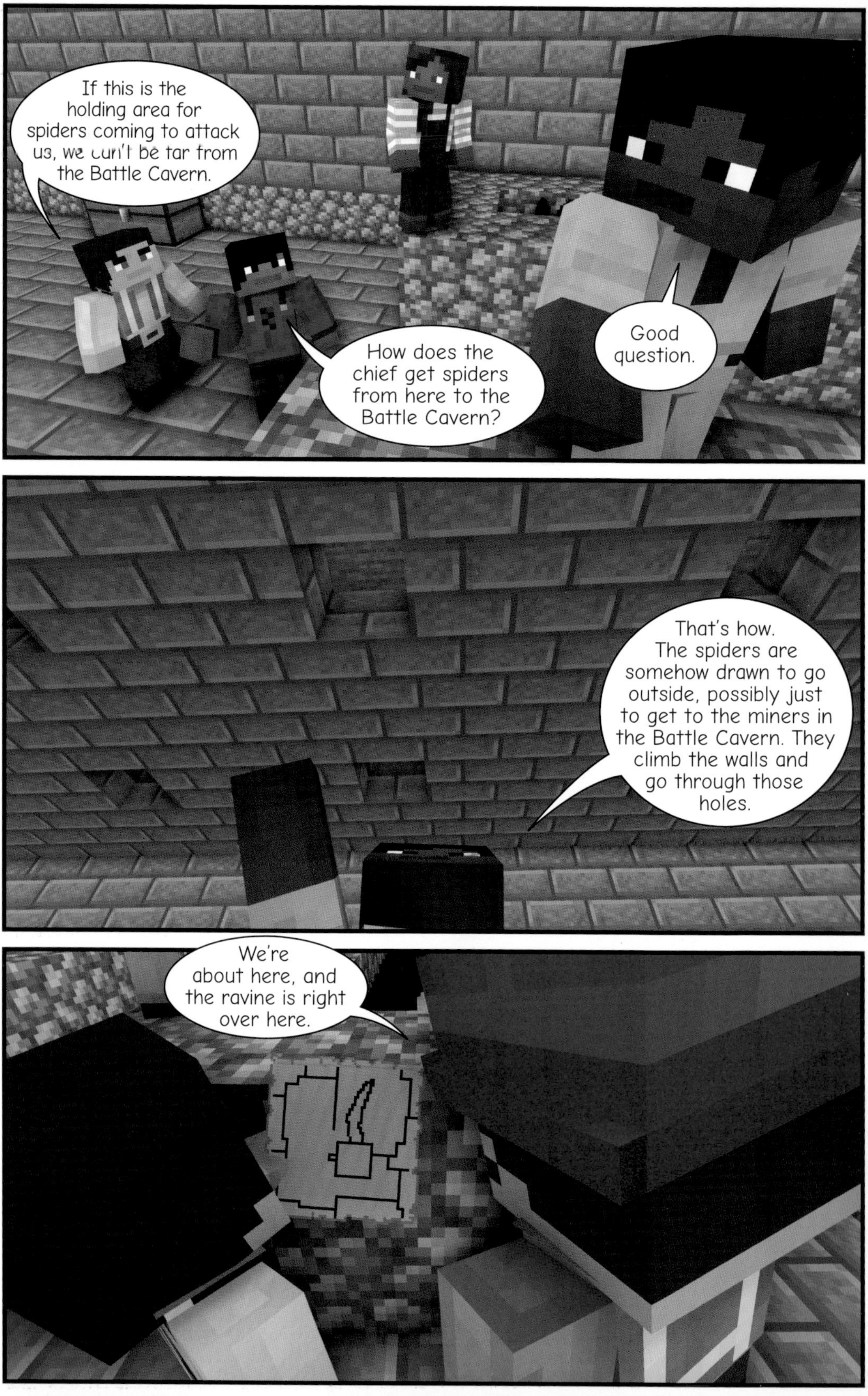

If this is the holding area for spiders coming to attack us, we can't be far from the Battle Cavern.
How does the chief get spiders from here to the Battle Cavern?
Good question.
That's how. The spiders are somehow drawn to go outside, possibly just to get to the miners in the Battle Cavern. They climb the walls and go through those holes.
We're about here, and the ravine is right over here.

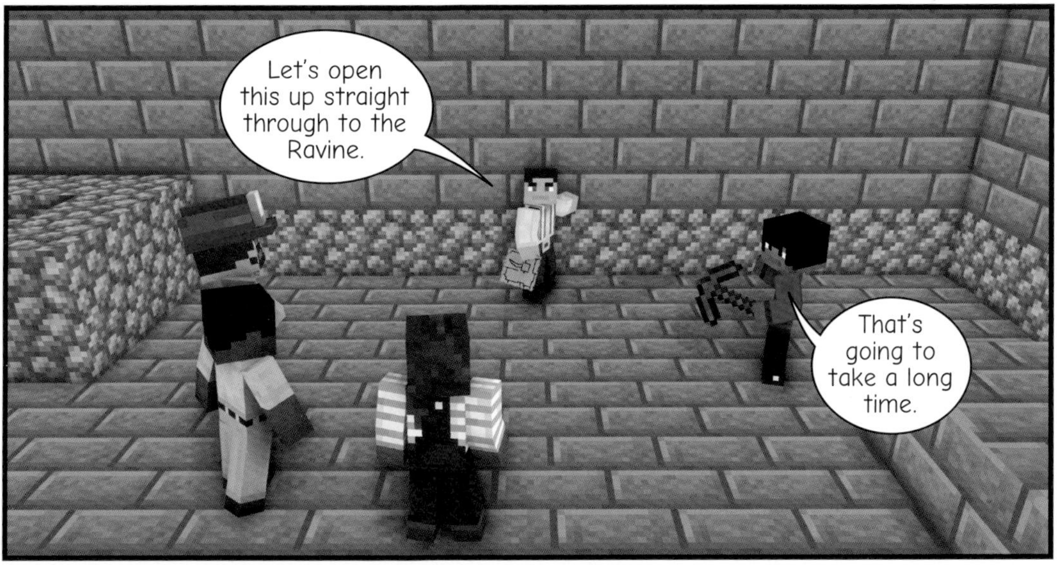

Let's open this up straight through to the Ravine.
That's going to take a long time.

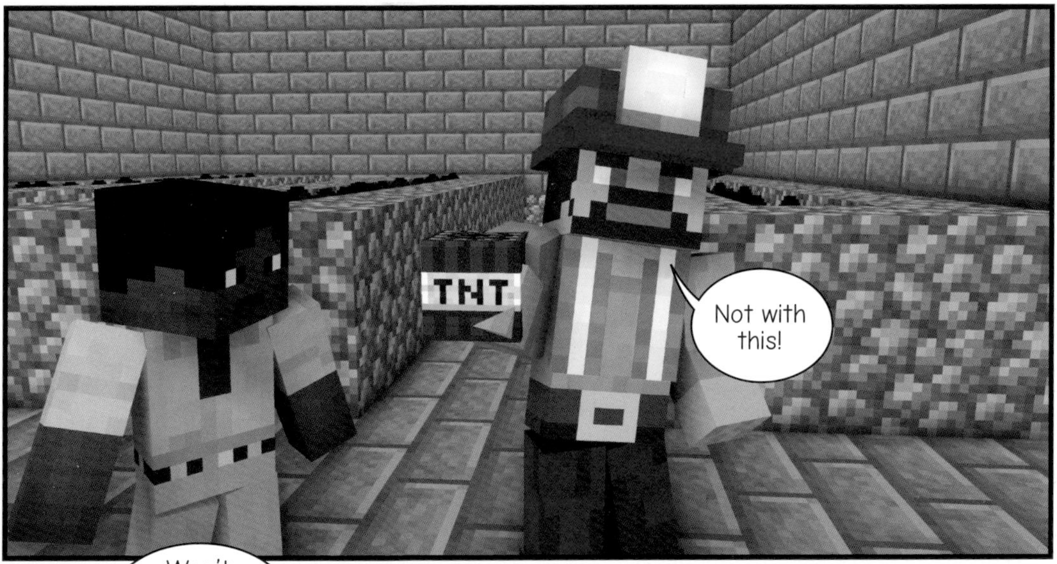

TNT
Not with this!

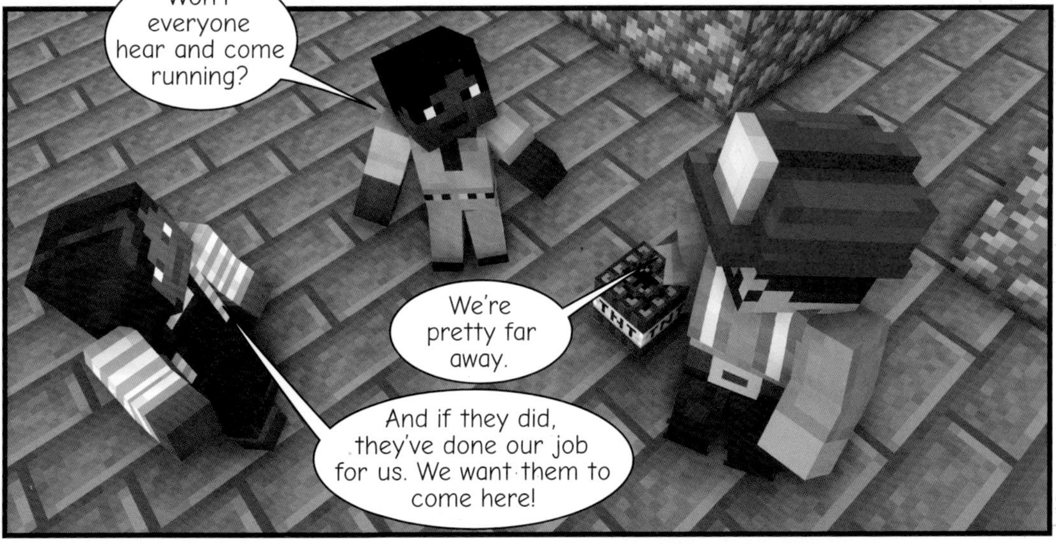

Won't everyone hear and come running?
We're pretty far away.
And if they did, they've done our job for us. We want them to come here!

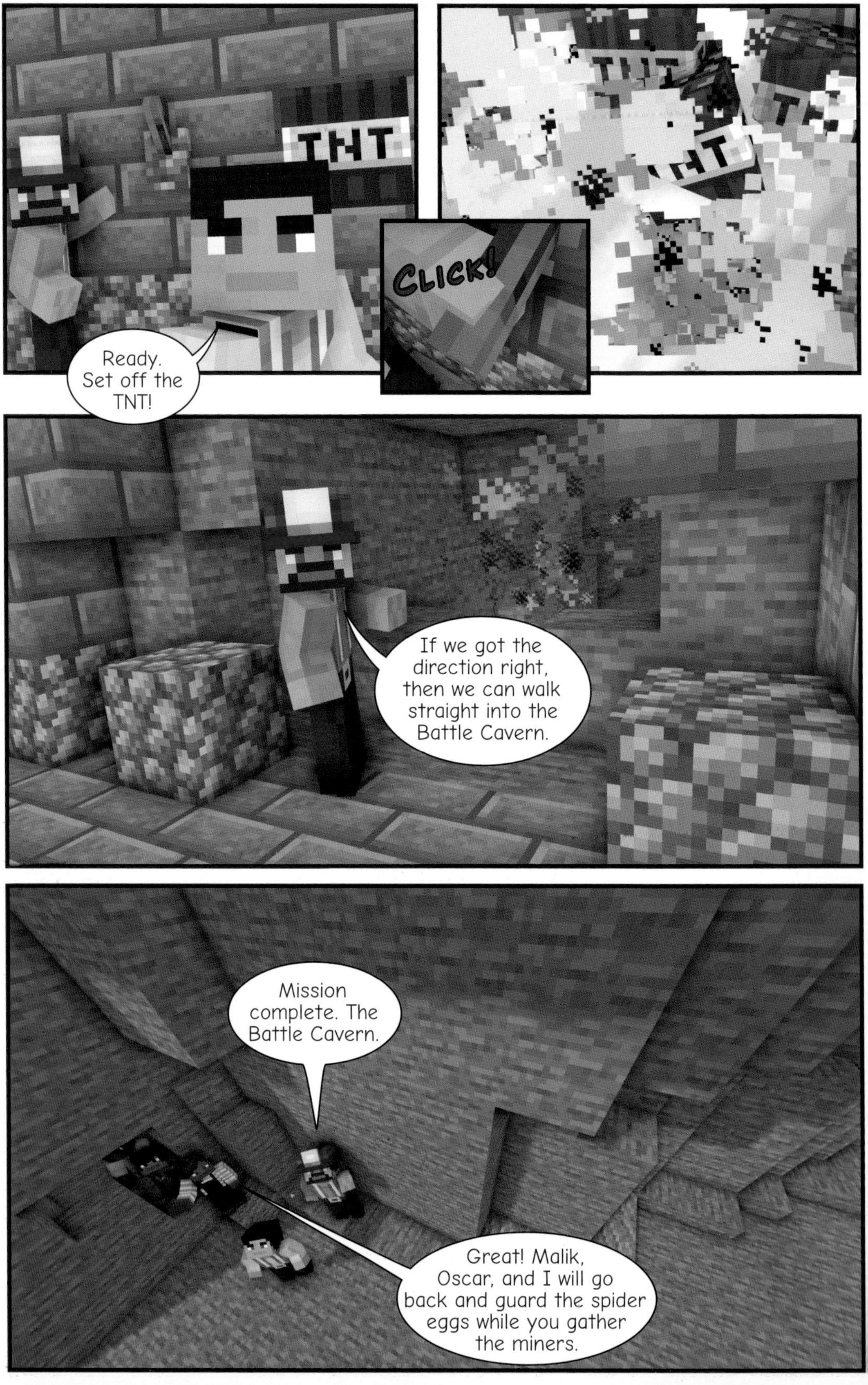
Ready. Set off the TNT!
CLICK!
TNT
If we got the direction right, then we can walk straight into the Battle Cavern.
Mission complete. The Battle Cavern.
Great! Malik, Oscar, and I will go back and guard the spider eggs while you gather the miners.

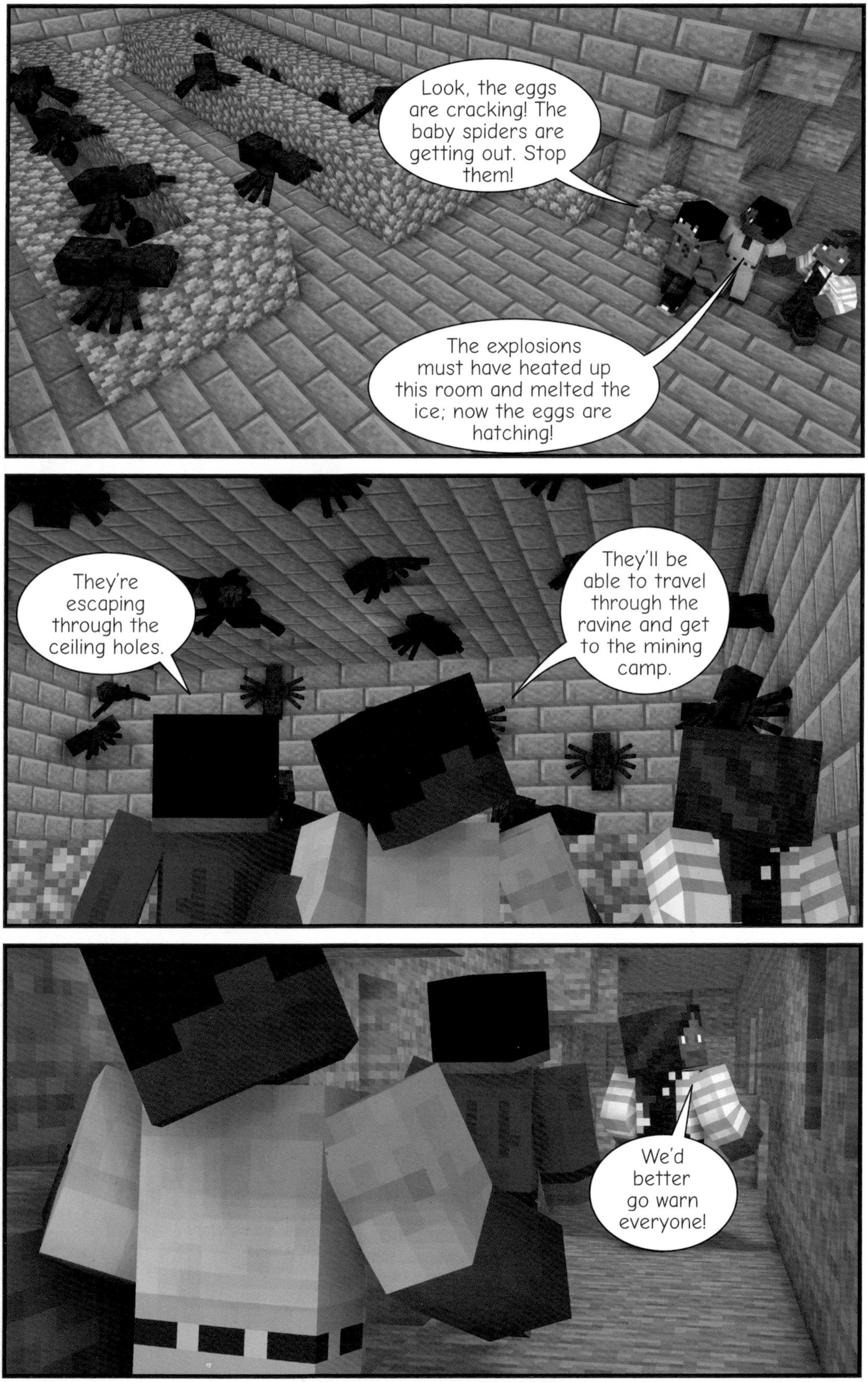
Look, the eggs are cracking! The baby spiders are getting out. Stop them!
The explosions must have heated up this room and melted the ice; now the eggs are hatching!
They're escaping through the ceiling holes.
They'll be able to travel through the ravine and get to the mining camp.
We'd better go warn everyone!

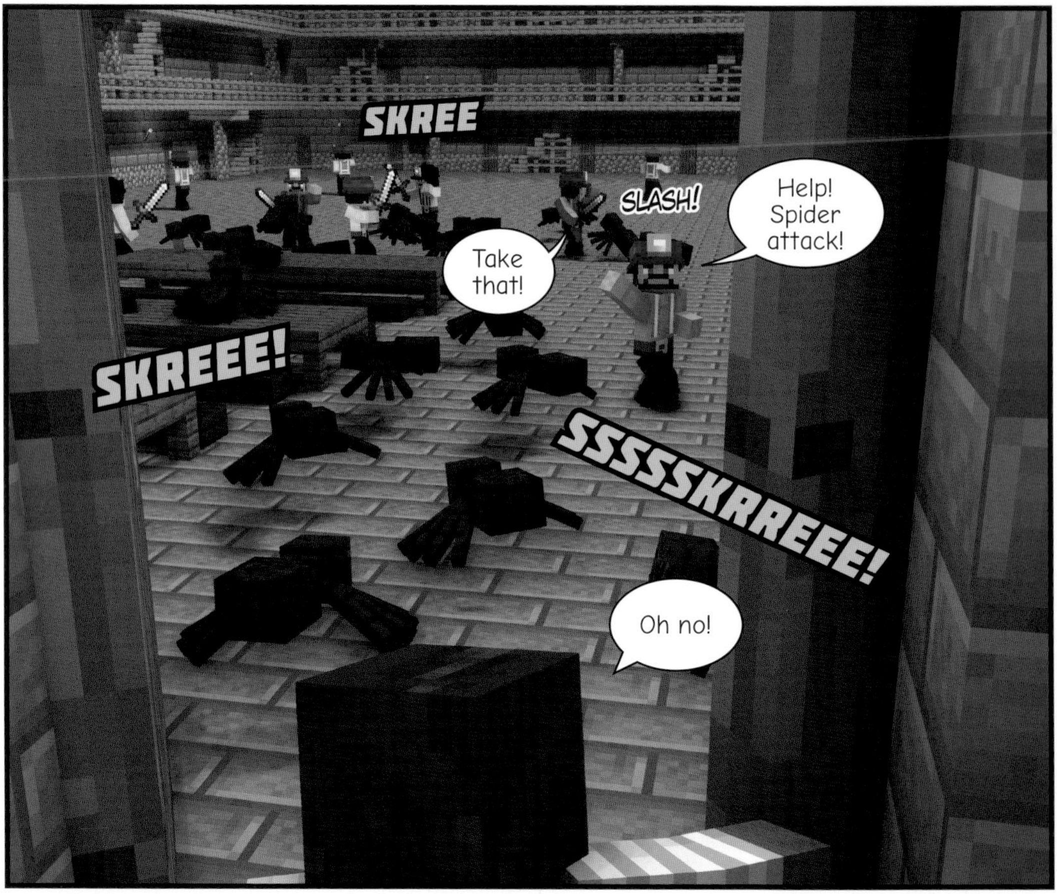
SKREE
Take that!
SLASH!
Help! Spider attack!
SKREEE!
SSSSSKRREEEE!
Oh no!

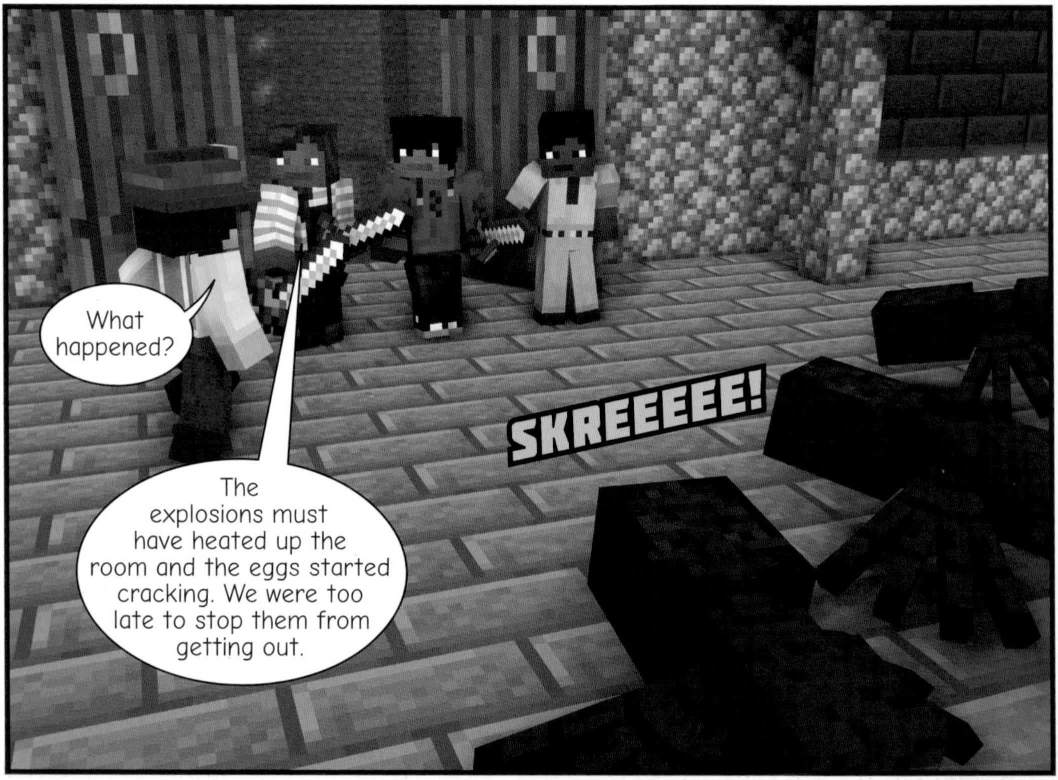
What happened?
The explosions must have heated up the room and the eggs started cracking. We were too late to stop them from getting out.
SKREEEEE!

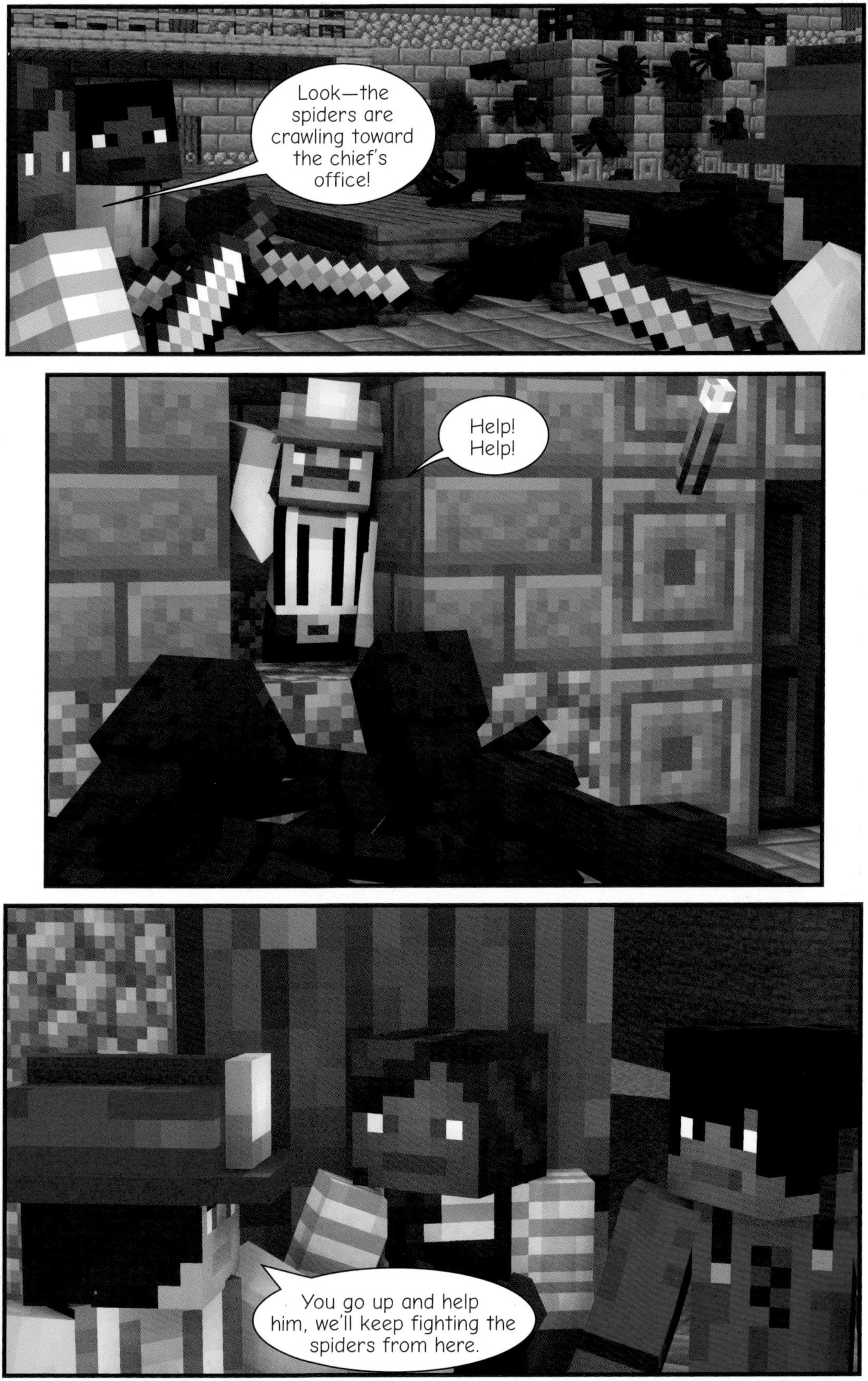
Look—the spiders are crawling toward the chief's office!
Help! Help!
You go up and help him, we'll keep fighting the spiders from here.

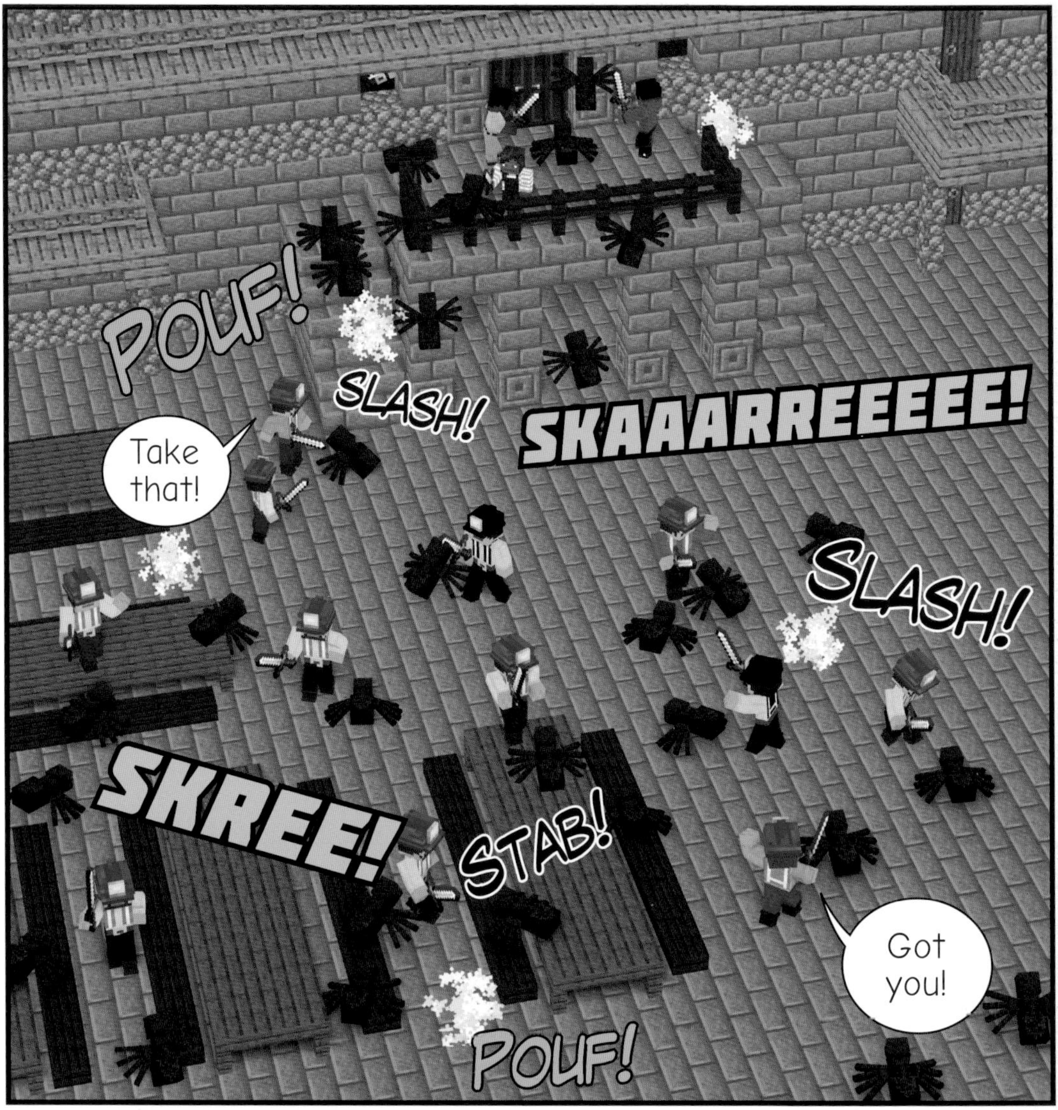
POUF!
SLASH!
SKAAARREEEEE!
Take that!
SLASH!
SKREE!
STAB!
Got you!
POUF!

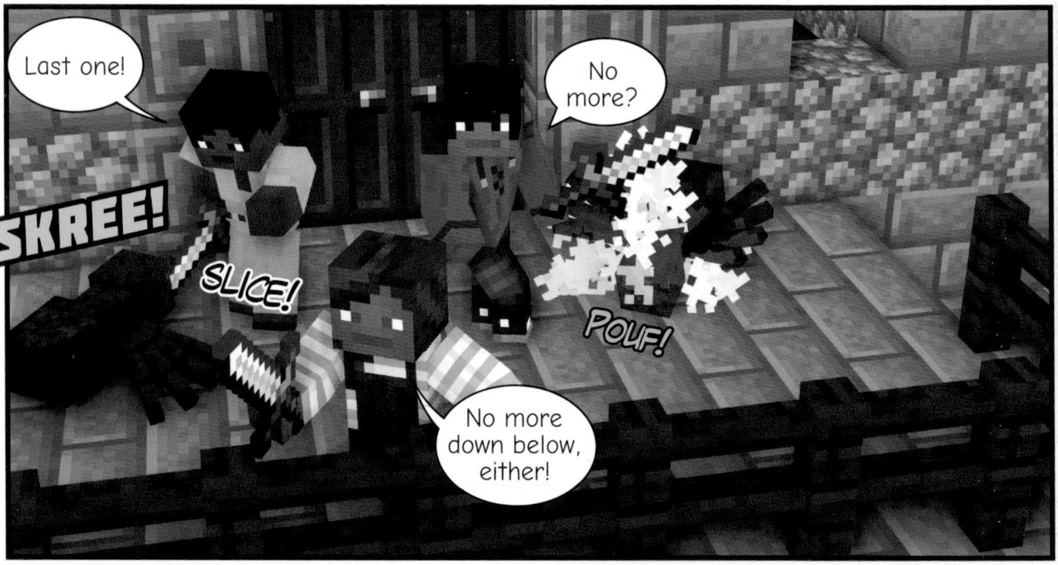
Last one!
No more?
SKREE!
SLICE!
POUF!
No more down below, either!

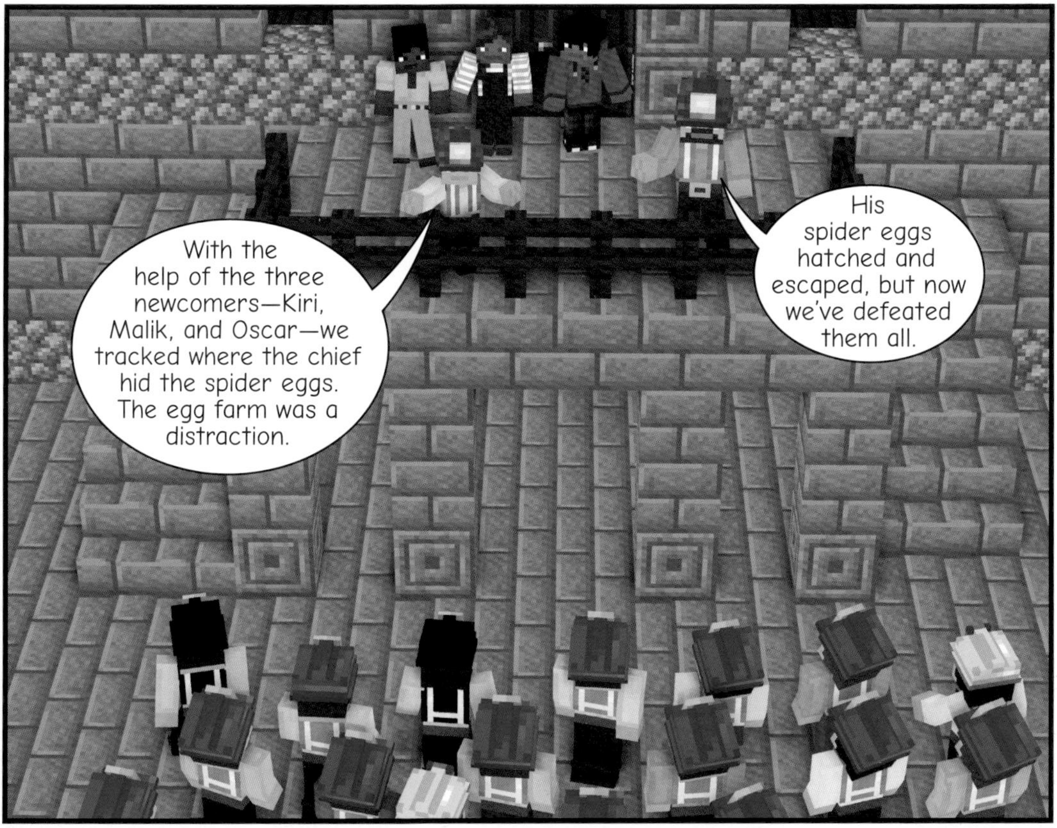
With the help of the three newcomers—Kiri, Malik, and Oscar—we tracked where the chief hid the spider eggs. The egg farm was a distraction.
His spider eggs hatched and escaped, but now we've defeated them all.

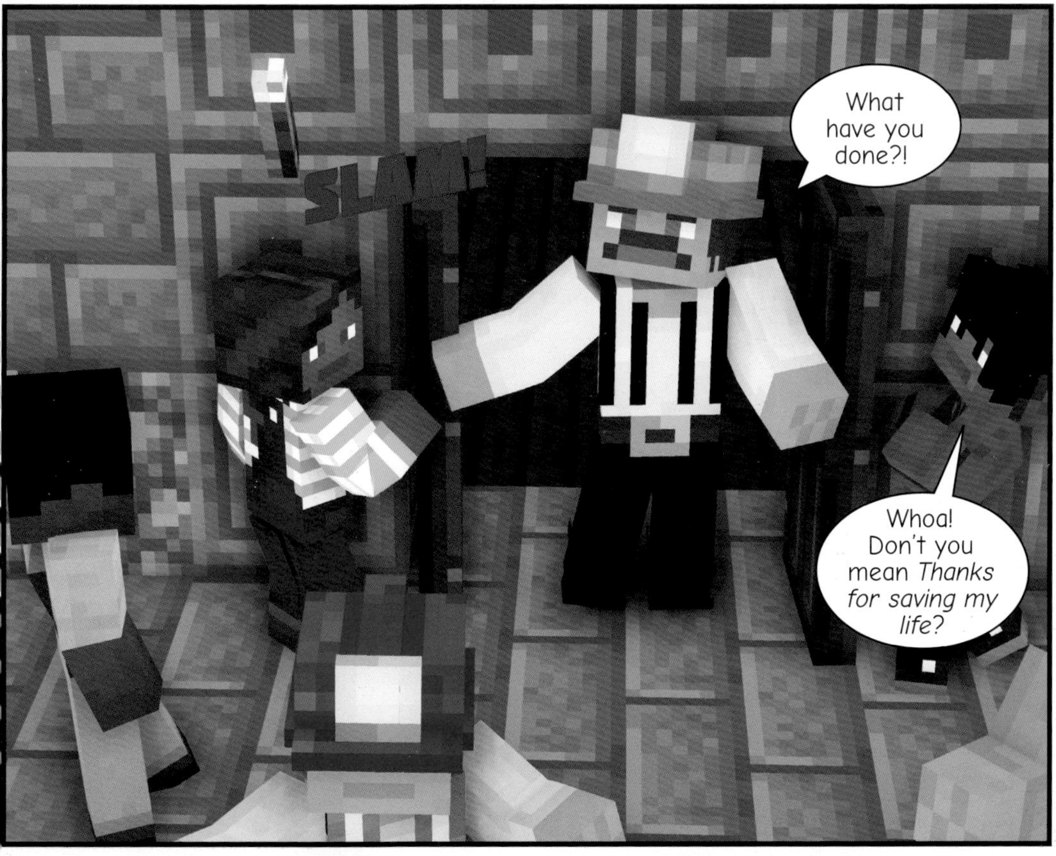
SLAM!
What have you done?!
Whoa! Don't you mean *Thanks for saving my life?*

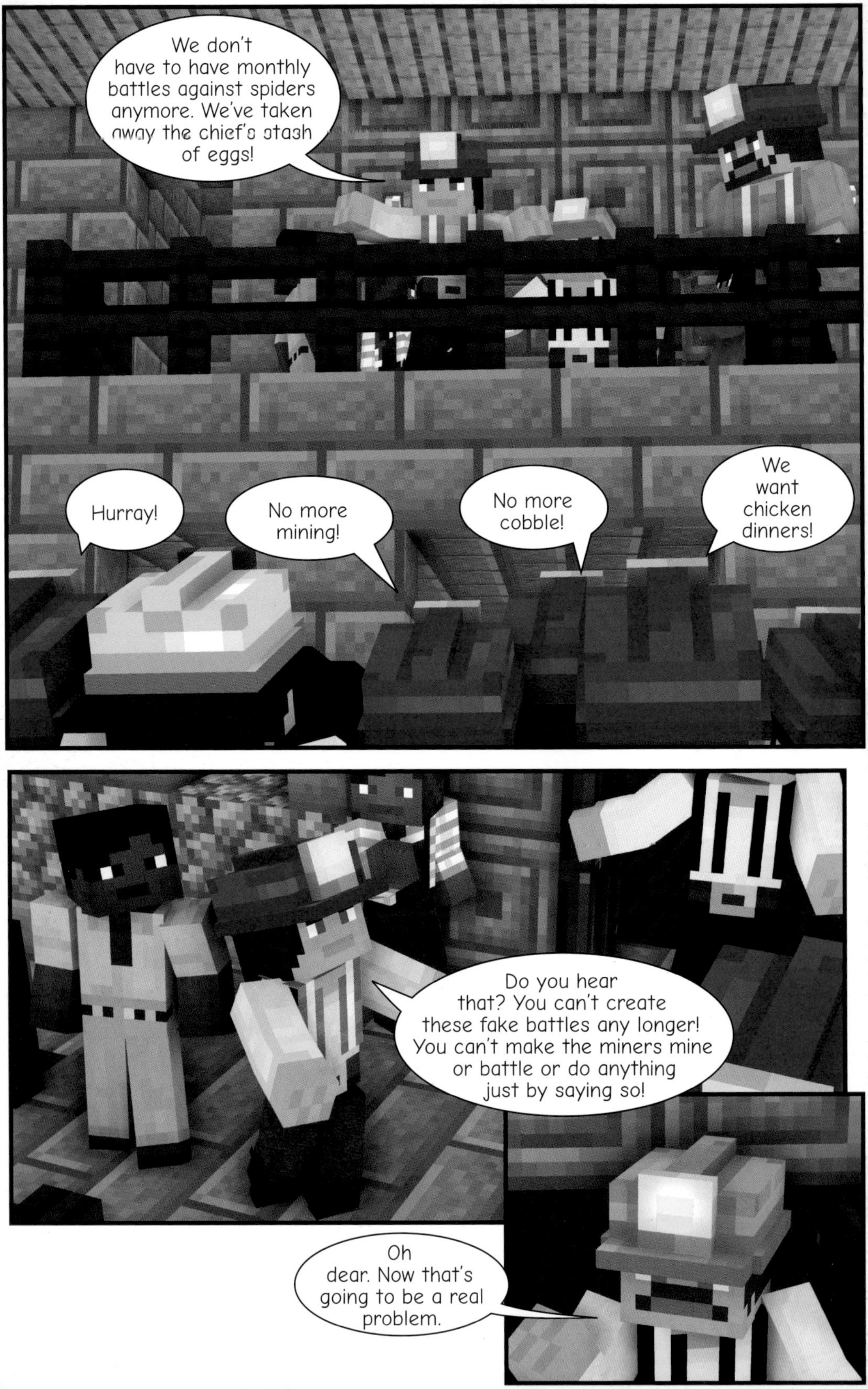
We don't have to have monthly battles against spiders anymore. We've taken away the chief's stash of eggs!
Hurray!
No more mining!
No more cobble!
We want chicken dinners!
Do you hear that? You can't create these fake battles any longer! You can't make the miners mine or battle or do anything just by saying so!
Oh dear. Now that's going to be a real problem.

Chapter 10

The Menace

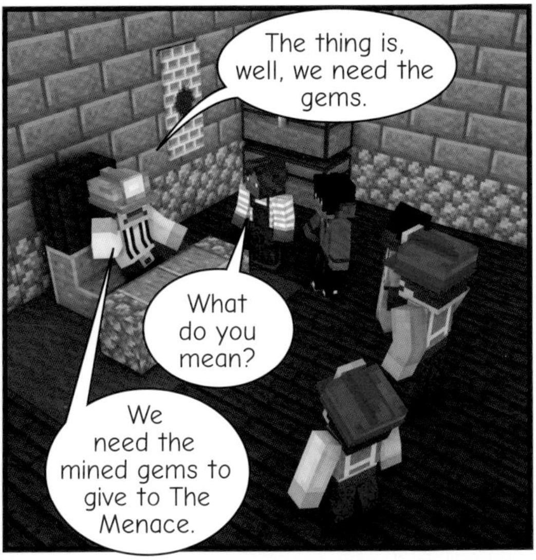
The thing is, well, we need the gems.
What do you mean?
We need the mined gems to give to The Menace.

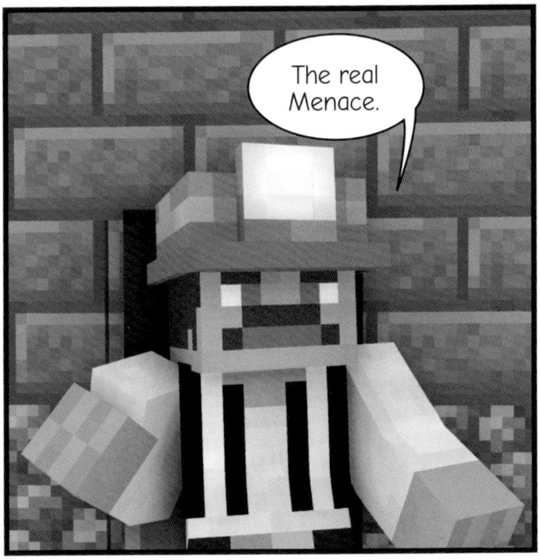
The real Menace.

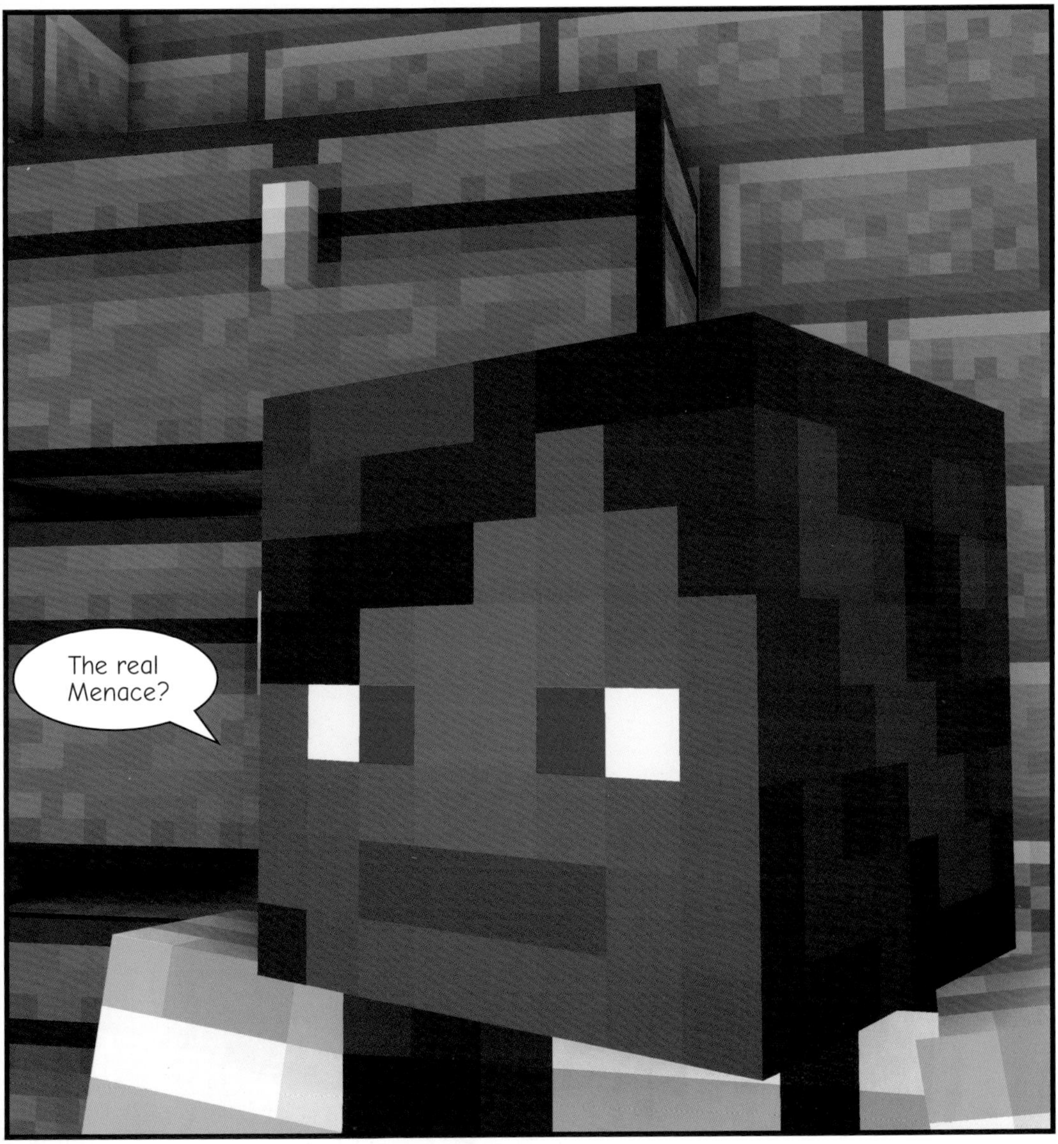
The real Menace?

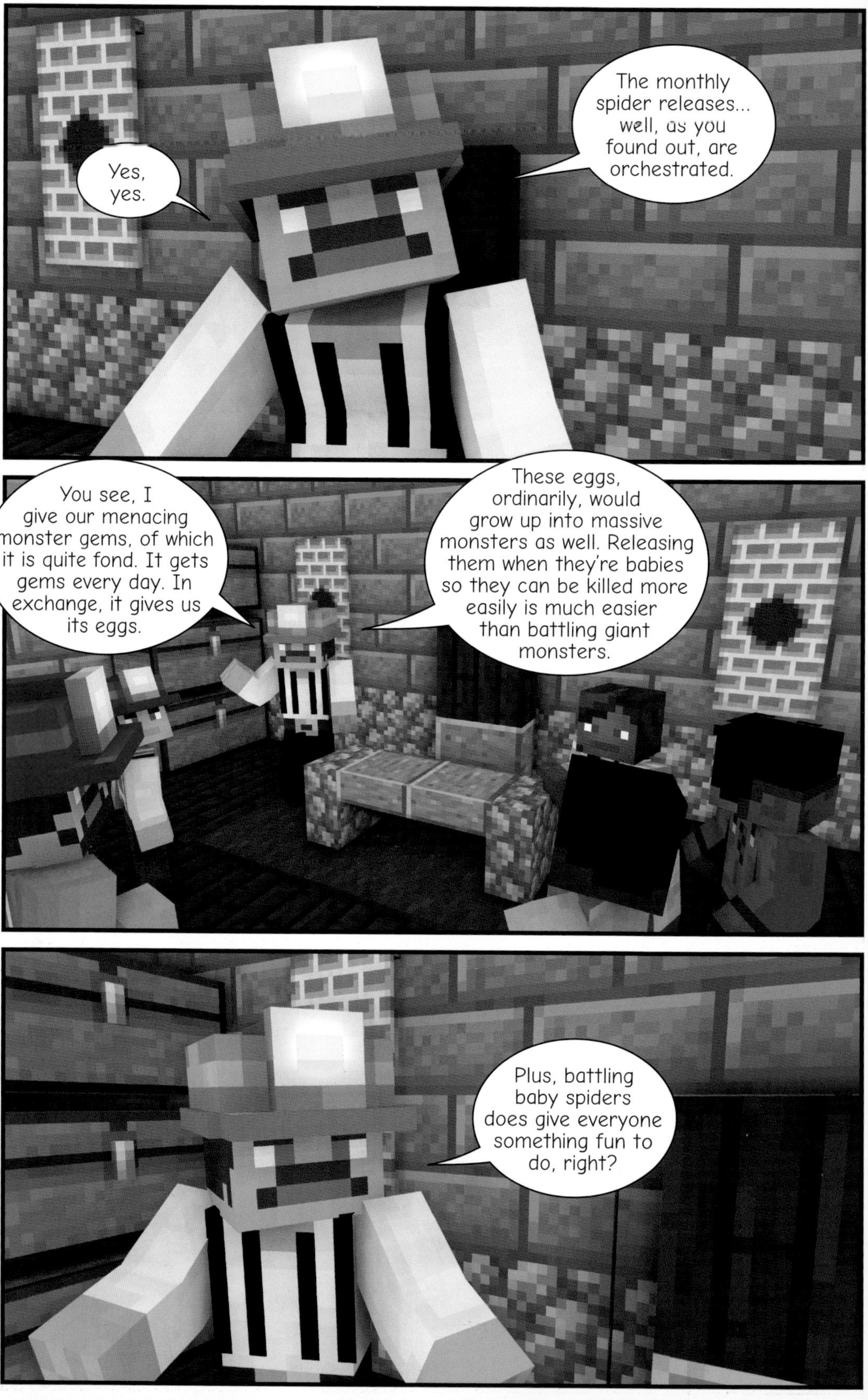
Yes, yes.
The monthly spider releases... well, as you found out, are orchestrated.
You see, I give our menacing monster gems, of which it is quite fond. It gets gems every day. In exchange, it gives us its eggs.
These eggs, ordinarily, would grow up into massive monsters as well. Releasing them when they're babies so they can be killed more easily is much easier than battling giant monsters.
Plus, battling baby spiders does give everyone something fun to do, right?

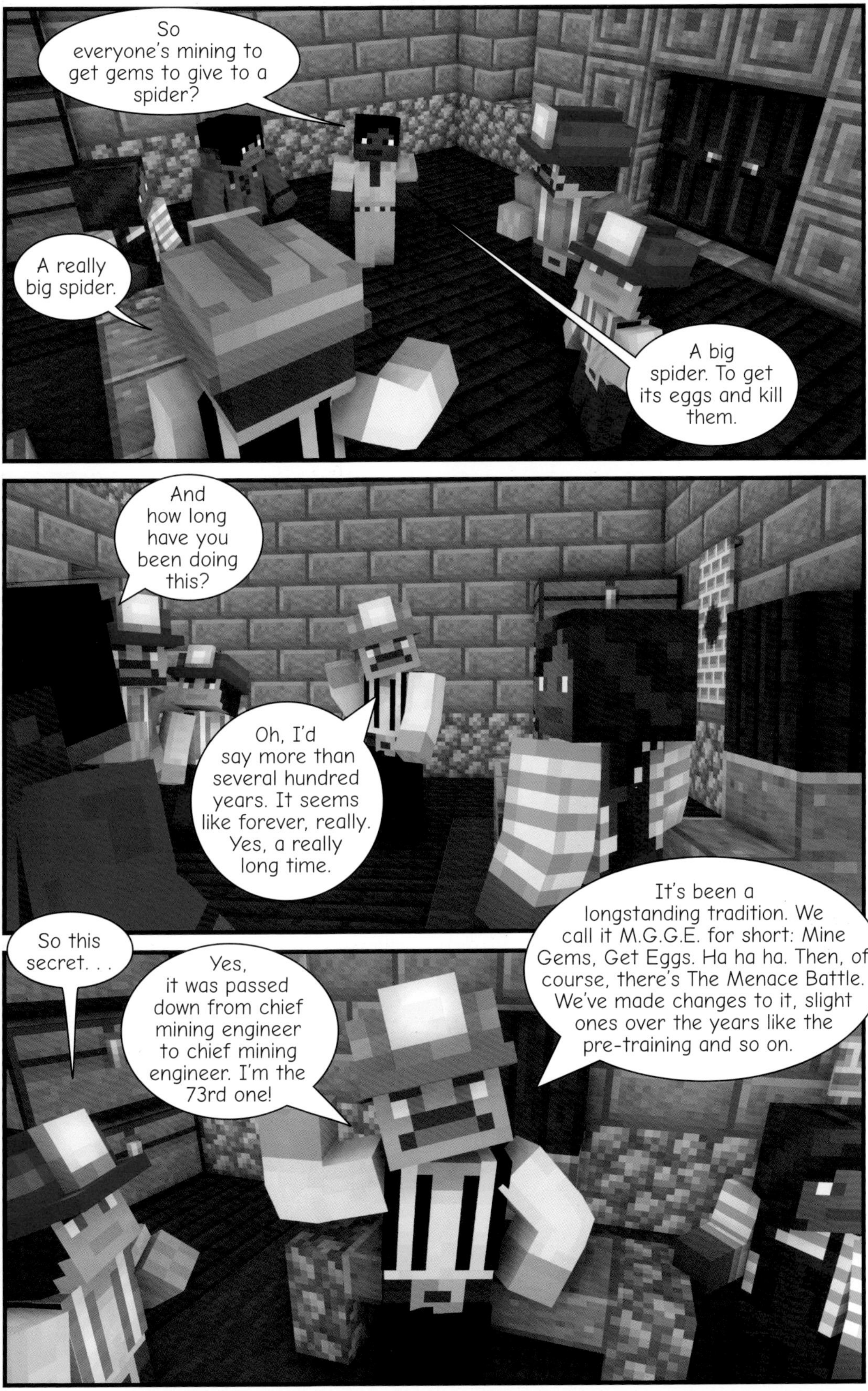
So everyone's mining to get gems to give to a spider?
A really big spider.
A big spider. To get its eggs and kill them.
And how long have you been doing this?
Oh, I'd say more than several hundred years. It seems like forever, really. Yes, a really long time.
It's been a longstanding tradition. We call it M.G.G.E. for short: Mine Gems, Get Eggs. Ha ha ha. Then, of course, there's The Menace Battle. We've made changes to it, slight ones over the years like the pre-training and so on.
So this secret. . .
Yes, it was passed down from chief mining engineer to chief mining engineer. I'm the 73rd one!

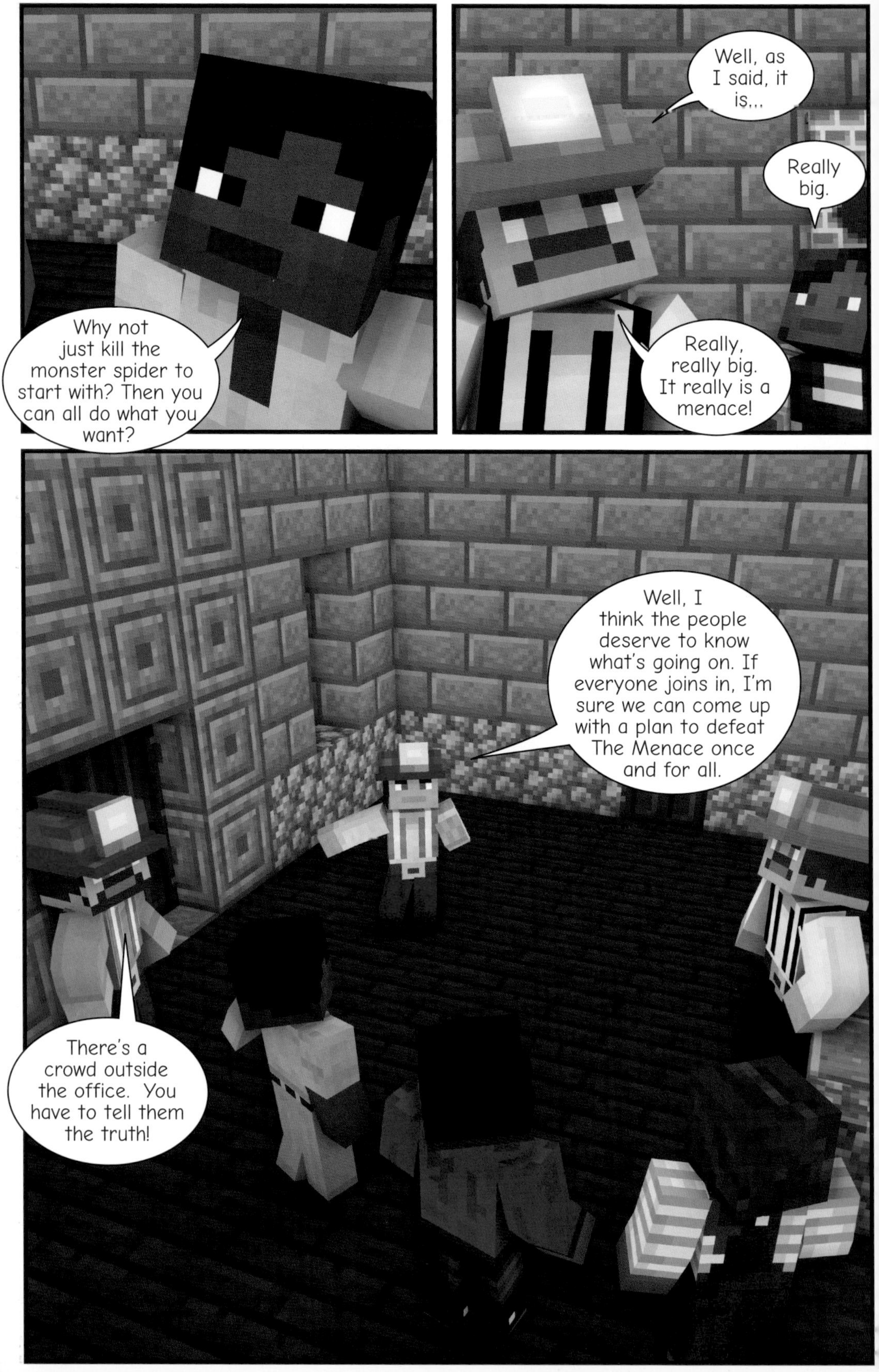

Why not just kill the monster spider to start with? Then you can all do what you want?
Well, as I said, it is...
Really big.
Really, really big. It really is a menace!
Well, I think the people deserve to know what's going on. If everyone joins in, I'm sure we can come up with a plan to defeat The Menace once and for all.
There's a crowd outside the office. You have to tell them the truth!

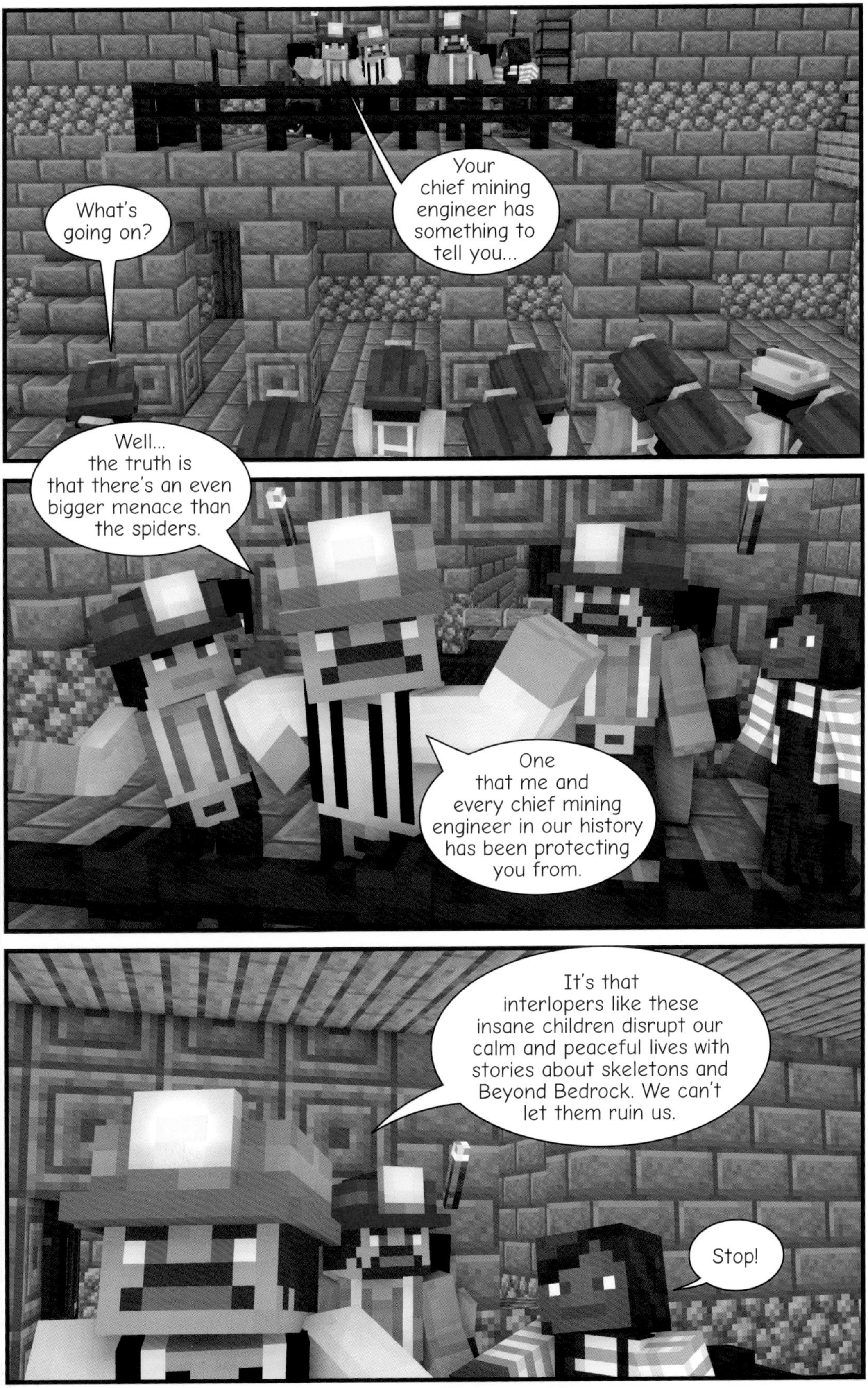
What's going on?
Your chief mining engineer has something to tell you...
Well... the truth is that there's an even bigger menace than the spiders.
One that me and every chief mining engineer in our history has been protecting you from.
It's that interlopers like these insane children disrupt our calm and peaceful lives with stories about skeletons and Beyond Bedrock. We can't let them ruin us.
Stop!

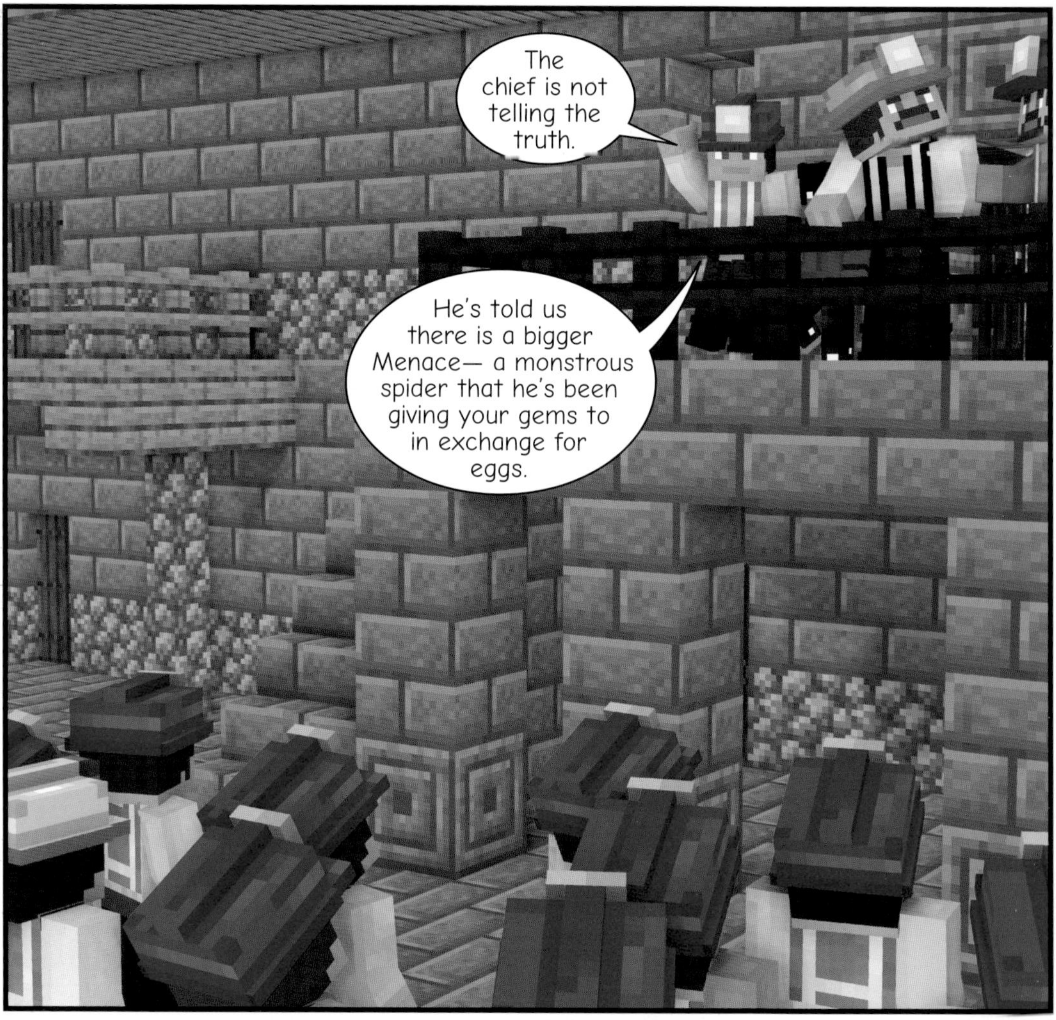
The chief is not telling the truth.
He's told us there is a bigger Menace— a monstrous spider that he's been giving your gems to in exchange for eggs.

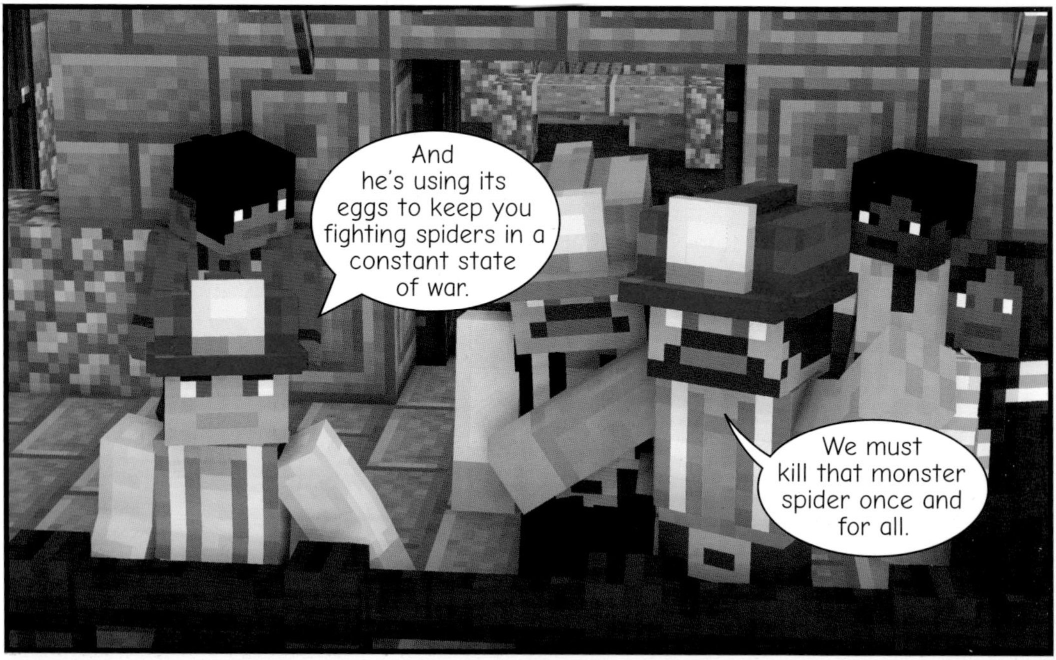
And he's using its eggs to keep you fighting spiders in a constant state of war.
We must kill that monster spider once and for all.

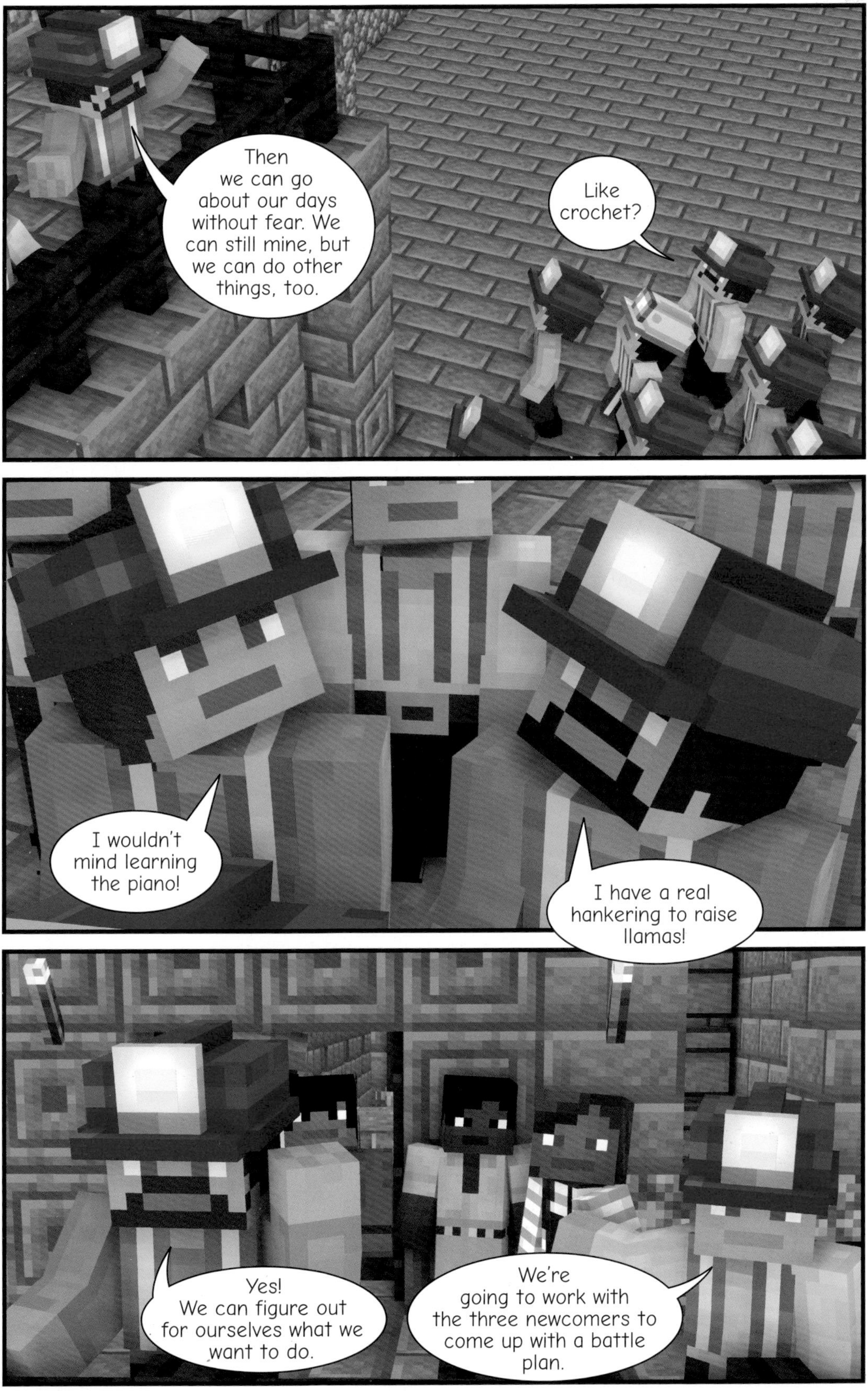
Then we can go about our days without fear. We can still mine, but we can do other things, too.
Like crochet?
I wouldn't mind learning the piano!
I have a real hankering to raise llamas!
Yes! We can figure out for ourselves what we want to do.
We're going to work with the three newcomers to come up with a battle plan.

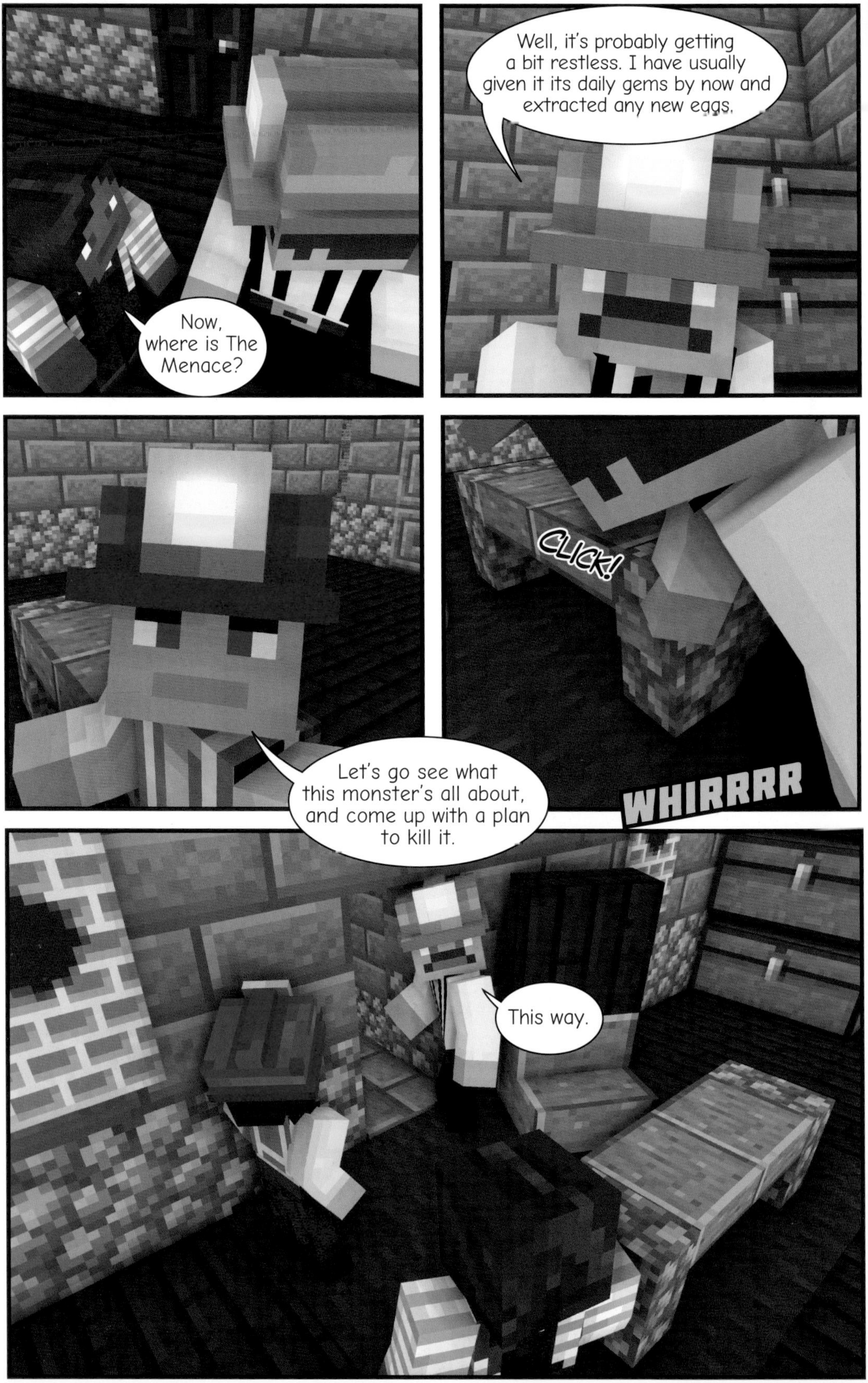
Now, where is The Menace?
Well, it's probably getting a bit restless. I have usually given it its daily gems by now and extracted any new eggs.
CLICK!
Let's go see what this monster's all about, and come up with a plan to kill it.
WHIRRRR
This way.

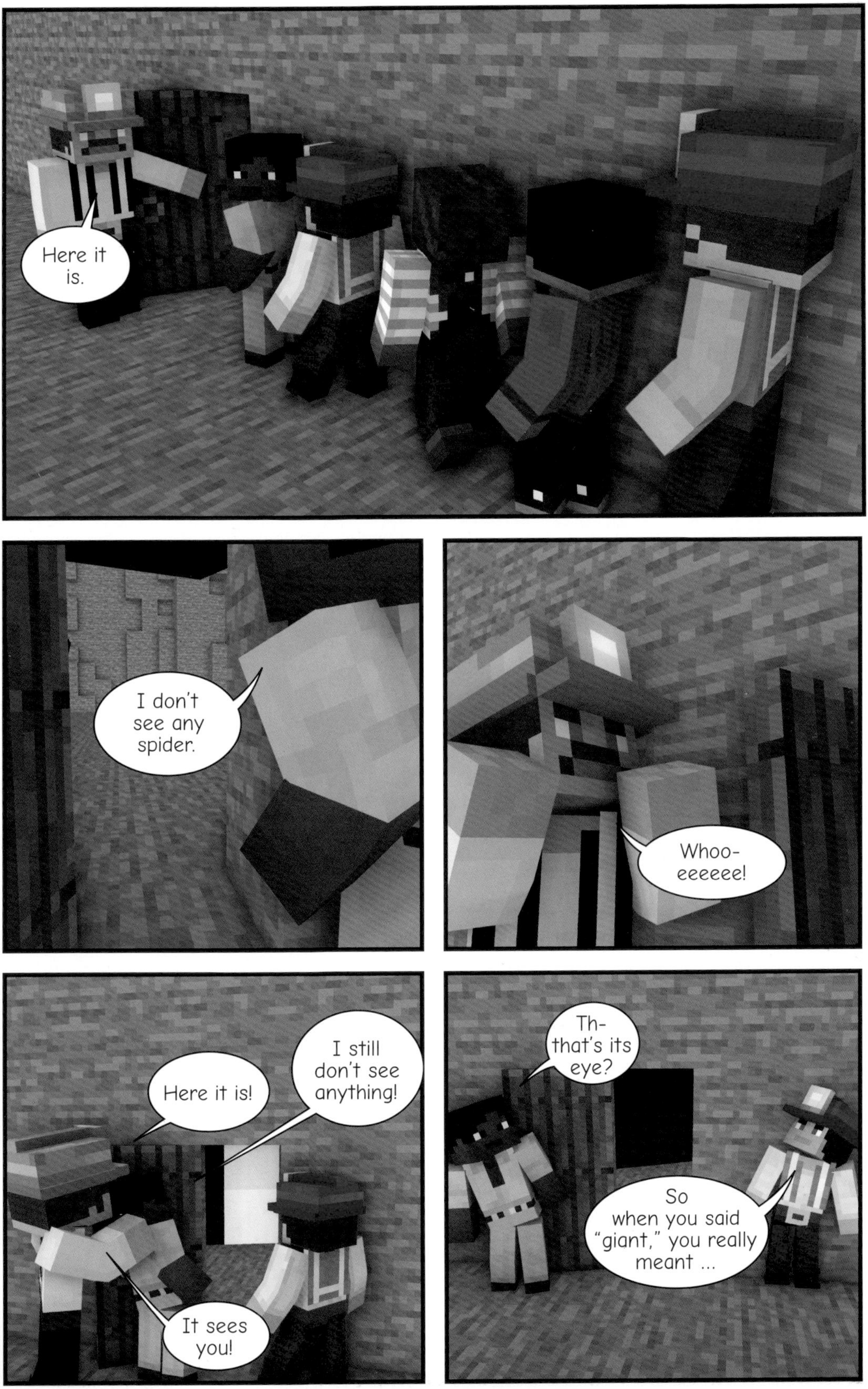
Here it is.
I don't see any spider.
Whoo-eeeeee!
Here it is!
I still don't see anything!
It sees you!
Th-that's its eye?
So when you said "giant," you really meant ...

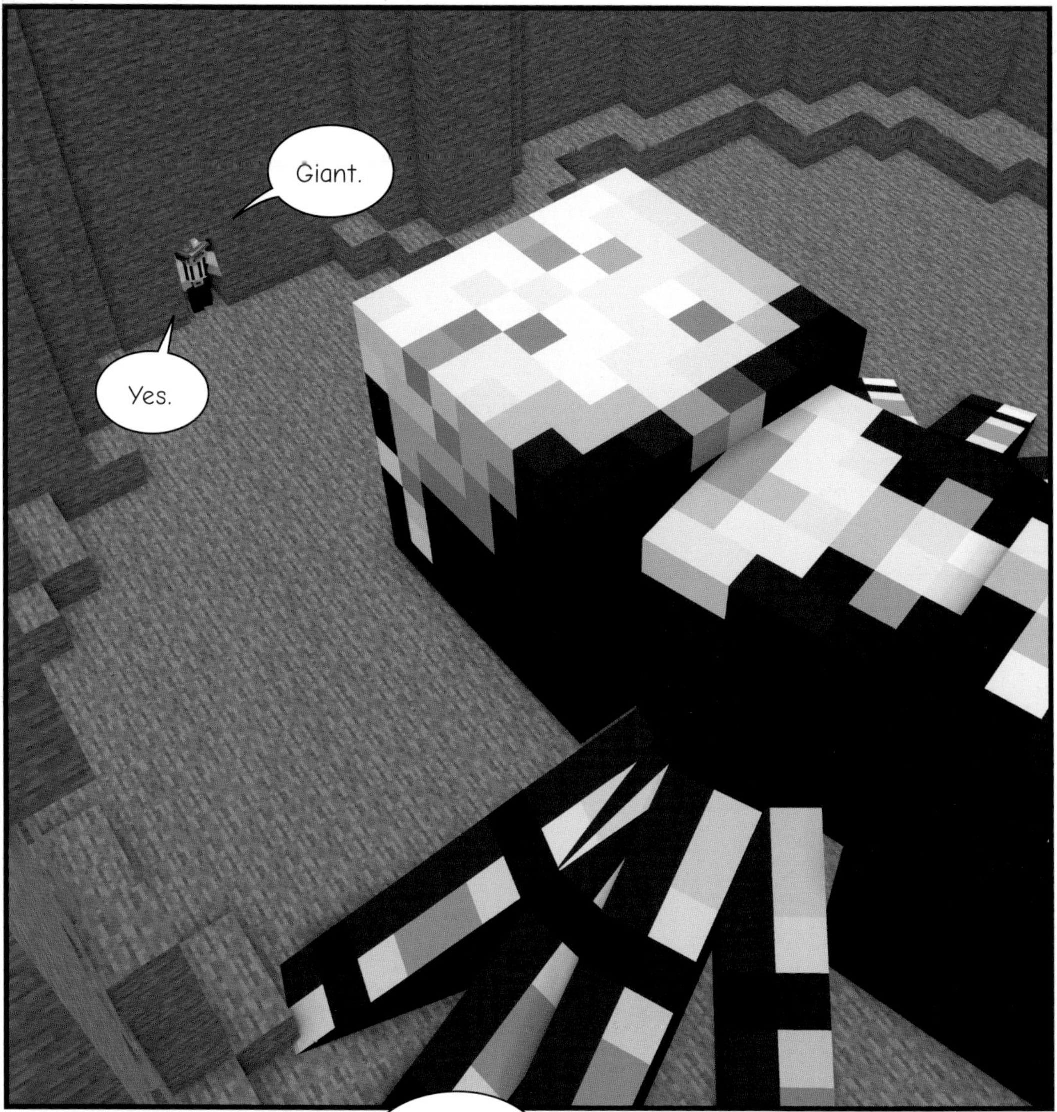
Giant.
Yes.

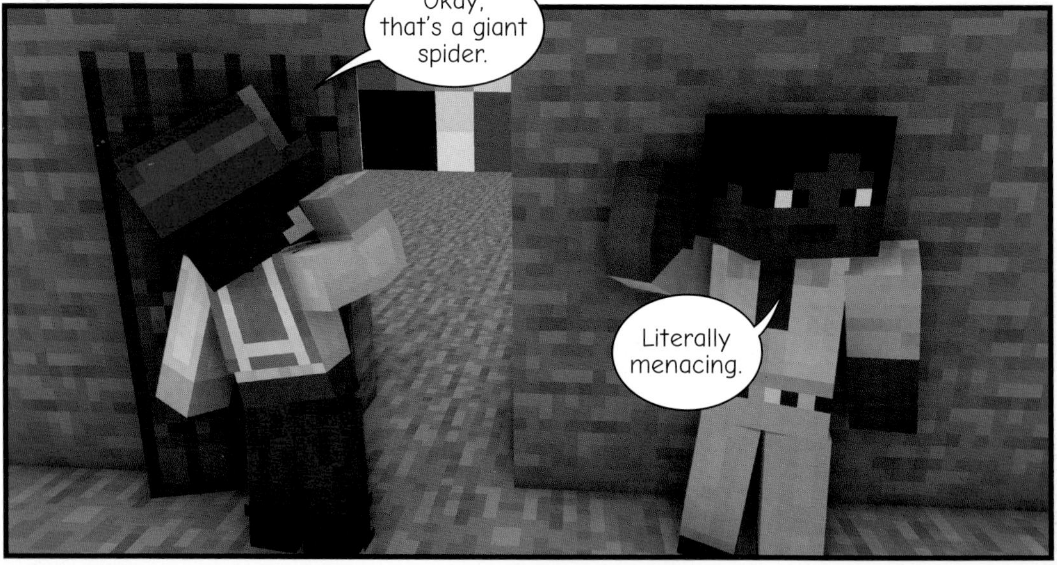
Okay, that's a giant spider.
Literally menacing.

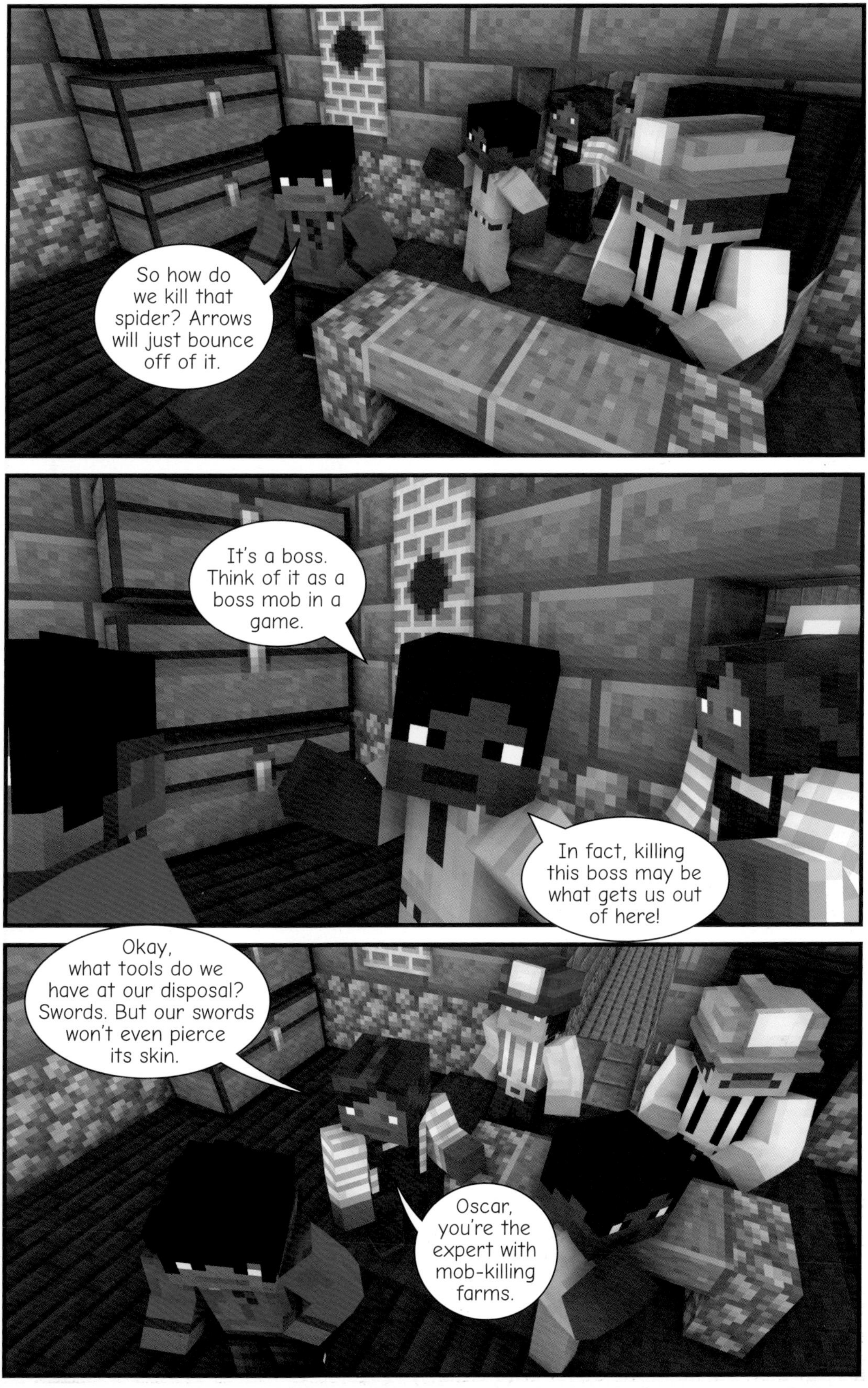
So how do we kill that spider? Arrows will just bounce off of it.
It's a boss. Think of it as a boss mob in a game.
In fact, killing this boss may be what gets us out of here!
Okay, what tools do we have at our disposal? Swords. But our swords won't even pierce its skin.
Oscar, you're the expert with mob-killing farms.

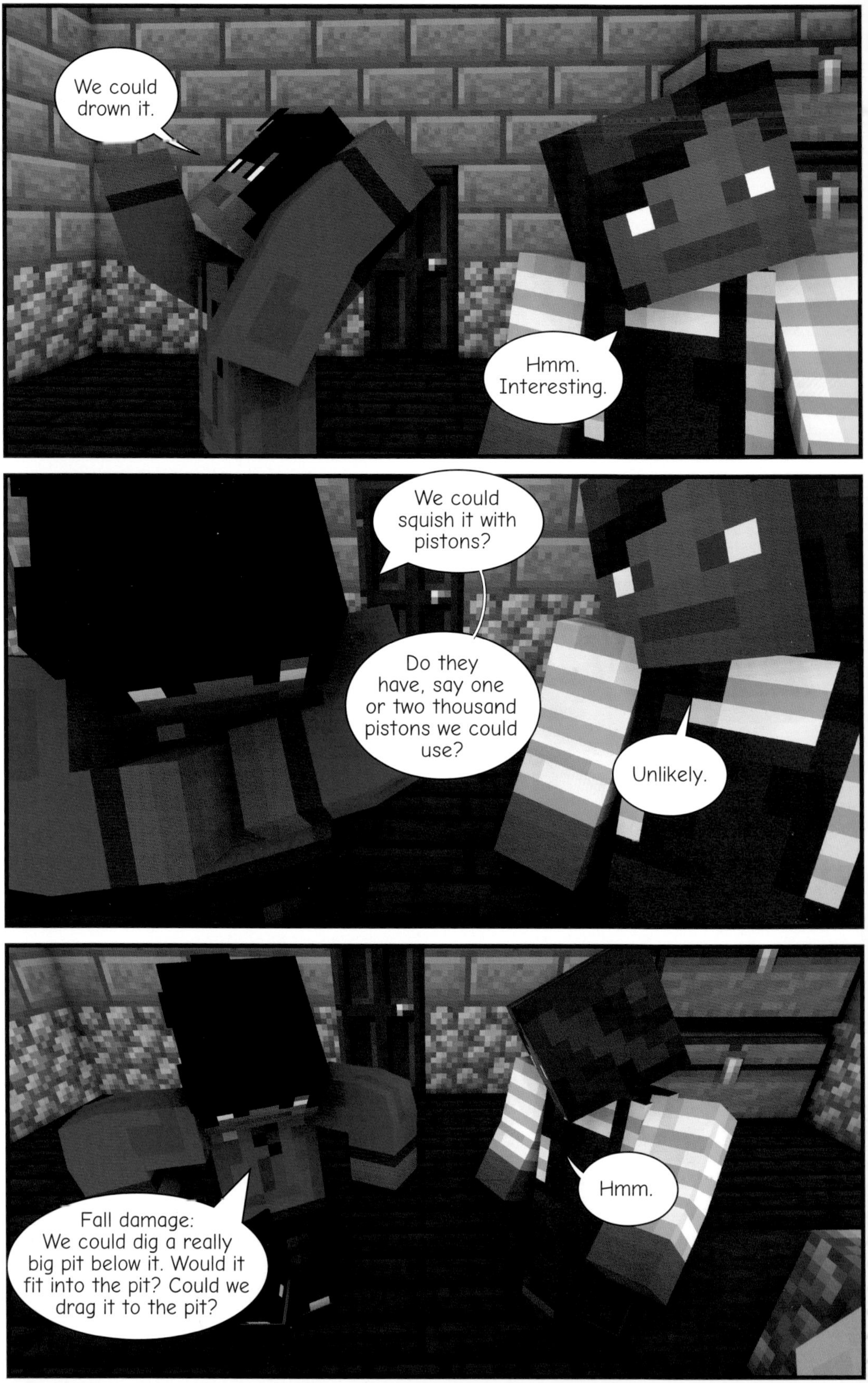
We could drown it.
Hmm. Interesting.
We could squish it with pistons?
Do they have, say one or two thousand pistons we could use?
Unlikely.
Fall damage: We could dig a really big pit below it. Would it fit into the pit? Could we drag it to the pit?
Hmm.

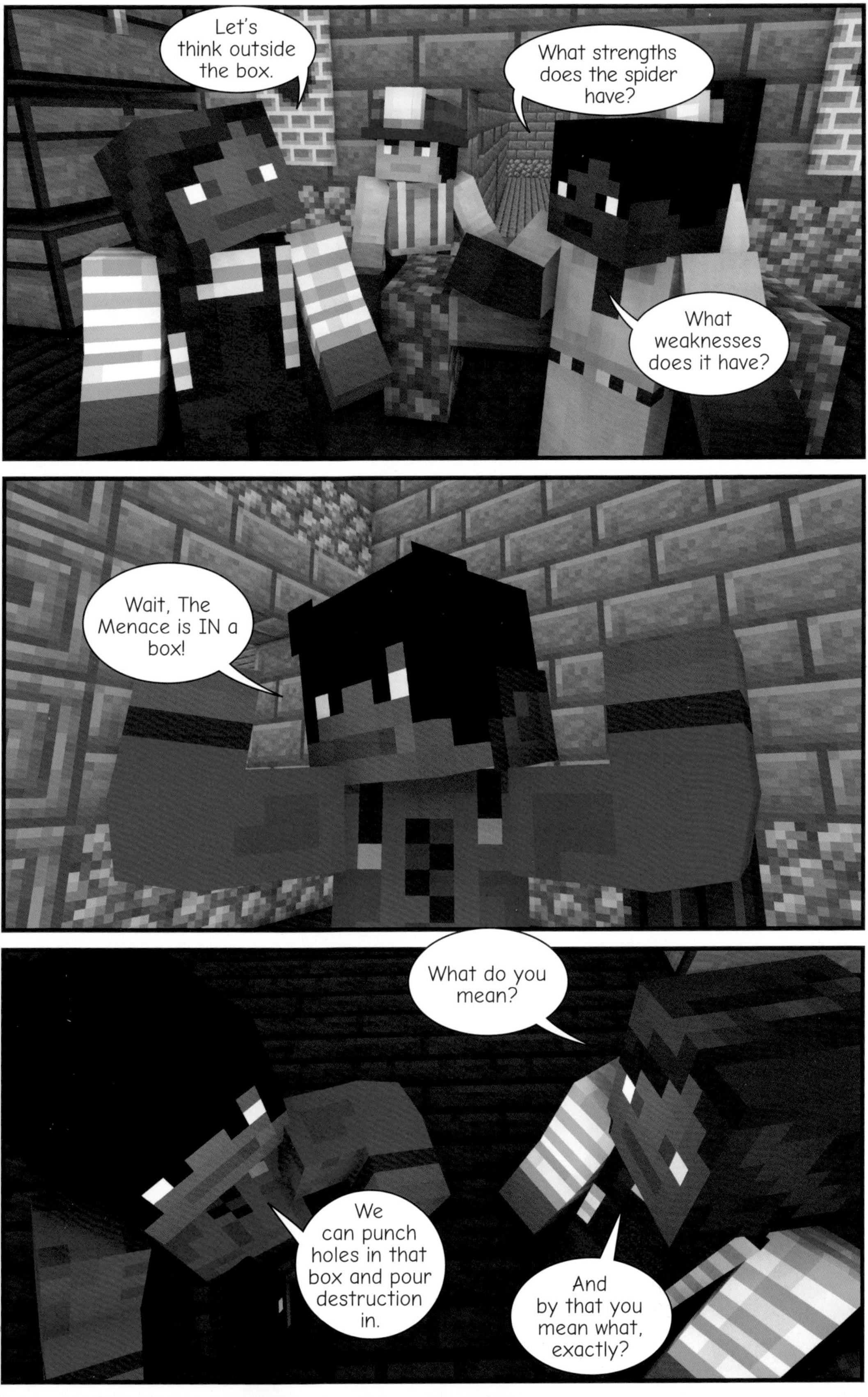
Let's think outside the box.
What strengths does the spider have?
What weaknesses does it have?
Wait, The Menace is IN a box!
What do you mean?
We can punch holes in that box and pour destruction in.
And by that you mean what, exactly?

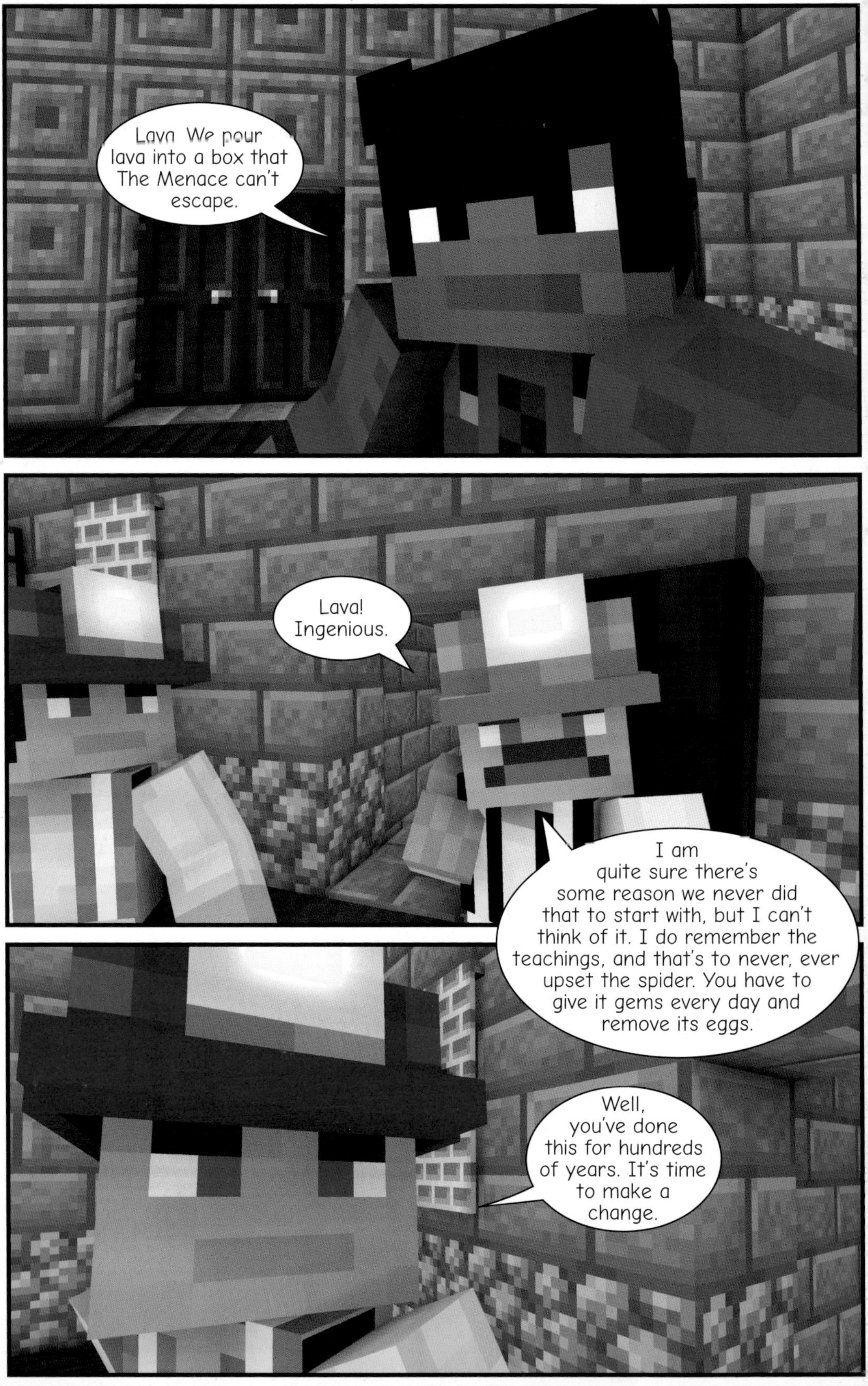
Lava We pour lava into a box that The Menace can't escape.
Lava! Ingenious.
I am quite sure there's some reason we never did that to start with, but I can't think of it. I do remember the teachings, and that's to never, ever upset the spider. You have to give it gems every day and remove its eggs.
Well, you've done this for hundreds of years. It's time to make a change.

Chapter 11

The Ceiling
Is Lava

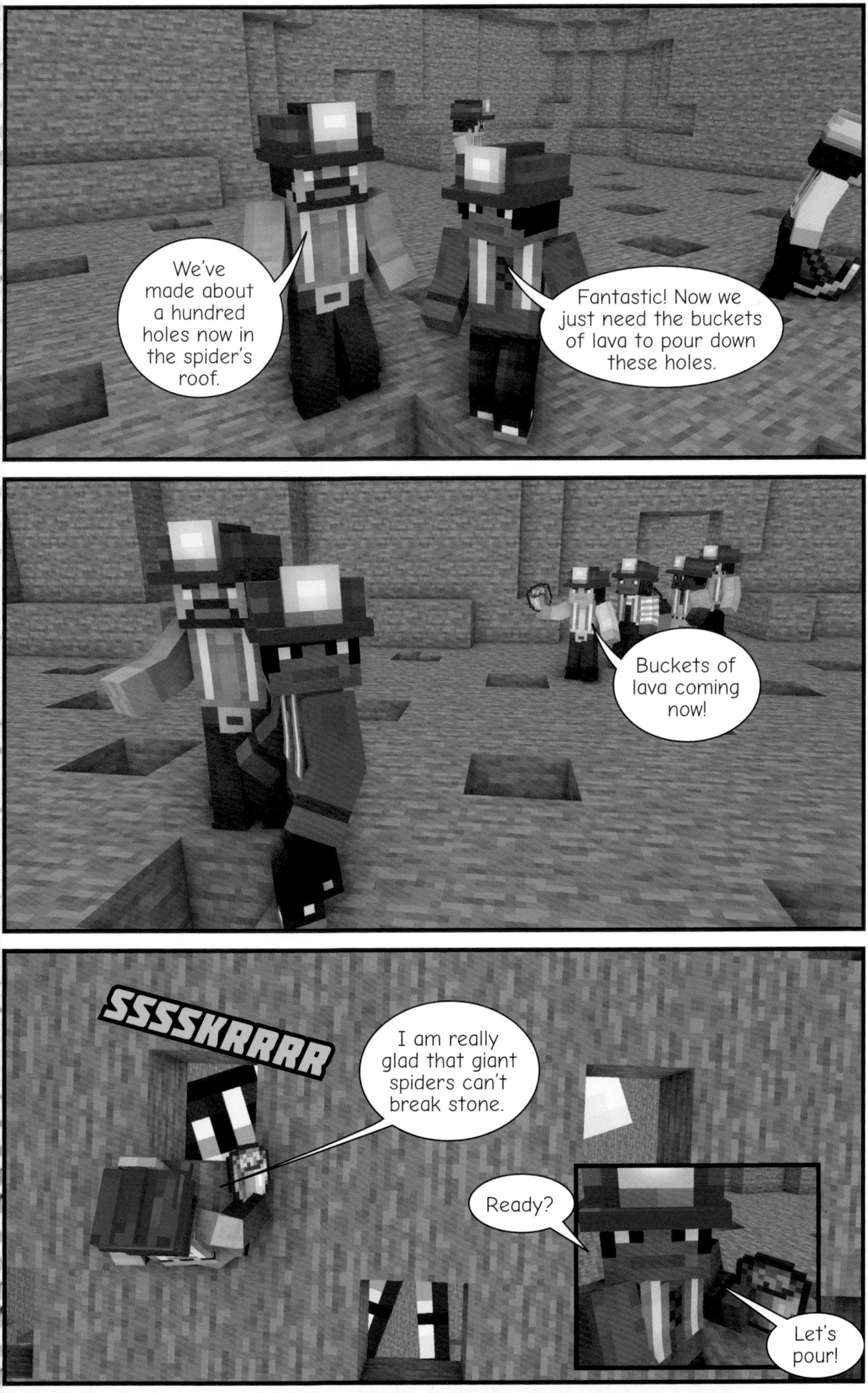
We've made about a hundred holes now in the spider's roof.
Fantastic! Now we just need the buckets of lava to pour down these holes.
Buckets of lava coming now!
SSSSKRRRR
I am really glad that giant spiders can't break stone.
Ready?
Let's pour!

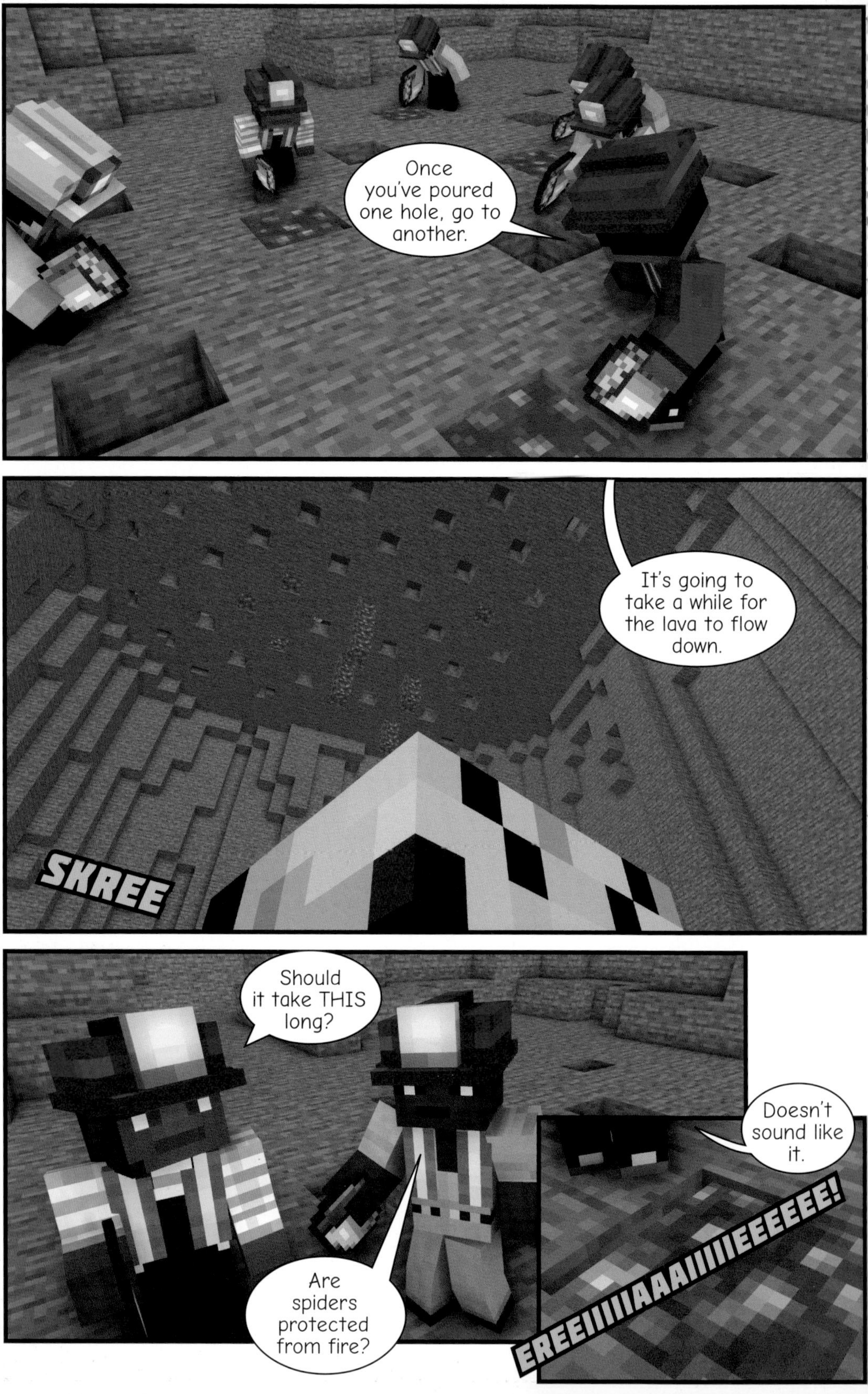
Once you've poured one hole, go to another.
It's going to take a while for the lava to flow down.
SKREE
Should it take THIS long?
Are spiders protected from fire?
Doesn't sound like it.
EREEIIIIIAAAIIIIIEEEEEE!

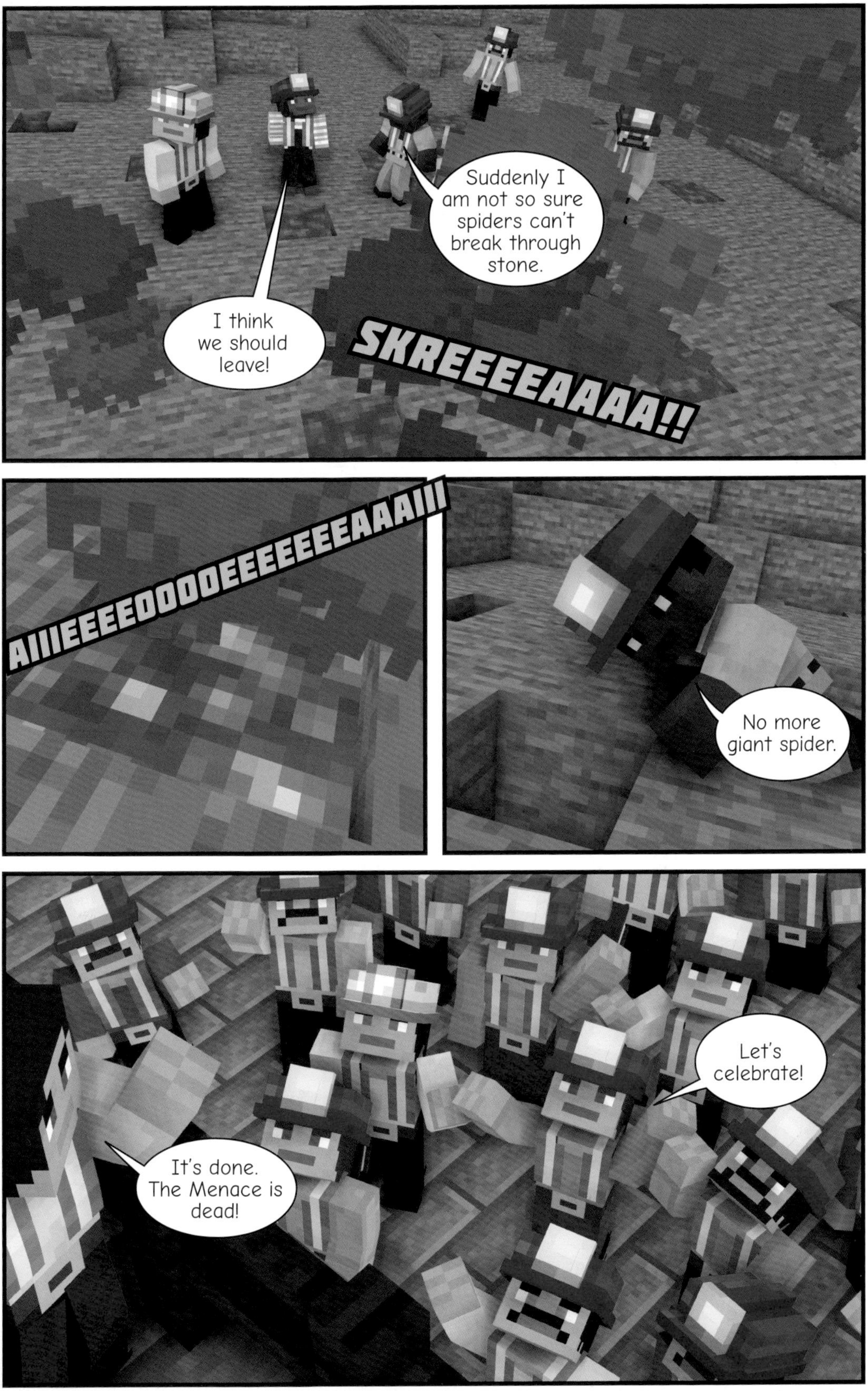
Suddenly I am not so sure spiders can't break through stone.
I think we should leave!
SKREEEEEAAAAA!!
AIIIEEEEOOOOEEEEEEEAAAIII
No more giant spider.
It's done. The Menace is dead!
Let's celebrate!

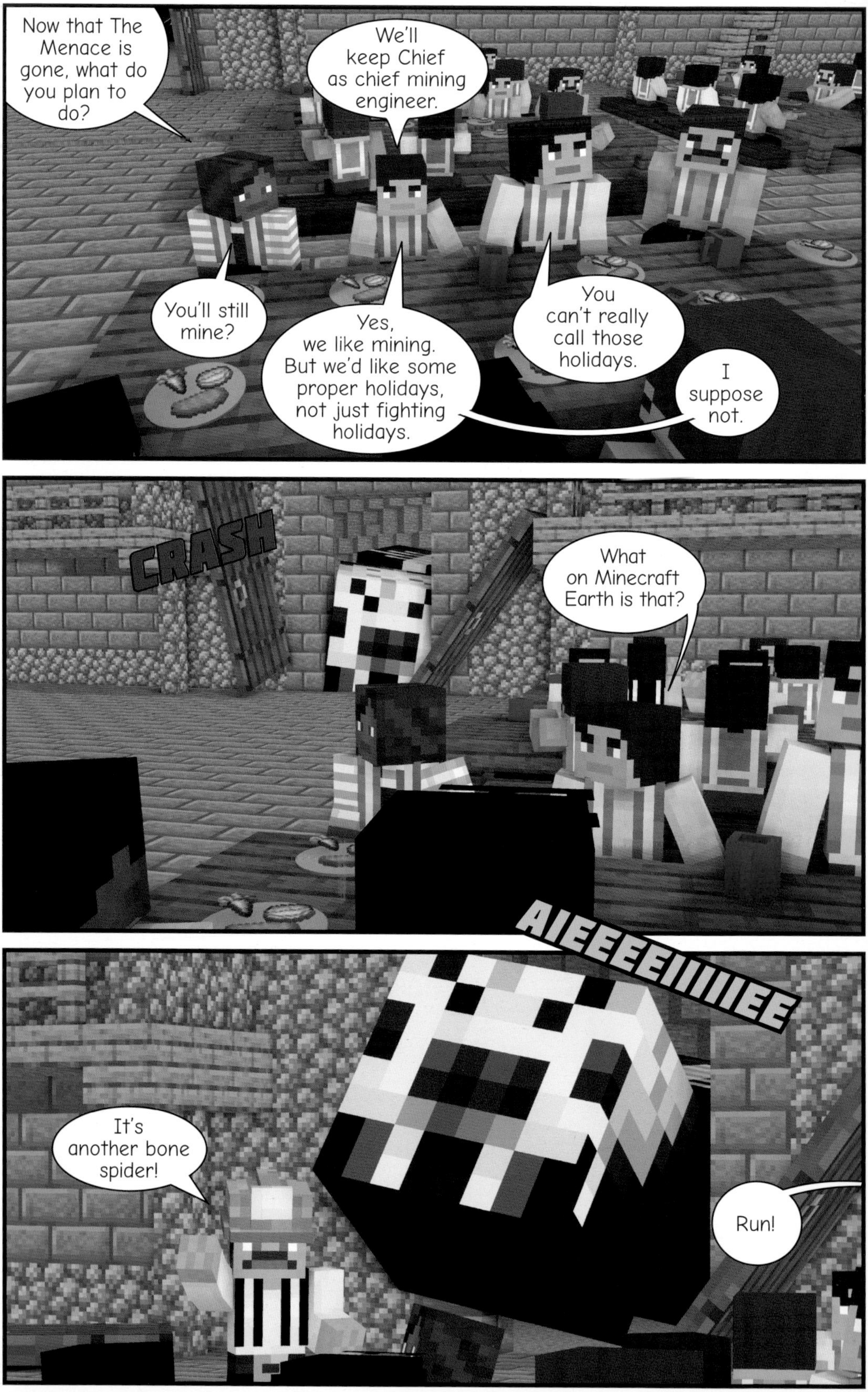
Now that The Menace is gone, what do you plan to do?
We'll keep Chief as chief mining engineer.
You'll still mine?
Yes, we like mining. But we'd like some proper holidays, not just fighting holidays.
You can't really call those holidays.
I suppose not.
CRASH
What on Minecraft Earth is that?
AIEEEEEIIIIIEE
It's another bone spider!
Run!

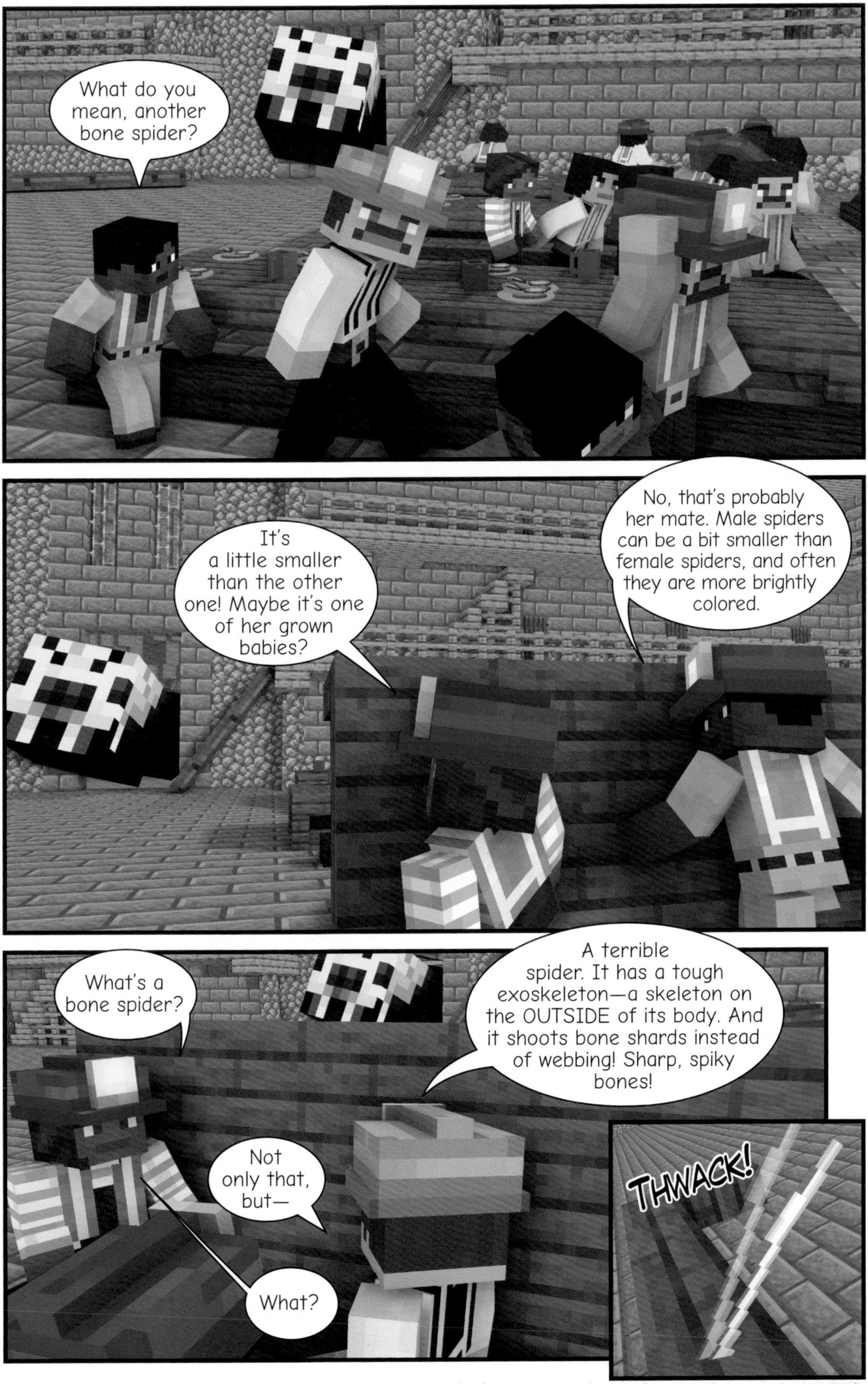
What do you mean, another bone spider?
It's a little smaller than the other one! Maybe it's one of her grown babies?
No, that's probably her mate. Male spiders can be a bit smaller than female spiders, and often they are more brightly colored.
What's a bone spider?
A terrible spider. It has a tough exoskeleton—a skeleton on the OUTSIDE of its body. And it shoots bone shards instead of webbing! Sharp, spiky bones!
Not only that, but—
What?
THWACK!

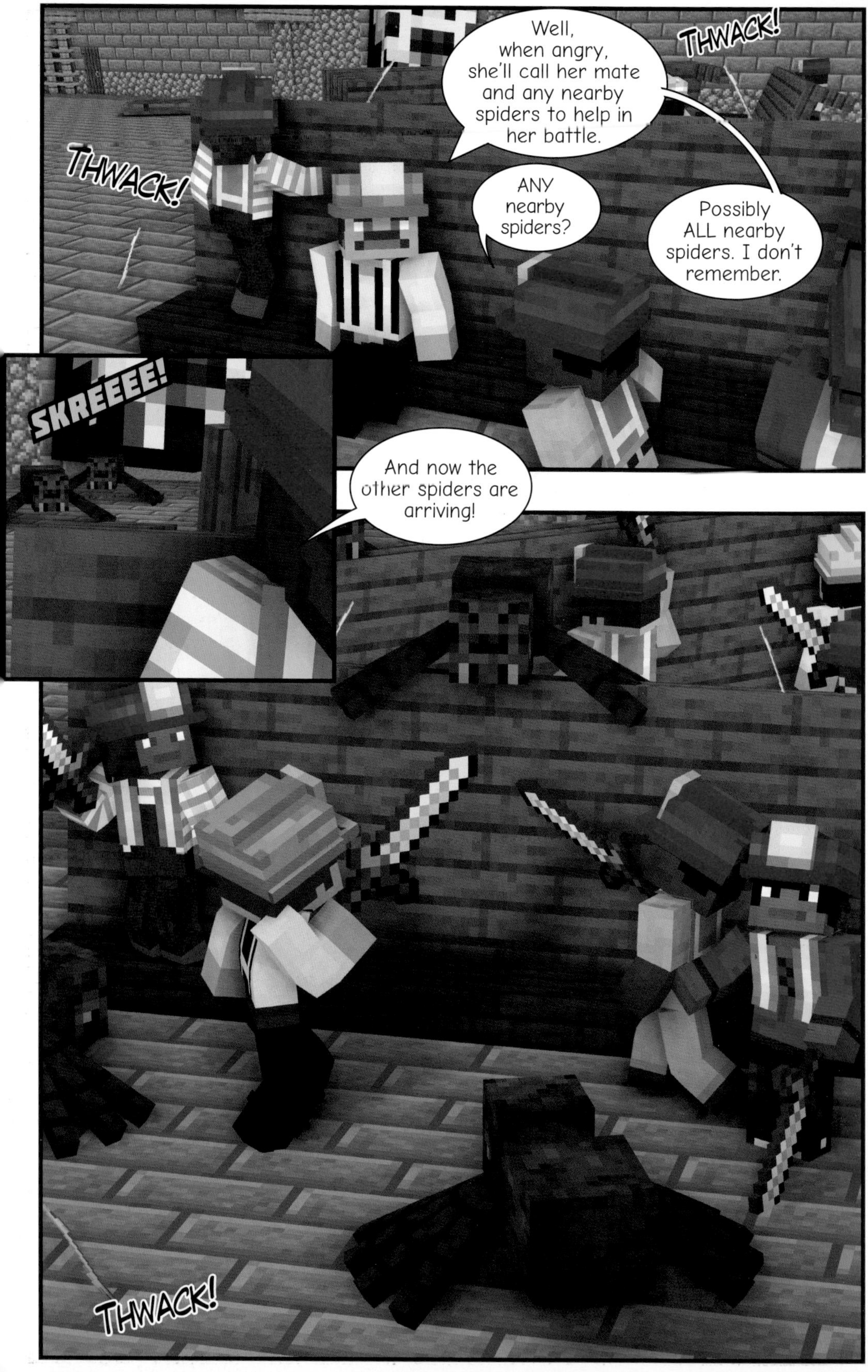
Well, when angry, she'll call her mate and any nearby spiders to help in her battle.
THWACK!
THWACK!
ANY nearby spiders?
Possibly ALL nearby spiders. I don't remember.
SKREEEEE!
And now the other spiders are arriving!
THWACK!

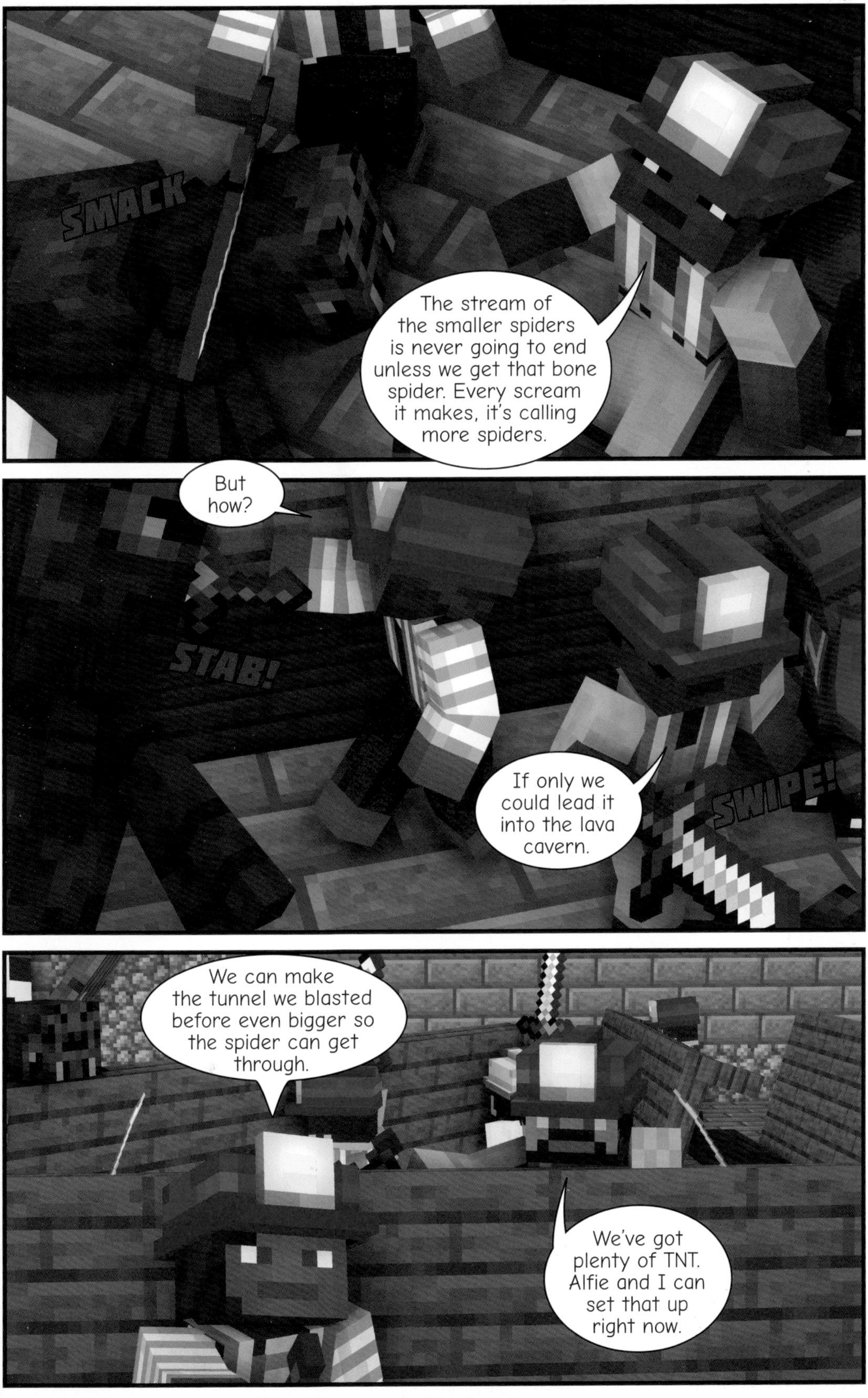
SMACK
The stream of the smaller spiders is never going to end unless we get that bone spider. Every scream it makes, it's calling more spiders.
But how?
STAB!
If only we could lead it into the lava cavern.
SWIPE!
We can make the tunnel we blasted before even bigger so the spider can get through.
We've got plenty of TNT. Alfie and I can set that up right now.

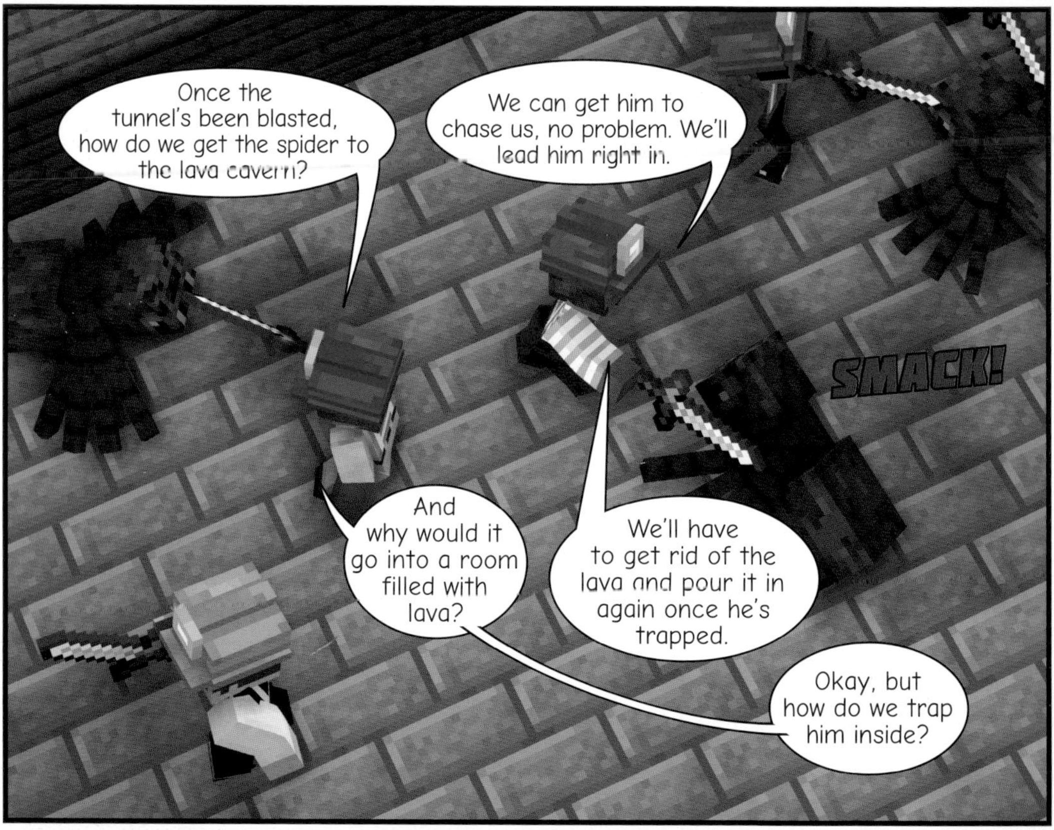
Once the tunnel's been blasted, how do we get the spider to the lava cavern?
We can get him to chase us, no problem. We'll lead him right in.
SMACK!
And why would it go into a room filled with lava?
We'll have to get rid of the lava and pour it in again once he's trapped.
Okay, but how do we trap him inside?

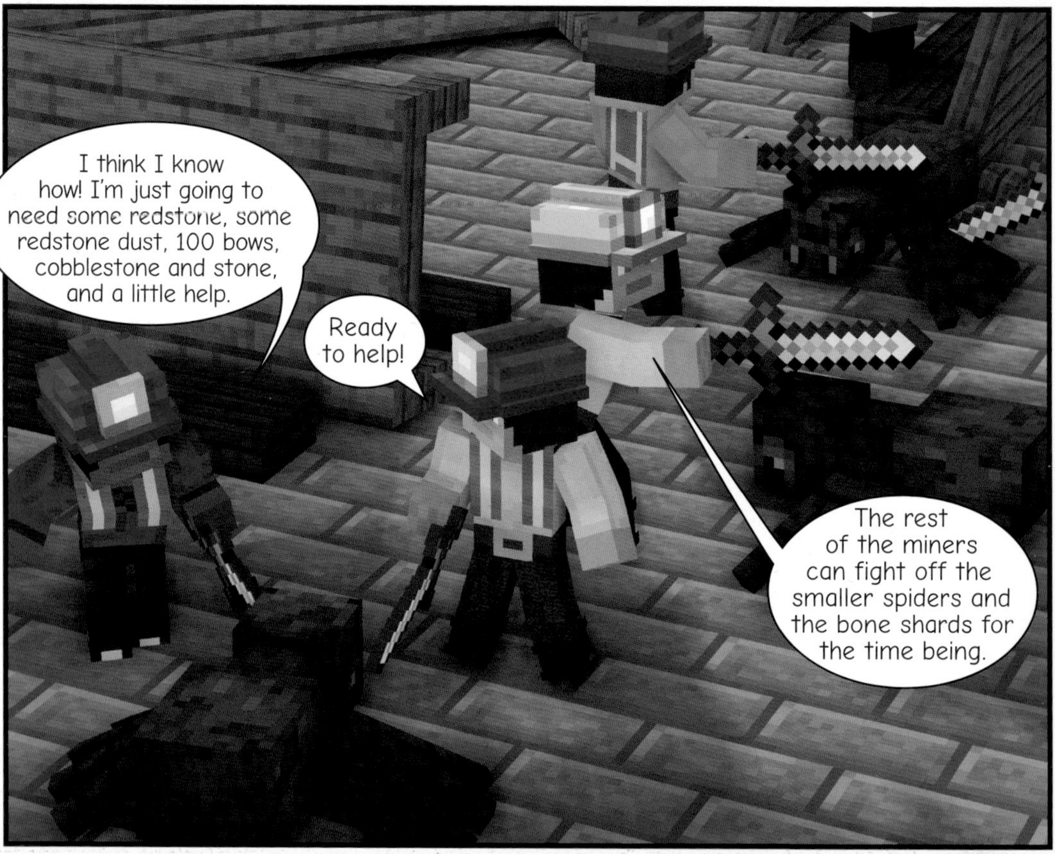
I think I know how! I'm just going to need some redstone, some redstone dust, 100 bows, cobblestone and stone, and a little help.
Ready to help!
The rest of the miners can fight off the smaller spiders and the bone shards for the time being.

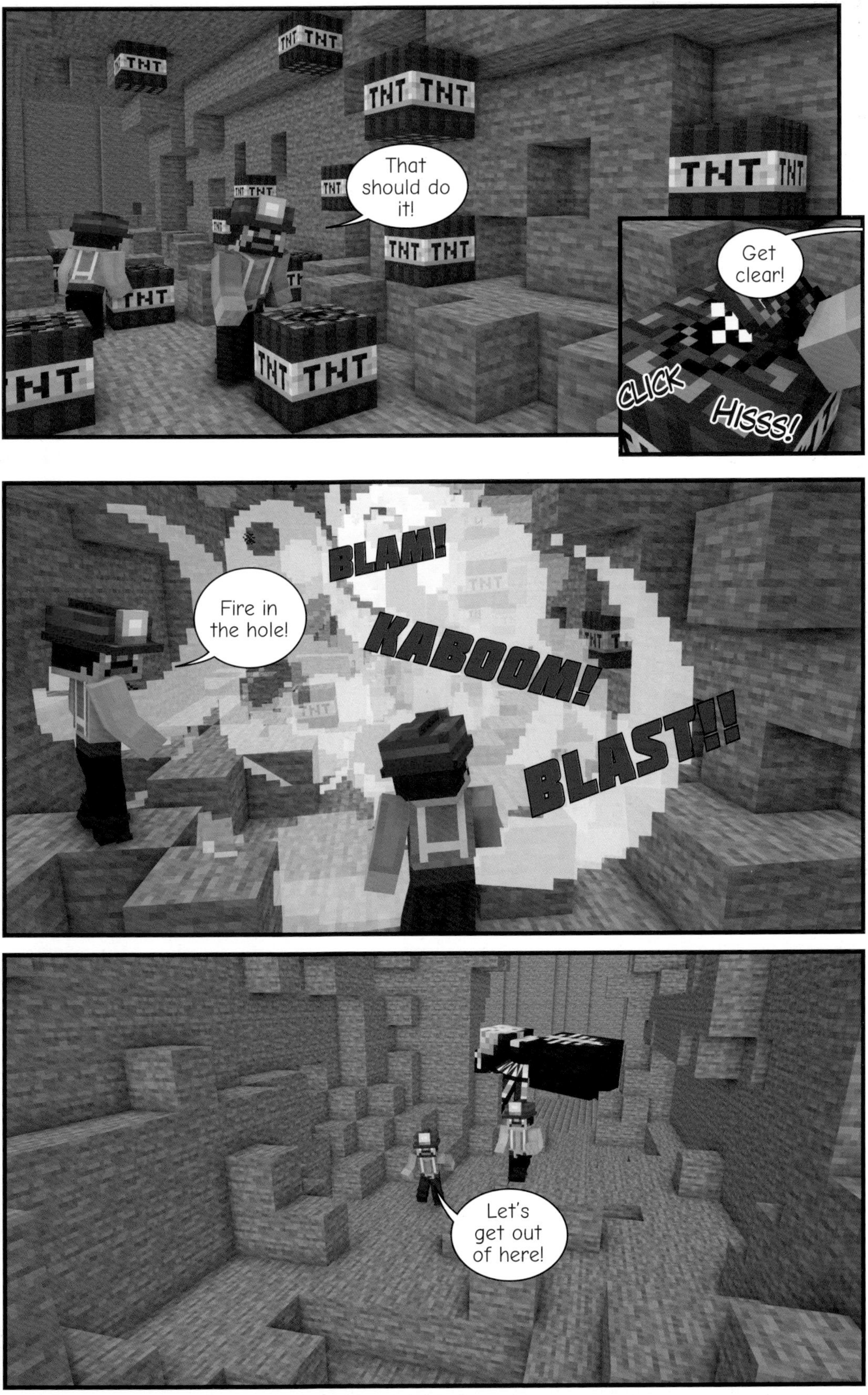

That should do it!
Get clear!
CLICK
HISSS!
Fire in the hole!
BLAM!
KABOOM!
BLAST!!
Let's get out of here!

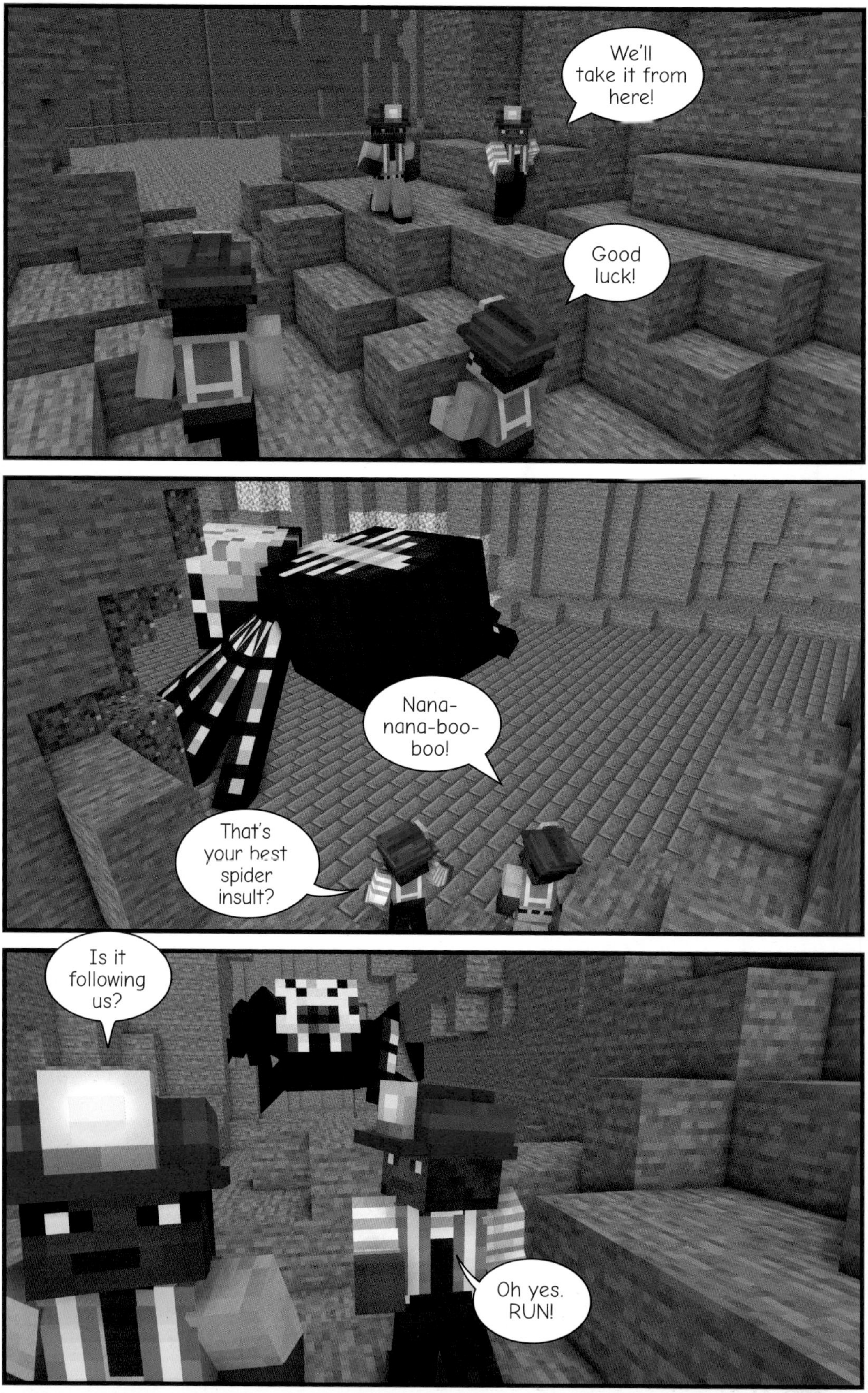
We'll take it from here!
Good luck!
Nana-nana-boo-boo!
That's your best spider insult?
Is it following us?
Oh yes. RUN!

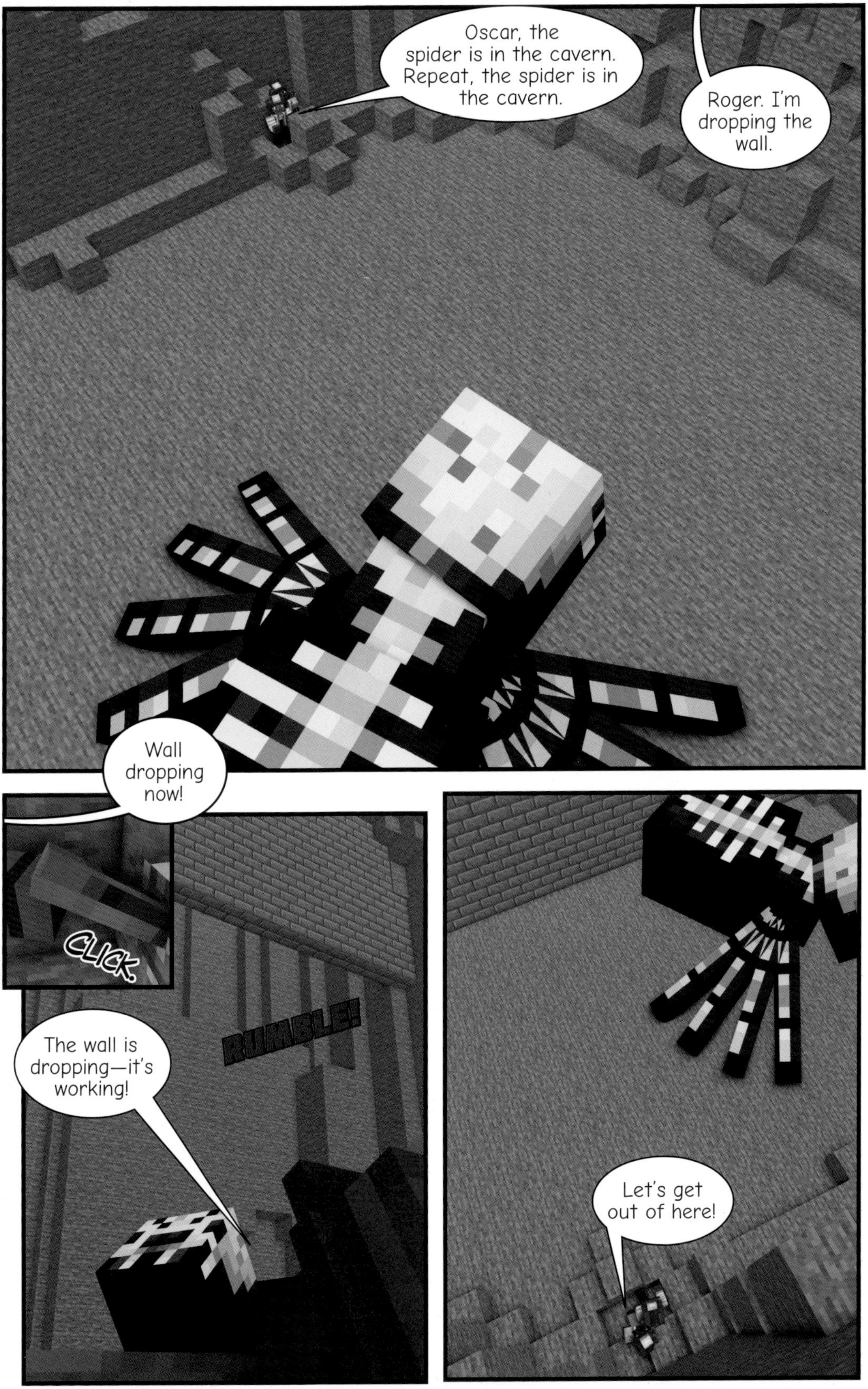

Oscar, the spider is in the cavern. Repeat, the spider is in the cavern.
Roger. I'm dropping the wall.
Wall dropping now!
CLICK.
RUMBLE!
The wall is dropping—it's working!
Let's get out of here!

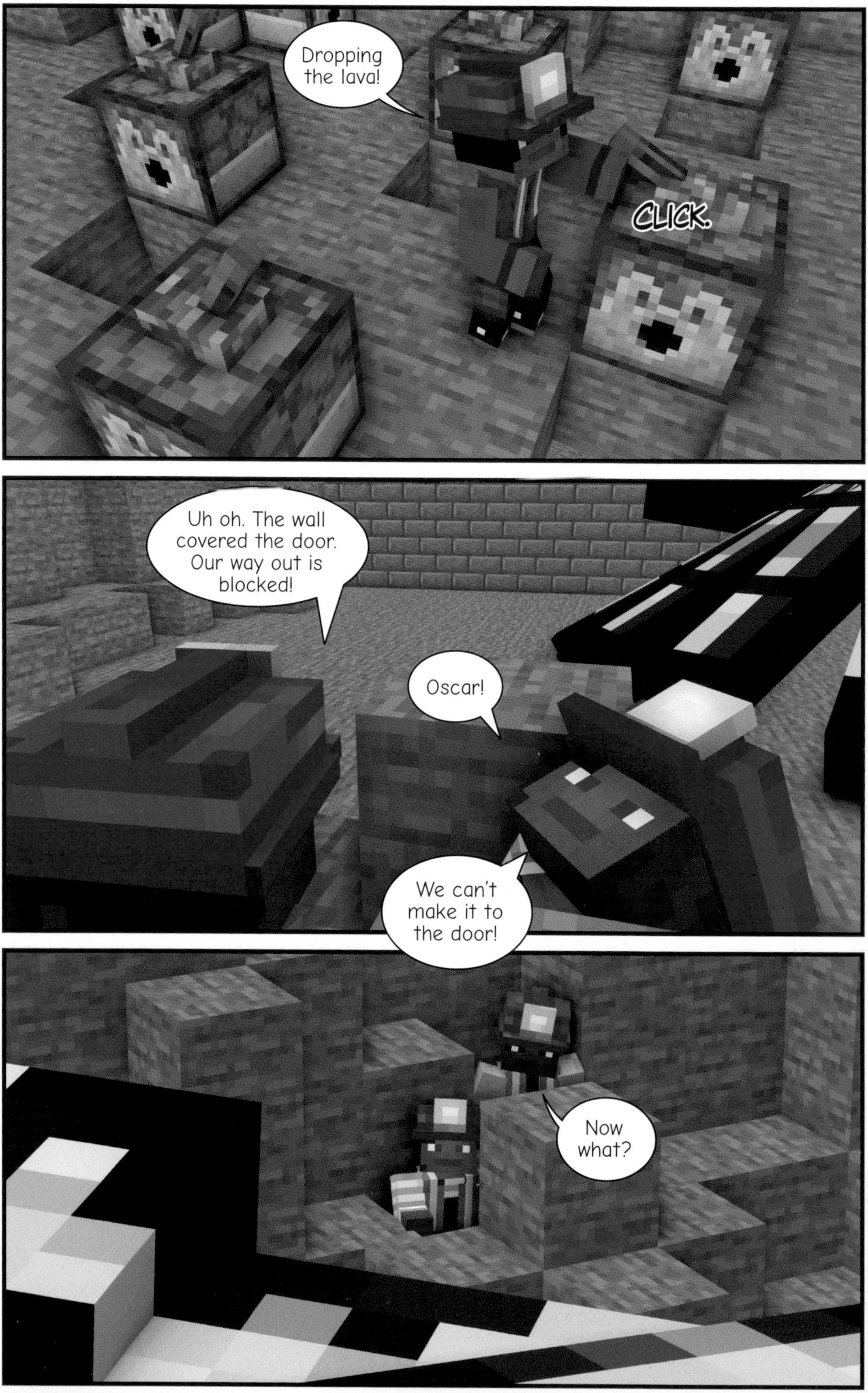
Dropping the lava!
CLICK.
Uh oh. The wall covered the door. Our way out is blocked!
Oscar!
We can't make it to the door!
Now what?

Chapter 12

Beyond Bedrock

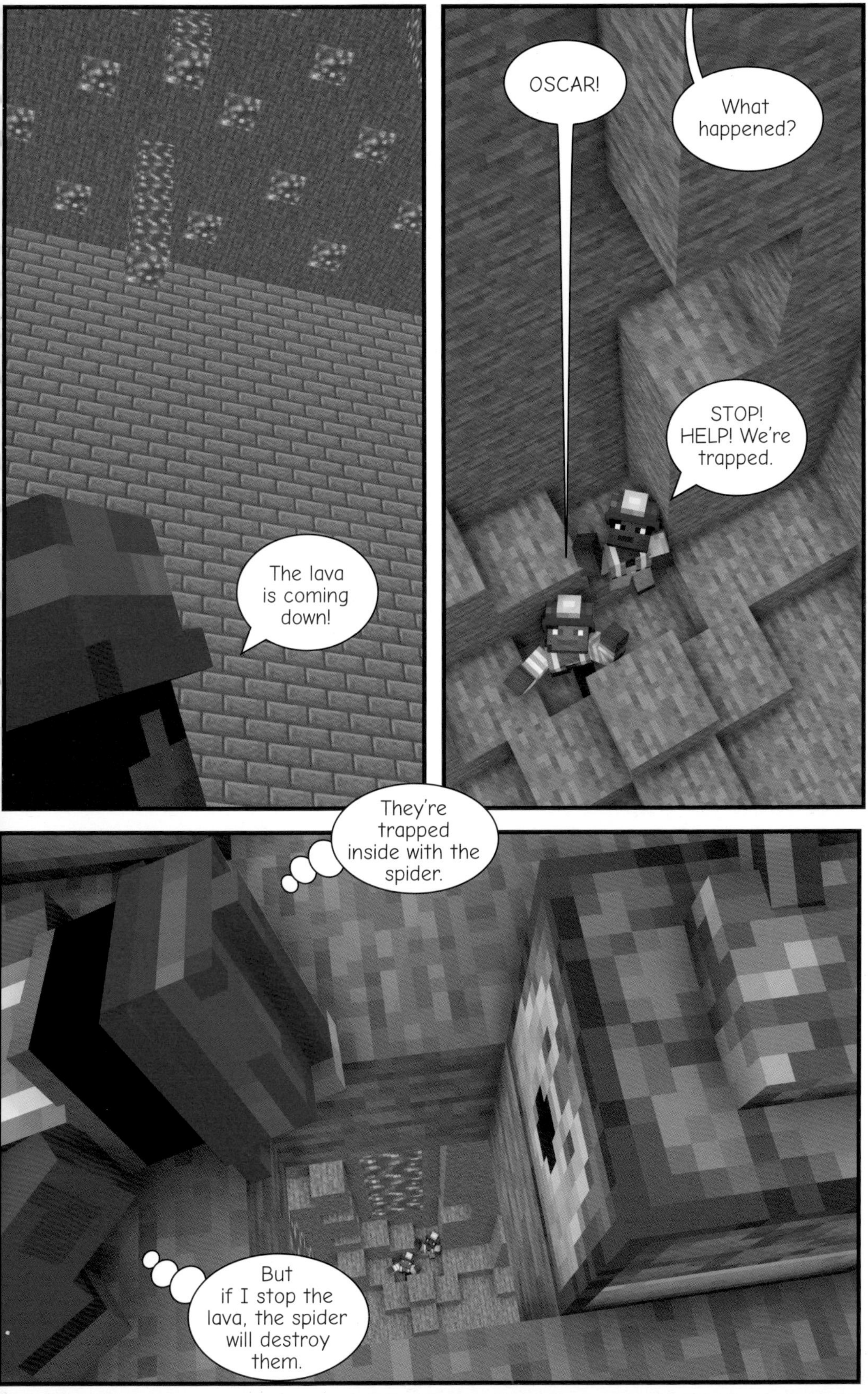
The lava is coming down!
OSCAR!
What happened?
STOP! HELP! We're trapped.
They're trapped inside with the spider.
But if I stop the lava, the spider will destroy them.

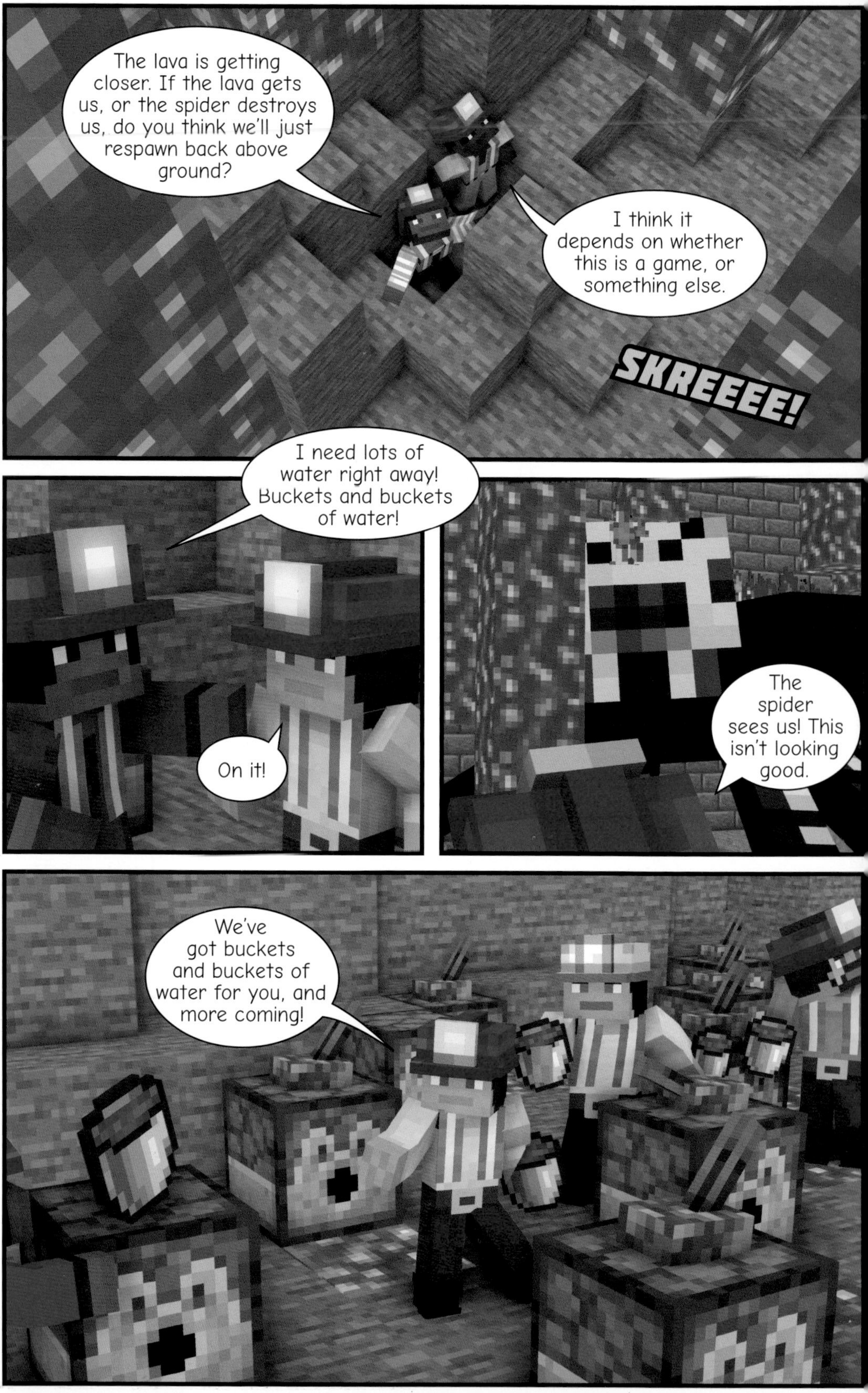

The lava is getting closer. If the lava gets us, or the spider destroys us, do you think we'll just respawn back above ground?
I think it depends on whether this is a game, or something else.
SKREEEEE!
I need lots of water right away! Buckets and buckets of water!
On it!
The spider sees us! This isn't looking good.
We've got buckets and buckets of water for you, and more coming!

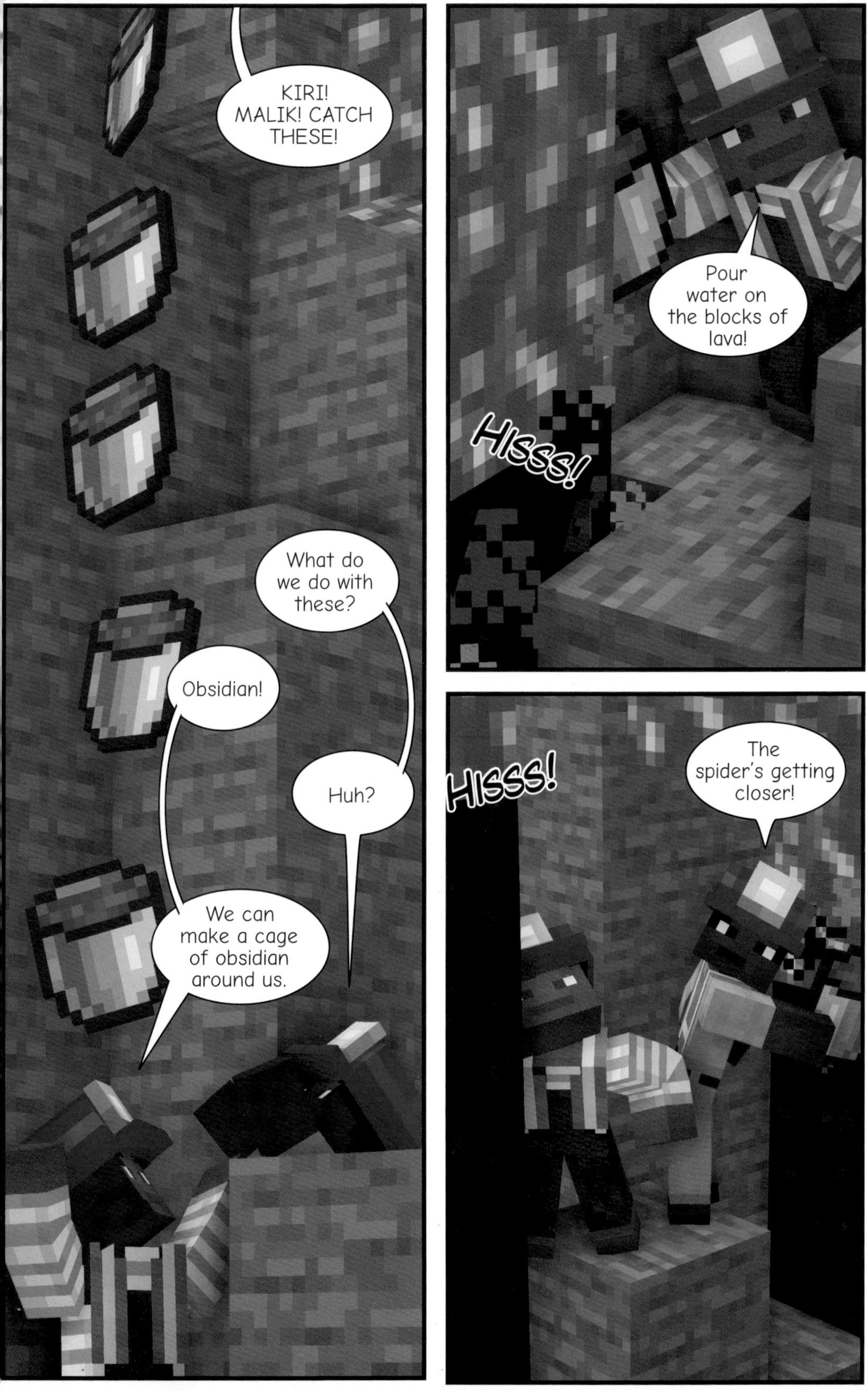
KIRI! MALIK! CATCH THESE!
What do we do with these?
Obsidian!
Huh?
We can make a cage of obsidian around us.
Pour water on the blocks of lava!
HISSS!
HISSS!
The spider's getting closer!

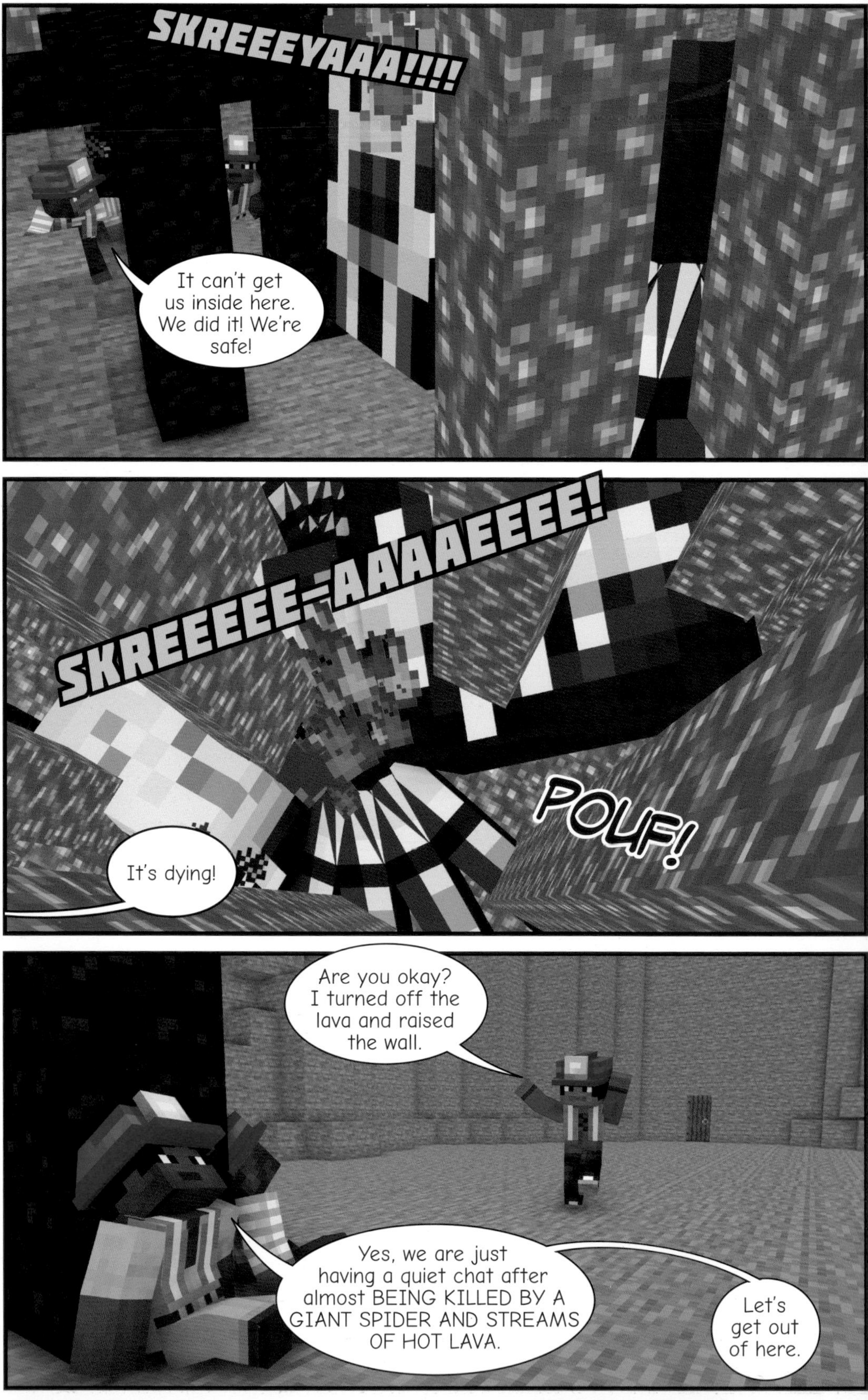
SKREEEYAAA!!!!
It can't get us inside here. We did it! We're safe!
SKREEEEEE-AAAAEEEE!
POUF!
It's dying!
Are you okay? I turned off the lava and raised the wall.
Yes, we are just having a quiet chat after almost BEING KILLED BY A GIANT SPIDER AND STREAMS OF HOT LAVA.
Let's get out of here.

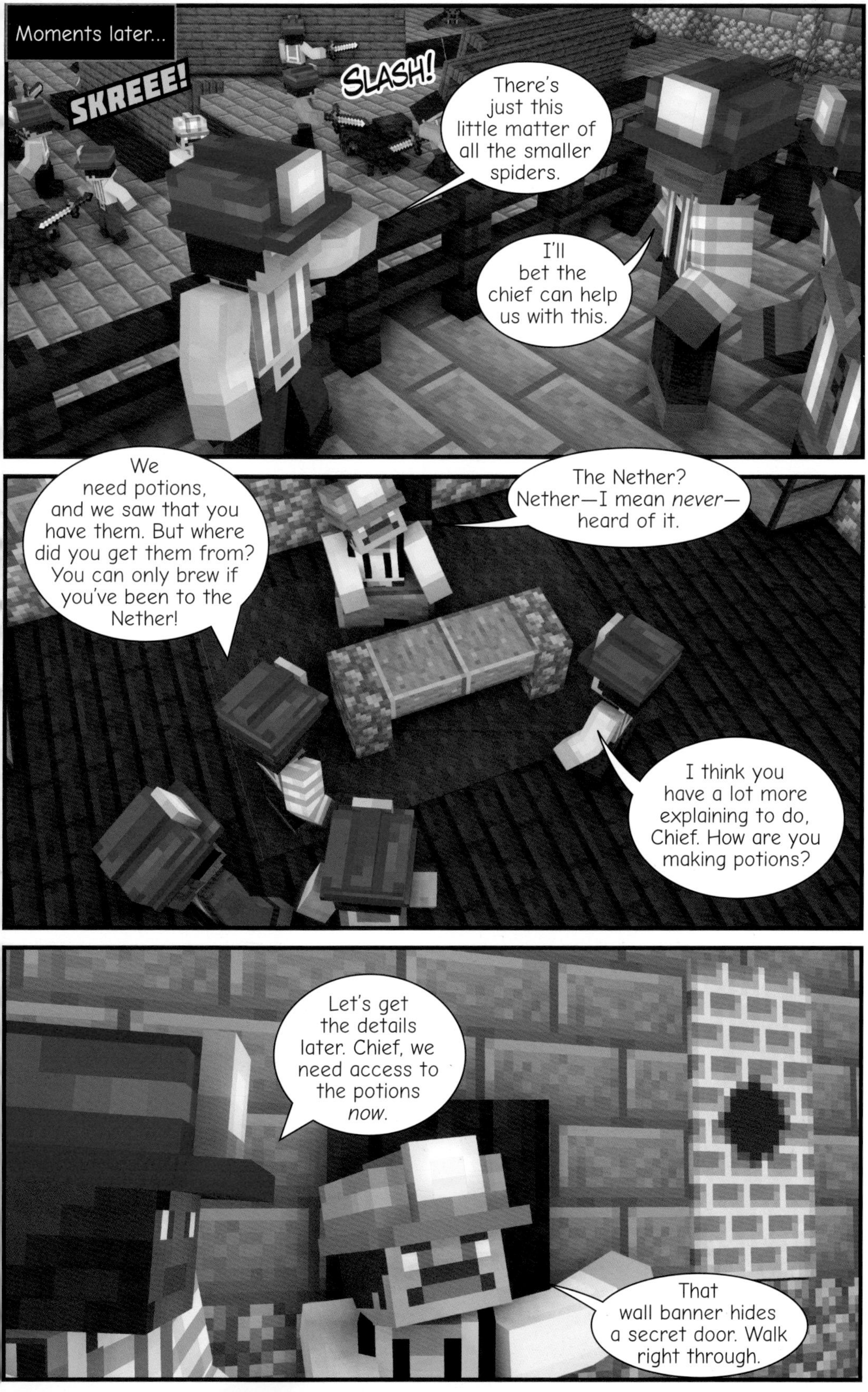
Moments later...
SKREEE!
SLASH!
There's just this little matter of all the smaller spiders.
I'll bet the chief can help us with this.
We need potions, and we saw that you have them. But where did you get them from? You can only brew if you've been to the Nether!
The Nether? Nether—I mean *never*—heard of it.
I think you have a lot more explaining to do, Chief. How are you making potions?
Let's get the details later. Chief, we need access to the potions *now*.
That wall banner hides a secret door. Walk right through.

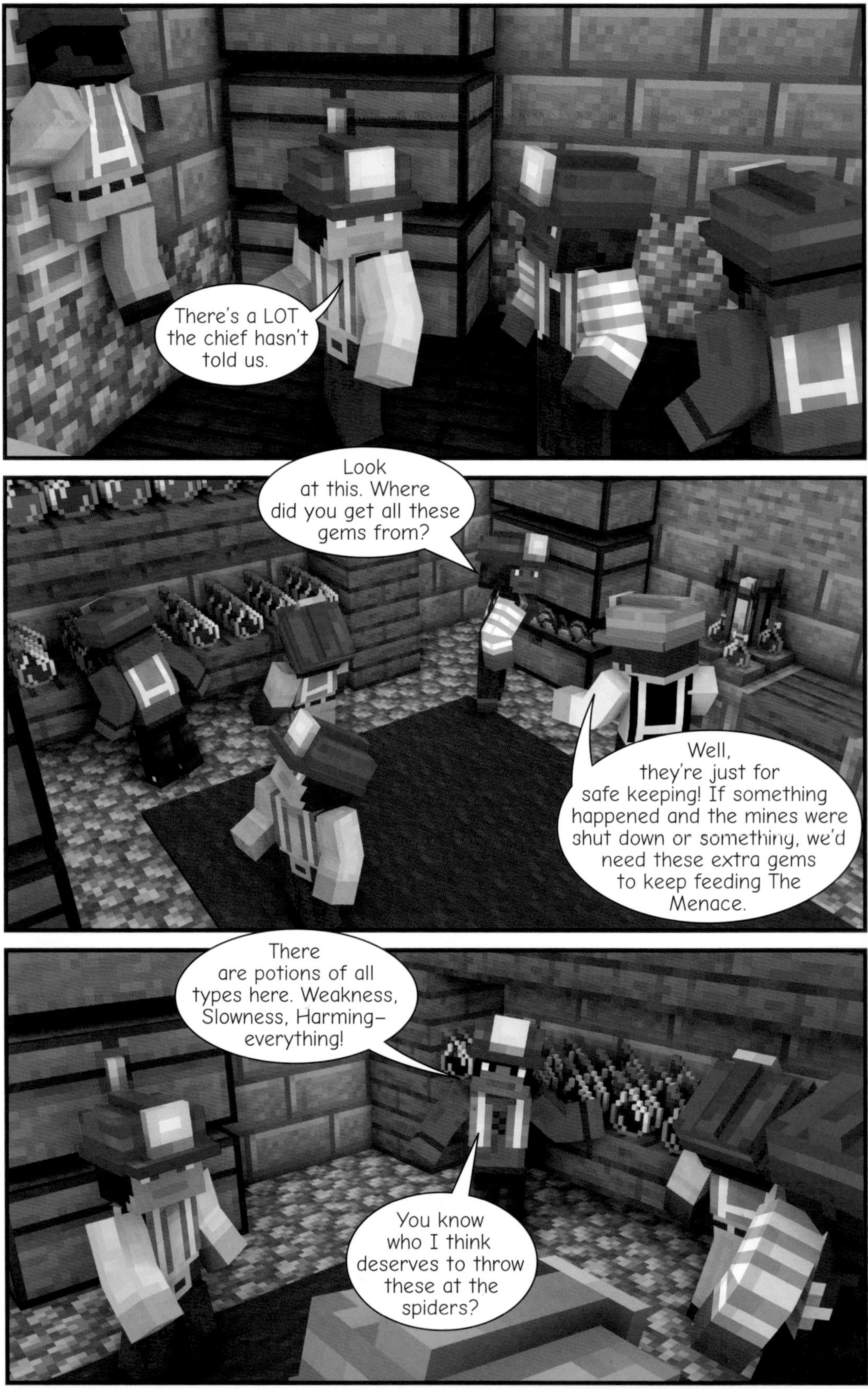
There's a LOT the chief hasn't told us.
Look at this. Where did you get all these gems from?
Well, they're just for safe keeping! If something happened and the mines were shut down or something, we'd need these extra gems to keep feeding The Menace.
There are potions of all types here. Weakness, Slowness, Harming–everything!
You know who I think deserves to throw these at the spiders?

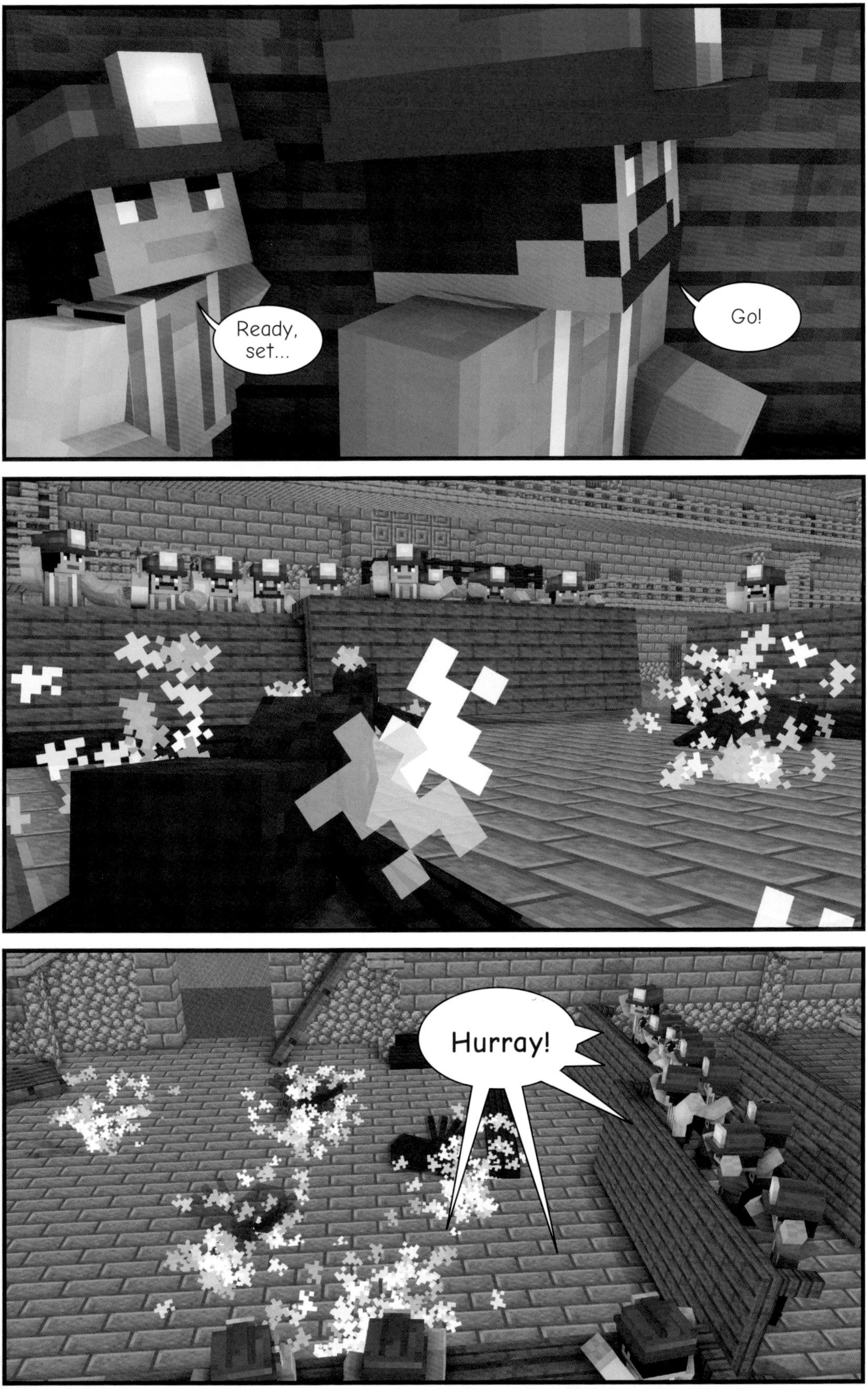

Ready, set...
Go!
Hurray!

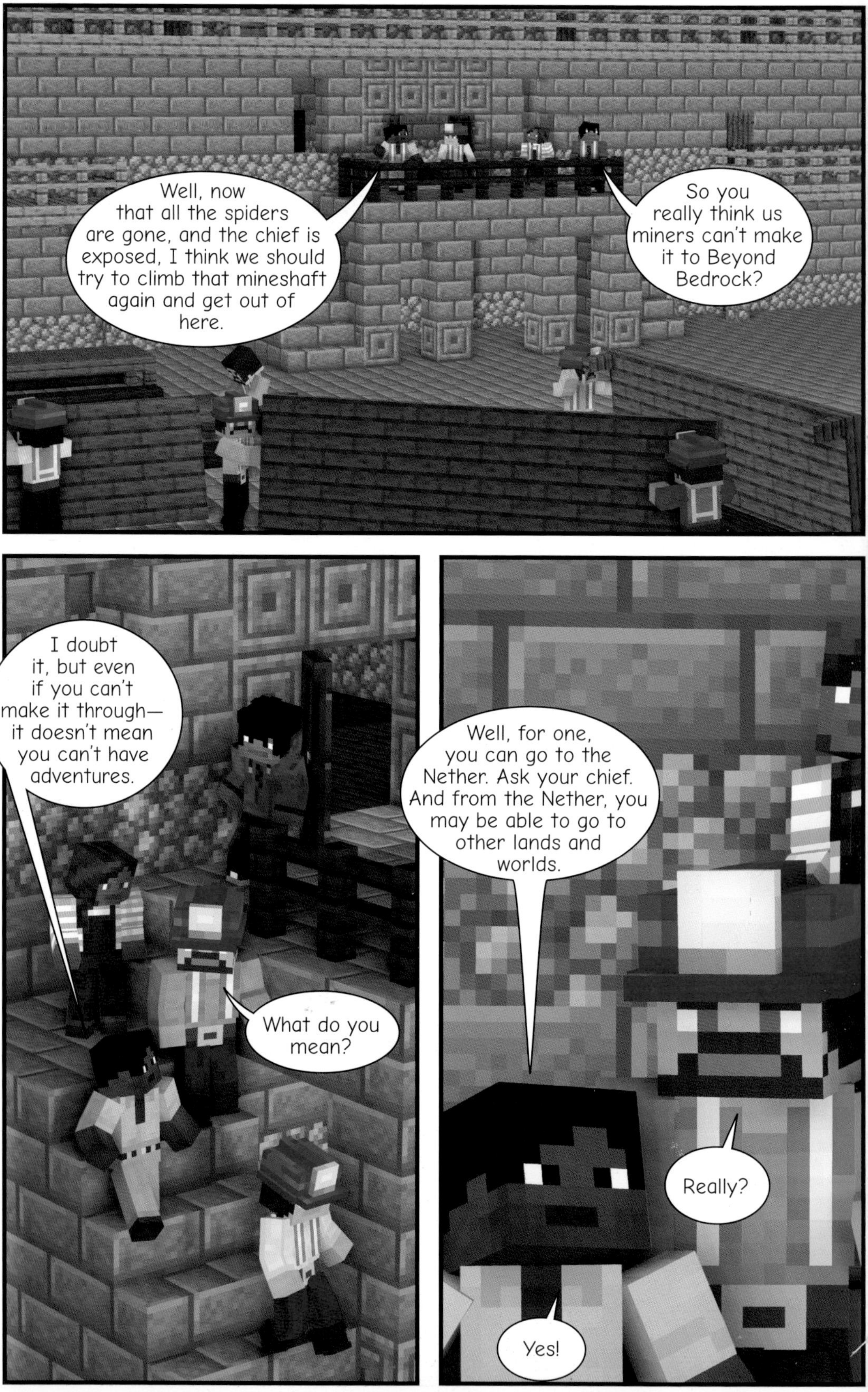
Well, now that all the spiders are gone, and the chief is exposed, I think we should try to climb that mineshaft again and get out of here.
So you really think us miners can't make it to Beyond Bedrock?
I doubt it, but even if you can't make it through—it doesn't mean you can't have adventures.
What do you mean?
Well, for one, you can go to the Nether. Ask your chief. And from the Nether, you may be able to go to other lands and worlds.
Really?
Yes!

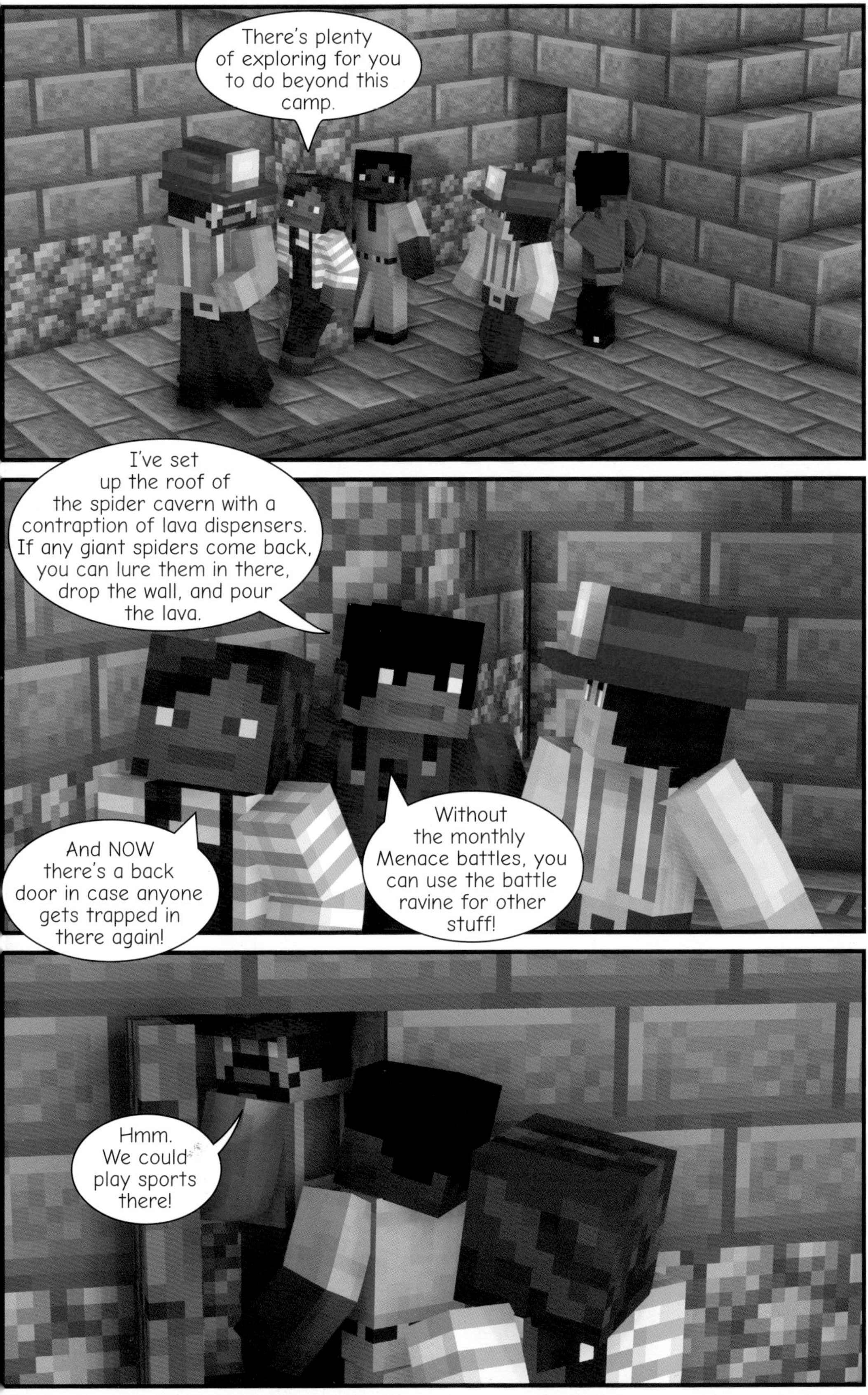
There's plenty of exploring for you to do beyond this camp.
I've set up the roof of the spider cavern with a contraption of lava dispensers. If any giant spiders come back, you can lure them in there, drop the wall, and pour the lava.
And NOW there's a back door in case anyone gets trapped in there again!
Without the monthly Menace battles, you can use the battle ravine for other stuff!
Hmm. We could play sports there!

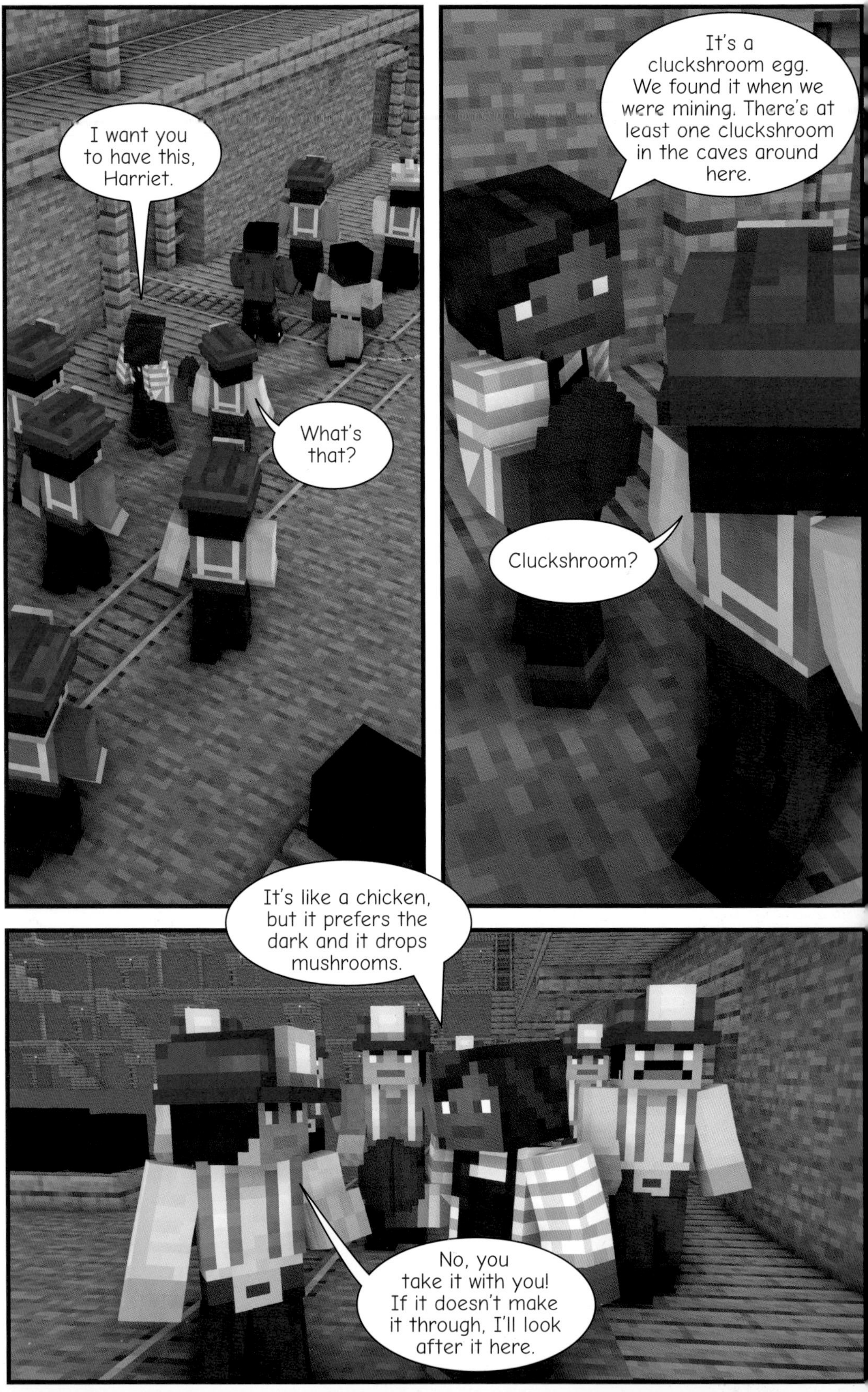
I want you to have this, Harriet.
What's that?
It's a cluckshroom egg. We found it when we were mining. There's at least one cluckshroom in the caves around here.
Cluckshroom?
It's like a chicken, but it prefers the dark and it drops mushrooms.
No, you take it with you! If it doesn't make it through, I'll look after it here.

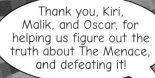

Thank you, Kiri, Malik, and Oscar, for helping us figure out the truth about The Menace, and defeating it!

No! It is YOU THREE that are the menace!

Sentries! Come take them to the pit!

Actually, about your sentries, Chief. They have something to tell you.

We're making a sports team with Rupert and Alfie.

And we've covered up that pit. No need for it.

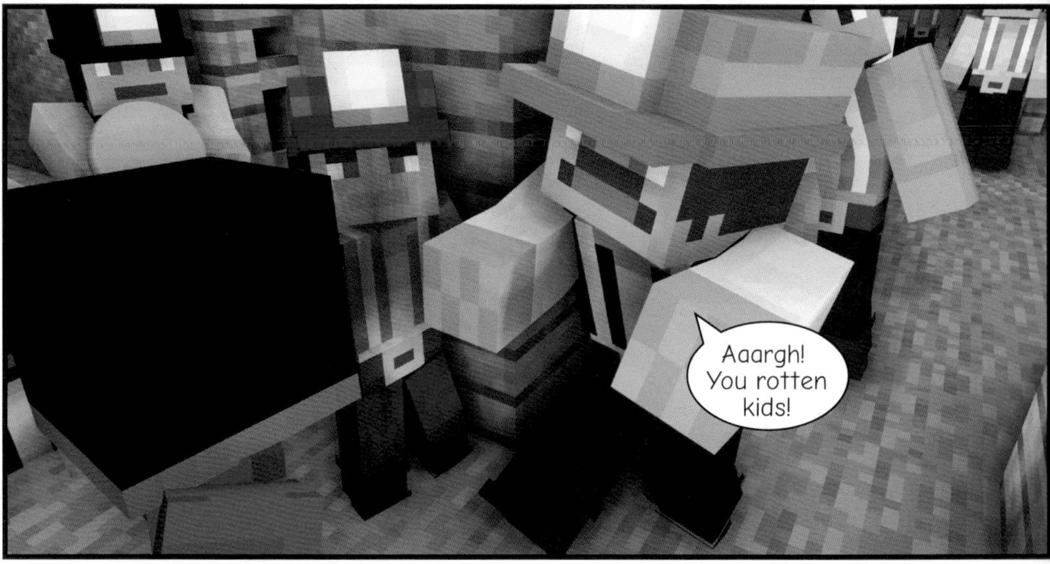
Aaargh! You rotten kids!

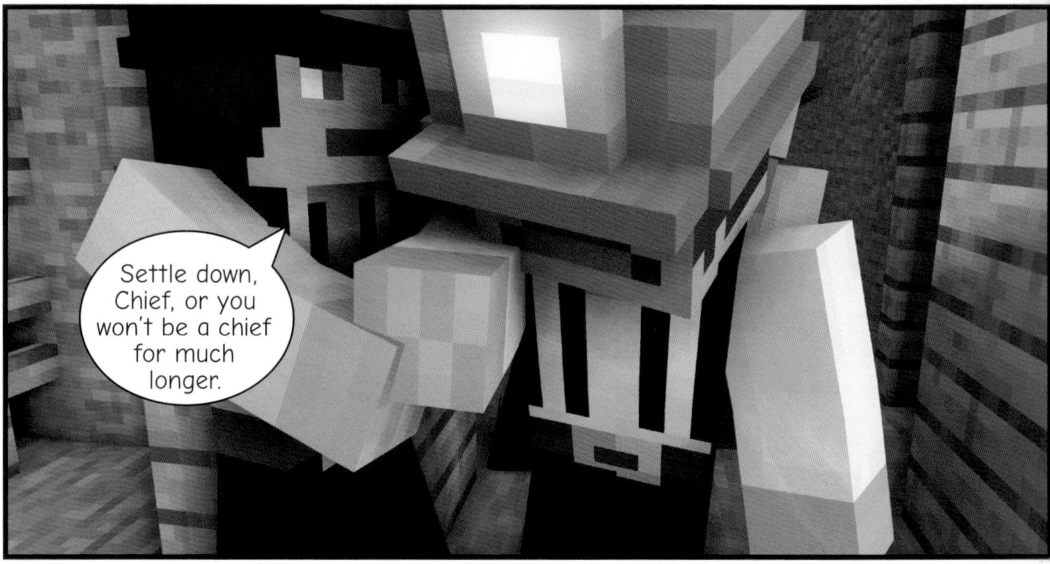
Settle down, Chief, or you won't be a chief for much longer.

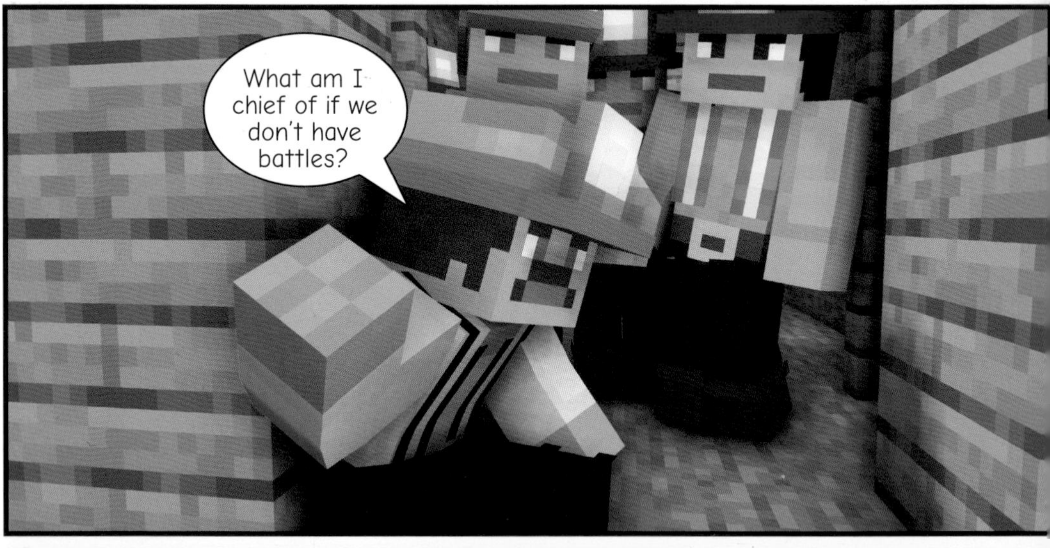
What am I chief of if we don't have battles?

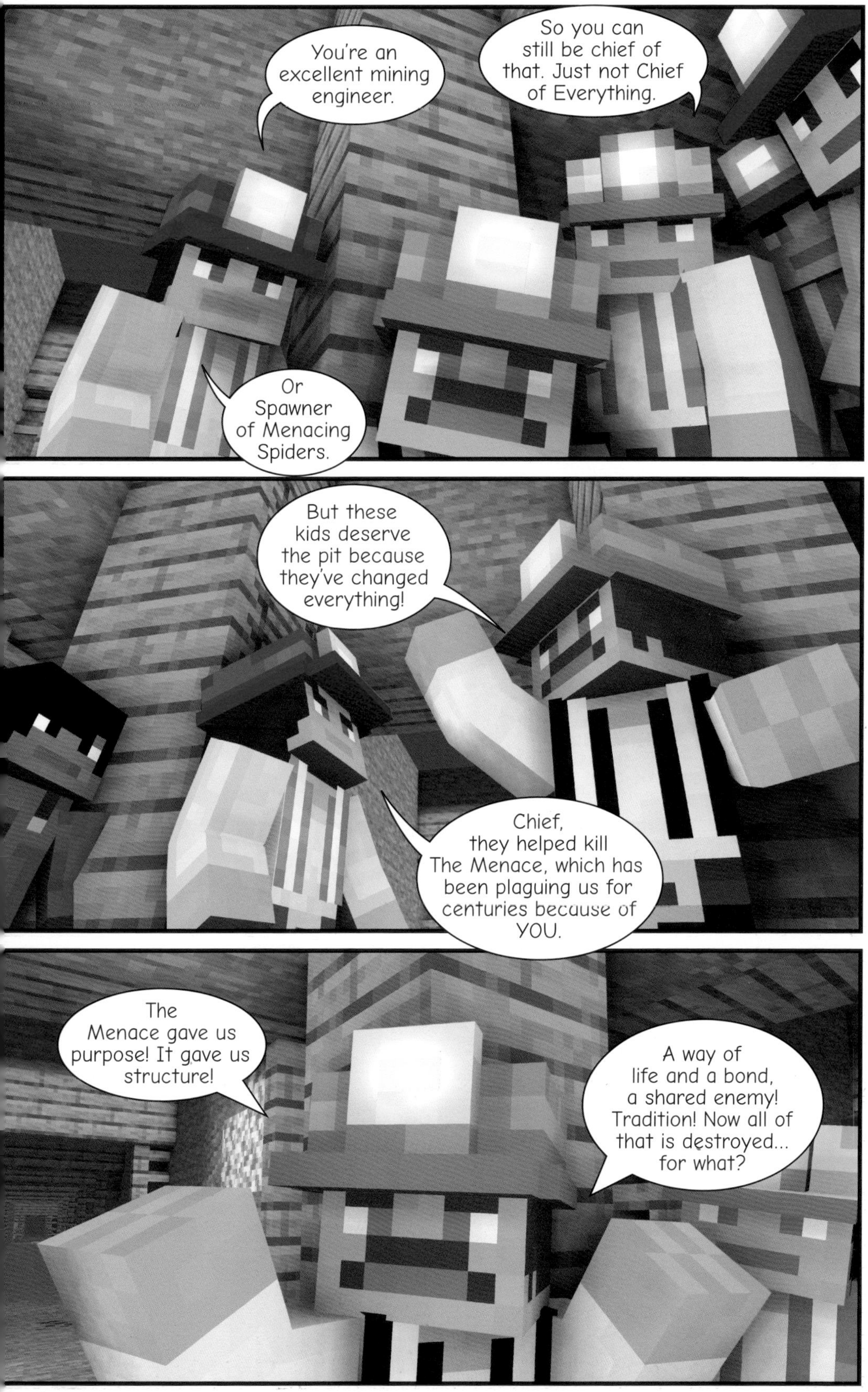
You're an excellent mining engineer.
So you can still be chief of that. Just not Chief of Everything.
Or Spawner of Menacing Spiders.
But these kids deserve the pit because they've changed everything!
Chief, they helped kill The Menace, which has been plaguing us for centuries because of YOU.
The Menace gave us purpose! It gave us structure!
A way of life and a bond, a shared enemy! Tradition! Now all of that is destroyed... for what?

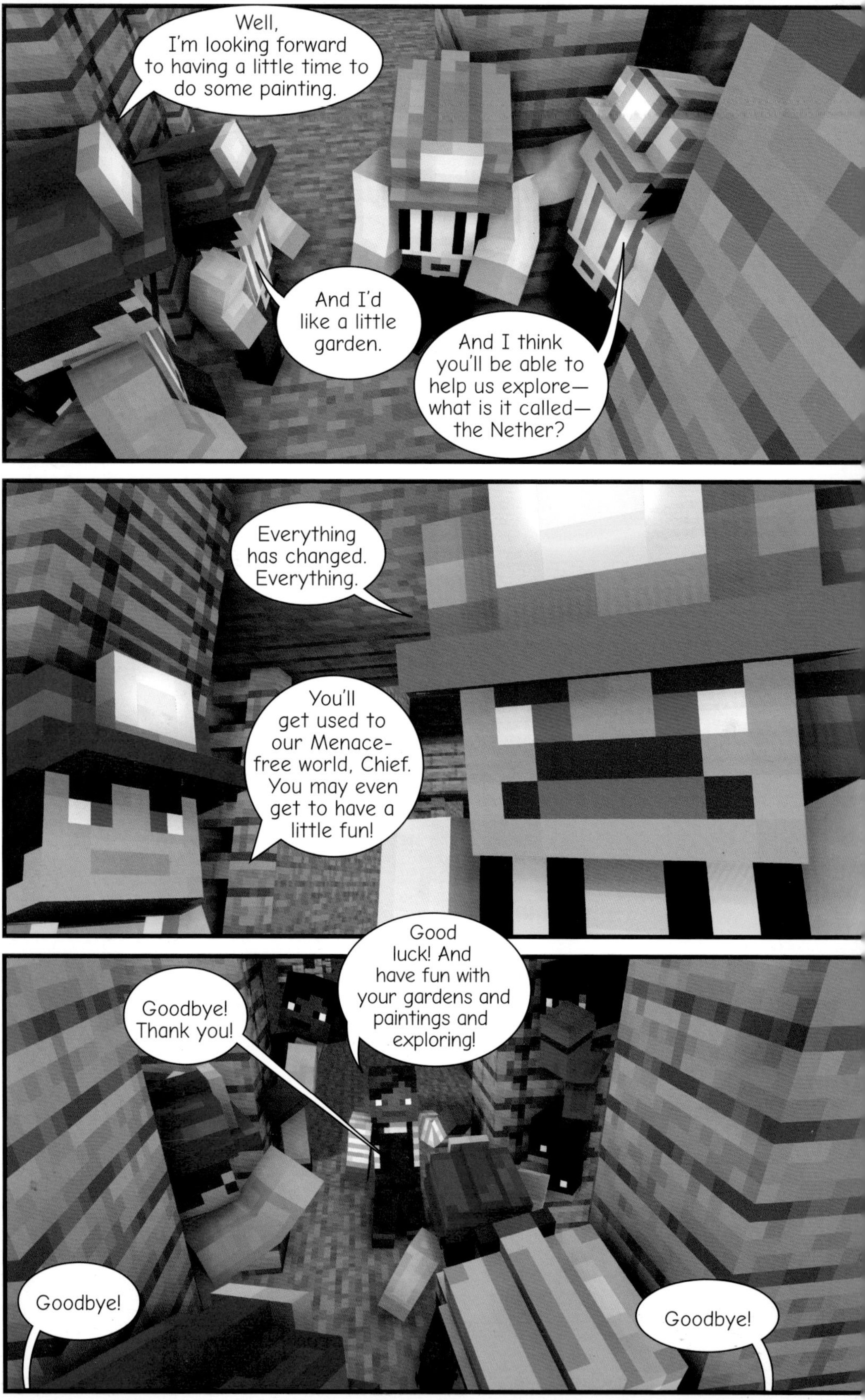
Well, I'm looking forward to having a little time to do some painting.
And I'd like a little garden.
And I think you'll be able to help us explore—what is it called—the Nether?
Everything has changed. Everything.
You'll get used to our Menace-free world, Chief. You may even get to have a little fun!
Goodbye! Thank you!
Good luck! And have fun with your gardens and paintings and exploring!
Goodbye!
Goodbye!

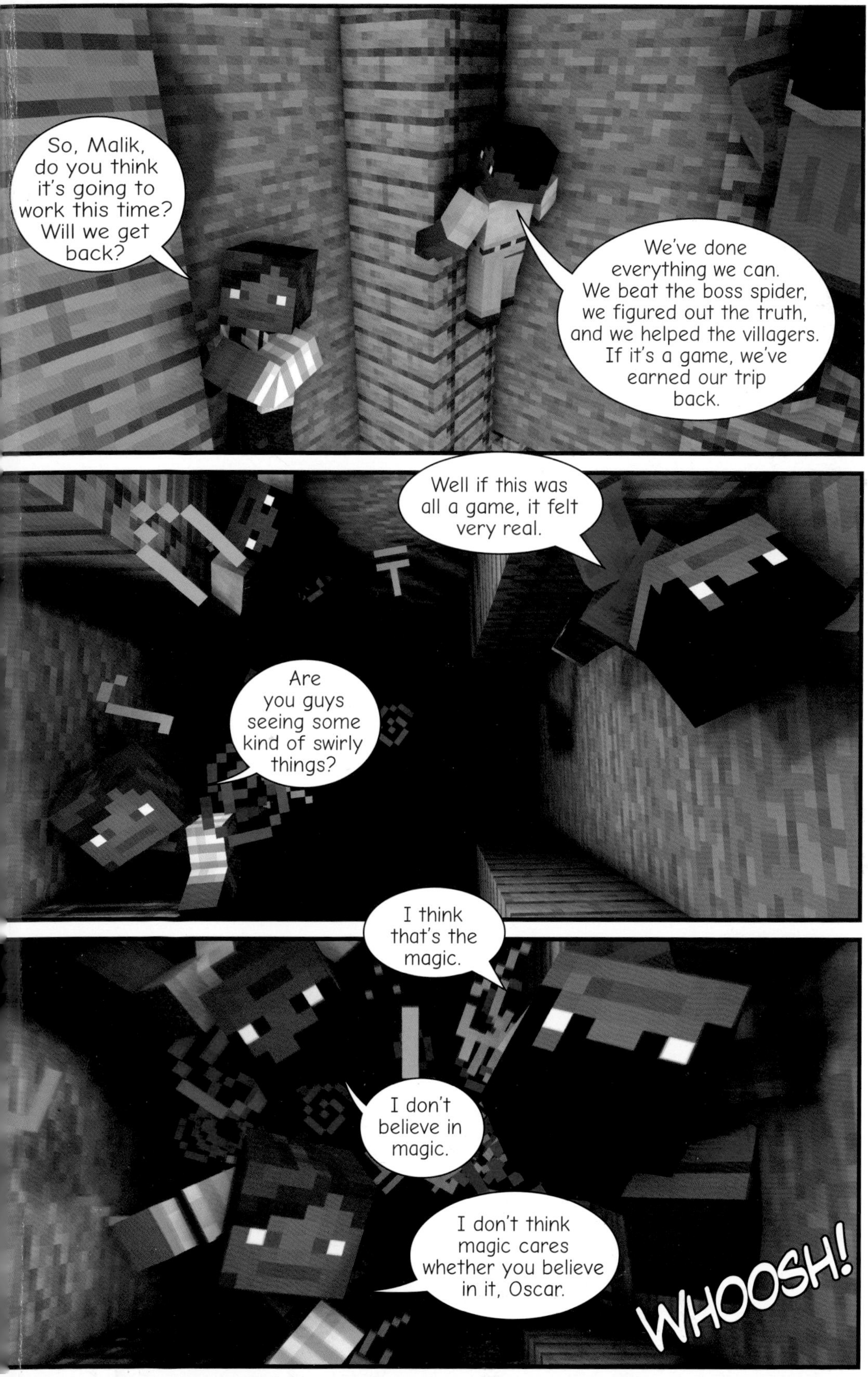
So, Malik, do you think it's going to work this time? Will we get back?
We've done everything we can. We beat the boss spider, we figured out the truth, and we helped the villagers. If it's a game, we've earned our trip back.
Well if this was all a game, it felt very real.
Are you guys seeing some kind of swirly things?
I think that's the magic.
I don't believe in magic.
I don't think magic cares whether you believe in it, Oscar.
WHOOSH!

And that's what happened.

Malik was right when he said that time was different inside Minecraft Earth. We made it back before lunch! It turns out we were only gone for a few minutes here, even though in the other world, a week had passed.

We're still not sure if the world we dropped into was real and the game allowed us in, or if it was all just a video game. I think it was real.

And Malik thought that there was no way the miners could follow us here because the two worlds couldn't collide. But that's not exactly true. Something did come back with us. I found it in my pocket, sleeping, the day we returned. It's the cluckshroom. It hatched! And it's really small.

O. M. G., y'all. I have a cluckshroom!

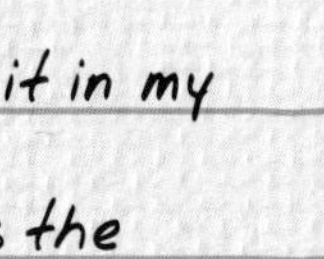

Here are its little feet markings so you can see how tiny it is. I think I'll name it Clucky.

Keep our secret safe, okay? And watch out when you're gaming. Things can get real real fast.

-Kiri